C000083528

The Gladio Pı

Philip M Cooper

Dedications

To all my family and friends who supported me during the long four years it took to write this book. The many friends who undertook editing and proofing duties but particularly Chris H, who used his magic proofing to give the book its final polish. Finally, to my understanding and beautiful partner Pauline who put up with my long absences to the study. Without all these lovely people I could never have finished this book.

Prologue

March 12th, 2010 - Berlin

The hotel suite was tightly guarded at all entrances by marines from Russia, Germany and Greece. Inside the room two men and two women were formulating a treacherous plan which if successful would make them all very rich. Themis Xenakis the Greek prime minister looked over at Elena Davilova the Russian deputy finance minister, her long shapely legs stretched out as she leaned back in her armchair and let out a long stream of smoke from her cheroot. Xenakis noticed that Dominik Vogel the German finance minister had his bird like eyes firmly fixed on Davilova's legs.

'Dominik,' said an exasperated Brigitte Neumann, the German Chancellor. 'Themis needs an answer. Once we have decided who will replace Antonopoulos when he goes, we can review the plan and then go back to our hotels.'

Vogel tore his eyes off Davilova and turned to Xenakis. 'Weren't you roommates with your justice minister in Boston?' he asked.

'I was,' confirmed Xenakis.

'Can we manipulate him into replacing Antonopoulos?' asked Vogel.

'How? Short of blackmail I don't see an answer. Anyway, he is a lawyer not an economist.'

'It doesn't matter that much Themis because he will be following orders from his advisors, us. He won't be deciding any economic policy, he'll be our puppet,' countered Vogel.

'He still might not agree, I can't force him, can I?'

'Blackmail would do it. Don't you have anything on him?'

'No,' said Xenakis. 'I mean could I blackmail him for indiscretions outside his marriage? Doesn't seem tangible enough though.'

'Do it,' chimed in Davilova. 'He has a reputation for cheating on his wife, doesn't he? So, catch him in a compromising position and use it as a bargaining chip. We've only six months before the announcement.'

'What if he doesn't play ball and cheat on his wife?' said Xenakis.

Davilova looked over at both Vogel and Neumann and raised her eyebrows in exasperation. 'Well fix it. You can use John Dexter's services for setting up blackmail traps as well as the odd assignation here and there,' she finished, grinning at Xenakis.

Xenakis wanted this badly, the 'this' being a successful partnership between the people in the room. He was not at all comfortable with talk of killings and blackmail. Had his greed for money and power led him down a path which he would later come to regret? Would he be able to stop events snowballing out of control? The other three felt comfortable with this kind of talk. He wasn't surprised about Vogel and Neumann, because both their backgrounds were steeped in ruthlessness and callous brutality, however he was shocked by the apparent mercilessness of model-like Davilova. He'd hate to be on the wrong side of her. More astounding was that she seemed to be the leader of the 'trinity' and the Germans were subservient to her demands. He pondered on what secrets Russia might be holding over them like the poised axe of the executioner.

'Let's recap on what we have decided.' Davilova interrupted Themis' thought process. 'Themis will sign contracts on behalf of the Greek Government giving Germany and Russia the sole rights to forty percent each of the oil reserves in the northern and western Aegean with Greece retaining twenty percent. Germany and Russia will be given first option for exploration of the eastern Aegean. In addition the Greek Government will issue contracts to Germany and Russia for the rights to the gas reserves in the southern Aegean with the same percentage split as the oil reserves. In return, in addition to the percentages Greece has been allocated, we will write off Greece's national debt to zero. Everyone agreed?'

Three heads nodded in unison. 'What about the American gas pipeline crossing northern Greece?' questioned Vogel.

'Themis will use John Dexter's black ops to destroy the American pipeline leaving our pipeline as the only gas supply through Greece into Europe.' Said Davilova.

'In addition Dominik will arrange a consortium consisting of a German, Russian and Greek international bank to start selling Euros against major currencies including the American dollar, British pound and Japanese yen. This will be done on the eve of 'Ochi' day so hopefully the announcement at the Bilderberg meeting will increase the pressure on the Euro and the consortium will be able to buy back the cheap Euro realising huge profits.'

'Right,' said Vogel. 'The announcement will be made the evening before the 'Ochi' day celebrations in Greece. Kalfas will lead the press conference at the Bilderberg meeting in Athens on the 27th October. He will detail the agreements that we will have put in place by then, monetary, political and territorial. Agree?'

'Agreed,' said Neumann.

'Agreed,' repeated Davilova. 'It's up to you now Themis. Don't let us down.'

The four leaders left the room one at a time, each one escorted by their respective marine guards. Once back in her hotel room Elena Davilova dialled the Russian Presidents mobile phone.

'Elena,' answered Igor Putilov. 'How was the meeting?'

'Hello Igor, the meeting went as well as we could expect. Xenakis is the weak link as we thought. He has no stomach for violence or blackmail. He must be watched very carefully.'

'Not unexpected in light of his background. Use JD to do all his dirty work. How about the other arrangements?'

'They agreed to split the extraction of the reserves in the Aegean and we have forty percent of the northern and western edge plus other gas reserves just south of Crete. We will also have sole licence for a gas pipe running across northern Greece as well as first option on the resources under the eastern Aegean.'

'Congratulations,' enthused Putilov. 'How much does Xenakis want in return?'

'Debt clearance and some,' replied Elena. 'A lot less than the assets however. It's a good deal.'

The line went quiet as Putilov digested the information. Elena waited knowing that Igor was calculating the numbers with the finance minister. Twenty minutes later she heard the phone at the other end of the line being picked up.

'Okay, we'll run with it for now. Once we have finished our surveys we will be in a better position to assess the monetary strategy. Enjoy your trip to the States Elena.'

Without waiting for a reply Putilov hung up. Elena stared at her phone for a few seconds. He could be so rude, she thought. Then with a shrug she signalled to her bodyguard to call a car to take them to the airport.

Chapter 1

October 23rd 2010 - Russian Beach – Poros Island Greece

The small boat glided out of the little bay as it tracked the silvery road laid down by the half-moon in the night sky. Kostas Triandafilos scanned the high cliffs dominating two sides of the bay and then looked back at the trees which served as a backdrop to the small sandy beach that during the summer teemed with beautiful young bodies sunning themselves in the hot sun. Now however in mid-October the beach was deserted during the day and at night the beach parties had long since finished for the season.

Behind the tree line Kostas could just make out the ruins of a large building which had once been the headquarters of the Russian fleet command in the Aegean Sea. In 1840 it was manned by over 200 naval personnel but now lay empty, a half-hearted tourist attraction during the summer months. It has served me well over the years thought Kostas. He had hidden himself from the eyes of the world many times in the last few years. Now he hoped tonight would be the last time. The tiny engine of the boat gave a small sputter and then resumed its steady low beat as Kostas steered it towards a small island just five hundred metres off shore. His destination was Daskelos (Teachers) Island, a tiny island barely big enough to hold its small church, a few trees and two small jetties', one facing Poros island and one on the seaward side.

Kostas was a full colonel in the Greek army and an ex-marine. At six-foot-tall with a full head of hair bleached blonde by the sun, he belied the fact he was pushing fifty-five years old.   Dressed in an old pair of jeans, a grubby shirt that had seen better days, he looked like one of the local fisherman, which was exactly what he wanted. On his head was an old beaten up captain's hat, on his feet wellington boots and he sported an old black knapsack on his back - no marine fatigues for him tonight. His knapsack contained a small pistol, a hunting knife and his cell phone which was set on vibrate. He didn't want it ringing as sounds carried a long way on a still night like this.

As the island became clearer in the faint moonlight, Kostas could just make out the church which stood forlorn in the centre of the island. He steered towards the jetty on the seaward side of the island and breathed a sigh of relief when he saw another small fishing smack moored to the jetty. When he was twenty yards from the wooden landing stage he cut the engine and allowed the boat to drift slowly towards the jetty. After securing his boat, he took his pistol and knife from his knapsack. The knife went into a shin sheath on his left leg and the pistol was held lightly in his right hand. He didn't really expect trouble but it wouldn't do any harm to be vigilant he thought to himself. A faint light came from within the church which confirmed to Kostas she had kept their meeting.

Two minutes later he was standing outside the church peering through the missing window pane. A woman and a man were inside the church. She was smoking and sitting on one of three chairs forming the first row which the congregation used during services. Nowadays the church was a popular summer venue for young couples to marry as they saw it as a romantic place, particularly as it was only accessible by boat. As the church was tiny with only forty chairs for a congregation, whenever a wedding took place most of the congregation listened to the service as it was piped from loudspeakers, out to the moored taxi boats, usually hired for the occasion and which anchored close to the shore around the island.

Kostas pushed open the door and stealthily entered the church. 'Kalispera,' (good-evening) he said as he pulled a chair from the first row and sat down facing the woman, 'Did anyone see you Ariadne?'

The woman got up and went over to Kostas, kissing him once on each cheek before replying. 'We were very careful Kostas. I don't think anyone saw us. Don't be so anxious.'

'Things are coming to a head Ariadne,' said Kostas. He looked over at the man sitting next to her. He was also dressed as a fisherman and the fact he was unshaven heightened this impression, giving him a swarthy appearance. He was Theodoros Halkias, also an ex-marine. He was code named 'the Gardener' and he was Ariadne's bodyguard, Lighthouse's main asset in Greece.

'Are you ready?' questioned Ariadne.

7

'Yes I am,' answered Kostas. 'All my resources are in place and ready for the word from Lighthouse. The identified targets can be taken within two hours of the go ahead if it comes.'

'It will come, don't worry about that,' said Ariadne. 'Lighthouse is confident that you will be needed to douse the flames of Gladio. Are you sure the men you are using are loyal to you?'

'They are and those that are not will be dealt with. I don't expect any problems at all.'

Ariadne's cell phone beeped from inside her clutch bag, interrupting their conversation. 'I'll take this outside,' she said, as she walked towards the door. Once outside she spoke softly into the phone. 'I'm with 'Tinos' and the 'Gardener' she referred to the code names of Kostas and Theodoros as she replied to the voice at the other end. 'Are you positive?' she asked. Just at that moment she heard a shot coming from within the church, 'There's trouble, I'll call you back.'

Ariadne ran to the church doorway, pulling a Glock pistol from her bag as she went. At the doorway she stopped and peered through the gap between the door frame and door. She saw Kostas, pistol in hand, standing over Theodoros who was lying spread-eagled on his back with blood gushing from a neck wound and a hunting knife resting in an outstretched hand.

'What happened?' shouted Ariadne.

'He came at me with a knife,' replied Kostas. 'The crazy malaka!

'That was Lighthouse on the phone. They were suspicious that Theodoros may compromise the operation. It looks as though their reservations were well founded. Fortunately, he didn't know all the details but I may be in danger now; however, I imagine that you are still in the clear. We'd better get going. Get rid of the body and get back to Athens. If something happens to me Lighthouse will communicate with you direct.'

Ariadne kissed Kostas and left the church. An hour later the calm sea was once again broken by the passing of two small boats as they glided silently into the shallows of Russian Beach.

Chapter 2

October 23rd 2010 - London

Sir Peter Bogart sat behind his antique mahogany desk, his laptop was open in front of him. He was playing computer Bridge and was good at it, proud that at the age of seventy-two he was as computer dexterous as his favourite grandson. There was a knock at the door and his secretary Janet popped her head around.

'Sir, Gregory is coming up in ten minutes. He said it was about Sheepskin,' she said. She secretly wondered how a man in his position could possibly enjoy computer games, although it was a thought that she never voiced, as you never knew what ears were listening in the building. It was rumoured that the building had more bugs in it than a world health organisation laboratory for dangerous diseases.

'Send him straight in,' said Sir Peter, 'Oh and give him my morning coffee as he passes you, will you?

'Yes sir,' replied Janet.

Sir Peter watched her walk out and reflected on their brief fling twenty years earlier. He had headed MI6 in those days and he had taken her on several foreign trips before the inevitable happened and they had an affair lasting six months. He ended it when he was asked to set up Lighthouse, a Government agency that reported to the prime minister and the foreign secretary. Their brief was to conduct covert operations independent of any ally, especially America. He had been surprised when Janet had agreed to be his secretary at Lighthouse given her feelings towards him, but it had worked out fine. Janet never mentioned the affair and never treated him informally, retaining her prim and proper role for the past twenty years.

Sir Peter's career had been spectacular to say the least. Educated at Cambridge where he studied politics and foreign affairs, his professor soon realised that he had an uncanny knack for 'best option analyses'. This in layman's terms means that he could analyse a situation and come up with the best option to move events in the favour of the interested party he represented. Two days before he graduated he was recruited by MI6 as an analyst. Recognising his leadership qualities, he moved up the ranks at unprecedented speed and by the time he was thirty-eight he was 'C's' number two. C was the acronym given to the head of MI6 after the initials of the first head of MI6, Captain Mansfield Smith Cumming. Unlike the 'M' depicted in the James Bond books. After C died of cancer Peter was promoted to head of MI6 becoming 'C' at the age of fifty-two. Knighted soon afterwards, he had ten successful years before being asked to head up Lighthouse.

Lighthouse was involved in a very delicate operation in Greece. Great Britain like America had not been happy that Greece was leaning towards Russia with its future energy and financial plans. Greece was practically bankrupt and the weight of the Troika's austerity measures was lowering the Greeks' standard of living every day. This was motivating the people towards two extremes, the left wing Syriza party or the right-wing Nazi party - The Golden Dawn – and these extremes were causing social unrest.

'Good morning Sir Peter,' greeted Gregory stepping into the office before striding across the room and placing a cup of coffee on Sir Peter's desk. Sitting down he stretched his long legs out on the thick pile crossing them at the ankles and sipped his coffee. Gregory had been head hunted from MI6 three years ago by Sir Peter, who made him his number two at Lighthouse. He was proud of his decision as over the last couple of years Gregory had proved himself a reliable field and case officer. Sir Peter had asked Gregory twice to go into the field and sort a problem out and both times Gregory had been successful. What's more he didn't flinch at eliminating those responsible for the problem, the details of which were never recorded in the official report, only verbally to Sir Peter, who did him the service of not recording their conversations as possible leverage in future years.

'We have a problem in Greece,' continued Gregory, 'there was a mole in our team there.'

'What do you mean by 'was',' asked Sir Peter.

'Tinos killed him,' said Gregory, 'it seems that 'Gardener', the mole, had decided to take matters into his own hands and failed. According to Ariadne, if he had blown the whistle he had no need to try and kill Tinos as his superiors could have simply arrested him or made him disappear.'

'Has it compromised the operation?' asked Sir Peter. Gregory had been warned that Sir Peter could be ruthless but until now had not believed that his normally kindly eyes could look so cold and steely.

'I don't believe it has,' replied Gregory, 'per Ariadne 'Tinos' is ready and has his men in place. He is waiting for our signal to go ahead.'

'Are the Americans in play yet?'

'Yes, but they don't know about our operation. They've brought Ariadne's son Alex into the game by default, as he has just been made Greece's economic minister. The asset they have been nurturing in Germany is standing by to mind Alex. They have no idea that Ariadne is working for both sides of the Atlantic. The trigger is still in place. The moment Alex goes public we will set the wheels in motion and Tinos will move his men into position.'

'I don't think the Americans will dislike the successful outcome of the operation at all. They might publicly condemn it, but in private they will be reassured that Greece is still in the fold. Although the referendum may alter things a little.'

'I presume current policy will change if the leave campaign wins a surprise majority,' said Gregory.

'Yes, and that could be a problem because the Government might then be happy to see the European Union break up. If so you would have to stop the coup at any cost. I don't know how you'd do it but it would have to before the tanks started rolling. You realise that, don't you?'

'I know sir,' Gregory said. 'Is there anything else?'

'No Gregory, just keep me in the loop will you. I want to know every detail, especially after you've given Tinos the green light.

'Right, I'll arrange for ops to provide you with a satellite phone so we can do face time.'

'Why do I need that Gregory? Are you going into the field on this one?' asked Sir Peter, with a look of puzzlement on his face. 'Surely your unique skills are not required for this one.'

'We can't leave anyone alive that could point to any 'Lighthouse' involvement sir, so I have to be in the field and make sure that whatever the outcome, our assets don't become liabilities,' reasoned Gregory.

Sir Peter gazed at Gregory without saying anything for a good twenty seconds. He hated violence and needless deaths. However, he realized that Gregory was right. The Americans must never suspect Britain's role in this operation. Unfortunately for their assets, who were risking their lives willingly for their beliefs, were going to lose their lives whatever the upshot of the operation. Rather reluctantly he said. 'I agree with the strategy but tread with care; nothing can be traced back to us, absolutely nothing.' With that he dismissed Gregory with a wave of his hand, and resumed his game of Bridge.

Chapter 3

October 25th 2010 – Berlin

Alex was as nervous as hell. Not only was it his first meeting with the German Finance Minister but it was his first official meeting in his new capacity as the Finance Minister of the Hellenic Republic. He was cold and shivering from his nervousness. Alex also had a problem with understanding complex economics, but it was more the thought of meeting with the stone faced, hook-nosed, former East German. Before the fall of the Berlin wall he had been a member of Stasi, the feared German secret police, and had suffered gunshot wounds which confined him to a wheelchair.

The limousine crawled slowly through the early morning commuter traffic towards the German department of finance. Alex decided to call Melina his wife and let her know his flight had been uneventful. He occasionally felt guilty that he was not the perfect husband to Melina. Although he was certain that he loved her and he knew that he was a lucky man to have married one of the most beautiful fashion models that Greece had produced, he could not help but wonder. He was a womaniser but was it his fault that women found him sexy? He wasn't an 'A' typical sexy guy, he wasn't tall, average at five foot ten, not slim, no six pack, in fact he was a little chunky with a glimmer of a rounded tummy. He had great hair though, dark and curly bordering on unruly. Alex always knew that his eyes were his best feature, a vulnerable dark brown. Women loved his seeming defencelessness and the way his eyes appeared to be on the verge of crying.

Alex had first realised that women were attracted to him in his late teenage years when he was still at private school in Georgetown Washington. He was staying overnight at a school friend's house. His friend Josh had an absolutely drop dead gorgeous mother with legs to die for. At least that was Alex's opinion and by all accounts half the neighbourhood too. That night Alex slept in his usual rooms when staying with Josh. It was fairly secluded from the rest of the house as it was set above their double garage. Comprising a small den, a shower room, separate closet and a double bedroom; Alex always felt comfortable there.

This particular night Alex had gone up to his room just after eleven. He showered then got into bed and watched several recorded episodes of the Big Bang Theory, his favourite TV show. He must have fallen asleep because he awoke with the realisation that somebody, to be more precise, a woman, a naked woman, was rubbing herself against his body. 'What the hell......', he started to utter but a finger was put against his lips. It crossed his mind that it smelt faintly of lavender. He realised that the naked body belonged to Mrs Cowan, Josh's mother.

The finger left his lips and traced a line down his body until it found the base of his now erect penis. Alex drew in a breath then let it out slowly, waiting for her next move. It soon came as she slid down his body, without letting go of his erection, until her mouth was against his member. Alex went through a myriad of sensations that he had never experienced before. She played with him with her tongue, mouth and finger always sensing when he was about to lose control and squeezing him in such a way as to delay his ejaculation. After playing with him for half an hour she mounted him and pulled his hands onto her breasts as she leaned forward kissing him on his lips and penetrating his mouth with her tongue. She told him to keep still as she moved rhythmically back and forth. Alex was unable to control himself for long and let himself go, exploding into her waiting orifice with wave after wave of pulsating sensations. After it was over and he had slipped out, she cleaned him up, kissed him on the lips and whispered 'Stay over more often, won't you.' Alex nodded in the dark and Mrs Cowan tiptoed out of his room giving him a glimpse of her long legs in the faint light from a nearby street lamp.

Alex stayed over many times that year and Mrs Cowan taught him how to make a woman have an orgasm and generally how to please her. He was a good pupil and he was talented enough to give her multiple orgasms in one session by the time the summer was over. During this time, they hardly said a word. She would come to his bed in the dead of night, show him what to do, have passionate sex and then leave the room. She never stayed the whole night. In losing his virginity Alex had become very aware that women found him attractive.

14

His thoughts were abruptly brought back to the present when the limousine slowed to a halt outside his destination.

Alex alighted from the limousine and entered the modern building on Friedrichstrasse. No bodyguards for him this trip as he was not well known to the general public and not a danger to anyone – not yet anyway. Slowly he climbed the stairs, avoiding the lifts and also getting some exercise, making his way to the third floor which held the offices of Dominik Vogel his counterpart in Germany. Alex's mother who had lived through the German occupation of Greece had told him many stories about the occupation and the German officers and soldiers she had met. None of the stories painted a good picture of the German race. Unfortunately, they had left Alex with a strong dislike of them and consequently he always tried to steer clear of Germans in Greece.

It made him nervous that he was meeting a man whom he would be working with. Could Alex cut through the bias and behave as if there had been no violent history between their people? They were after all quite bizarrely Greece's main partners in Europe.

Alex pressed the buzzer next to a plaque engraved 'German Republic Ministry of Finance' and smiled into the camera positioned above the door. The door was opened by a long legged tall blonde girl wearing a white blouse and a blue skirt barely brushing her knees and exposing her long shapely legs. On her pert left breast was a name tag informing Alex she was Gitta Lehrer. In German 'Lehrer' means teacher and Alex thought being taught anything by Gitta would be a delight.

'Good morning Mr Kalfas, welcome to Berlin,' she said, showing Alex a set of flawless white teeth. 'My name is Gitta. Can I take your coat?'

Alex managed to drag his eyes away from her left breast and locked onto a set of beautifully expressive green eyes which remained cold and bore a look of disdain as she caught him staring too hard.

'Good morning Gitta,' Alex replied. 'Yes, thank you very much,' as he pulled off his coat and handed it to her.

'Come this way, Mr Vogel is expecting you.'

15

Alex did as she requested and kept his eyes on her impeccable rear as it sashayed its way towards the set of double glazed glass doors that led into Vogel's office. She drew back the doors and stood to one side to let Alex pass. She had hardly left him enough room and his arm inadvertently brushed against her right breast.

'Thank you Gitta.' Alex smiled at her and although her teeth smiled back her eyes didn't.

'Hello Kalfas, please come in.'

Vogel was sitting in his wheelchair behind a huge red mahogany desk. As Alex entered the office Vogel wheeled towards Alex. He thrust out a hand and held Alex in a vice like grip, wanting to show that although he was in a wheelchair he was as strong as any other man.

'Welcome to my ministry,' He said. 'Did you have a good journey? It must have been very rushed for you, short notice wasn't it?'

'Thank you and well…yes it was short notice but the flight was fine and although it's a little cold at least the weather is good,' Alex replied, trying not to stare too hard at Vogel's nose, which was hooked like the beak of an eagle. In fact, his whole posture even in his wheelchair was one of a bird of prey. He was tall, slim and bird like with eyes that bore into you but did not give a clue as to what he was thinking. Even his name 'Vogel' translated to 'bird' in German.

'Sit down over here.' Vogel said indicating a leather chair opposite his. 'Have you been briefed by your Prime Minister?'

'I have,' Alex replied. 'I am fairly well versed on the forthcoming closeness of the partnership between our two countries at the expense of the International Monetary Fund and the European Central Bank, although I haven't been told who will replace them, if anyone.' Then he lied, 'But I am confident that we can move forward without any problems.'

'Never mind for now,' expressed Vogel impatiently as he moved behind his desk and opened a file that had the word 'Hellas' stamped in a deep blue on its cover. He felt a little uneasy because he did not detect sincerity in Alex's reply. Not that he cared that much because he was quite

16

certain that Alex would be persuaded to do everything asked of him. As he began looking through some of the papers in the file, Alex took the opportunity to study Vogel's desk. He had seen one exactly like this before. He had to know.

'Your desk is very similar to a desk that Marcus Opel the former Chairman of the Swiss Bank had in his office. Is it from the same carpenter?' Alex enquired.

'You are very observant.' Vogel replied. 'In fact it is the same desk. He gave it to me as a gift on the day that Union Bank of Switzerland merged with Swiss Bank Corporation and he was forced to resign. Now will you excuse me for a few minutes while I catch up with some of these documents which the ECB has prepared for our meeting? Gitta, does Mr Kalfas want a coffee?'

Alex turned round in his chair and realised that Gitta had never left the office. She smiled at him and asked. 'White or black?' 'Black with two sugars please,' he replied.

While he waited for his coffee and for Vogel to finish reviewing the documents Alex reflected on how he had arrived at this point in time.

Chapter 4

October 23rd 2010 - Athens

It was only two days earlier that Alex had been called into the office of the Prime Minister in the Mansion Maximou on Herodou Attikou Street in Athens.

'Alex do come in and sit down. Would you like anything to drink?'

'Do you mean a beverage or a real drink?' Alex answered feeling slightly stupid.

'You'll need a real drink to lessen the shock of what I've got to say to you Alex,' laughed Themis Xenakis. 'What will it be?'

'Well if you insist I'll have a gin and tonic,' he replied without much conviction. 'Now tell me why I need a drink or should I wait until I've taken a few sips?'

Alex was feeling quite anxious now and he started combing his memory banks for something that he might have done which prompted this call to the Prime Minister's office. He was even more anxious when Themis treated his question as rhetorical and buzzed out to his secretary to bring him his gin and tonic.

Themis and Alex went back years. They had both studied in Boston and shared a student rooming house. However, most of the Greek media had them both attending Harvard when in fact Alex had attended Harvard and Themis, Boston University. Themis was still slim and tall and quite distinguished, although up close the slight tic in his left eye rather spoilt the overall picture of the leader of a beleaguered people. The door opened and Rena the Prime Minister's personal secretary brought in Alex's drink, setting it down beside him on a small side table.

'Thank you Rena,' he said and his politeness was rewarded with a wide smile, as indeed he had hoped it would be. Alex watched her leave the office and as she shut the door he turned towards Themis who had sat opposite him in a large leather chair. A smile was playing around his lips; no doubt he had caught him staring at Rena's shapely rear. He was right.

'I see you're admiring one of Rena's many assets, probably her best. Doesn't Melina get fed up with your wanderings? I'm sure she must suspect what you get up to when you're away from home.'

'You misjudge me Themis. I have never strayed from my marriage vows. Occasionally I might look at a beautiful woman but that is all.' Alex lied.

Themis roared with laughter and when he'd calmed down said, 'You're a consummate liar Alex. You have lied your way through life without regret or guilt and even when we were roommates in Boston you lied when I accused you of having sex with my girlfriend.'

'I didn't fuck her,' Alex interrupted. 'She gave me a blow job and I fondled her breasts. That was all there was to it,' he finished lamely.

'You're as bad as Clinton. However, that is exactly why I invited you to my office. I have a proposition for you which will enable you to use your prowess as a liar and will probably also satisfy your sexual appetite at the same time. But I must warn you it's not going to be easy. It will mean hard work, a clear mind and a lot of energy.'

Alex stared at Themis not believing his ears. His major failings were suddenly becoming assets, tools of his trade. What was his trade to be? Was he being promoted to run the Greek secret service, was he to become the Greek equivalent of 007, licensed to lie and to cheat all in the name of the Greek Republic.

'Are you offering me a new post?' Alex inquired.

'Yes Alex, I am. Antonopoulos is handing in his resignation at four o'clock and you will be replacing him in my cabinet.'

'But he is the Chancellor of the Exchequer Themis, and I know nothing about economics. My degree from Harvard was in law, you know that and it's perfect for my job as Minister of Justice. Now you want to appoint me as your economics minister. Well I'm sure there are far more qualified ministers or indeed members of parliament than me who could do the job. You can't be serious?' he ended in almost a plea.

'That's just the point Alex. Yes, there are far better qualified people than you who are economists, but unlike you they don't or won't tell lies and they are not womanisers, you are the best qualified in those departments. This is your opportunity to completely pull the wool over the Greek people's eyes and the rest of the world for that matter,' Themis ended with a flourish and looked him in the eye.

Alex stared back, his thoughts racing, why would I have to lie, he thought? Something did not add up here. The PASOK (Panhellenic Socialist) party had only just won the election so why would Themis force Antonopoulos to resign so soon? Had he done something wrong? Was there something about the numbers PASOK had inherited from the New Democracy party that were causing a problem?

'Is there a bigger problem with the economic situation in the country than people realise?' he questioned.

'Yes Alex,' grinned Themis, 'Greece is not in good shape. Our biggest problem is that Greece has the beginnings of a debt mountain which we have to get rid of.'

Then he said something that caused Alex to shudder as if someone had walked over his grave.

'With your help we are going to convince the world that Greece needs a lot more monetary help than it really does. We are going to fudge the numbers and call in the International Monetary Fund who of course will not trust our numbers and decline to help. We will then turn to Germany and Russia and with their help we will all become rich while Greece grows from strength to strength. Except.... well...apart from the collateral damage.'

Alex sat there speechless for a full minute.

'I would be party to one of the biggest frauds Europe or even the world had ever seen,' Alex blurted out. Then he had a sudden thought. 'What if I decline now that you have told me the truth?' Alex looked

Themis straight in the eye. 'Will I have one of those suicides that look like accidents?'

Themis stared at Alex and then suddenly burst out laughing. 'No Alex I would not hurt you if you declined. Somehow I don't think you will,' continued Themis as he passed a buff folder over to Alex. 'You have no choice Alex. Take a look at these.' Inside were several photographs showing Alex in compromising positions with Zoe Lafazanis, the current deputy minister of finance.

'If these ever got into the public domain your career and marriage would be destroyed. As well as Zoe's.'

Alex looked at Themis and for the first time noticed a hardness in his eyes. Yes, he thought Themis wasn't making an idle threat.

'No need for these to leave this room,' said Alex. 'I'll do it.'

'Good,' agreed Themis. 'I hope I never have to use those photographs. Why don't you keep them as a reminder of your loyalty and your addiction?'

Alex thought that was a little low but didn't give Themis the satisfaction of seeing him embarrassed or ashamed in reaction to his comment. Admittedly women were his weakness, well actually much more than a weakness, more of an addiction, but he would never admit to that. He often berated himself for cheating on his wife. Any other man would not dream of even thinking about another woman. She was tall, taller than Alex in high heels, slim and wore her clothes very well, looking good in minis or long evening gowns. She had the most piercing green eyes Alex had ever seen and wore her auburn hair shoulder length. Her body was perfectly shaped except perhaps her breasts which were slightly smaller than most men liked but in a tight pair of jeans, high heels and a halter top she turned more heads than the passing of a Hollywood star. Melina was also a little subservient in the bedroom and did whatever Alex commanded. He knew he was an idiot for going astray time and time again but like cigarettes he wasn't ready to give up his addiction just yet.

'Have you heard of Gladio, Alex?' said Themis interrupting Alex's thoughts.

'No I haven't,' replied Alex. 'What is it?'.

'Gladio is a code name taken from the Italian word - Gladius - a type of short Roman sword - for a clandestine NATO 'stay-behind' operation in Italy after the war. It was set up to continue anti-communist resistance in the event of a Warsaw Pact invasion. 'Operation Gladio' as it became known was used as an informal name for all stay-behind paramilitary organisations in Europe, whether CIA, MI6 or BND backed. When Greece joined NATO (in 1952, the country's Special Forces, the LOK (Lochoi Oreinōn Katadromōn, or 'Mountain Raiders') were merged into the European stay-behind network. This network stayed in place until just before Greece joined the Eurozone at the turn of the millennium.'

'I'm sorry,' interjected Alex. 'Who or what is BND?'

'It's the German federal secret service.'

'What happened in 2000?'

'The CIA and MI6 closed down their ends and left Gladio to LOK and BND to run, probably thinking that a united Europe had nothing to fear from extreme left wing ideologies.'

Alex pondered Themis's revelations. 'So the military coup in 1967, the attempted assignation of Makarios in Cyprus and the November 17th self-styled terrorist group were all sponsored by Gladio?'

'Spot on Alex! Of course not all the twenty-five assassinations conducted by the November 17th group were sponsored by the CIA. Once the CIA had left the building LOK and BND sanctioned targets associated with the American Embassy, including CIA operatives, in a clean-up operation.'

'I have often thought it odd that the November 17 group targeted Americans, now I see why, they were leaving no loose ends.'

'Exactly,' agreed Themis. 'Back to the business at hand. As both the Germans and Greece control Gladio we can now manipulate it to form a solid economic partnership with Germany and Russia.'

'What's the plan?' enquired Alex.

'You will meet with Vogel on the twenty-fifth and then attend the Bilderberg at the Astir Palace on the twenty-seventh. Vogel will explain everything. I'll see you at five-thirty in the office of the President of the Greek Democracy, for the ceremony to swear you in to the office of Minister of Economics.'

'I'll be there,' confirmed Alex. Although he did not feel very comfortable with any of it. But what could he do? He was backed into a corner with no escape.

Themis looked surreptitiously at his watch. Time was getting on he thought to himself. I can't give the team the go ahead while Alex is here. Alex is no fool and once he heard the news about Antonopoulos he would realise that I was involved. It was already 16.00 and Antonopoulos would be leaving his office in the parliament building fairly soon. He should get Alex out of here in the next few minutes.

'Good, let's talk again Alex. You should leave now before Antonopoulos gets here. I'll see you later.' With that Themis rose from his chair and proffered a hand to Alex and guided him towards the door. He opened it and beckoned Rena to escort Alex to his car.

Once he was sure that Alex had actually left the building he went back into his office, shut the door and walked swiftly to the phone on his desk. He dialled a number and on the third ring the phone was answered. Themis uttered one word 'Gladio' and put the phone down. That one word started a chain of events that would eventually rock the foundation of democracy in Europe.

Chapter 5

October 23rd 2010 – Athens, Greece

As Christos Antonopoulos left the parliament building through the doorway which led down onto the expansive rear garden of the building, he wondered why he had been summoned to the Prime Minister's Office. Over the last few months he had become more and more disillusioned with the way that the Eurozone were demanding more and more from Greece. Germany in particular was bleeding Greece dry with their demands to buy German goods and services, which Greece didn't need; nor could pay for, placing them in the position of having to borrow money from German banks to pay for them.

He was convinced that if Germany could re-arm they would have re-occupied the country, even perhaps the rest of Europe. But because they had no army they were conducting an economic war of the most hurtful kind, both unfair to the poorest in the Greek population and destructive for the future economic strength of the country. However, what caused him more concern than anything was an email he had received from an anonymous Hotmail account, warning him to watch his back.

Christos knew that there were certain elements in the Greek cabinet that had met with Elena Davilova in an attempt to persuade her to persuade Igor Putilov, the Russian premier, to support Greece's application for a substantial loan to complete major urban and countryside infrastructure projects. This program had already been halted by the European Union because they had correctly suspected that the funds had been diverted into other areas of the economy which directly benefited ministers and other interested parties in the country.

He had vowed to himself not to give in to peer pressure as he was certain that there was a hidden agenda which would not bode well for Greece. From now on he would be very careful and not commit himself in any way until he had formed strong alliances in Europe. That was the purpose for his upcoming visit to Brussels and his unofficial meeting with the director of the International Monetary Fund, Madame Christine

DuPont. On the quiet he would meet with her and attempt to use her as an ally against a cabinet which, he suspected, was leaning more and more towards new Russian money to avoid more of the severe austerity program which was currently crippling Greece.

Nor did he trust Themis because he was sure that he was behind the increasing Russian influence in Greece which was gaining a lot of momentum. In the last few weeks there has been unrest in several towns in western Thrace. That region had become very important to both America and Russia and also Germany, since huge deposits of oil had been discovered just offshore in the western Aegean. Western Thrace was also the region where the gas pipelines from Russian and American interests entered a terminal where the gas was then routed into the huge gas pipeline that traversed northern Greece before going under the Ionian Sea into Italy and on into Europe.

The unrest seemed to emanate from the ethnic Muslim minorities who lived in the region. It was reported that the minority Turkish Muslims were behind the unrest, but Christos believed otherwise and had recently vented his scepticism in cabinet meetings, theorising that pro-Russian elements were trying to destabilize the region for their own agenda. All this rushed through Christos's mind as he walked through the parliament building's gardens.

Today Christos had his usual two bodyguards with him, but as they were very sure that he was in no danger on a walk he and many before him had made many times in the past, they walked a few metres behind him. The garden at the rear of the parliament building is split by a hundred metres of path bordered with rhododendron bushes, and the path runs down to the Harry Truman gate, which opens out onto Herodou Attikou Avenue, there guarded by the statue of Harry Truman. This tree lined avenue borders the length of the parliament building gardens and is blocked at both ends by metal barriers, guarded by presidential guards.

Only official cars were allowed onto Herodou Attikou and the two shorter avenues which formed a 'T' with Herodou Attikou. All had guard houses preventing access by public traffic, except official and diplomatic cars belonging to the many embassies set back from the road in their capacious private gardens.

At one end of Herodou Attikou stood the Prime Minister's residence, just two hundred yards from the Harry Truman gate. At the opposite end stood the Presidential Palace.

As Christos neared the Harry Truman gate he noticed that the barriers at the end of Likiou Avenue, which formed a 'T' with Herodou Attikou, had opened and a black Nissan Navara Black Star was being let through. If he had stopped and continued watching, he would have seen a figure run out of the guard house and leap into the car. The car began to pick up speed and the barriers remained open. He saw none of this as his view was obscured by the Harry Truman statue. It was only as he exited the gate and turned right and started walking towards the Prime Minister's residence that he noticed that the Nissan had almost reached the corner. His guards must have sensed something was not quite right because they began to quickly close the gap between themselves and Christos, but as the Nissan turned right onto Herodou Attikou Avenue, its rear window, which had been hidden from view until then, was fully open with an ugly looking AK-47 protruding out that immediately started to spit a hail of lead towards Christos and his bodyguards.

One of the bodyguards managed to throw himself in front of Christos and took five lethal bullets in his chest. As the guard fell to the ground leaving Christos exposed to the gun fire, Christos threw himself to the pavement wincing in pain as a bullet passed through his neck at the instant the second bodyguard landed on top of him. With his breath knocked out of him and an excruciating pain in his neck Christos suddenly realised that he should attempt to get back into the parliament building gardens and try to escape. He noticed quietness had descended on the street as if someone had turned the sound off on the television, but the picture still played. The Nissan had stopped a few yards from where Christos lay and in the distance he could see the presidential guards streaming out of their barracks towards the Nissan. Christos tried to push the motionless bodyguard from on top of him but only managed to get his upper torso free of the dead weight. Suddenly a cacophony of sounds split the silence; the Nissan's wheel's screeching as the driver attempted to reverse at speed, and the shouts and gunfire coming from the presidential guards who were only fifty yards from the scene. The Nissans wheel's gripped the road as the driver threw the steering wheel to the left and the car reversed up onto the pavement. Too late, Christos realised that the car was reversing towards him. With a superhuman effort he tried to free himself from the bodyguard. One leg came free and then the other but it was too late,

The last thing Christos saw was the deep treads of the Nissans rear left wheel a split second before it passed over his head crushing the life out of him.

Chapter 6

October 23rd 2010 – Langley, Virginia

Laura Foot stared hard at her screen. For several days she had been watching Athens because there was intelligence about impending violent demonstrations against austerity in Syntagma Square in front of the Greek parliament building. She was head of operations for the Balkans region and had only been in the Balkans section of 'Overlook' for three days. She realised that something was going on. She needed confirmation, she needed more eyes.

'Jim,' she shouted, to a large man who had a tuna and mayo sandwich in one hand and a coffee in the other, 'I need another birds eye view of Athens. I've got GEO37 online; can you get another one that's just passed over Greece?'

Jim was the sections geek, although he didn't look anything like a typical geek at all. At least not to his colleagues. He was a large man, not overweight but muscular. Laura suspected he worked out in his spare time. He wore a round face with brown unruly hair continually falling into his eyes so he was continually swatting it away from his forehead. He rarely came into work in a suit even though he obviously owned a few as he quite often spoke about the dinner parties he had been invited to through his current girlfriend, the daughter of a Washington socialite. His favourite casual wear was old fashioned corduroys and long sleeved checked shirts. Jim certainly knew his technology, machines were his passion as was jazz, this he let slip one evening when he, Barry and Laura had an after work drink to celebrate his forty second birthday last month.

'On it, Laura,' confirmed Jim, 'what do you think you've seen?'

'Something's going on behind the parliament building. It's not clear but I thought I picked up muzzle flashes. GEO37 got a side view, I need an overhead. Have you got one?'

'I think we have two overheads, one is ours, GEO41, and the other belongs to Turkey.' I'll download the video from forty-one straight away. What's the time window?'

'Ten minutes either side of 4pm GMT plus two,' said Laura. 'Ask Barry to pull in a favour from the Turks so we can get confirmation.'

'Right, I'm feeding the video to the wall now. I'll split screen it with your stuff and we can compare. I'll call Barry.'

Laura, watching the video from GEO41, saw a figure walking through the gardens at the rear of the parliament building in Athens with two men about two yards behind. She also saw a black Nissan pass in front of the three figures as they turned right onto the street. The muzzle flashes were coming from the back left hand side of the Nissan. All three figures fell to the pavement and then the Nissan reversed onto the pavement and seemed to run over the three figures lying on the ground before speeding away up the road from where it had come.

'Can we get in closer?' asked Laura as she moved over to where Jim was typing furiously on his computer console. It had to be someone important she thought as she knew there were a series of high level meetings in the area of the parliament building today. The door opened and Barry Lightfoot, Laura's boss and the Balkan Station Chief in Washington, walked quickly towards her.

'What have we got?' Barry said to the room in general.

'Looks like a shooting in Athens,' answered Laura, 'but we don't have any details just yet. Jim is trying to get us a closer look and also bring a Turkish bird on-line. I'm guessing it's a Government minister with two security guards.'

'Damn,' vented Barry, 'can you enhance Jim?'

'I'm trying sir, but even if I get a clear frame, the subjects face is looking down and we won't capture any recognizable features.'

'Body type…is the subject slim, portly, short or tall? Can you tell?'

'Difficult to tell but I would say portlier than slim. Wait, the Turkish bird is now on-line so maybe we can get something more concrete,' replied Jim, as he turned towards the wall screen pointing out the fresh video being streamed in from the Turkish satellite.

They watched as Jim manipulated the incoming data to show the three men actually leaving the rear door of the parliament building. He centred on the leading man and started to zoom and enhance so that within a minute they had a clear picture of Christos Antonopoulos.

'It's the Greek Economics Minister,' exclaimed Laura, 'why would he be an assassination target?' she asked.

'He was a friend, that's why,' exclaimed Barry, 'too good a friend it seems. I wouldn't mind betting there has been a major policy change in Greece with regard to allies. Can you get hold of the Athens Station Chief, what's his name? Chris something isn't it?'

'Chris Horsman sir,' answered Laura, 'I'll call him now.' Laura punched in a set of numbers on her cell phone and then placed it in a speaker phone cradle. After five rings it was answered and a voice sounding as if it was coming from a tin can penetrated the room.

'You've seen it, that's why you're calling,' stated Chris at once.

'We have Chris and we're puzzled. Why would Antonopoulos be an assassin's target? There is no logic to such an act; can you shed some light on this dreadful event?'

'I'll try,' said Chris. 'There have been rumours around for a few weeks now that Antonopoulos had stumbled across some information and he was about to talk to IMF. No-one is clear what he had found out, but it must have been big because he wanted Brussels to know about it. He was on his way to the Prime Minister's office when it happened. We are hearing that a major policy change is about to take place. What it is exactly we don't know, but obviously it has something to do with the beans that Antonopoulos was about to spill. Interestingly enough, Elena Davilova was in Athens yesterday meeting with Xenakis and not with Antonopoulos, so that might point to a move towards former allies. On the other hand, we are also hearing that Germany is looking for more natural resources and is looking towards the Aegean, so we aren't sure where Greece is heading but something is definitely brewing. My guess is that within a few hours a group will claim responsibility for the assassination and soon after that some evidence of CIA backing will emerge.'

'This could be messy, and just as we thought it was safe to holiday in Greece,' he chuckled. 'Do we know who will step into Antonopoulos's shoes?' he asked.

'No idea,' said Chris, 'but I would imagine we will learn very soon. I'm going to make a few phone calls and if I get anything new I'll get back to you.'

'Thanks Chris, see what you can find out,' reiterated Barry and signalled to Laura to cut the connection. 'Okay, I've got to take this upstairs, how soon can you put a package together? 'One hour tops,' replied Laura. 'I'll have it on your desk at one o'clock.'

Chapter 7

Central Greece October 24th 2010

Alex watched as his mother stopped and sat down on a small rock by the cobbled road. She looked up and saw that she had a hundred more yards to the summit, thankfully she didn't see him. The summit was a rock that stood like a sentinel, one hundred and seventy metres above the village. She was tired and even though it was late in the evening and approaching late September, the temperature was still up in the mid-twenties centigrade. There was no need to hurry she thought; the dead are not going anywhere. The cemetery that overlooked the village of Achinos had been part of the village for thousands of years.

She was still as lithe, slim and beautiful as she had been many years ago, but since her husband had died of cancer when she was still only thirty-six years old; she had led a life of mourning and solitude. She was alone because of two events. One was that she had given birth to Alex and the other was that on her husband's death bed she had made a foolish promise.

'Ariadne?' Vassili whispered, as he lay pale and gaunt on his hospital bed in the armed forces hospital in Athens.

'Yes Vassili,' answered Ariadne, squeezing his hand to let him know she was close by. 'What is it?'

'When we get home I'll fix the wooden bench so that we can sit out in the garden and watch the sun set over the sea.'

Tears filled Ariadne's eyes for she knew that Vassili was never going home. Vassili was going to God's home. 'When you are strong enough we will go home together,' she answered, a tear dropping onto Vassili's hand.

'Ariadne, don't cry, I know I'm never going home. I just wanted to cheer you up. You look so beautiful today. Promise me one thing Ariadne.'

'Anything Vassili.'

'I wouldn't like it if another man touched you Ariadne. You know how jealous I get. Please promise me you won't marry again.'

Ariadne didn't know what to say. She kept smiling down at her husband as images from the past cleaved through her brain. She had met him for the first time when she was 23 years old, at a dinner party held on her behalf by her uncle in Conakry, New Guinea. Her first real vivid memory was standing on a dock at the port of Piraeus in 1948 when she was 21 years old. The woman she was with said she was her aunt and had taken her to the port to catch a ship to Marseille in France to be with her father.

The ship was not a proper passenger liner, it was a cargo ship that had a few cabins for passengers and friends but it was clean and the crew were friendly, particularly as Ariadne was the only young female passenger on the ship. The trip was uneventful however and the highlight of the five-day trip was dinner at the Captain's table on the last night of the voyage.

It was raining hard when the ship docked in Marseille. Her father had met her at the port holding a large golfing umbrella over a woman who turned out to be his live-in girlfriend. She recalled that she thought the girlfriend, who was French, was very beautiful and sexy. She wore clothes that showed off her slim body and long shapely legs. He greeted her just like a father would, but underneath his excitement at seeing her she detected a falseness that puzzled her. It was as if he was acting a part and what's more she failed to see a likeness to him at all, although after a few days she began to realise that perhaps the likeness was not physical but that they had similar personalities. He was stubborn just like her and hated to admit that he was wrong, also he was outgoing and liked to regale others with stories of his life.

Her father lived in a small but pretty cottage in Nice not far from the promenade. He owned a small Greek bakery business which provided bread to the community of Greeks who lived in Nice and the surrounding areas. The girlfriend said she was a model but never elaborated on what type of model she was, although later Ariadne discovered that the girlfriend worked in a bar as a stripper.

33

Ariadne became bored with her life in Nice very quickly. Her father was very strict and did not allow her to go out on her own. Whenever she ventured out she had to be accompanied either by her father, his girlfriend or on occasions one of his not too kosher friends. The only places she went to were the beach if the weather was nice, or to some sort of men's club where her father played poker for money, or very occasionally a cinema or restaurant. The truth of the matter was that in 1948 in the aftermath of the Second World War southern France was full of suspicious and unsavoury characters, so for a beautiful young girl venturing out at night on her own there were inherent dangers.

She dared not tell her father about her boredom. She was smart enough to know how she could get round him. Her father had a brother who had a bakery in the small Greek community in Conakry in New Guinea, so she had persuaded him to let her visit his brother in Africa. Actually, he seemed almost relieved that she was getting out of the house, but pleased she wanted to visit his brother. Within a month she was on a ship steaming towards Conakry and it was in Conakry that she met Vassili. Was she in love with him? No she wasn't, but she was in love with the prospect of being away from her father and on an adventure.

Although she was warned against getting too friendly with him, the moment she met Vassili at a dinner party given in her honour by her uncle, she vowed to marry him and help him with his Festika nut business in the hinterlands of New Guinea. To this day everyone had said that she had done it to spite her father and her uncle. She knew differently however as she knew that she had done it to be independent and have her own business. Vassili was 20 years older than her and had never been married. He could never have rejected the attentions of a beautiful Greek girl. On the night they met she had coaxed him to accompany her to the warehouse at the back of her uncle's house. There his life was changed forever as she made love to him with an expertise that belied her innocent demeanour. They were to meet nightly and after six days he was putty in her hands, proposing marriage on the seventh day.

She accepted his proposal without hesitation, even though it had been alleged that he had been in involved in one or two sex scandals with under age black girls, but nothing had ever been proven and he had never been charged. Some years after she had married Vassili she found him having sex with a 13-year-old black girl in the store room of their shop. She had forgiven him because they were about to return to Greece with the money they had made and she thought that in a more familiar environment Vassili would not repeat his actions. She was to be proved wrong.

In Greece Vassili got a job as a French interpreter in the offices of the military police, acquired through his brother Dimitris who was an officer in the Greek army. It was an easy job that paid well, so with the money they had accumulated in Africa and with his salary, Ariadne and Vassili had bought a villa by the sea in the district of Vouliagmeni, just 25 kilometres along the coast from Athens. He was then transferred to the Greek Embassy in Rumania as the assistant to the military attaché. The Rumanian secret police used young girls to seduce Vassili in the hope that he would talk about his job and unwittingly give away important information. He never gave anything away, and despite Ariadne and the Greek Ambassador warning him to stop seeing Rumanian girls, he continued to see them and finally, while driving one of his girl's home one night the Rumanian secret police rammed his car in an attempt to kill him. They failed, but the injuries he sustained led to him protracting cancer and being in the hospital he now occupied. These thoughts raced around Ariadne's head in a flash and then she answered.

'Yes, Vassili I promise not to marry again,' Ariadne whispered. Then she bit her lip and regretted saying those words the moment she had said them. But she kept to her promise and after Vassili had died she lived alone and never considered marriage despite numerous introductions to eligible men.

Only once did she stray, this was into a secret affair with an American naval officer but she broke it off when she realized that she was pregnant. She dropped out of sight until she had given birth because in Greece at that time an unmarried mother was likely to be ostracised by family and friends. She then gave the baby up to be fostered by a couple who were close friends of the naval officer. They brought up her son whom she had named Alex after his father and sent him to America to live with his father in Washington DC. While he was there she had been sent a plane ticket, with a letter requesting her to attend a meeting which had something to do with her son. What she had been told had frightened her, but she had agreed to do as they had requested. Now twenty-six years on, as of yesterday, Alex was Greece's minister of finance and she was proud of him and loved him dearly.

Now she was sitting on the small rock by the road resting her tired legs before she attempted the final one hundred steep yards to the summit to sit at the graveside of her Vassili.

She looked down on the village that had been there for thousands of years. The present village was built upon the ruins of ancient Echinos, and is still guarded over by its impressive castle, which dates back to the fourth century BC and sits on the side of a rocky mound one hundred and fifty meters tall. On the summit of the rock sits a cemetery and a small church. The church dates back to 786AD and was the place of worship for the villagers before the modern church of Saint Ekaterina was built in the village square.

Today the small cemetery church is used to store the bones of the dead after they have been extracted from rotting coffins to make room for the new dead. The cemetery was small and the average age of the villagers was up in the mid-fifties, so the church of Saint Ekaterina had more than its fair share of funerals and the small church in the cemetery has more than its fair share of bones. Before the cemetery was built the rocky mound was part of the fortifications of the ancient village. In those days the sea was much higher than it is now and almost lapped at the doors of the ancient village. Just over twelve kilometres south of the village across the Bay of Maliakos is the pass of Thermopylae where in 500BC, three hundred Spartans died delaying the Persian armies from their march south into Athens by defending the only pass that allowed passage from the north between the sea and the mountains.

Nowadays the sea has receded so that today it is two kilometres from the village and the relinquished land supports thousands of olive trees. The fortified homes of more recent periods suggest that the history of Achinos remained impressive throughout the ages. Because as it was in direct line of raiding hordes from Salonika and northern Greece passing through on their way to Athens, they needed a means of repelling pirate raids. Over hundreds of years Achinos suffered victories and defeats, but was never entirely vanquished. Today, beneath the houses and gardens of the village lie coffins buried in haste. Villagers excavating to build their homes often had to repatriate coffins and skeletons to the cemetery at the top of the rocky mound.

Most of the archaeological treasures they found in between the coffins didn't end up in the cemetery or the local museum; after initially being hidden they were later smuggled out of Greece to Europe and America. Some families in the village were extremely well off, although they did not work or own olive groves. Also, it was not unusual for German tourists to spend time near the village digging up the treasures they had left buried there during their occupation of Stylida, a small port twelve kilometres south of Achinos.

As the old woman gazed out over the village towards the sea, the sun slipped over the horizon, and dusk started to cast its dark shadow over the countryside. Some lights had already been switched on in the village below, the most prominent being the blue cross that sits atop the dome of Saint Ekaterina, the village church. Further down from the church the lights of the cafés and the souvlakia eating places were just coming on and a group of Albanian workers were sitting in the only caffenion and souvlaki place. They had finished harvesting in the olive groves for the day and were now taking a break before the job of grading the day's olives began.

Ariadne could see people walking along the village's main street, some carrying plastic bags holding the shopping they had just purchased from the supermarket owned by Maria Antonopoulos. It was the only supermarket in the village and had been there in one form or another since 1947. It was in that year that Maria's husband was handed the keys of a small dairy by his father. Over the years the small dairy became a mini market and then a small supermarket and except for one son Christos, who yesterday had been cut down in the streets of Athens, the whole family worked in the business. She wondered how the supermarket could survive in the economic climate of present day Greece. Achinos was a village that had a population of nine hundred and almost a third of those were pensioners. Over the last two years they had seen their purchasing power reduced by fifty percent as had every other pensioner in Greece.

Alex watched as his mother slowly got to her feet and started to climb the last one hundred yards of road that led to the cemetery. Just inside the cemetery Ariadne walked to the small church and disappeared inside. Alex followed. He entered the church and in the gloom saw his mother standing looking at one of the many icons that adorned the walls of the old church. Alex walked over to her and pulled her to him giving her a long hug.

'We must hurry,' urged Ariadne, 'anyone could walk in here and see us together. Take this,' she continued, as she handed Alex a folded piece of paper. 'Memorize it and then burn it.'

Alex took the paper, unfolded it and read what it said.

'How are you?' asked Alex, as he started to memorize the numbers written on the paper. 'What are these numbers?'

'They are the access code to the Balkans section of the CIA. Although I work for British intelligence I am also a liaison with the CIA. The British and Americans are supposed to work close together, although there are times when political pressures or national interests get in the way. You Alex have just been woken up. Actually the moment you accepted Themis' job offer you became a CIA operative. You will get help from a Stazi double agent so don't worry. You will be protected,' finished Ariadne.

'How do you feel about Christos?' asked Alex.

'Better than I should,' volunteered Ariadne. 'When I heard about the assassination yesterday I knew that the final stages of the dismantlement of 'Gladio' had begun, and I was afraid for you. But, I was also proud because I know that you will succeed, you have to be successful and bring the corrupt Greek elite to their knees once and for all. You must finish Operation Gladio as it was originally envisaged!'

Before Alex could respond, the door of the church opened and a family from the village walked in. Alex turned his back on the door and wandered deeper into the gloom of the church. His mother nodded a greeting to the family and walked out into the twilight. Alex followed at a discreet distance and once outside the church walked to the grave of his mother's husband. Around the grave were several candles burning within glass holders. He took one last look at the paper he had been given, then folded it up into a cigar shape and set it alight with one of the candles. He watched it burn and when he was quite sure it was completely burnt he blew the ashes to scatter them. He then strolled towards the cemetery entrance fearful about the immense responsibility that had been thrust upon him.

Ariadne walked through the cemetery and stopped to tend Vassili's grave. She then slipped through a break in the low wall surrounding the cemetery and walked to the north facing edge of the rock mound. She stopped and sat on a small rock and gazed out over the landscape. She loved this view of the central Pindus mountain chain that separated Greece vertically east to west. Her eyes settled on Mount Othrys rising a majestic eighteen hundred metres which still had a little snow from last winter. These days the view was spoilt by the ugly scar of a new highway being built between Athens and Salonika which ran through the olive groves dressing the valleys and hills between the rock and the mountain.

Suddenly Ariadne heard a noise. She turned around and saw a man smiling down at her.

'What are you doing in Greece?' she asked.

'We were concerned,' said the man. He was a good lair. 'So I was sent to see you. Do you think Gladio has been compromised?'

'If it had been there would have been arrests and an armed forces cull. I would have been arrested for starters,' She replied as she stood up and faced the man.

'Dramatic view,' suggested the man. Ariadne turned around and looked out in the same direction as the man. She felt his hand on her back but before she could turn around the pressure increased and she felt herself being forcefully pushed towards the edge of the rock mound. She stepped forward to ease the pressure but she was already off balance and forced to take another step to get her balance back. It was one step too many. The slope was now too steep and she simply stepped out into a void. Silently she fell the one hundred and fifty metres to the olive grove slopes below. Her last thoughts were a prayer that her son would be victorious and snuff out the threat to democracy in Europe.

Chapter 8

October 25th 2010 – Berlin

Vogel shuffled the papers he had been reading and slid them back into the blue folder that had 'Hellas' stamped on the front, opened a drawer, put the folder into it and then closed it with a flourish. He looked up at Alex, but Alex was deep in his own thoughts and didn't notice that Vogel had finished reading.

'Alex,' said Vogel, a smile playing around his lips. 'Are you still with us?'

Alex jumped at the sudden interruption of his thoughts and looked up to see that Vogel was looking at him with a strange smile on his face. He felt that Vogel thought of him as a plaything and that he would be putty in the hands of the plans stakeholders which he knew Vogel would start to present to him in the next few seconds.

'Sorry Dominik,' replied Alex. 'I hope using your Christian name isn't out of order? If it is, then please tell me.'

'No my dear Alex, I don't mind at all. Now, let's get down to the business at hand shall we. By the way I'm sorry about the unfortunate death of Antonopoulos as he was a fine man, a good diplomat and a good friend of the German people. Do the police have any idea who murdered him?'

'No, not yet,' replied Alex thinking that Vogel was as sad as a man who had just won the lottery. 'I don't consider it a murder, it was an assassination, a brutal unnecessary violent act,' he continued vehemently.

'Perhaps,' murmured Vogel, 'let's see who claims responsibility for the act. We might be surprised at the outcome.'

'You sound as if you already know which group will claim the killing,' said Alex, looking hard across the desk at Vogel. He was surprised to see that Vogel was wheeling himself around his desk towards him with what seemed to be a smirk on his face, that is, if his bird-like features could actually produce a smirk. If Alex needed prompting that he should not trust Vogel he need look no further, his sarcastic comment and smirk confirmed it all.

'You have a lot to learn Alex,' said Vogel as he stopped in front of Alex, 'and we don't have much time. We have decided that you will conduct a press conference in Athens at the Bilderberg meeting in two days' time. At this press conference you will announce that your country is bankrupt and that you have asked the International Monetary Fund, the Eurozone countries, and the European Central Bank for financial help. They agreed but in return they want Greece to enter a very hard financial austerity program. So Greece has decided to look elsewhere for help. Tomorrow you will travel to attend the Bilderberg meeting at the Astir Palace Hotel in Vouliagmeni Greece. You are booked on a Lufthansa flight in the morning. It's only an hour and forty-five-minute flight and Gitta will travel with you.'

'Who will be at the meeting?' asked Alex, 'and why is Gitta coming with me?' Even as he said it Alex knew what the answer would be. Gitta would be keeping an eye on him.

'My dear Alex, we imagined you would enjoy the company of a beautiful woman as otherwise we thought you might get bored,' he chuckled and then he carried on. 'Seriously though, Gitta is not just a pretty face, she is an excellent economist and has a sharp business mind, she is my number two as well as my bodyguard and she will be your personal bodyguard at the meeting. Gitta will be invaluable to you as she knows most of the attendees at the meeting. She will pick you up from your hotel tomorrow morning and take you to the airport. Now is there anything else we need to talk about?'

'Who will vet my press conference speech?' asked Alex.

'The speech will be constructed by a committee of people outside the official meeting who will form a working group to include you. Gitta will organise this so you will have no need to worry.'

'Who will be at the meeting? Do you have a guest list?'

'Gitta will fill you in on those details later. Why don't you go to your hotel and freshen up and Gitta can come over and keep you company and answer all your questions about the meeting over dinner.'

Alex actually didn't think it was a good idea at all. He wanted to be alone for a few hours as he had things to do and he was also feeling rather tired after the events of the last few days. Normally he would have welcomed the company of such a beautiful woman as Gitta, but he didn't want to be distracted by her tonight. However, he could not think of a decent excuse so he acquiesced.

'Yes, I could do with some company,' lied Alex, 'and Gitta's knowledge and input will be invaluable to me. Shall we say the lobby at 20.00? Oh, by the way, which hotel am I staying in?'

'Good, I'll inform Gitta of the arrangements,' replied Vogel. 'She doesn't live far from your hotel anyway. The hotel is the Adlon Kempinski on Unter den Linden near where the old Berlin Wall used to be. It's a luxurious hotel, you will enjoy your stay I'm sure, the floor manager has been instructed to cater for whatever you might need, including female company if you so desire it,' said Vogel, a smug smile forming on his thin lips.

Later that Saturday afternoon Alex was being shown into his suite at the Adlon. No single doors with a card key here, thought Alex. The floor manager unlocked the door using two golden keys. The plaque on the door read Brandenburg Gate Suite and as the doors were opened Alex saw the Gate itself through the huge windows that flanked one side of the big living room. The room itself had a lush thick pile beige carpet which set off the four huge armchairs which were positioned around a glass topped coffee table set on silver legs. In the corner of the room was a gold lamp standard dressed with a black shade and next to that was a small teak table. The only acknowledgement of the contemporary was a huge flat screen television, standing on what looked like a drinks cabinet. Alex walked through the living room and slid open the oak doors that led into the bedroom. This was decorated in the same luxurious style as the living room and duplicated much of the furniture except of course the king size bed which was book ended by two oak bedside tables. Off the bedroom was a shower room which could literally hold five or six people and through the shower room a bathroom with a Jacuzzi, bidet and toilet. Both rooms were decked in black floor tiles that continued half way up the walls, the upper half being mirrored.

'Thank you, I don't want to be disturbed except by the porter when he brings up my bags,' Alex said to the floor manager before dismissing him with a wave of his hand.

'Yes sir,' replied the floor manager, 'if you need anything just press the blue button on any of the phones in the room, it's a direct line to me. My name is Kurt and am at your disposal twenty-four hours a day,' continued Kurt, as he backed out of the room with a slight bow.

After Kurt had left Alex walked over to the window and looked out at the Brandenburg Gate. He recalled from history that it was once the gateway to Berlin and now formed the entry to the famous Linden tree lined avenue of Unter den Linden, which used to lead to the city palace of the Prussian monarchs. It was only since the fall of the Berlin Wall that the Brandenburg Gate has once more come into prominence as one of the most well-known landmarks of Germany. It was here in 1989 that the Berlin Wall was breached and the Brandenburg Gate became accessible again.

He looked at his watch and saw that it was almost five o'clock. Gitta would be here at eight, so he had only three hours alone and he had a lot to do. He needed his laptop in a hurry but it was with the rest of his bags and the porter still had not arrived. Alex needed a drink and walked over to the cabinet on which stood the television. He pulled open the door and saw that it was a safe and not a drinks cabinet. He looked around loosening his tie as he did so. Not spotting a drinks cabinet in the living area he went into the bedroom and immediately noticed it in the corner. Alex poured himself a whisky and topped up the glass with water, dropped in two cubes of ice and sipped it a few times enjoying the slight burning sensation in his throat and the warm feeling filling his mid region.

He toyed with his glass while he waited for the porter and his mind tried to sort out what lay in store for him in the coming days. His mind drifted to thoughts of the Bilderberg meeting. He didn't know too much about these meetings but he did know that it was an annual conference established in 1954 which was intended to foster discussion between Europe and North America but now included participants from Russia, Asia, South America and Australasia. The group's programme, originally to prevent another world war, is now clearly defined as emphasising a consensus around free market Western capitalism and its interests around the globe. Attendees include political leaders, industry experts, finance experts, academics, and the media, usually numbering between one hundred and twenty to one hundred and fifty participants. Attendees are entitled to use information gained at the meetings, but not to attribute it to a named speaker. This is supposed to encourage frank debate, while maintaining complete privacy. Invariably this meeting was often associated with some sort of conspiracy theory but none was ever proven. Alex wondered who the attendees in Athens might be. Waste of time trying to guess he would be informed in good time. Perhaps Langley had that information.

He would have to communicate with them of course, once his laptop was delivered with the rest of his bags. Then there was Gitta. Alex had never laid eyes on such a beautiful woman before, however he knew that she would never let him anywhere near her, he had seen it in her eyes that afternoon. Alex was no fool and he had seen the way she looked at him. Her eyes did not smile at him at all. She probably wasn't looking forward to spending her evening chaperoning a stranger, answering his questions and discussing boring details about the Bilderberg meeting instead of being out on a hot date. It crossed Alex's mind that she might be married although he hadn't noticed a ring, but modern women seem to shun such symbols of belonging and are far more independently minded. Alex had a feeling that Gitta was a career women and marriage was not one of her ambitions. For her men were no problem, it was keeping them at bay that was a headache for her.

Alex's thoughts were interrupted by a knock on the double doors leading to the suite.

'Who is it?' shouted Alex.

'Your bags sir,' replied the porter.

'Come on in,' said Alex. The porter stepped into the room and asked Alex. 'Shall I put them in the bedroom sir?'

Alex nodded and the porter shuffled into the bedroom and placed Alex's bags at the foot of the bed. On the way out the porter took the five euro note that Alex proffered, made a one fingered salute and shuffled out of the suite closing the door behind him. Alex decided to shower and shave before he used his laptop; after all it was still only midday in Langley.

Chapter 9

October 25th 2010 – Langley, Virginia

In the operations room of the Balkans Overlook team in the CIA building, several people sat round an oval desk chatting aimlessly about anything but the situation at hand. They were waiting for Barry Lightfoot the Balkans Station Chief and their boss, who was being briefed by the Head of Operations European Region about the situation in Europe but specifically Greece. Laura Foot couldn't contain her excitement and tried hard not to show the others how eager she was to contribute to whatever project was about to be set in motion. She had been in the department as Head of Operations for just 5 days and now she had a major event to handle. Not bad, she thought, for a gangly girl from Westerville, a small town twenty or so miles from Columbus, Ohio.

No longer a gangly girl, she had filled out nicely, although tall at five foot seven without heels. Laura favoured above the knee skirts showed off her toned thighs to maximum effect. Lately she was aware that men eyeing her up and down. This was a far cry from her university days at Ohio State where she was the only girl in her year who never had a steady boyfriend. It wasn't that she was ugly, but boys tended to be intimidated by her intelligence and shunned her.

Laura had once attempted, in a clumsy way, to ask a third year student to go out. He was fit, but she wasn't the only one to think so, most of the girls fancied him. After going out on a date they were sitting in the campus bistro. She had taken great care with what she wore that night, choosing a slightly transparent blouse without a bra, knowing her nipples would be noticeable. Her skirt was short, and her heels high, giving her gangly legs some semblance of a womanly shape. They talked, he about sport and family, she about physics, electronics and politics, all the things she loved.

Whilst she was talking the strangest thing happened. She had been bored with his small talk and he was obviously not interested in what she had to say, but as she talked and took over the conversation, she started to become turned on by her own words and she felt herself becoming wet, her thighs becoming moist. Still engaging him with conversation she suddenly grabbed his hand and before he understood what was happening had placed it on the moist patch on her thigh. Her very first orgasm was instantaneous and strong and she could barely stop herself from groaning, letting out a barely perceptible wheezing sound.

The boy looked at her in bewilderment as he pulled away his hand and asked 'Are you alright Laura?'

'Err…yes…I mean no…. I had an orgasm', she blurted out as her face coloured a deep red, 'I'm so sorry', she finished lamely.

Laura didn't wait for the boy to say anything else. Getting up from the table, Laura threw a ten-dollar bill down and rushed out of the bistro, leaving the astonished boy staring after her. She didn't slow down till having reached the safety of her dormitory room where she burst into tears as she threw herself on the bed. Ten minutes later her analytical mind had reasoned out why she had cried and what had caused the orgasm. The tears were not because she felt embarrassed or that she had ruined her reputation, they were because she had become a woman. She also reasoned that she should be dating older men, men who could discourse on her level and excite her, men with the experience to satisfy her sexual desires. Laura did exactly that, three months later found her having an affair with one of her university professors.

It was he who had pushed her to become a CIA analyst. His brother worked as a political analyst for 'Overlook' South America and after she had gained her master's degree in Political Science and International Relations, he invited her into Langley for an interview. She impressed everyone and was immediately offered the position of deputy Head of Overlook Operations Panama. Six days ago Laura was promoted to Head of Overlook Operations Balkans, just four years after joining the CIA. Now her department were in the middle of a European crisis and she couldn't wait for the meeting to begin. Her thoughts were disrupted by the sound of the door opening and Barry Lightfoot, the Balkans Station Chief, walked in.

Barry sat down at the head of the oval table, opened his briefcase took out a file and then called the meeting to start.

'Good morning', he said as he loosened his tie. 'We have a lot to cover today so the first decision is what you want to eat during our working lunch. Write down what you fancy and I'll get someone to order it in. Laura could you please sort that out whilst Jim gets hold of Chris in Athens? Jim the line needs to be completely secure and also set up for an incoming encrypted SCIPTS call'.

'Who is calling in?' questioned Laura as she punched a button and at each place at the table a panel opened and a flat screen monitor silently rose into view. Laura chuckled to herself as she thought about the Satellite Communications International Protocol Telephony System -SCIPTS. It was the most popular free internet telephone and messaging system in the world and nobody knew what it stood for, that is except CIA personnel. As a CIA stealth tool and one of their greatest successes, it enabled them to listen in to every internet conversation taking place over SCIPTS and nobody had a clue.

'We have activated an asset, in fact two assets. The caller is Alex Kalfas who has just been appointed the successor to Antonopoulos. He has no idea who the other asset is yet', said Barry. 'I haven't got a written agenda but I think the day's proceedings should go something like this'.

While Barry talked Laura was gathering her thoughts. With her IQ of one hundred and seventy, she had no problem in listening and thinking at the same time. She knew that Barry would ask her for her analysis on the situation and she was quite confident that her analysis would be spot on. After all she had unique informants, dangerous at that. Suddenly Laura's ears pricked up as she heard Barry say that Geoffrey Stevens, the Head of Operations European Region, wanted their section to stop monitoring the whole Balkan region and concentrate on Greece and the key individuals involved in Germany, Greece and Russia. Another section would temporarily take over the rest of the Balkan countries. This must be really big, thought Laura realising that her analysis couldn't be complete because there was a lot of information which she didn't possess.

49

'Jim we need birds covering Athens and Berlin and maybe Moscow as well as key individuals. Geoffrey has given us the clearance to commandeer any satellite whether it is ours or an ally. We need full satellite coverage by the end of the day. Now, I'll give you the intelligence we have available. Jim is Chris listening in?'

A tinny voice boomed across the room. 'I'm here Barry; carry on it's a clean line'.

'Right', said Barry, 'jump in if you have something to add. It seems the one thing which we were afraid of happened. After the CIA pulled out of Gladio and left it to LOK and the BND to run, they have completely ignored its original ethos and under its umbrella covertly moved down the opposite path from its intended direction.'

'You're right,' agreed Chris. 'It does look like they are moving over to the other side of the street.'

'Also becoming greedy for natural resources and green energy. The only untapped resources left in Europe are the oil and gas reserves under the Aegean and Ionian seas and the abundance of land which is owned by the Orthodox Church,' interjected Barry. 'Russia is keen to have a foothold in Eastern Europe and Germany is keen to get their hands on cheap resources. To do this they need to do two things. Firstly, discredit the United States and secondly they must destroy the economic potential of the country. The discretisation of the USA started with the assassination of Antonopoulos and the admission of the killing by the November 17th terrorist group. According to the Greek authorities this group was supposedly destroyed when the ring leaders were tried and imprisoned in 2002. Over the last few days' sources in the Greek Government have been leaking snippets of information which discredits the USA. Do you have any more on that Chris?'

'Yes, I do', confirmed Chris. 'Greek parliament members have always been keen to appear on television and most days will see four or five on each of the main stream channels. They like hearing their own voices but more than that they get paid appearance money of one hundred and fifty euro per appearance. It's a tremendous supplement to their income and analysts estimate that many members of parliament earn an extra fifty thousand euro in untaxed cash payments each year from their television channel appearances. However, in the last few days there has been a huge increase in appearances on political chat and news programmes by senior members of the Government. All, either directly or with innuendo, making sure the general public know which country is behind November 17th. Only today there were violent demonstrations outside the American Embassy in Athens'.

Chris paused as a phone was heard ringing in the background. He excused himself and answered the phone. They heard him talking and seemingly asking for clarification on several points. The phone was put down and Chris came back and said. 'Alex's mother is dead'.

The room went silent and no-one moved for a moment. Then they all spoke at once.

'How?' asked Barry.

'Was she murdered?' questioned Laura.

'What playing field should I be mapping?' asked Jim.

'She was found at the bottom of the rocky escarpment on which Achinos cemetery is situated', said Chris. 'It appears she wandered behind the cemetery while she waited for Alex to go down the hill yesterday and missed her footing in the dark. That's the official statement anyway'.

While Jim mapped the satellites which had passed over that area of Greece yesterday, Laura started to piece together the intelligence they had so far. They hadn't expected another death and even though it still might be an accident, Ariadne had been one of their assets in Greece, albeit a sleeper until a few months ago. Ironic thought Laura that she is now sleeping forever. Was Alex one of their assets she asked herself? According to Chris he had met with her at the cemetery and shortly after that she was dead. What had they spoken about? If Alex was one of theirs they had a senior Greek minister in place to cause some damage, but what could he do? Were there strategies in place that she didn't know about? If there was, Barry would know and most likely put them on the table today. 'Is Alex one of ours?' asked Laura to no-one in particular.

Barry looked up and nodded. Before Laura could get a follow up question in, Jim announced that he had located yesterday's satellite pictures for the area of central Greece where Achinos is located and was about to put them on the video wall. Everyone turned towards the video and watched in silence as it showed Alex leaving the small church at the cemetery and starting to walk down the cobbled road towards the village. They then saw his mother leave the church and walk amongst the gravestones before stopping at a particularly ornate grave. She tidied up the flowers which had been spilled onto the grave from an upturned vase and lit a couple of candles. She then walked to the far side of the cemetery and slipped in-between a broken section of the low wall which surrounded the cemetery. As she sat down on a low rock at the side of the escarpment a male figure detached himself from a group of people who were gathered outside the gates of the cemetery and made his way around the outside towards Ariadne. As he approached her she stood up and appeared to talk to him. It was obvious to the Overlook team that she knew him. They talked for a couple of minutes until the man pointed at something in the distance. Ariadne turned to look at what he was indicating and as she did so the man shoved her in her back and she disappeared over the edge. The man then wandered back to re-join the group still talking outside the cemetery gates.

There was silence in the room. Only the hum of the air-conditioning could be heard. Barry clearing his throat addressed the room. 'So it was murder and not an accident'. It was a statement not a question.

'Jim it's almost 18:30 in Berlin, our asset should be calling in on the half hour, clear all traffic and make sure the line is secure', said Barry as he signalled to the others to stop talking by making a zipping motion over his lips.

Chapter 10

October 25th 2010 – 18:30 Berlin

In his room at the Adler, Alex dressed and shaved, opened his laptop and the SCIPTS application. He clicked on the dialling window and entered the first five numbers of the sequence he had memorized in the church at Achinos. He heard a ringing tone which lasted five seconds and then a metallic like voice said 'Secure, enter your ten-digit code'. Alex complied and heard a sequence of pings similar to a submarines sonar system. Then a voice said, 'Good evening Alex, you're through to Overlook. Speak freely; you are on a secure network'.

Alex's voice boomed across the room. 'Good evening gentlemen'. Nobody mentioned that there was a lady in the room. 'I'm afraid I'm completely out of my depth here. I haven't a clue what I'm supposed to do or accomplish or even how to go about it'.

'Calm down', said Barry. 'You are not alone. You have a whole team of people who are watching your back plus we have someone on the ground not far away from you. Now tell us about your meetings, any clues as to why Antonopoulos was killed?'

'He must have found out something about what Themis Xenakis was planning to do and was going to let the cat out of the bag,' surmised Alex.

Alex then began telling them about his meeting with Themis Xenakis, the Prime Minister. He emphasised the point that he had been told he was required to lie about the financial state of Greece, although he didn't know to what degree, however, all should be clearer at the Bilderberg meeting. He also told them about the blackmail and assured the room that he did not sleep with Lafazanis.

'We know that,' interrupted Barry. 'We set that up. All doctored photographs, brilliant.'

'Xenakis certainly believed them,' continued Alex. 'How on earth.......

As Alex was talking it occurred to Barry that perhaps Alex didn't know about his mother. Now Barry was preoccupied with whether he should tell him or not. Certainly telling someone that their mother had died over the phone was not the best of ideas but there was no doubt in Barry's mind that Alex should be told. He would get their other asset to do it. After all she was seeing him in a couple of hours. Barry scribbled a note and handed it to Laura. 'Get this to her as quickly as possible', he whispered.

Laura glanced at the note and blanched. She nodded her assent and turned to her computer. So Gitta is our other asset she mused. How on earth had they managed such a high level insertion without the German Government getting a whiff of what was going on under their noses?

Alex was still talking when Laura received an email from Gitta which simply said 'affirmative'. She signalled Barry that Gitta had agreed, then turned her thoughts to trying to analyse what was going on in Greece. She felt sure that Barry was going to ask her to offer her analysis while Alex was still on the line.

Alex meanwhile was talking them through the Bilderberg meeting. 'Is Gitta going to be there with you?' asked Barry.

'Yes she is', said Alex. 'I suspect she is there to keep an eye on me and make sure I toe the party line'.

'Do you know what the party line is?' asked Barry.

'As far as I can gather I'm supposed to be the deliverer of bad tidings to the world, highly overstating Greece's debt mountain and current account deficit. Unfortunately, I don't know why the Prime Minister wants these numbers to be published and also why Germany is becoming such a close ally in this matter. Perhaps you know more on the why? I must admit I'm feeling threatened especially after the demise of Antonopoulos'.

'Laura will give us her take on this in a while Alex. Meanwhile we will assess your risk profile and try and mitigate as much of the danger as we can. In the worst case scenario, you may never be able to go back to Greece again. However, we believe that if anyone wanted you dead, they would not attempt anything outside of Greece. The Greek police are not renowned for their criminology skills, so assassinating you in Greece gives them their best chance of getting away with it. Outside of Greece the police were more advanced and are better equipped to deal with the situation particularly in Germany, the United Kingdom and the United States'.

'That's a relief', laughed Alex. 'I can probably live a danger free life as long as I avoid my home country'.

Alex wasn't feeling like laughing, he suddenly felt very lonely. He suppressed an urge to call his mother; little knowing that he would never call her again. He shut the lid of his laptop effectively ending the communication.

Chapter 11

October 25th – 2010 – 19:30 Berlin

Alex had poured himself a small brandy when the phone rang and the concierge asked him if he was expecting a Gitta Lehrer. Alex said he was and asked them to send her up. He suddenly felt a little excited about seeing her again and soon forgot the anxiousness he had felt when talking to Langley. Alex left the door of his suite open and sat down in a chair which offered him a view of the open door.

Gitta pressed the button for Alex's floor and her thoughts turned to breaking the news of his mother's death. She knew that Alex and his mother were close and Alex had always been anxious whenever she was involved in any operation for the CIA. Gitta was sure that Alex had only allowed himself to be recruited because of his mother's persuasive skills. Now she was dead. There was a danger that because of her death, Alex would just decide to not go along with the CIA and follow the instructions of his Prime Minister to the letter. On the other hand, perhaps he would want to get back at the people who had eliminated her. Her thoughts were interrupted by the doors of the elevator sliding back. She stepped out into the luxuriously carpeted corridor and walked towards Alex's room.

When she was a few feet from the double doors of Alex's suite she noticed the doors were slightly ajar. She was immediately suspicious and stopped in her tracks, listening intently for any sounds coming from the room. She heard none. Now alert, adrenalin flowing through her veins she slid her hand through the slit in her knee high dress and pulled a small Beretta from the holster sitting between her thighs. Checking the safety was off; she crept silently towards the double doors. She noted that the doors opened inwards and the right hand door was the one that was ajar. Gitta eased up to the gap in the doors, careful not to cast any shadow into the room and alert anyone who might be in there.

Her view of the suite was very limited, all she could see was a partial wall and curtained window but at least the lights were on, albeit not that brightly. She reasoned that she needed a brief distraction to enable her to enter the room and have a chance at the first shot if needed. Quietly opening her bag Gitta pulled out a small lipstick applicator. This will do, she thought. With the applicator in her left hand and gun in her right she positioned herself beside the gap in the double doors. She took a deep breath; flicked the applicator as far as she could into the room as a distraction; then in one fluid movement she threw open the right hand door, dropped down on one knee holding her gun in the normal two handed grip, scanned the room from right to left and then back to the centre of the room. Alex sat wide eyes with astonishment having just shattered his brandy glass in his surprise at suddenly looking down the barrel of Gitta's gun.

Gitta put a finger to her lips to indicate that Alex shouldn't say anything. She saw that the door leading to the bedroom was open and she moved very quickly to the wall adjacent to the door and flattened herself against it so she was hidden from whoever was in the room.

'Hello Gitta,' said Alex. 'Why the James Bond act? There's no one here you know.'

Gitta breathed a sigh of relief and slipped her gun into its thigh holster. 'Your door was ajar,' she explained. 'I was just being careful. I could have been anyone; you should always close the door to your room.' She sat down opposite Alex as she rebuked him. She stretched her legs out flexing her ankles to ease out the dull ache caused by her crouching entrance, at the same time giving Alex a view of her perfectly shaped legs as her skirt rode higher.

Alex momentarily forgot his nervousness as he took in Gitta's long legs. Then he walked to the bar, poured another brandy and took a long gulp before asking. 'How does the assistant to the German Minister of Finance know how to use a gun and what's more know how to enter a room ready to use a gun in earnest?' Alex giggled, the brandy must be getting to me he thought to himself. 'Don't tell me you're a female equivalent of James Bond and you work for MI6?' Alex expected Gitta to laugh out loud at his half-hearted attempt at humour.

'Not MI6,' said Gitta, 'the CIA.'

Alex stared at Gitta. How many people I know work for the CIA, he thought. Gitta, my mother and me for starters, I wonder how many people I have met during my life also work for the CIA that I have no knowledge of.

'I know it's hard to believe and your brain must be frazzled with the speed of events that have carried you through the last few days,' said Gitta.

Alex said nothing as he stared into her eyes. His mind was racing and not for the first time he felt he was very much out of his depth. I'm an amateur compared to these people he thought. A reluctant spy who's had no training in analysis, martial arts or firearms. I'm simply a man who has been thrown into the deep end by a strong mother and her CIA buddies and who because of a reputation as a womaniser and general 'bad egg' as the British would say, elected into a political job that was beyond him.

'Yes,' said Alex. 'I'm very much out of my depth, very frightened and not at all sure who my friends are, or indeed if I can pull off.... whatever it is I'm meant to do.' Alex spoke the last few words in a rush and immediately took a long swig of brandy as if to quell the torrent of words.

'Get a hold of yourself,' said Gitta. 'I'll be around to make sure you don't get into trouble.'

'You mean you are my guard, guardian angel or whatever the official CIA term is? Talking of CIA, you'd better tell me how you came to be involved with them. I need reassurance that you are as professional as you looked when you made your James Bond-esque entrance.'

Gitta realised that Alex needed the whole story otherwise he was going to go to pieces. She dared not tell him about his mother, not now at least. She thought about getting clearance from Langley especially as they had tasked her to tell Alex about the murder of his mother. In his current state that news would probably finish him off so better not chance it. She would clear it with Langley later. She had to calm him down and show him that he was in good hands.

'Handler....' Gitta smiled, this time the smile reached her eyes. 'Pour me a drink.... a whisky,' she said, 'sit down and make yourself comfortable. If you don't mind, I need to use your bathroom to clean up. I'll be five minutes.' Before Alex could say anything Gitta had grabbed her bag and disappeared into the ensuite of the bedroom.

As Alex poured Gitta her drink he reflected on how he had arrived at this uncomfortable moment in his life. It was only a few days after his twelfth birthday when his father had sat him down and explained that the person he had always known as 'mother' was in fact a surrogate. He wasn't told about the affair between his real mother and his father but was told that his mother was unable to keep him in Greece and was forced to send him to America with his father. His father had married soon afterwards and his wife had accepted Alex as her son. Alex was schooled in a private Georgetown school where he proved to be an able student with an aptitude for languages. He learned ancient Greek, Latin and Modern Greek with some ease and by the time he reached his fourteenth birthday he was fluent in all three classical languages.

In 1976 on his sixteenth birthday his father took him out of school after morning assembly and drove him to his office. Already waiting there was a woman. She was introduced to Alex as his mother, a mother he had not seen since he was a baby. Alex felt nothing towards her but he did find that he liked her so he was friendly towards her. She stayed a week spending most of her time with Alex, talking, walking and telling him that he was going to be a hero of Greece one day. Alex warmed to his mother more and more throughout the week and by the time the week was up he had become very fond of her. On the day before she left they were sitting in one of Georgetown's most elegant patisseries enjoying iced Lattes and a Greek styled truffle.

'There is something that I have to tell you,' said his mother. 'You know of course that your father works for the Central Intelligence Agency?'

'Of course I do,' interrupted Alex impatiently.

'Well there is no easy way to break this to you,' smiled his mother. 'So do I and you will too when you are ready.'

Alex stared at his mother in total disbelief. 'Is this a joke mother?'

'Unfortunately, it's not a joke Alex. I paid a price for having you out of wedlock. Your father was an officer in the American Armed Forces and attached to the CIA. I was nothing; a simple peasant girl.' Ariadne spread her arms as if in submission, then she took Alex's hands. 'I wanted more for you. If I had kept you with me in Greece, you would never have had the education your father has been able to give you. To give you a decent start in life I had to let you go for a while. I had to agree to work for the CIA and I had to promise that I wouldn't stand against your father's wishes that you too work for the CIA.'

'Have you been involved in any operations yet?' asked Alex. He was gradually warming to the idea that his mother was a spy. What would he tell his friends he thought? Bad idea was his next thought. He couldn't tell anyone because he would become a spy too. His thoughts were interrupted by his mother's reply.

'Only one......I helped the Americans make sure that the colonels overthrew the then unsteady Government of Greece in 1968. Greece became a stable country under the colonels despite the people's protests. Economically there was growth and more important everyone had jobs and the country did not owe anything. Now Greece has Karamanlis and democracy is back and the country is being Europeanised. It was unfortunate about the invasion of Cyprus of course but Turkey had to be given a carrot by the west.'

'What happens now?' questioned Alex.

'When you are eighteen your father will induct you into the CIA and you will become what is commonly called a 'sleeper'. Your studies will groom you for a life of politics in Greece. Your father reasoned that if we could place you in a high Government position we could monitor what was going on much more efficiently. The CIA will train you in truth avoidance and behavioural sciences. Don't worry, you won't need to do anything physical or have to carry a gun. You won't be a spy in the field. All you will be asked to do is observe, report and lie to whoever you are having a relationship with; be it girlfriend, lover or wife.'

Alex's thoughts were suddenly interrupted by the sound of Gitta returning from the bathroom. He placed her whisky on the small table beside her armchair and sat down opposite her. He noticed that even though her skirt was revealing a good portion of her thigh there was no sign of her thigh holster or her gun. Alex waited expectantly for Gitta to tell her story.

Chapter 12

October 25th 2010 – Milos Island – Cyclades - Greece

Kostas Triandafilos sat in a waterfront café on the island of Milos in the main port of Adamas, drinking a Greek coffee and smoking his favourite AB brand of cigarettes. He looked out at the bay shaped like the letter 'C' but with the gap out to sea much narrower than a conventional letter 'C'. The Germans had used the bay as their Mediterranean navy base during the Second World War with much success as it was difficult to attack by sea and the surrounding mountains provided natural defences for their anti-aircraft gunners.

Now with the summer over even the private yachts had hibernated to the Athens Riviera or to the marinas of the port of Piraeus on the Greek mainland. Just a few fishing boats were moored in the bay and once a day a ferry from the mainland would bring food, newspapers and other essential goods to stock the shops. But it was not cold; with the temperature around 22 degrees centigrade and most people, like Kostas, still wore short sleeved shirts.

He was waiting for Stavros Blounas and Christos Mavrides, both colonels in the Greek army. They were due on the ferry that had just docked not more than five hundred yards from the caffenion where Kostas was sitting. Kostas reasoned that they would be at the café pretty soon, as this time of year as the ferries were fairly empty. Once the school year started in September the Greeks, who made up 70% of the tourist trade to this largely unknown island, left for the mainland. Kostas was in two minds about the island having only 30% of foreign tourists as it was a beautiful island with much to offer to the discerning foreigner. However, the thought of thousands of package holiday tourists flooding the island would compromise the mystical allure the island currently held. Everyone who flew into the island loved the quaint little runway and the husband and wife team who between them were part time air traffic controller, weather man, customs officer, check in desk clerk, security officer and ground hostess escort. Yes, he thought, the airport has a unique personality.

'Kalispera Kostas,' said Stavros and Christos in unison, cutting into Kostas's thoughts.

Kostas looked up smiling. 'Kalispera pedia, ti kanete?' he replied. 'How was the journey? No-one recognised you I hope.'

'Quite uneventful,' said Stavros. 'It's amazing what a little hair dye and a beard can do. Don't you think I look rather like a university professor?' said Stavros laughingly.

'Amazing!' agreed Kostas, 'Fancy a beer?'

'Mythos for both of us,' answered Christos.

'Okay let's drink our beers and then we can go to a quiet, less public place to finalise our plans.'

'Where?' Said Stavros as he swigged back half his beer in one huge gulp.

'Well,' said Kostas. 'You remember the caves which the Germans turned into their underground bomb shelter and headquarters during their occupation of this island? It's a museum now and one of my cousins is the curator there. I told him that a couple of friends were visiting tonight and leaving first thing in the morning and they had never visited the museum. He gave me the key. There is one cave which has been set up as a replica of the German command office. We can use that to finalise our plans.'

October 25th 2010 – Alexandroupoli, Western Thrace – Greece

At the same time as Kostas Triandafilos and his two colleagues were making their way to the bomb shelter on Milos, Themis Xenakis was in Greece's version of Air Force One, a retired Olympic Airways Boeing 737-400, heading to Alexandroupoli in Western Thrace, near the Turkish border. He did not care for this region of Greece as it had caused many problems not only for his Government but for previous Greek Governments too. The region had a population of nearly four hundred thousand people of which half were Greek Orthodox and the other half

Muslim, mostly of Turkish origin but also some Romani. This area, which is bordered by Bulgaria to the north, the Eastern Thrace region of Turkey to the east, the Aegean Sea to the south and Greek Macedonia to the west had been in political turmoil for years. There were certain elements who advocated that Macedonia should be an independent state as it had been in Alexander the Great's time. The Former Yugoslavian Republic of Macedonia was claiming that Greek Macedonia was their own, and Turkey had eyes on Western Thrace claiming its people's human rights were being violated.

Themis, as the prime minister of Greece had grown tired of the problems that had beset this area for many years now. But he was approaching this region tonight because the very troubles that had bothered Greek Governments for decades in the past would now become a weapon which he could use to shoot down the flak he knew the Greek Government would receive when their strategy was revealed after the Bilderberg meeting.

The Boeing's 'seat belt on' signs pinged on as the plane decelerated with its air brakes full on. Themis saw the lights of Alexandroupoli drift past his window whilst hearing the hydraulics rolling out the wing flaps of the 737; at the same time the giant wheels locked into place as the pilot readied the plane for landing. Ten minutes later the pilot banged the plane down on the runway, applied the reverse thrust braking system and exited the runway on the furthest taxiway from the main terminal. It then taxied to an isolated apron at the far end of the airport where a black four by four, with dark tinted bullet proof windows, was parked with its engine running.

Themis walked down the steps pulling his coat up around his ears to keep out the biting cold. He had forgotten how cold it could get up here in Thrace during the winter. One of his bodyguards opened the rear door of the four by four and he stepped into the warmth of the rear seat. He switched on the reading light and took out a folder from the briefcase that had been put on the seat beside him. The car with the briefcase had been supplied by the man Themis was going to meet. A man who had managed to remain anonymous for more than twenty years although he was the chief executive officer of one of the biggest private armies in the world. Not that Themis needed an army but he did need subterfuge and he did need men who knew how to cause a lot of trouble and social unrest without being caught. The man he was meeting could arrange that – for a fee of course – a big fee. Still, Themis reckoned, it would be worth the money.

The folder contained a map of the gas pipelines that entered Thrace from Turkey. There were three in total: one started at the Exxon gas and oil terminal in Azerbaijan, crossing Armenia before entering Turkey at Kars, then traversing Turkey before entering Thrace at Soufli. It then continued through northern Greece entering Albania and passing through Fier, crossing the Adriatic into northern Italy at the San Foca terminal. This pipeline was owned by the Americans. Pipeline two started in Georgia, crossed Turkey at almost the same latitude as the American pipeline, entering Thrace ten miles north of Soufli before following the same route as the American pipeline to San Foca. This pipeline was owned by the Russians. The third pipeline was also Russian and would follow the proposed route from the Crimea across the Black Sea into Bulgaria at Burgas and then southwards into Thrace to connect with the existing Russian pipeline. Themis turned the page and read the capacities of the existing and proposed pipelines.

Pipeline one was transporting twenty-five billion cubic metres of gas per annum through to Europe. Pipeline two was also conveying fifteen billion cubic metres of gas per annum to Europe but when the planned pipeline is connected to pipeline two it would carry fifty billion cubic metres per annum. Themis allowed himself a wry smile…fifty million cubic metres per annum was equivalent to a nice windfall for the Greek Government and also he would not come out of it too badly either. The transit fees he had successfully negotiated with the Russians were eighteen pence a barrel which equated to almost one point three billion dollars per annum.

He'd probably have to reward Alex at some point with a couple of million, he thought, but there was enough to go around and perhaps he would get lucky and Alex would have an accident. Themis realised that the powers in play, would in the next few days complicate matters and make things more dangerous than they were now. So there was every chance that some people would not see Christmas this year.

His thoughts were disturbed by the brakes being applied and the car drawing up at the open front door of a large villa. Themis alighted from the car and walked through the front door into a small hall that contained a table with a mirror above it and an umbrella stand to one side. Themis walked through the hall and through another door which led into a salon furnished in the traditional Greek manner. Sliding doors which were wide open led to an elongated lounge area furnished in a more modern style with both walls down the length of the lounge consisting of metal framed glass sliding panels. In the centre of the L shaped lounge was a huge square shaped wood burning fire place with an ornate chimney that disappeared into the ceiling. As Themis approached the warmth of the fireplace he was able to see round into the space behind. He stopped short in surprise, causing his two bodyguards to draw their weapons against an unseen foe.

There on a chaise lounge next to the fire place were three people; two adults, one a male and one a female as well as a small child, probably male, with their wrists and ankles tied together and wearing gags. All three stared at him with frightened eyes.

'Good evening Themis,' said an American accented voice. 'Welcome to Thrace.'

Themis looked up to see a stocky, fairly tall man with amazing blonde swept back hair. His eyes were an icy blue under bushy eyebrows and he was wearing a dark blue suit, black shirt and a yellow tie. He looked and smelt ex-marine and walked with the air of a man who exuded confidence and was certain of his destiny. 'My name is John Dexter and I'm the CEO of Black Hawke.' He continued as he walked over to Themis offering his hand.

Themis took his hand and replied 'Nice to meet you.'

'Sit down,' said Dexter, although it sounded more like a command. 'How was your flight?'

'Trouble free I'm glad to say and thanks for supplying the transport. I take it that this is not a company villa and these trussed up people are the real owners,' said Themis glancing towards the prisoners. 'Are they going to keep their mouths shut after seeing us?'

'Yes you're right; our company does not have any property in this part of the world. I'm afraid that they will have to be silenced for good,' added Dexter. 'Does that bother you?'

Themis shook his head hoping that he wouldn't have to ask one of his bodyguards to commit cold blooded murder.

Dexter looked at Themis and smiled as if he had read his mind. 'Don't worry Themis; Black Hawke will take care of all the loose ends. Now dismiss your bodyguards and we can talk business. I take it you have read the documents I left for you in the car?'

'Perimenai sto aftokinito,' instructed Themis in Greek. 'Yes I have,' he replied after telling his guards to wait in the car for him.

'So if you are happy with the revenue numbers let me tell you my plan for causing sectarian mayhem in Thrace thereby giving the Greek Government an excuse to close down the American gas pipeline and announcing a deal with the Russians. Firstly, however, let me complete some unfinished business. If you're squeamish, don't look.'

Without waiting for a reply Dexter drew out a pistol from his shoulder holster, screwed on a silencer, walked over behind the prisoners and very calmly shot each once in the back of the head.

Chapter 13

October 25th 2010 – Langley – Virginia

Laura watched patiently as Jim Broadbent brought the screens that were embedded into the wall of the operations room to life. She had earlier briefed him on the live feeds and recordings she wanted from the various spy satellites they controlled in the European and Balkans region. These screens would add credibility to her analysis which she had typed up and placed in the folders around the desk. At least she hoped that would be the case. She was especially interested in the screen that had followed the Greek prime minister's plane from Tatoi; the military base close to Athens; to Alexandropoulos in Thrace. It now showed an overhead view of a villa with a black four by four standing in the drive.

Laura marvelled at the technology leaps which had enabled Governments to watch and listen to what was going on around the world. She estimated there were approximately one thousand one hundred operational satellites in orbit around the Earth, fifty percent of which were sent into orbit by the United States. Half of that number are in a low earth orbit just a few hundred kilometres above the surface; including the International Space Station, the Hubble Space Telescope and many observation satellites. About a twentieth are in a medium earth orbit around 20,000 kilometres up. These are mostly global positioning satellite for navigation, like household satnav's and cell phone GPS apps. A small handful are in an elliptical orbit which brings them closer and further from the earth. The rest are in geostationary orbit at an altitude of almost thirty-six thousand kilometres. If we could see these satellites from earth they would seem to hang motionless in the sky. By remaining over one geographic area they provide the perfect platform for telecommunications, broadcasting, weather observations and of course spying. Just like the ones broadcasting to the screens Laura was looking at, twenty-four hours a day. What was more remarkable was that it was possible to change the direction of a satellite's orbit or switch it from a normal orbit to a geostatic or vice versa at the flick of a switch.

Yes, she thought, it was all a bit 1984-ish but she had embraced it. Her philosophy was that if you had done nothing wrong you had nothing to fear. Except, she had done something wrong and now she could not go back.

She has met Arcady six months ago at a Washington function. She had been attracted to him instantly and even though she knew that he was a Russian Embassy attaché she took a chance and introduced herself. They found a quiet corner where they could talk and as the evening went on she realized she was becoming more and more attracted to him. Arcady wasn't a young man he was in his mid-fifties but that was the age that Laura liked her men. As they talked she felt the familiar moistness on her thighs. Arcady sensed that she was ready and suggested they find somewhere even quieter to talk. The room they found was obviously a dressing room for the lady of the house and once inside Laura asked.

'Are you wired?'

'No!' Arcady replied.

'I have to be sure,' said Laura. 'Please take off all your clothes.'

'Of course,' said Arcady, 'but you must take your clothes off too.'

'You first,' said Laura. Arcady complied. He had no wire but then Laura had figured that he wouldn't have had one anyway. She studied him for a while. He had a slight paunch but she quite liked that in a man. He was very hairy and she thought it strange that his body was covered in black hair yet his head had grey hair.

'Your turn, 'said Arcady. Laura slowly got undressed and as she did so she could feel her nipples hardening and the wetness around her thighs increasing. By the time she had finished getting undressed Arcady's manhood had become extremely hard.

'Well neither of us is wired,' said Arcady smiling.

'I might have a microphone hidden somewhere which isn't obvious,' purred Laura, as she walked towards Arcady. She put his hand between her thighs. He knelt in front of her. Some minutes later she gasped and said. 'Do you normally look for hidden microphones with your tongue?'

69

An hour later they re-joined the main party both of them glowing after their love making. As their relationship grew they became lovers and Laura began to spy for the Russians.

Gradually over time Arcady won her over and persuaded her to tell him what the CIA was doing. Laura convinced herself that she wasn't a traitor, after all she wasn't giving away top secret information. She only gave him small bytes of information, nothing that would really compromise the position of the United States. In return he provided her with an intellectual companion and an excellent lover. They met several times a week on the outskirts of Washington in a small motel which Arcady himself had hand-picked. They remained an ecstatically happy couple for several months until one day Arcady changed the venue of their clandestine meets. The meeting was in a big house just over the Maryland state line in Virginia. Arcady himself opened the door and showed her into a spacious lounge area. There was a woman seated on a chaise lounge, a beautiful woman, it took Laura several moments to realize that the woman was Elena Davilova the Russian deputy minister of economics.

Laura stared at her; then Elena smiled warmly and said 'Hello Laura, Arcady has told me a lot about you. Come sit!' Elena patted the chaise-longue indicating to Laura that she wanted her to sit down next to her.

Laura walked over and sat rather stiffly. She had been taken aback with Elena Davilova being there with Arcady. Elena leaned towards Laura until their lips were almost touching. Just close enough for Laura to smell the subtle fragrance of her scent and the sweet bouquet of her breath. It was then that Laura realised with astonishment that she could desire another woman. Elena leaned forward once more and this time let her lips brush Laura's while at the same time she laid her hand softly on Laura's exposed thigh. Arcady had asked Laura to wear something sexy when he had told her about the change of venue for their meeting. So Laura was wearing a backless, strapless, short evening dress in matt silver.

Laura covered Elena's hand with her own, uncrossed her legs and pulled the hand gently between her thighs. Elena leaned in again and this time parted Laura's lips with her tongue. Laura let out a low moan as Elena's hand touched the outside of her now very moist panties.

Laura couldn't clearly recall how she had got undressed nor who had undressed her but an hour later as she lay eyes closed in complete abandonment in Elena's arms with Arcady naked, cuddling her from behind, she knew she was smitten by Elena's raw sexuality. She wanted more. That night she was pampered by both Elena and Arcady for several hours until finally she fell into a deep contented sleep completely exhausted.

While she slept Arcady and Elena talked about Arcady's progress in turning Laura. Arcady said he was confident that Laura would continue to supply them with enough data to keep them one step ahead of the Americans and the British as well as keep Laura the safe side of having too much of a guilt complex.

Laura herself was very good at justifying all her actions whether they be good or bad. This particular characteristic had served her well throughout her university life, her career and in particular her sexual desires with her penchants of wanting married elderly men with brains in the normal place. This trait enabled her to avoid nasty guilt complexes. So now she had two lovers, one of each sex. Both high profile Russian diplomats and she was giving them, not secrets – Laura didn't believe keeping them informed of what her section was doing or where it was doing it – was giving away state secrets. After all she reasoned with the technology both sides had at their disposal, both sides could monitor the movements of the other. No, she considered her thought process perfectly valid and leaking information to Arcady and by default Elena would not harm anyone and it would keep certain parties pleased with her. This might have been true six months ago but now events had a momentum of their own and there had been collateral damage with more to come. Unbeknown to Laura she was not immune to being a damage limitation target by any of the powers that were in play.

'Laura!' Barry threw a pencil rubber across the desk at Laura. 'Are you with us or far away in another universe?

Laura jumped, startled out of her thoughts of Arcady and Elena. 'Sorry,' she muttered. 'Just trying to pull things together in my head.'

71

'Then tell us,' said Barry. 'Have you managed to make sense of this at all?

Laura looked around the faces at the table. Barry was looking anxious as always. She knew he would have to report to Geoffrey as soon as she had finished her briefing. Jim was probably more focused on his technological gadgets than her analysis. Chris Horsman looked very tired and why shouldn't he be. He had just flown in from Athens and had spent the previous two hours being debriefed by Laura herself. She cleared her throat and began her analysis, hoping against hope that she had got it right and that they would not suspect that some of her sources were very close to home. Whether the U.S.A. could act or stop whatever was going to happen or just let 'others' pick up the pieces was not her decision. After all she was just a conduit she reasoned and couldn't influence her Government or anyone else's. Or so she thought.

October 25th 2010 – Alexandroupoli, Western Thrace - Greece

Themis Xenakis tried not to notice the ever-extending pool of blood as it crawled across the grey marble floor like the incoming tide on a shingle beach inching ever closer to the dining room table he was sitting at. He felt sick but he couldn't show it. He couldn't let Dexter see any weaknesses as he would be the first to exploit them. He probably had two minutes, before he returned from the bathroom, to compose himself and steel himself for the negotiations that lay ahead. He felt quite alone for a moment. He had no real allies in the Government and he was essentially going it alone with the Russians and Germans, while at the same time convincing himself he was saving Greece from an economic meltdown. Even the collateral damage and the riches he would garner from the coming events were simply by-lines to the main theme he mused.

The hiring of John Dexter was an essential part of the strategy even though the man had a reputation for treating his customers aggressively and rather rudely. Once you had done business with Black Hawke you were tied to them for life and Dexter never let you forget it. In some ways Black Hawke was the most powerful organisation in the world, second only to Goldman Sachs and the U.S. Government.

Dexter was an ex-marine who had seen four tours in Iraq shared between both gulf wars, and one tour in Afghanistan. He was awarded the medal of honour after he was captured and tortured for thirty days by the Iraqis on his second tour in the first gulf war, before he managed to escape and make his way on foot across the desert to Jordan. On leaving the marines he set up Black Hawke which initially hired mercenaries for small one off projects. As the company grew in size and reputation it became more and more involved in major conflicts in Syria, Libya, Iraq, Georgia and Ukraine. Guns for hire with no particular loyalty to western or eastern Governments, just an allegiance to money.

Despite all that, he would show Dexter that he was not in awe of him and that he was not going to be bulldozed into doing anything he didn't like.

'You didn't have to kill them, did you?' Themis questioned as Dexter entered the room. 'You could have blindfolded them before I came here.'

'Sure, and they wouldn't have recognised your voice,' replied Dexter as he sat down opposite Themis.

'There had to be a way of not having to kill them,' continued Themis.

Dexter didn't reply at first as he busily retrieved some papers from the end of the table and handed them to Themis. 'Don't be so naïve, you yourself ordered the killing of your economics minister.'

Touché thought Themis, he was right of course. He hadn't thought twice about arranging the assassination of Antonopoulos. He had felt it necessary to prevent the information that he had to leak out. Then there was Alex's mother. That was a strange one because his sources were sure that she had been pushed. However, no-one knew why. It was probably one of those unexplained coincidences and had nothing to do with the current operation.

'Tomorrow we will begin our end of the operation. I have two hundred of my best men strategically placed around Thrace and three demolition experts surveying the most vulnerable sections of the pipeline,' explained Dexter. 'My people have confirmed the first tranche of money has arrived in our account. As per our agreement we will receive the remaining ten million dollars when the job is complete.'

'Yes,' agreed Themis, nodding as if to emphasise his compliance. Don't worry the money will be in your account by close of business on the 27th. You have forty-eight hours to complete the operation.'

'Then we are done. All the details are in these documents which you can take with you. I would recommend you destroy them once the operation is complete,' said Dexter, a conspiratorial smile hovering around his mouth. 'After all we wouldn't want to leave a trail to either of our doors, now would we?'

'No,' said Themis as he got up while putting the documents that Dexter had given him into a file. He leant forward and extended his hand towards Dexter. 'Good luck.'

Dexter shook Themis hand saying. 'I'll walk you to the door, it was nice doing business with you.'

Chapter 14

October 25th 2010 – Milos Island – Greece

Kostas Triandafilos stared upwards at the dark rock escarpment which soared above him. It bounded one side of the narrow waterway which was the entrance to Milos's harbour and protected it in tandem with the five-hundred-metre-high mountain guarding the opposite side of the waterway. Where the escarpment met the road there was a heavy oak double door strengthened with metal bars around every edge of the doors and slightly hidden beneath a rocky overhang. Next to the door was a metal sign on four spindly metal legs. It read 'Bunker Museum' entrance fee '7 euro'.

As Stavros and Christos caught up with Kostas outside the museum, one side of the double doors opened and a man wearing the blue uniform of a guide appeared in the doorway and beckoned them inside. Once they had crossed the threshold Kostas introduced his friends.

'Michalis these fine fellows are my good friends Stavros and Christos,' said Kostas, pointing to each in turn.

'Kalos orises,' greeted Michalis with a smile. 'Welcome to my museum.' 'Let me show you around and then I'll leave you to your business. Kostas has told me that your meeting is a matter of national security and that is why you need a place where no prying eyes or ears can find you.'

'That's right, 'answered Stavros. 'We would appreciate a tour of this place.'

'Michalis was born on Milos and was a teenager when the Germans invaded and took over the island in 1941,' explained Kostas. 'He knows everything about the island and has over the years fought against those who wished to destroy the cultural and physical heritage of the island by building huge tourist hotels and complexes. That is the reason the islands tourist board nominated him to turn this place into a museum and gave him the responsibility of curator.'

'The museum opened only last year,' said Michalis extending his hand to guide them forward into a long barely lit tunnel that was ten metres wide and three metres high. The walls and ceiling were bare jagged rock. 'This tunnel has been hewn out of the rock that makes up the escarpment above us, as have all the rooms and smaller tunnels. As you can see no attempt has been made to clad the rocks or paint them. This particular tunnel is one and a half kilometres long and has ten rooms on either side, with each room being roughly the same size. The tunnel here,' continued Michalis as he pointed out a tunnel that branched off the main tunnel to their left, 'runs around the back of all the rooms off to the left side of the main tunnel and served as a massive storage area. It is half the size of the main tunnel but still big enough for its purpose.'

As Michalis took the three friends around, childhood memories came flooding back to him. He could almost hear the whistling of the bombs dropped from the allied planes as they roared over the hilltops where Michalis and his friends laid amongst the rocks watching the fireworks display taking place over Milos's harbour. Night after night, he, his friends and many other children spent their nights watching the allies trying to destroy the German fleet. They watched as the islanders banded together in small groups of resistance fighters and attempted to blow up the entrance to the bunker or destroy the array of aerials which sat atop the escarpment above the bunker. However, no matter how many times the aerials were destroyed by the resistance or by the allied bombs within twenty-four hours they were back up again and transmitting to their forces.

On occasion the Germans rounded up thirty or forty children and took them into the bunker and put them to work. Michalis himself had worked in the bunker making gas masks out of ad hoc materials such as bottles and balloons. It was during the occupation of the Germans in Milos that Michalis decided that he wanted a career in the armed forces.

Kostas interrupted Michalis's reminisces. 'Didn't you once work in one of these rooms Michalis? he asked, as they were shown into a huge room furnished with two lines of old wooden trestle tables and around the walls what looked like old fashioned rudimentary gas masks.

'Yes,' answered Michalis. 'I actually toiled in this very room making gas masks like the ones you see around the room. The masks are now exhibits in this museum. Why don't you settle yourselves here; there is an abundance of tables to select from. I'll go and organise some elliniko (Greek) coffee and ouzo.'

'Epharisto,' Kostas said thanking Michalis as he put his arm around his shoulders. Michalis left the three friends and headed back down the tunnel.

Once they were seated Kostas asked Stavros if his part of the operation was on track.

'Yes,' replied Stavros. 'My squadron of thirteen tanks will roll out of our base at Marathon at 2am on the morning of the twenty eighth. It should only take a couple of hours to reach the forest a short distance from the air force base at Tatoi. '

'What about the noise and your noticeability?' Interrupted Kostas. 'Isn't there a danger that people will be wondering what an echelon of tanks is doing at that time of the morning?'

'I don't think so. Of course there is a risk but I believe that it is a small one. People will naturally assume that the tanks are going to take part in the 'Ochi Day' parade in Athens. Our route doesn't take us through any major Athens suburbs, only the outskirts and a few small villages. The riskiest part of the operation is once we reach the forest. We'll have to hide the tanks far enough away from the air force base that we won't be detected but near enough that we can surprise them at precisely 10:30am, half an hour after the parade begins,' finished Stavros.

'I agree with you,' said Kostas. 'People will assume that the tanks are heading for Athens and the parade. It's ironic that on the anniversary of the day that Metaxas gave Mussolini a big fat 'no' and rejected his request for his Italian army to invade Greece without a fight. We are giving a big fat 'no' to Themis Xenakis because he is going to give away the sovereignty of Greece without a fight and for his own gains.' Kostas looked into the eyes of each of his friends in turn and said in a low voice that resonated a determination that they hadn't seen before.

'We must not fail.'

'We won't,' said Christos enthusiastically. 'My tank squadron will leave the Marathon base at the same time as Stavros. That way we won't arouse suspicion and as Stavros said, the people that are awakened by the noise will assume that the tanks are on their way to Athens for the parade. We will head for Athens Airport and park up on the overpass which straddles the motorway between the airport and Athens. We will leave a platoon on the road on the other side of the airport. We will make it look like they have broken down; their engine cowlings will be open and we will place cones around them so the breakdown looks natural enough. At exactly 10:30am these tanks will shell the runways and break through the perimeter fencing of the airport itself. At the same time the remaining tanks parked on the overpass will target the air traffic control tower and take it out. Unfortunately, there may be loss of life but it should be at a minimum because the air traffic controllers are taking strike action from nine o'clock in the morning and no-one should be in the tower.'

At that moment Michalis came in with tray of coffees and three glasses of ouzo and a flagon of water. He placed them on the table and not wanting to interrupt their discussion, walked away back down the tunnel.

'Yes it would be unfortunate,' concurred Kostas. 'But we can't afford a warning shot, it's too dangerous. Will the tanks on the overpass enter the airport?

'No need. The two on the runways will be enough to stop any landings or take-offs. The overpass tanks will spread out and block the motorway routes into and out of the airport.'

'Sounds solid enough Christos,' praised Kostas. 'Now Stavros how are you taking Tatoi?'

'At precisely 10:30am we will storm the air force base from the forest side. There should not be any shooting as my contacts within the base have confirmed that the Xenakis Government has pissed them off a number of times and any coup against the Government would be supported.'

'My contacts in the air force have led me to believe that too,' confirmed Kostas. 'Good job,' he said smiling at his friend.

'As for my part,' continued Kostas. 'My squadron is scheduled to take the salute from the prime minister and the President of the Republic at precisely 10:30am as you know. We will take that salute, however, before we join the parade we will be parked up with all the other military vehicles in Zapion Park towards the eastern side near to 'Vasilios Sophia' Avenue. At 10:00am all the vehicles will turn their engines on to warm them up and allow the engineers to conduct final checks. Under cover of engine noises, a platoon of three tanks will slip away from the main body of vehicles and head north towards the grounds of the parliament building. The boundary between the park and the gardens is only five hundred metres from where we will be parked and it's a low wall so it won't any trouble for a Leopard 2A6 tank to punch through.'

'How long will you wait?' asked Christos.

'The platoon will wait for my okay, which I shall give once we have secured the main dais where the Prime Minister, the President of the Republic and the military chiefs will be taking the salute. They will then break through the wall and one will guard the back entrance of the parliament building. As the main dais is opposite the main entrance to the parliament our squadron will be able to stand sentinel in front. The rest of the platoon will head for Herodou Attikou street, split into two and one will take up position outside the prime minister's official home and the other tank will position itself outside the home of the President of the Republic. By 10:35am we should have secured the two airports and Athens. The TV and Radio stations will be put out of action when the generating stations in Papagou are blown. We can then secure the buildings later in the morning.'

Kostas stood up stretching his legs. He was never one for sitting in one position too long. Even his marine training didn't help his restlessness and he was often the target of disparaging remarks from his commanding officer. However, once he had proved himself in a number of clandestine missions in North Africa and Turkey no-one gave him negative feedback any more, just praise and a respectful salute. 'Any questions?' he said.

Christos and Stavros shook their heads. 'Endaxi pedia, off you go. Enjoy yourselves tonight, I'm going to stay and catch up with Michalis. Don't forget that I'll text you 'Gladio' if it's a go as planned for the twenty eighth. If I don't text then stay at your bases. Okay?'

'We understand,' said Christos and Stavros in unison, as they disappeared down the tunnel towards the entrance to the museum.

Kostas watched them go then sat down again. He looked at his watch – it was almost time. He pulled a flip top cell phone from his pocket and turned it on. It wasn't a recognisable make. Not even the young geeks of the computer or gaming age would know of this phone. It was MI6 standard issue – but it was far from a standard cell phone. From another pocket he pulled out a small grey box about the size of a match box. The box had a mini USB attachment which he inserted into a socket on the cell phone. He then plugged the grey box into the electric socket on the wall behind him. The grey box was a VME encryption mobile unit. It enabled the cell phone user to make calls worldwide in absolute safety without risk of the encryption algorithms being cracked.

Kostas looked at his watch again – it was time. He keyed in the name 'Gregory'. The name was immediately encrypted and two encrypted signals were sent to a clandestine base station somewhere in Turkey. In less than half a second the base station had randomly created two cell phone numbers, one it returned to the cell Kostas was using and the other to the cell phone in Gregory's pocket. It beeped and on pulling it out Gregory saw the name 'Kostas' flashing in the display. He opened the flip top and spoke into the phone.

'Hello Kostas.'

'Yassou Gregory,' answered Kostas. 'We've just finished concluding the plans for the 28th. Unless Lighthouse has any reservations it's a go at our end.'

'He won't. He has left the final decision to me and as of now the clock is ticking down. If anything changes, I'll contact you but I don't believe it will. Good luck!'

The connection went dead as Kostas uttered a verbal 'thank you' into a now dead line. Gregory was very curt mused Kostas, rather as if he didn't want to get too friendly. I wonder.......no......but Kostas sixth sense was ticking away in his brain. Not alarm bells as yet, but more a warning to be vigilant. He needed someone to watch his back. Someone who they'd never suspect, a non-army type, but able to merge into the background while keeping watch....

'Kostas,' said Michalis as he walked into the room. 'You look troubled. Why don't we grab a beer on the waterfront?'

Kostas looked at Michalis and then smiled. Perfect he thought. 'Good idea Michalis, let's go, I want to run something passed you anyway.' Kostas put a hand on Michalis shoulder as he steered Michalis out of the room.

Chapter 15

October 25th 2010 – Central Aegean – Greece

Captain Naismith reached for the red phone shrilling for attention on the wall to the right of his chair on the bridge of HMS Stallworth.

'Go ahead John,' answered Naismith.

John Talbot was the chief communications officer aboard the Stallworth, charged with overseeing the multitude of listening devices the ship had at its disposal. To the uninitiated the ship was an oceanographic survey ship and looked every inch the part. But it wasn't. The ship carried an immense range of viewing and listening devices which enabled it to directly support the Navy by using both passive and active low frequency sonar arrays to detect and track undersea threats. Serving as a platform for monitoring missile and satellite launches, collecting data that could be used to improve missile efficiency and accuracy, the ship also had the ability to monitor foreign missile and weapons tests that may pose potential threats to air or surface navigation. Monitoring wireless traffic from satellite, aircraft and sea based platforms as well as cell and cable telephone communication systems was another of its abilities. In short the frigate was a very powerful floating listening platform, probably the most lethal in the world.

'Picked up an interested flight pattern emanating from North Eastern Greece sir.' Talbot's voice crackled through the phone line. 'Military or commercial?' asked Naismith.

'Well sir, it's a Boeing 737-400 which left Alexandroupoli Airport a short while ago.'

'What's strange about that,' asked Naismith, 'it's an airport is it not?'

'No sir, I mean yes, it is an airport but the usual traffic is short haul prop planes of Greece's domestic carrier Olympic Air. This aircraft has not filed a flight plan and is flying rather erratically so it's difficult to say where it's heading except that the direction is more south west than any other compass point.'

'Ideas John?'

'Well sir, I'm pretty sure it's the Hellenic Airforce One. I used Spyglass and got a pretty good view of the plane, including its tail number.' Spyglass was a system developed by the British Ministry of Defence as an enhancement to satellite technology. It took images of a targeted subject or object from several satellites and restructured them pixel by pixel producing a three dimensional image of the targeted objective. Without this technology Talbot could never have accurately identified the tail number of the 737 Xenakis was travelling in.

'Well done John,' congratulated Naismith. 'I wonder what he was doing in the Thrace region of Greece. We should report this to Lighthouse – they did ask us unofficially to report the movements of Xenakis if we spotted him.'

'Right sir,' said Talbot, 'I'll get on to it right away. Anything else you want to add?'

'No John, just give the facts. Show them we are doing our bit to help,' Naismith chuckled, 'If the public at large knew how some of their tax pounds are being used, they would have difficulty in believing it, or they would be very afraid. Actually, they probably should be.'

October 25th 2010 – London

Sir Peter Bogart put down the phone after getting the message from the communications officer of the HMS Stallworth.

What was Xenakis up to, he asked himself. Why was he in Thrace? What was so important and secretive that he didn't file a flight plan? Sir Peter picked up the cell phone that was his communication with Gregory. He punched in a code and password, waited for several seconds while what sounded like cogs churning together filled his ear. 'Sir Peter,' answered Gregory. 'Is everything alright?'

'Nothing's wrong,' said Sir Peter. 'Something puzzling has happened down in Greece. By the way where are you? In the UK or Greece?'

'I'm sitting in Kolonaki Square,' he lied, 'in the centre of Athens looking at the out of season tourists drinking coffees side by side with the rich, famous and beautiful people of the Athens social scene. They certainly know how to charge for a cup of coffee here, it's three times the price of a coffee elsewhere in Athens.'

'It's way past your bedtime isn't it?' said Sir Peter with a hint of sarcasm, which wasn't lost on Gregory.

'It's only 11pm here…. the time that Athens wakes up,' said Gregory.

'Well as you are awake perhaps you can come up with ideas as to why Xenakis travelled to Thrace this evening without filing a flight plan. What's so secretive that he doesn't want anyone to know where he's been?'

'Pipelines,' exclaimed Gregory. 'There has been a lot of unrest there in the last few days. I guess Xenakis doesn't trust the levels of security around the pipelines and decided to make a visit to see for himself.'

'How many are there?'

'Three, one American owned and two Russian owned, one of which has just come online or is about to come online.'

'So he is worried that one or all would be compromised. I guess he wouldn't want to piss either of his partners off, would he?'

'Possibly,' murmured Gregory thoughtfully. 'You know sir it could be that he went to Thrace to orchestrate an event. He could use the clashes between the Muslim and Greek Orthodox groups to attach blame if anything happened to the pipelines. Then he would have an excuse for closing the border to ethnic Muslim minorities.'

'Doesn't make sense,' replied Sir Peter. 'The ethnic minorities might be a problem, but nothing worthy of a personal visit. By the way didn't Elena Davilova visit Athens a few days ago?'

'Yes, she did.'

'What if the capacity of the Russian pipelines were bigger than that of the American's? With Greece moving closer to the Russians it would make sense to have just one pipeline, without a loss of revenue of course, thereby cementing their relationship with Russia?'

'It would at that,' agreed Gregory. 'You know sir you might just have hit the nail on the head. Xenakis could also have negotiated a better deal on revenues by giving them exclusive access of Northern Greece to run their raw energy through to Europe.'

'Can we stop them?' asked Sir Peter.

'Once 'Gladio' has been activated on the twenty eighth and we have our people in place, we could then nullify any agreement between Greece and Russia, if our suspicions are correct of course,' explained Gregory. 'I'm afraid if they are planning to sabotage the American pipeline we don't have the assets on the ground to thwart them,' added Gregory.

'I'll forewarn the Americans through discreet channels. They might have assets in Northern Greece.'

'Right,' said Gregory. 'Let's hope they have. I'll contact you on the morning of the twenty eighth to let you know if it's a go or not. At the moment it looks good for a successful operation. Everything is in place.'

'Good, let's hope our efforts are effective. And don't forget, keep me in the loop at all times. Bye for now.'

'Bye sir.'

October 25th 2010 – Milos Island - Greece

On Milos Island Gregory carefully put the phone down on the table. He had stayed close to Kostas and his friends since they had arrived on the island. In fact, he had followed them there, traveling on the same ferry from Piraeus. He wanted to stay close to make sure they did not talk to anyone not directly involved with the operation. He was the perfect tourist and enjoyed looking the part, knowing that as he passed, women would turn to stare. Even though it was late November he sported a pair of white Chinos, an orange polo shirt and casual tan deck shoes. In the cool of the evening he wore a lightweight jacket with a man's city bag slung over his shoulder. His attention now turned to the man trussed up and gagged at his feet.

Michalis stared up at him whilst struggling to free his bonds, a look of stark fear in his eyes. Deep down he knew it would be impossible to untie his restraints and he also knew that he didn't have long to live. Gregory suddenly bent down and tore the duct tape that he had used to gag Michalis, from his face.

Pain mingled with relief as Michalis spluttered. 'Who are you? Why are you doing this to me?'

'Nothing personal old chap it's just that you were in the wrong place at the wrong time. You let Kostas Triandafilos and his two friends into this bunker tonight didn't you?' said Gregory surprisingly enough smiling with both his mouth and eyes.

'Yes I did,' said Michalis, 'but I don't know why they were here or what they were talking about.'

'Unfortunately for you I can't take that chance,' said Gregory as he extracted a syringe filled with a clear liquid from his city bag. 'This will be painless,' he added.

'Please…no…. please don't,' cried Michalis. 'I don't want to die.'

Gregory crouched down in front of Michalis and said 'I'm sorry, I really am.' Then he thrust the syringe into the side of Michalis's neck and pressed the plunger until the cylinder was empty. Michalis immediately felt sleepy and by the time his heart stopped beating a few seconds later he was aware of nothing. Gregory easily lifted the dead weight body of Michalis and sat it in the chair by the table with his head laying on the table top surface. Gregory didn't bother to wipe for fingerprints or DNA. There were no records that police or law enforcement agencies could access to identify Gregory. He was literally a ghost, completely untraceable and able to do what he did best with impunity. Only Lighthouse had a record of his fingerprints and DNA, however that information was for their eyes only.

Chapter 16

October 25th 2010 – 23:30 - Berlin

Gitta stretched out her long legs as she lay beside Alex on his king size bed. She turned her head to the right and saw that Alex was fast asleep. She slipped off the bed grabbed her bag and tip toed to the bathroom. Gitta had heard her cell phone warble, announcing an incoming message. She opened her phone and read the message.

'Probable imminent destruction of American gas pipeline in Thrace Northern Greece. Warn Langley. Lighthouse.'

Gitta opened up the SCIPTS application on her phone and keyed in a series of numbers, then typed in a message for her handler in Langley. Two seconds later the encrypted message was being decoded by the SCIPTS software on her handler's cell phone and being displayed. She closed her phone, slipped it back into her bag, then after making sure Alex was still sleeping she stepped into the shower.

As she showered she thought back to her conversation earlier that evening when she had told Alex how she had become a CIA agent.

Her story had started in East Germany in a small town called Penkun where she was born, some 20 kilometres from the Polish border.

'My father who was in the 'Spezialisierte Einsatzkräfte Marine Corps', the German equivalent of the Marines or SAS, had been captured by the Americans at the end of the second world war and taken to the United States where he was trained by the CIA. He was then sent back to East Germany with a completely new German identity created under the umbrella of a joint British and American operation sending agents back to their homeland within the Soviet Bloc for the sole purpose of infiltrating the secret police of their home countries.'

'I had heard about that operation,' said Alex. 'I never really believed it was possible to keep such a secret.'

Gitta ignored his remark and continued. 'Within three years my father had been accepted into the Stazi – the East German secret police. He managed to work his way to the top, keeping both his masters happy with the work he did and the information he supplied them. In 1970 I was born and my father immediately started planning how to get me out of East Germany and into the West. Over the years he managed to persuade his CIA masters to take me in hand if he could get me out of Germany when I turned eighteen.'

'Why eighteen and not before?' interjected Alex.

'Because East Germans could not get travel documents before the age of eighteen,' said Gitta. 'However his plan was made much easier when fate intervened and the Berlin wall came down in November 1989 just two weeks before my nineteenth birthday.'

Gitta had then told Alex that she was able to travel without restrictions, and in the January of 1990 she found herself at the gates of 'Camp Peary' the CIA's special training centre in Virginia.

Camp Peary was actually a nine-thousand-acre military reservation in York County near Williamsburg, Virginia. Officially referred to as the Armed Forces Experimental Training Activity (AFETA) under the auspices of the Department of Defence, Camp Peary hosted the covert CIA training facility known as 'The Farm'. This was never formally acknowledged by the U.S. Government, despite media pressure over the years. An airport with a five-thousand-foot runway was added to the facility near the site of Bugler Hill to facilitate operatives' departures off continent and enable them to avoid nuisance customs officials at regular airports.

Gitta spent five years training as a field operative and passed her finals exams with an A plus grade. She was trained in covert surveillance, sleight of hand, con-artistry, manipulation tactics, personality-type identification, lying, cheating, stealing, trickery, camouflage, evasion, escape, weaponry improvisation, self-defence, analytical combat and espionage. Gitta had excelled in all disciplines and had passed out fourth best of all agents trained by the CIA. She also won the 'sharpshooter rookie of the year' award in her three final years at 'The Farm'. Gitta had entered the CIA academy a gangling teenager, shy and without a great deal of self-confidence. During her training she blossomed into an extremely attractive athletic woman who oozed self-confidence and had a commanding presence wherever she went.

On her penultimate day at 'The Farm' her commanding officer called her into his office and handed her a file.

'I want you to read this,' said Cartwright.

'What is it sir?' she said taking the file. Cartwright had been very supportive of her throughout her time at 'The Farm'. She respected him and moreover liked him a lot. He was tall with not an ounce of fat on his body; damn good looking as well. He wore his ginger hair short and had kindly brown eyes that seemed to turn black when angry or wanting to make a point. Gitta did not fancy him despite his good looks and there was never any hint of a student teacher infatuation. The physical characteristic she really liked about him was the way he walked, giving him an air of unflappability whatever speed he was walking at. It reminded her of the way Clint Eastwood walked.

'Your assignment in Europe. You don't have to take it if you don't want to. We have an alternative assignment for you if you don't take this one. My opinion is that it's perfect for a first assignment and will enable you to hone your field skills admirably. Let's meet tomorrow in this office at 16:00 hours to discuss.'

'Thank you,' said Gitta as she stood up. 'Have a good afternoon sir.'

Once Gitta had closed the door Cartwright put a call through to Gitta's father in Berlin.

'Boris,' he said as soon as the phone picked up. 'How are you?'

Boris recognised the voice immediately. 'Hello Alan, I'm fine and how is my daughter?

'She has been given the file,' replied Alan. 'I've given her until this time tomorrow for a decision.'

'Do you think she'll accept the assignment?'

'Once she sees that she is perfect for it she will agree to it. Don't worry, you will be able to retire in peace Boris,' said Cartwright with a chuckle.

Boris laughed into the phone. 'Smart arse!' he said laughing as he spoke. 'But joking aside, from what you've told me about her progress in the academy I agree with you.'

'She's good Boris, very good, one of the best to pass through here. You'll see first-hand when she returns which won't be long now. If or rather when she accepts the assignment, you'll have to oil the wheels to make sure she gets the job of Vogel's personal assistant. Her CV will be impeccable but you must make sure the references stand the test of Vogel's ex-Stazi cronies.'

'Don't worry Alan, it's all in hand. We'll talk again when Gitta gets here.'

'Yes, goodbye Boris.'

As her father and her boss were exchanging pleasantries Gitta started to read the file. After leaving her bosses office she had dropped by the canteen to pick up three slices of pizza and a choc-ice before heading back to her apartment on the grounds of 'The Farm'. Closing the door behind her she kicked off her shoes, threw the pizza into the microwave, the choc-ice in the freezer and headed for the bathroom.

After showering and dressed in shorts and a skimpy tee-shirt Gitta settled down on her veranda, pizza in one hand and file in the other, she started to leaf through the loose sheets. It contained two biographies, both built up over several decades by CIA operatives in East Germany, and both about two current high level leaders in the German Government; Dominik Vogel, the finance minister and Brigitte Neumann, the German Chancellor.

As Gitta read the biographies she began to comprehend how similar their rise to power was. Both were Stazi trained and both were born in the then East German town of Leipzig. Although Vogel was older than Neumann their paths initially crossed at the Leipzig Academy of Intelligence and Dis-information. The academy was a separate school at the Leipzig University and only the top East German students ended up there. It was the equivalent of Yale in the United States or Cambridge in the UK for recruiting operatives.

During the time that Gitta had been at The Farm, Neumann and Vogel had joined forces and made a lot of money through taking advantage of the chaos in the former East Germany after the fall of the Berlin wall. That day over two million East Germans poured through the open border into West Germany within seventy-two hours of the Berlin Wall crashing open. After a week, more than eight million frustrated people had slid through for at least a gander at the other Germany.

The blitz swamped shops and stores in West Berlin and West German border towns, with the East Germans astonished by the spectacle of goods they only fantasied about in the east. Shelves were emptied of much valued blue jeans and beauty products. Fruit disappeared from fruit stands while fast food restaurants were overcome by orders for burgers.

But as the celebrations wore away, East Germans rapidly realised they were paupers in a promised land. Their marks were worthless in the West, and the one hundred deutsche marks 'hospitable money' from the West German Government, worth about sixty dollars in new money, were quickly spent. Soon the anti-regime protests in East Germany furthered a new demand to calls for reforms. They wanted the deutsche mark which meant that somehow Germany had to be united. In the following months, the West German Government set in motion the first phase of a gigantic transfusion of financial and social subsidies and within a year managed to make whole a country that had been divided for some forty years.

As fast as East Germans left their apartments and moved into what was West Germany both Neumann and Vogel made deals with a close ally of theirs in the KGB. A man who rose to the top of the KBG and eventually became the Russian President - Igor Putilov. Together the three of them bought up for a pittance the properties and land that the Germans moving in to West Germany had left behind. They changed the titles of the deeds and then sold them at enormous profits to land and housing developers.

As their wealth built up they both managed to buy their way into the Social Democratic party.

'Without any degree, well relevant degree?' Alex had interjected.

'Don't forget they both attended Leipzig University and apart from getting honours in the so called 'espionage school' Vogel attained a PhD in Economics and Neumann a PhD in Political Science,' replied Gitta.

'I don't get it,' said Alex. 'Why would your assignment be to spy on those two?'

'Because they were from Eastern Germany and Stazi at that. Their ideals and values were not honed in a western democracy.'

'How did you manage to become Vogel's personal assistant?' asked Alex.

'When I returned from 'The Farm' to Germany my father had already paved the way for me to be on Vogel's staff. How he did it I don't know and I never asked.'

'So you got Vogel and someone else got Neumann?'

'Yes, someone who was also at 'The Farm' with me was assigned to Bridget Neumann. He was smart, fit and his name was Rolf. His parents were German but he was born in the States. He eventually became her lover.' What Gitta didn't tell Alex was that Rolf during the final months of her stay at 'The Farm' had become her lover too.

Alex stared at her and Gitta guessed what he was thinking. Was she Vogel's lover?

'I know what you're thinking. You are wondering whether I became Vogel's lover. It's actually none of your business but if it helps you to trust me. I didn't, but if I needed to I would have, it's part of my job.'

Gitta smiled as she recalled Alex's face, when after she had said that it was part of her job, she stood up and walked over to where Alex was sitting, hitched up her skirt and stood astride his lap giving him a close up view of her thighs and black panties. She then pressed herself against his face while staring into his now astonished eyes. Eyes that quickly turned to wanton lust. Gitta sat on his lap and started to grind into his crotch as she parted his lips with her tongue. It didn't take much effort and soon he was kissing her passionately. Somehow they had made it to the bedroom and had made love twice, the first time in a frenzy of passion and the second time long and slow.

Why she had done it she couldn't fathom. Alex wasn't really her type. Although he was quite good looking he was in no way fit. But there was something about him, a kind of vulnerability which appealed to her.

Gitta turned the shower off and stepped into one of the two courtesy bathrobes hanging on the back of the door. She tiptoed back into the bedroom and slid between the sheets next to Alex so as not to wake him. He looked so serene with a semblance of a smile seemingly playing around his lips. One arm nonchalantly thrown over his head. Gitta leant over and gently kissed his smile. For a brief moment she wondered what Alex would think when he finds out she worked for the CIA but also had special liaison responsibilities to Lighthouse, the opposite of his mother who had worked for Lighthouse but also had special liaison responsibilities to the CIA. Before she finally dropped off to sleep she thought about the awkwardness that might herald their waking in the same bed. Then her thoughts quickly turned to the day ahead and the Bilderberg Conference at ironically enough, the Astir Palace Hotel in Vouliagmeni Greece.

Chapter 17

October 25th 2010 – 17:30 - Langley – Virginia

'As you know,' Laura began. 'Greece has suffered more than most European countries because of the global economic meltdown which started in 2008. If they asked for economic help they would be forced into a severe austerity program by the so called Troika, the European Central Bank, the International Monetary Fund and the Eurozone. The Eurozone is essentially controlled by Germany as they are the economic powerhouse of Europe. Greece's unemployment rate is rising and the standard of living of the middle classes is falling rapidly. Their debt mountain is rising rapidly and now at a point where it will be impossible for Greece to repay any of the money they owe. The country is running out of money because of four things; the corruption which has been endemic in Government circles for thirty years now; secondly the huge growth in the public sector resources; thirdly the culture that paying taxes is optional, especially by private companies and the upper class, the so called oligarchs; lastly the constitution which protects Government employees and their friends from prosecution whilst they are in power.'

'I would concur with that,' said Chris nodding his head. 'I would also add that since the downfall of the Colonels in 1974, political family dynasties have been running Greece. When I say families I mean cousins, second cousins and aunts five times removed. Politicians in Greece are very rich people. For example, the former leader of the communist party retired with fifty-two properties to his name.'

'Why on earth were they let into the Eurozone then,' exclaimed Barry. 'They should have been excluded with a record like that.'

'Another financial trick,' explained Chris. 'They were helped by the German Government through the then Bundesbank who turned a blind eye to a deal Goldman Sachs put together with the Greek Government which shrank its fiscal deficit from five point two percent of GDP to one point two percent of GDP. So it seemed that Greece was within the three percent Brussels imposed ceiling and therefore able to join the European club. A clever trick which has been used since by Italy. The motive behind allowing such a move was that Germany wanted another export market. With Greece part of the Eurozone they had access to cheap funds which they used to buy German products.'

'Okay Chris, but that's not enough to warrant the current events is it?' Barry questioned. 'Do go on please Laura and try not to confuse me with financial numbers,' he said with a wry smile on his face.

'No, you're right. That is only a side-line. Greece's finances have deteriorated so dramatically over the last few years that the Government seems to be looking for long term solutions rather than short term fixes. Ironically the so called Troika would want the same thing but at a major cost, for Greece that is. The traditional austerity measures which the International Monetary Fund would impose would eventually bring Greece to its knees, simply because these measures failed in the past.'

'Countries such as Turkey, Argentina and several other countries rejected the IMF austerity programmes, or cost cutting as the IMF like to describe them, when they began to suffer and their economies got worse. Apparently these countries are now thriving economically,' continued Laura.

'However, there might be an added value in the shape of valuable fodder for the rest of Europe, particularly Germany. What is the fodder? Greece is sitting on an immeasurably large amount of oil and natural gas resources in both the Aegean and Ionian seas and up to now they haven't touched it because Turkey is claiming that half of it belongs to them.'

'Surely not the natural resources in the Ionian Seas?' exclaimed Barry. 'Turkey surely can't lay claim to those. I can sort of understand their claims in the Aegean but not the Ionian.'

'True,' replied Laura, 'but any company given drilling rights in the Ionian Sea would want the same rights in the Aegean too. Economies of scale, spread the cost around.'

'Hold on,' interrupted Jim. 'We have an incoming.'

'Who from?' said Barry.

'Gitta! She says that there will be a probable destruction of the American gas pipeline in Thrace Northern Greece.'

'How does she know?' exclaimed Chris.

'I don't know,' replied Barry. 'But her sources have always been trustworthy in the past, so we can safely say that what she has conveyed is probably going to happen. Do we have any field agents in that area Laura?'

Laura shook her head as she tapped into her computer. 'The quickest we can get anybody there is tomorrow evening central European time,' she said.

'Probably too late. Who would want to do away with the American pipeline? Any ideas Laura?' questioned Barry looking straight at Laura.

For a moment Laura felt herself start to redden as it flashed through her mind that Barry somehow knew she was having an affair with Arcady. She rubbed her eyes and pulled herself together rebuking herself for such idiotic thoughts. If Barry had suspected anything she wouldn't be here. 'It might be something related to the Greek prime minister's clandestine visit to the outskirts of Alexandropoulos,' she ventured.

'You mean that black four by four that met his plane at the airport?'

'Yes, it took him to a villa near the village of Loutro just ten kilometres from Alexandropoulos airport,' said Laura.

'Do we know who owns the villa?'

'I'm on it,' replied Jim.

'Okay, any ideas why Xenakis would travel to Thrace? Was it a scheduled Government visit? Did he have his usual entourage?'

Chris was busy on his computer. 'Just onto my sources in Athens,' he said in response to Barry's questions. 'I'll have an answer shortly.'

'Right Laura, while we're waiting for Chris continue your analysis please.'

Laura looked over at Barry, who was reading a report in front of him on the desk. She gathered her thoughts. Even sitting down he looked tall she thought. Perhaps the fact that he was thin and lanky made him seem tall. Not that he was clumsy but he was certainly loose jointed. Maybe thin was not the right word, more like lean. It was difficult to tell whether he was muscular under his suit, which was his mode of attire. She had never seen him in anything more casual. Mind you, the suit and the brushed back hair made him look even more distinguished especially as he was starting to grey around his sideburns which matched his piercing grey eyes she thought.

Barry looked up from his reading and lifted his eyebrows at Laura as if to say 'well come on then let's hear what you have to say'.

'If the Xenakis Government is looking for a way to borrow money but not become embroiled in an austerity project then it could conceivably be thinking about letting Russia share its bed. However, such a scenario doesn't quite fit with Greece's other new bedfellow, Germany.'

'We, I mean the United States, would not be pleased to see Russia having a foothold in southern Europe,' said Barry. 'Greece is in NATO and the European Union. How would….'

'The Xenakis trip was not official,' interrupted Chris. 'Not only was it not official but the flight plan was filed for Thessaloniki, the second largest city in Greece. It was changed just before his plane was due to get landing instructions from air traffic control.'

'What about his entourage?'

'Just two men,' replied Chris. 'Which is very unusual for Xenakis, he usually has at least six bodyguards.'

'Perhaps he gave the rest a night off,' said Barry dryly. 'If he's taking the bare minimum for bodyguards he must be desperate to keep his visit a secret.'

'The family that live in the villa are not Greek they are Italians. A married couple and their son. The husband works at the Soufli oil terminal,' said Jim.

'That sounds suspicious. Doesn't the American pipeline run through Soufli? Asked Barry looking at Laura.

'Yes,' agreed Laura. 'We should get the authorities to that villa quickly before the terminal is compromised.'

'I agree. Jim get onto our consulate in Salonika and ask them to put pressure on the authorities in Alexandroupoli to go and take a look at that villa.'

While Jim was warming up to his task of getting the local authorities to the villa to take a look, Chris was deep in conversation with one of his contacts in the Greek air force. He was talking to Air Marshall Mitsos Aslanides chief of Tactical Air Force Command based at Larisa in central Greece.

'Hello Mitsos,' said Chris. 'I'll get right to the point. Do you know why 'Aristotle' took an alternative route this evening?' Aristotle was the traditional code name assigned to Greek prime ministers since Karamanlis came out of exile from Paris in 1974. Such was the fear of an assassination in the aftermath of the Colonels reign it was decided to refer to the prime minister as 'Aristotle' whenever he moved around Greece. This was unlike the codenames assigned to American presidents and their families which are generally unambiguous words such as 'scoreboard' which was Eisenhower's codename, or 'Lark' John F Kennedy's codename. The Greek security services had decided that something from their classic era would be more appropriate as it would dovetail from the cradle of democracy to modern Greek democracy, which in reality they hadn't had for the best part of eight years.

'Well I didn't at the time,' said Mitsos. 'But I do now, I learnt about it half an hour ago. Everyone here is clueless why he did it although most have concluded he has a secret girlfriend in that area.'

'You're kidding; he went all that way to fuck his girlfriend. Not plausible. He could do that in Athens without causing a stir. Why would he change a flight plan for a bit on the side? Did you know he visited a house owned by a family of Italians where the husband works at the oil terminal in Soufli?'

'Of course I didn't. How do you know that anyway?'

'We have been keeping a close eye on events since the assassination of Christos Antonopoulos. We have eyes everywhere now,' revealed Chris. 'Something is going on right under your noses and you haven't a clue. Perhaps you should start calling in some markers and see if you can get some hard information,' finished Chris.

'Okay, 'agreed Mitsos. 'I'll do some digging. Call me in three hours.' With that he cut the connection and Chris was left listening to a silent noise.

As he slowly replaced the hand set to its cradle Chris heard Jim say that the consulate had contacted the Greek authorities in Western Greece and they had despatched a squad of E.K.A.M. Eidiki Katastalkiti Antitromokratiki Monada to the villa near Soufli. 'They should be there in less than half an hour,' said Jim.

'Well we can't do anything else until we have a report back from the consulate. Seems a bit over the top to send in an anti-terrorist squad doesn't it?' Barry questioned to no-one in particular. 'There are a number of events that just don't make sense or at least seem rather unrelated. We have had two murders, Antonopoulos and Ariadne Kalfas. The Greek prime minister takes a clandestine trip to a village in Thrace, Alex is asked to lie about Greece's economic situation and we get a strange warning about a pipeline being blown up. None of it adds up.'

'We just have to find the thread that binds these events. There has to be a connection,' said Laura. Without waiting for an answer Laura retrieved her bag from under her desk saying. 'Need a minute to powder my nose,' as she closed the door behind her.

Laura hurried to the bathroom and into the cubicle furthest from the door. She retrieved the cell phone that she used for communication to Arcady and dialled.

'Laura,' answered Arcady from his office in the Russian embassy. 'Anything wrong?'

'I know I don't normally call during the working day,' she answered breathlessly. 'I haven't got much time but I need to know something. Aristotle took an unscheduled trip to Thrace this evening and our contacts in Europe suspect that it has something to do with gas pipelines. Do you know why he went?' asked Laura using the Greek prime minister's code name just in case anyone was listening.

'Yes, he was visiting a friend,' replied Arcady.

'Then this friend could be in danger,' continued Laura. 'The authorities are on the their way as we speak. You have twenty minutes' tops. I've got to go. Bye.'

Without waiting for a response she closed her phone, slipped it back into her bag and walked quickly back to the others.

Arcady lifted the receiver of his landline and dialled a number. When the phone answered he said. 'You have twenty minutes before the Greek authorities get to you.'

'Don't worry I have covered my tracks; the authorities will have a not so nice surprise,' said the voice.

'Good luck,' said Arcady and put the receiver down. 'What sort of surprise are they going to get?' he wondered out loud.

Chapter 18

October 26th 2010 – 02:00 – Western Thrace – Greece

Three dark blue armoured vehicles belonging to the Greek anti-terrorist squad drew up outside the villa on the outskirts of Alexandroupoli, which Xenakis had vacated only a few hours before. Sakis Rouvas, the chief of the squad, alighted from the lead vehicle and gave the signal to spread out around the villa. He had already discussed tactics with the crew while approaching the property and each man knew what position to take up. Sakis himself would be with the three-man crew breaking in through the front door. He watched as his men surrounded the villa, each one moving to his assigned spot.

'Ella pame,' said Rouvas telling the three men at his side to follow him towards the front door. Once there he pressed the door bell and stepped back. The door remained shut and the villa continued to be eerily silent.

'Any lights around the back?' whispered Rouvas into his helmet microphone. Everyone gave a negative reply. 'On my mark enter the premises but watch out for any booby traps,' said Rouvas. Turning to the two men who held a metal battering ram he said. 'Get ready.' They moved into position.

'Mark!', yelled Rouvas. The front doors gave way easily as his men employed the battering ram. The noises coming from the other side of the villa assured Rouvas that his men had breached the premises on all sides through doors or windows. He immediately led the way into the hallway, moving quickly they burst through the salon and into the lounge. On the far side of the lounge area the men who had entered the villa from the back, were congregated and staring at something on the floor. Rouvas moved closer and saw three bound bodies lying in their own blood on the floor besides a couch.

'Don't touch anything,' said Rouvas. 'Let's get forensics in here. Captain Trakas, go and call them from one of the vehicles immediately.' Rouvas watched Trakas leave the villa then turned to his men. 'I want the whole villa searched for signs of life. Nobody touches anything unless they are wearing surgical gloves,' he ordered. 'Now get on with it!' Rouvas turned around and went after Captain Trakas to remind him that they should also update the American Consulate in Salonika.

Twenty kilometres to the north John Dexter huddled over a laptop staring at the screen. It showed a night vision birds-eye view, from twenty-four thousand feet, of the terrain to the north of Alexandroupoli. He was watching the camera view of a guided drone which was being meticulously piloted by a drone controller sitting in a Black Hawke facility in Soufli, forty-five kilometres further north. The drone was the latest version of the MQ-9 military weapons carrier. It carried two AGM-114 Hellfire II air to ground missiles, each with a range of twenty miles. Dexter marvelled at the technology which put powerful weaponry into the hands of people who only needed to be as dexterous as kids skilful at using a hand held game controller. Sometimes he actually felt like they were playing a global video game. The controller deftly guided the drone towards the villa where Dexter had recently met with Themis Xenakis. Two minutes later he saw the villa below the drone and in the roadway several military vehicles with two men talking on a radio to one side of the lead vehicle. He made sure the targeting crosshairs were dead centre on the roof of the villa and said, 'Dexter I am green to go. Target is locked on.'

'Proceed,' said Dexter from his four by four vehicle, 'Good luck!'

The drone ground controller took a deep breath, then pressed the red knob on top of his joystick.

'On their way, thirty seconds to impact.'

Chapter 19

October 26th 2010 – 19:00 – Langley

Eight thousand kilometres away in Langley the members of the Overlook team were glued to their satellite feed watching the anti-terrorist operation unfold in front of them. They had witnessed the incursion into the villa and then seen both Trakas and Rouvas leave the villa minutes later to talk on the radio phone by the lead vehicle. Suddenly they saw two simultaneous flashes, then a huge ball of flame engulfed the villa as it exploded, sending out shock waves which bowled the military vehicles over as if they were made of papier maché as well as destroying two villas on the other side of the road.

'What the hell!' cried out Barry. 'What was that? A bomb? Was the villa booby trapped?'

'Can't we get a better angle,' asked Laura. She couldn't take her eyes off the satellite feed. What have I done she thought. I'm responsible for this! If I hadn't spoken to Arcady this would never had happened.

'I'm going to get a wide angle view from just before the villa went up,' confirmed Jim.

They watched as Jim manipulated the satellite feed so the view was as if the picture was taken thirty thousand feet up instead of fifty feet. Their eyes never left the screens as the feed did a fast rewind and the view angle became wider and wider.

'There!' shouted Chris. What's that?

They stared at an object that looked like a miniature aeroplane. It was just over forty-foot-long and had a wing span of about sixty foot. Slung under each wing was a missile.

'It's a drone,' confirmed Jim. 'Looks like an MQ-9 Predator with the latest specs too.'

'What are the missiles,' asked Chris.

'They look like two AGM-114 Hellfire air to ground missiles,' said Jim. 'That drone is one of the most technically advanced the USA has produced. It has a range of eighteen hundred miles from its ground controller and can stay aloft for eighteen hours at a cruise speed of over four hundred miles an hour'

'You mean it's one of ours?' questioned Barry.

'I don't think it's being controlled by our armed forces,' said Jim, 'but I'd love to know who is controlling it.'

'Considering the villa had the Greek prime minister in it just over half an hour ago, the ground controller can't be that far away,' reasoned Laura.

'You may be right Laura,' said Jim as he narrowed the field of vision to approximately five thousand feet above the terrain. 'Look over there in the lower right hand corner of the screen. There's a black four by four parked on top of a rise.'

'Looks like one of the four by fours we saw earlier outside the villa,' said Laura. 'Could the ground controller be in there?'

'I doubt it,' said Jim. 'In all probability whoever is in the four by four is directing the operation.'

'Who does it belong to?' asked Laura.

'Jim can you get closer? Could we identify the owner of the vehicle?' asked Barry.

'I'm zooming in now. Here we go. Unless whoever's in the vehicle or the vehicle turns itself around we won't have a chance of recognition,' Jim added.

They all stared at the screen as Jim zoomed down over the black four by four. As luck would have it the driver's side of the vehicle was facing the camera and a silhouette of a head could be seen by the driver's side window.

'Initiating recognition protocol,' confirmed Jim.

The recognition protocol was clever technology which converted an image, pixel by pixel, into a 3D image and this 3D image was processed through the CIA's database of some three million high profile people looking for a match.

Twenty seconds later a photograph of John Dexter was displayed on the screen. Laura studied the screen. She recognised the face but could not recall the name or what he did.

'Jim, who is that?' asked Barry.

'On screen now,' replied Jim as a caption was displayed over the photograph of Dexter.

'John Dexter,' mused Barry. 'Isn't he the CEO of Black Hawke? What the hell is he doing in northern Greece? Laura, we must have a file on him if he's on our database. Get it would you.'

'I know Dexter. I met him at a dinner in Athens during a business conference hosted by the Greek Government,' said Chris, 'and I didn't like the man,' he added.

'Why not?' asked Barry.

'He comes over as extremely arrogant and there's something about him which disturbed me. I couldn't put my finger on it but I imagine he would be a dangerous man to cross. He seemed very chummy with Xenakis though.'

'Got the file. Coming up on screen now,' said Laura.

'Summarize it for us Laura,' said Barry. 'We can all get the same information in the same timeframe.'

'Give me a couple of minutes to assimilate the information.'

'Fine, in the meantime do we know if the two men outside the villa managed to give some sort of report before the villa exploded?' asked Barry.

'It couldn't be more mysterious,' said Chris as he put his cell phone down. 'The consulate says that there were three bodies found in the villa. Shot through the back of the head. A professional hit according to the men that managed a radio call before the villa got hit. By the way, neither man made it. Those missiles wiped out the whole anti-terrorist squad in northern Greece. Twenty-one men in total.'

Laura kept her head down to avoid anyone noticing the panic in her eyes. I'm responsible for those deaths she thought. Giving bites of information to Arcady is one thing but giving out intel that leads to innocent deaths is another. What is the connection between Arcady and Dexter? Could Russia and Greece be in bed together? But how and what for? And this John Dexter fellow seems to have a lot of power. Laura vowed to herself that she would see Arcady that night and confront him with the information she had. 'Barry, I'm ready,' she said.

'Go ahead,' said Barry. 'Listen up everyone!'

Laura gave a little cough and then started. 'As Barry said earlier John Dexter is the CEO of Black Hawke, a company which has the largest army of mercenaries in the world. It hires out men and the most up-to-date technology and arms equipment to countries or wealthy individuals who can afford to pay for the expertise of Black Hawke's personnel. The company has been involved in all the major conflicts of the last ten years. It has no loyalties and has provided men and arms to both eastern and western Governments. Dexter himself is suspected of several low level assassinations in Europe and the middle east, being an ex-marine and a medal of honour recipient he is considered a dangerous man to cross. That's it,' finished Laura.

'Thank you, Laura. Okay anyone any ideas what a man like John Dexter is doing in northern Greece? Do we think he met with Xenakis in the villa and what would Xenakis want with Dexter?' asked Barry, looking around the room.

'Let's step back a little,' suggested Chris. 'We know from Alex an announcement will be made concerning Greece's finances at the Bilderberg meeting tomorrow in Athens. We also suspect that somehow Germany and Greece are involved in a strategic manoeuvre, although we don't know the details as yet. Also we have Xenakis making a secret trip to northern Greece to the very same villa which has just been destroyed. Presumably its destruction was to erase all forensics. And don't forget there have been two assassinations; Antonopoulos and Alex's mother.'

'We were also forewarned about a possible destruction of a gas pipeline in or around Soufli which suggests conceivable Russian influence, particularly as Elena Davilova, the Russian Finance Minister has visited Athens three times in the last six months,' added Barry.

At the mention of Davilova's name Laura felt herself flush. She felt as if they were all noticing her discomfort although logically they could not know about her meetings with Arcady or Elena. She knew she had to contribute to the discussion as after all she was supposed to be the analyst around here. Already she had reasoned in her own mind that something was going to happen in northern Greece, an event of some significance was imminent. However, she was unable to reason what it could be and also she had no idea where was Dexter heading?

'Jim, can we follow Dexter's vehicle?' she asked.

'Only if we have use of a drone,' answered Jim. 'I can try and locate his vehicle on the next pass of a satellite over eastern Europe in ten minutes' time. But where do I start, it's a big area?'

'Soufli,' answered Laura. 'It's got to be Soufli because that's where the pipelines are,' she added.

'You've got something there,' said Barry. 'Jim, can't we get a drone out of Cyprus?'

'The British won't loan us one of theirs but the Harry S Truman aircraft carrier is in the Persian Gulf.'

'Right, I'll move this up to Stevens. We'll need the Secretary of States permission to use a drone in a friendly country and only he has the authority to speak to State. I don't have enough to convince him we need a drone yet though. Give me some ideas people,' implored Barry putting his hands together in prayer-like fashion.

'If Greece has decided to ally with Russia and get funding from them how would Russia benefit?' asked Laura. Then she answered her own question. 'Of course, Russia gets sole rights to transport gas through northern Greece into Europe and probably a promise of a share in Greece's so far untapped oil and gas resources in the Aegean Sea. That would mean having to disable the American pipeline running through Soufli.'

'A possible attempt on an American asset overseas is probably enough reason to activate a drone. I'll talk to Stevens right now,' said Barry as he left the room. 'This could be a long night for all of us.'

Chapter 20

October 27th 2010 – 09:00 – Hong Kong

Forrest Collier looked out of his office window at the traders@ floor stretched out in front of him. His office was raised a metre higher than the main floor so he could oversee what was going on at each of the fifty trader's desks below him on the trading floor. He was the Head of Treasury at Deutschland Bank in Hong Kong and presided over a currency position of one billion dollars. In other words, the bank trusted him enough that he could risk and invest those amounts of funds at any one time into the global currency market.

Collier was in his element with risk. From the day that he walked into Deutschland Bank's London trading room twenty years ago he felt at home trading currencies and taking informed risks. His career path was dramatic to say the least. Within five years he was head of the sterling desk in the London branch. Over the next ten years he was moved to other Deutschland Bank's branches in the major financial centres of Frankfurt, then New York, then Singapore and now Hong Kong, where five years ago he was appointed to his current position.

Most people think of a market as a physical place where people get together and trade. However, Collier revelled in seeing the look on people's faces whenever he explained that the currency market was a worldwide network of banks, large corporations and brokers where the business of buying and selling currencies takes place twenty-four hours a day. Average daily volumes in this market are close to five trillion dollars. Collier reckoned most people sort of got their heads around this but what they couldn't fathom was the fact that it was a non-regulated market which started its day in Sydney and finished its day on the west coast of America just as Sydney was opening again. It was a market that spanned three major overlapping time zones, Asia, Europe and the Americas. Colliers thoughts were interrupted by Mike Mitchell his head trader.

'Everything's ready boss,' he said. 'Everyone knows what to do.'

Half an hour earlier at 'prayers', a slang term for traders early morning strategy meetings, Forrest had told his traders that head office had instructed him to dump one billion euros into the Asian markets over a period of eight hours. Each trader would trade up to a maximum of ten million euros on each trade so as not to tip off the market too soon about their strategy. They were to bring in their affiliate banks in Tokyo and Singapore to help them.

Forrest looked at his watch. It was seven fifty-five, nearly time to start the ball rolling.

'Thanks Mike. You are sure they know the parameters of the trades?'

'Yes, they are all going to trade between five and ten million per trade. They will spread their calls over the whole of the far east and Australia. We will also place sell orders at our European and American affiliates ready for their markets opening. By the time New York is in play the damage will be done,' finished Mike.

'Okay,' said Collier. 'Don't forget, mainly sell the euro against the dollar, yen and pound. Do a little against the Hong Kong dollar and Australian dollar but not too much.'

'Right boss,' said Mitchell.

Collier watched as Mitchell strode out to his work station, picked up a small hand bell and furiously rang it, signalling the start of their trading day. The silence on the floor was broken as fifty traders picked up their handsets, pressed a button on one of their direct bank to bank lines and barked into their phones 'Deutsch here, spot euro dollar please.' Each trader had seventy direct lines to banks all over Asia and the far east and within fifteen minutes between them they had sold two hundred and fifty million euros. The euro's value against the dollar, pound and yen began to fall. Slowly at first, but as more and more euros were dumped into the markets its price began to plummet. By ten forty-five it had lost one percent of its value and by ten minutes past eleven, two percent had been shorn from its value.

Collier was confident that the strategy was working at least at the moment. Other participants in the market hadn't yet realised that

111

Deutschland bank was selling huge amounts of euros into the market. The Deutschland Bank would be able to buy back the euros they sold at a much cheaper price and make a hefty profit. While the German bank was doing this, Greek and Russian banks were following the same strategy, helping to push the euro even further down. By the time the Asian markets were ending their trading day the euro had lost three percent of its value against the dollar.

Time for some profit taking decided Collier. He signalled Mitchell into his office.

'How many points has the Euro fallen so far?'

'About four hundred points almost three percent.'

'Okay, start buying and let's make some profit. How much will we make if we buy back one hundred million Euro?'

Mitchell didn't need a calculator to work out the answer as these sorts of maths were bread and butter for experienced traders.

'Four million easy,' replied Mitchell in a flash.

'Right, easy does it though we have a couple of hours before the European market opens and our branches in Europe start selling again. Once we have the four million in the bag lay off our position to head office in Frankfurt.'

Laying off positions was a common procedure amongst global banks. By passing a currency position to a branch that was active in an open market in another time zone they effectively hedge against any unforeseen event which could see their profits wiped out and huge losses taken. Of course, an unforeseen negative event may occur in the receiving branch's time zone but at least they would be able to react quickly in an open market and avert the damage.

Collier watched Mitchell passing amongst his traders giving them their instructions. He was a good trader and had helped Collier make big profits for Deutschland bank in Hong Kong. When Collier was tired of the trading game he would recommend that Mitchell take over his job. He swivelled in his chair and looked out over the Hong Kong skyline of towering skyscrapers. He looked at his watch. It was two o'clock. Europe would be opening in three hours and New York in twelve. By the time, New York opened, he reasoned, the Euro would have gone through the floor.

Chapter 21

October 27th 2010 – 00:00 – East Coast

Thirteen thousand kilometres away in Washington DC, Sean Hughes dragged himself awake from his sleep. He checked the clock on the bedside table and saw that it was midnight. Why had he woken up? He twisted around and saw that Carole was still fast asleep. So, the alarm hadn't gone off, she would have woken up. Then as his head gradually cleared its fuzziness he heard a low buzzing sound coming from the pile of clothes he had dumped on a chair after undressing earlier that evening. Instantly he realised that the sound was coming from his Reuters Alert, a small gadget half the size of a mobile phone. He jumped out of bed and rummaged in the clothes pile; his fingers found the culprit and automatically clicked on the display button. The buzzing stopped and the small screen lit up displaying 'eur/usd 300 down'.

Sean was the head trader on the Euro desk at Citicorp and after the currency markets closed on the east coast he never failed to set his Reuters Alert to warn him whenever a currency made any unusual movements. He stared at the numbers. So the Euro was down in the far east, but why? As far as he remembered there wasn't any economic events which could affect the eur/usd exchange rate. He decided to call his counterpart Roger Vaughan in Tokyo.

'Chris, is that you?' asked Sean as soon as the phone was picked up.

'Yes Sean. I recognised that Irish brogue immediately. How have you been?

'I'm good Roger. How are you? How's business?

'Business is good,' said Roger. 'But you didn't call to see how I was doing did you? I bet next month's bonus you called about the tumbling Euro.'

Sean felt himself blush with embarrassment even though he was thousands of miles away. He chided himself for not being the type of

114

person that kept in touch. It was the same with his friends as well as with colleagues in business.

'No, you're right,' he admitted. 'I know I'm bad at keeping in touch Roger but it's unintentional. I don't sort of think about it really.

'Try harder Sean because it's not an endearing trait. Okay let's forget about that now I've chewed you out and talk about the fall of the Euro. There are no technical reasons for the decline, the price wasn't at a resistance or support point when it began to drop. Neither was there any economic news to trigger the decline. So we don't know why. However, we have noticed that the major sellers are Deutschland Bank, the Moscow Trade Bank and Alpha Bank.'

'A German bank, a Russian bank and a Greek bank, strange bedfellows,' said Sean. 'There must be something to connect them or perhaps there is an economic event coming up and it's being priced in.'

'We looked at the economic calendar for today, tomorrow and the next day but there is nothing that would affect all three countries except perhaps the Bilderberg Meeting in Athens later today. I should imagine that there are representatives of all three countries at the meeting but what it's got to do with the Euro I don't know.'

'Greece does have some economic problems,' said Sean. 'Perhaps that has something to do with it. Are you selling?'

'Some, but without knowledge of the reason those banks are dumping Euros I don't want to risk too much. The price has come down another fifty points since we started this call. Don't you have any contacts at the Federal Reserve you could call?' asked Roger.

Sean was quiet for a minute as he mentally went through his contacts. Eureka, he thought Jim Broadbent. 'I don't have anyone at the Fed but I do know a technical analyst for the European desk at the CIA. He might know something.'

'Get on to him Sean. He might be very interested in what's going on with the Euro. You never know.'

115

I'll get on it right away. Nice talking to you again Roger. Promise I'll keep in closer touch in future.'

'Yeah right,' laughed Roger. 'Good luck with your friend and let me know what's going on. Don't forget me!'

Sean shut the call down and looked up Jim Broadbent's mobile number. They had met at MIT where they both studied international relations, technology and economics, a fairly new hybrid degree which had been developed for those who had ambitions to become top traders in the financial markets. However, the CIA also recruited graduates from this programme who showed excellent analytical and technological skills.

In a townhouse in the Georgetown district of Washington DC, Jim Broadbent extended his arm towards his cell which was buzzing like an angry bee on his bedside table. He saw Sean's name on the screen. Oh Frell! What the hezmana does Sean want this time of night or should I say morning? he thought.

Jim never cussed because he was brought up not to swear. He had never heard his parents utter a single swear word, not even a 'damn'. So he and his twin sister never used a swear word before they were twelve years old. Then they watched Farscape the Jim Henson Sci-fi series. As the series was shown before the watershed Henson knew that if he had the characters utter swear words the television watchdogs would either not show the programme or show it after the watershed when kids were supposedly in bed. So he made up cuss words and the programme was aired before nine o'clock. Both he and his sister and many millions of kids began to use Henson's made up swear words instead of the real ones. Jim himself even approaching middle age, still used Henson's words in preference to more common ones. Frell was a substitute for 'fucking hell' and 'hezmana' was a substitute for 'dammit'.

'What time do you call this Sean,' moaned Jim putting the phone to his ear. 'This better be good.'

'I don't know about good, it's certainly puzzling.

'What's puzzling?'

'The Euro has fallen over three points in the far eastern and Asian markets without any substantive reason for the move except that three banks seem to be the institutions driving it.'

'Which banks,' asked Jim.

'Ivan, Deutschland Bank and Alpha Bank. Ivan is traders pet name for the Moscow State Bank,' explained Sean.

Jim went quiet for a moment. Could it be that this has something to do with Greece he thought? But what? It's not as if Greece, Germany and Russia are partners in anything. Or are they? Maybe the whole purpose of the Bilderberg meeting and the announcement that Alex will make is aimed at frightening the financial markets. Jim knew that the financial markets were not his forte, neither was it the forte of the rest of the team. Should he convene them at this hour of the morning? He pondered whether it was important enough. Too many questions and not enough answers, he was out of his comfort zone on this.

'Sean, why would a small bunch of banks sell-off a currency? Could it be some kind of strategy?'

'When there is a currency sell-off there is usually an economic or bad news reason for it. In a case like that all the banks would join in. Occasionally one bank might try and sell off a currency if it was caught with its pants down because it had bought a currency that was expensive in the belief it would strengthen and they could sell it at a profit, but instead, it had weakened significantly and become cheaper, so they had to sell to minimise their loss. But this case is different. There are three banks working in unison which makes me believe they have inside information about a forthcoming event or some hard-economic news which they are certain will weaken the Euro. What the news is I can't begin to imagine.'

Jim thought fast. He had to inform the rest of the team. He was now certain that this had something to do with the assignment they were on. But he was feeling very uncomfortable about trying to explain currency movements to the team. Sean had to come along as his expert.

'Sean I'm going to gather my troops together for a meeting at Langley and I want you with me to give them the benefit of your knowledge of currency movements and likely economic scenarios.'

'How long have I got,' asked Sean.

'I'll pick you up in one hour,' said Jim firmly. 'Don't make me wait. This is important.'

'I'll be ready,' confirmed Sean and closed his phone.

Once the line had gone dead Jim sent out a text message to the other members of his team. It was four simple words 'code red ninety minutes'. They would think that something had broken in Greece of course but let them sweat it out a little. Besides the drone will be on station soon so they would be able to observe the goings on in Soufli.

Chapter 22

October 27th 2010 – 02:30 – Langley

'Who is this?' said Barry pointing rather rudely at Sean who was standing somewhat nervously by the door.

'I brought Sean in,' explained Jim. 'There has been an attack on the Euro in the far east. It seems to be isolated among three major banks at the moment. Moscow State, Alpha and Deutschland Bank. They are the only banks involved so far. Sean is the head trader for the Euro desk at Citicorp and I felt that he was the best person to help us figure out what might be going on. I….

'Does he have clearance?' interrupted Barry.

'Yes,' confirmed Jim. I got him a level four clearance. I figured that was high enough for what he hears and sees here tonight. Oh and by the way the drone is on station and awaiting our orders.'

'Okay Jim, good work. Level four seems about right. Sean before you leave here tonight you will be required to sign a document wherein you agree to never mention what you see or hear while you are in this room for at least ten years. Not even to your wife. Is that understood?'

'Yes sir,' said Sean.

'Enough of the sir, my name is Barry, this is Laura, over there is Chris and of course you know Jim.'

Sean acknowledged the team and then took the seat that Barry had directed him to. He sat down and looked around in awe at the technology that was evident within the room. The others sat down at the table with him except for Jim who was busy with a bank of screens and a computer.

'Before we start hearing what Sean has to say let's get this drone doing some work. Jim where is it now?'

'It's on station circling over Soufli now,' answered Jim. 'I can send a composite of John Dexter to the pilots on the carrier which will make their task of identifying him much easier.'

'Good idea Jim,' said Barry. 'Laura what do you think the surveillance strategy should be?'

'I suggest the drones' search pattern is split into three ten-minute sector runs. That way we'll cover the important ground three times in each hour. Start with circling over the gas terminal, then the next sector should probably be the area of Soufli where the well off people live. John Dexter is more likely to have a residence there. Finally, the last sector should be a section of the American pipeline to the east of the terminal where it is not parallel to the Russian one. Reasoning that if the American pipeline is to be sabotaged it will be where there is no danger of damaging the Russian pipeline.'

'I agree. Jim, can you get that in the works while we talk to Sean.'

'On it,' acknowledged Jim.

'Right young man,' said Barry looking directly at Sean. 'Tell us why you believe that the plight of the Euro in the far east overnight is not a normal phenomenon.'

Sean looked around at the people around the table as he gathered his thoughts.

'There are only really two reasons why a currency will have a large percent change in its value against another currency,' began Sean. Firstly, if there has been a fundamental change in the economy of a country investors will buy the local currency if its good news or sell it if its bad news. For example, if statistics are released which show that consumer spending in a particular country is slowing down investors might see that as a worsening economy and start to sell that country's currency. It wouldn't just be two or three banks but thousands of banks and corporate investors around the world selling the currency.

Secondly, a large currency movement might be precipitated by insider knowledge of an upcoming announcement which could trigger sharp movements up or down depending on whether the news is good or bad. In such a case it might only be one, two or even three banks who have this knowledge and are prepared to use it for earning huge profits.

In my opinion what is happening in the far east with the Euro is the latter reason, but I have no idea what knowledge the Greeks, Germans and Russians have or any inkling of any major announcements being made.'

'Thank you Sean,' said Barry. 'So you are pretty certain that they have some knowledge which no-one else has?'

'Yes I am. And to risk the amount of money they are risking to push the Euro down probably means they know something pretty mind-blowing is going to happen.'

'What do you think Laura?' asked Barry.

'Well let's look at what we know and maybe we can anticipate what could happen and why that event would support a weakening of the Euro. We know that later on today Alex will be making some sort of announcement that involves the rest of Europe, particularly Germany. That alone could account for Greek and German banks seemingly working in tandem to bring the Euro down. We also know that the Greek prime minister is involved in something highly irregular in the Thrace region of Greece and has been meeting with John Dexter who at this moment is somewhere near the Soufli gas terminal. We know that Dexter directed a missile attack on the very house in Thrace where he had met with Xenakis. Finally, we have also received a warning that the American gas pipeline in Thrace may be damaged or even destroyed.'

'Where is the Russian link?' asked Barry.

'I think I know what that is,' answered Chris. 'Energy. The Russians want to transport their gas exclusively into Europe via northern Greece. With the American pipeline, out of the way they will have the de-facto rights. I wouldn't mind betting that Xenakis has already done a deal with them.'

'Chris could be right. I'm bringing up the big screen for you,' said Jim.

They all swivelled in their chairs to look at the screen.

'This is fifteen kilometres east of Soufli and the pipeline is the American one,' explained Jim.

The picture from the drone's camera showed a four by four moving parallel to the metal fencing which protected the pipeline which itself was hardly visible as ninety percent of it was buried in the ground. The four by four looked to be the one John Dexter was driving earlier. Two hundred yards in front of the four by four they could see one of the many maintenance access stations which were inserted in the pipeline every ten kilometres. The access station looked like a concrete hut with a metal door and no windows.

'The maintenance crews use these stations to access the pipeline,' observed Jim. 'The pipeline comes up above ground within the stations so the crews can access them easily. Of course, that makes them especially vulnerable at these locations.'

They watched as the four-by-four stopped adjacent to the station and three men wearing commando fatigues jumped from the vehicle. One of them was carrying wire cutters and the other three each carried what looked like sports holdalls. The fence was breached in no time and they saw the man with the wire cutters produce what looked like a long thin strip of blue tack from his lapel pocket and place it so it circled around the lock on the door of the station. He then inserted a short thin straw like object into the blue tack, lit the end and stepped back.

There was a bright flash and the lock and handle of the door just fell out leaving a gaping hole where they had been. The commandos pushed open the door, entered the hut and disappeared.

'What are they doing?' asked Sean staring at the screen.

'I presume they are planting explosives and are planning to blow up the pipeline,' answered Barry.

'Can't you stop them?'

'The drone does have missiles on board but if we fired them we couldn't help but destroy the pipeline instead of the terrorists. It's better not to waste tax payer's money in firing the missiles for a wasted cause.'

'What's your assessment Laura,' asked Barry.

'Same as yours. We can only watch them sabotage the pipeline and then follow them back to their base and possibly take the base out. Hopefully with John Dexter in it. Look their leaving,' said Laura pointing at the screen.

'Right, track them Jim. Don't lose them,' said Barry.

Jim relayed the instructions to the drone pilots sitting aboard the Harry S Truman aircraft carrier. Moments later the three commandos ran out into the sunlight and jumped into the four by four. The driver gunned the accelerator and they surged off in a cloud of dust. Jim panned the drone camera out so they could see both the vehicle and the maintenance block it was racing away from. They didn't have to wait very long before the maintenance station and several metres of pipeline were engulfed in a ball of flame from which spewed upwards chunks of concrete and metal. Sean thought it was slightly eerie watching the explosion as there was no sound. It was a silent explosion as the drone did not transmit sound. A minute later once the flames and dust had settled down all they saw was a large crater where the maintenance station and the adjoining pipeline had been.

The vehicle careened along the dirt track leaving a head of dust behind it that could be seen for miles. The drone kept pace and on the odd occasion it lost sight because the track wound its way through woodlands, it soon recaptioned them when they emerged from cover. After three kilometres, the dirt track hit a tarmac road and the four by four turned west towards Soufli. The terrain was a rolling landscape of hills and forests and now and again the terrorist's vehicle was hidden from view by trees overhanging the road. Four kilometres from Soufli the four by four turned off the road onto what looked like a gravel track and after a further kilometre stopped in front of a pair of metal gates. A commando exited the vehicle, walked up to a small box which was at waist height, and seemed to key in some sort of code. The gates immediately began to swing inwards. The vehicle passed through the gates, waited for the commando to re-board and sped off down the gravel trail again. The gate behind them slowly closed They were passing through a denser area of the forest now and again slipped in and out of view of the eyes of the drone.

The people watching the progress of the four by four were fascinated as they followed the vehicle from the safety of their desks some five thousand miles away. They all thought the same question but none verbalised it. Where were, they going? Finally, after a further five kilometres the forest canopy became very dense and the drone lost the vehicle altogether. It circled around a couple of minutes before heading to where the road re-appeared a kilometre from where it had disappeared under the canopy. The vehicle did not re-appear.

'Jim, can we see what's below the canopy at all?' Barry asked.

'I can ask them to transmit an infra-red composite.'

'Do it Jim and while you're about it check that the drone is primed for missile launch.'

Jim responded with thumbs up then keyed his microphone headset. The others waited and then a couple of seconds later the screen changed from a clear high definition picture to an infra-red composite showing several hundred white blobs moving seemingly aimlessly around.

'It's a camp,' exclaimed Barry. 'There must be over two hundred men down there plus whatever equipment they have. Look on the right! That must be the heat signature of the stationary four by four.'

'No! it's not,' yelled Jim. The drone pilots have detected that the drone is being 'painted' by enemy radar and the heat signature is similar to a land to air missile powering up. They want to know what to do.'

Without hesitation Barry turned to Jim and said 'Take it out.'

Two seconds later the watchers saw two flames hurtling downwards from the drone.

'Ten seconds to impact,' yelled Jim.

The missiles spread apart one heading to the northern end of the camp where there were the most heat signatures of human beings, while the other headed for the centre of the camp. Only Laura noticed another heat signature moving at speed towards the southern end of the camp. Before she could say anything, the camp was obliterated by two plumes of flames and smoke. As the smoke cleared they saw an area devoid of trees, filled with the rubble of burning buildings and they could almost smell the stench of burning flesh.

They looked at each other without saying anything then Barry said 'I hope John Dexter was in the camp.'

'Look!' said Laura as she pointed to the screen. It showed a vehicle moving at speed towards the gates that the commandos had entered only a few minutes earlier. 'It's the same four by four and I'm betting that John Dexter is at the wheel.'

Later that morning Laura would find out to her cost that she had been right.

Chapter 23

October 27th 2010 – 09:30 – Athens

Alex and Gitta sat in the front of a dark blue Mercedes C class as it cruised north on route 83 towards Nea Makri to the east of Athens. Their plan was to give Alex some shooting practice in a remote area, take a slow lunch and then watch a spectacular sunset at five o'clock on the Sounion peninsular. An hour earlier their Lufthansa flight from Berlin had touched down at Athens International Airport dead on time. They had no luggage, just knapsacks, so they were through customs very quickly and were first in line at the Hertz desk. The Mercedes was Alex's choice, he loved that car; he loved the way it quietly and smoothly moved serenely over Greece's less than perfect road surfaces.

While he was doing the paperwork Gitta had disappeared into a lady's rest room to assemble the two pistols she had smuggled in, both in Alex's knapsack as he was less likely to be searched considering his VIP status. The guns were of a plastic compound very strong and in pieces virtually undetectable as components from a gun. The bullets however needed some fancy masking and Gitta used a specially made belt which had small metal fake derringers around the outside and on the buckle itself, were several bullets. The bullets were real but coated in the same colour as the fake derringers. The security officers always believed the bullets to be as ornamental as the derringers and never stopped her. When Gitta came out of the ladies room she had lost her jeans and was wearing her trade mark slit skirt with a thigh holster tucked between her legs.

Now Gitta stretched out her legs letting her skirt ride higher up her thighs.

'Hey, stop that,' said Alex half-heartedly. 'You're distracting me.'

'In that case, we could always stop in a quiet spot. I'm sure you know plenty around here,' Gitta said, giving Alex a knowing smile and a quick wink. 'By the way your gun is now in your knapsack fully loaded.'

'But I don't know how to use a gun,' protested Alex.

'I'll show you how when you stop in a quiet spot,' she said smiling, giving Alex another wink. For a man who had only that morning learned he had lost his mother he was bearing up well, she thought. He had wept when she told him and then she led him into the shower to wash away his tears and hurt. It's surprising how easily men can be diverted from their pain to something more pleasant. And making sure he enjoyed her was pleasurable to her as well. This surprised her somewhat as Alex was no hunk but for some reason she was attracted to him. Why? She didn't know.

Earlier that morning after she had consoled Alex, she had managed to bring his mind back to focus on what needed to be done that day. They had spoken to Barry Lightfoot and learnt that the intel on the pipeline had been accurate. Barry gave her a blow by blow account of the attack on the pipeline and the subsequent obliteration of the commando camp. The information that there was an attack on the Euro currency by three banks was a surprise to both at first but then after digesting this news Alex suggested that if Xenakis was cosying up to Russia and Germany and forming some sort of tripartite, it would make sense to hammer the Euro and weaken the European Union. They concluded that there was more information needed and that Alex would probably be privy to that during the Bilderberg conference. Barry suggested that as a courtesy Gitta should call Lighthouse and fill them in on what had happened overnight.

They had agreed that Alex would call in at midnight Eastern European Time, five o'clock Eastern Standard Time. A key issue was where Gitta should stay overnight. As Alex's bodyguard and handler, she should stick close to him, but with the security at the Astor Palace being extremely high due to the importance of the dignitaries staying there for the meeting, it would be difficult to smuggle Gitta in. She couldn't pose as Alex's wife as his wife was well known in Greece and the charade would be blown very quickly. The solution came from Laura who suggested that as the American Secretary of State was attending the conference they could see to it that Gitta was sequestered onto his bodyguard team. It would also enable Gitta to acquire a decent firearm and not have to rely on a couple of derringers. Suddenly Gitta realised that Alex had been talking to her.

'Sorry Alex, I was miles away,' she said, giving him an ashamed smile. 'What did you say?'

Alex pointed ahead. 'We are approaching an area that is free of houses and is a very popular camping area in the summer, see it has many trees and a sandy soil. I should think that this time of year there won't be anyone around to disturb our shooting practice.'

Gitta smiled. 'Is shooting practice, our code for more sex?' she laughed and briefly caressed his thigh.

Alex smiled. He recalled fondly that as a young boy his guardians had brought him down here to Nea Makri camping many times. It was a perfect area for young children. Five kilometres of sandy beaches covered in tamarisk trees to a depth of one kilometre from the sea. In the summer hundreds of families descended on Nea Makri in cars, caravans and buses. Tents were erected and hammocks slung between the trees. For young children and early teenagers, it was idyllic and many a young person experienced their first kiss or taste of sex during the balmy starlit nights.

Alex remembered little Sophie from his neighbourhood and how they always played together. Then in the summer before he went to the States they had ventured further than their usual peck on the cheek. One night they had undressed and lay down facing each other. She let him fondle and kiss her small tight breasts but not touch her where he really wanted to. She had held his penis in her cupped hand caressing it until he orgasmed, covering her hand in his sperm. Finally, at the end of the summer she consented to rubbing their naked bodies against each other. This time when he orgasmed his sperm covered her thighs and for an instant she was afraid she would get pregnant.

Alex laughed out loud at that thought and Gitta asked, 'What are you laughing about Alex?'

'I'll tell you later,' he said. 'Shall I find a spot for my shooting lesson as this area is as good as any. Afterwards, we can head south to see the sunset at Sounion. It's magnificent at this time of year.'

'Yes, go ahead. I'd like that'

Alex looked for a suitable area of sand which was packed hard and would allow him to drive deep into the trees. Within a minute, he was turning into the trees and when he was sure they were well hidden from the road he stopped the car. Alex looked at Gitta for reassurance that this was a good place to stop. She nodded her head imperceptibly, opened her door, and stepped out onto the sand. Looking around she saw that there was enough space between trees to mark out a makeshift firing range. Moving to the nearest tree she then stepped out twenty metres to a tree that had clear line of site from the one she had just left. Opening her bag, she pulled out a plastic compact with about a seven centimetres' radius and placed it on a protruding knot about the level of her head.

Alex was waiting for her by the tree that was to be the firing position.

'Ready? Asked Gitta.

'Isn't it a rather small target? Questioned Alex squinting as if he had difficulty in seeing the target.'

'Don't be an ass Alex. Now take one of the Derringers.'

Alex picked up one of the pistols and looked at it.

'It's got two barrels. I thought Derringers were one shot pistols,' he exclaimed.

'Some are but most are two shot now but there are also some specialised four shot COP Derringers like these two. They both fire .357 Magnum bullets and they are still the smallest pistols around today. They call them muff guns because a woman can holster them to her inside thigh,' Gitta said, winking at Alex.

'What's the range of this toy,' asked Alex.

'Maximum headshot kill is twenty yards, body shot ten to fifteen yards. Accuracy good for twenty yards but degrades fast after that. Now watch me.'

Gitta stood facing the target with her pistol in her right hand down at her side. She started to pull her right arm up and at the same time her left hand came up and held her right wrist. With both arms straight out in front she slowly brought the pistol up until it was sighted at the target. She squeezed the trigger. The gun jumped slightly from the force of the bullet leaving the chamber. The compact that she had placed on the tree spun into the air and fell to the ground.

'Good shot!' cried Alex.

'Not really. I just nicked it. A hit would have smashed it to pieces. Your turn. Prepare yourself exactly as I did.'

While Gitta retrieved the compact and placed it back into its original position Alex practiced preparing for the shot. The Derringer is surprisingly heavy for such a small pistol, he thought. He had fired a gun before when younger. His father had dragged him along to his gun club on a couple of occasions and made him fire a few rounds. Alex hated the noise and the smell of cordite. It hadn't been an enjoyable experience.

Gitta interrupted his thoughts. 'Ready? Off you go! Now remember slowly aim and squeeze the trigger, don't wrench it.'

Alex brought the gun up slowly, aimed, squeezed the trigger and fired. Nothing!

'Where did it go?' he asked.

'You missed by a mile. Don't close one of your eyes. You should keep both eyes open. Try again.'

Alex tried again and again. His fourth shot hit the tree and after that success gave him confidence, his shooting got better. His eighth shot was an inch from the target and so were his ninth and tenth shots.

'Enough for now,' said Gitta. 'You have done really well. Let's pack up and head back to the car. Wear this shoulder holster under your jacket. I'll fix it for you when we get back to the car. Let's stop for a long lazy lunch somewhere. It's a nice warm day we could find a small cove and relax on a beach for the afternoon before we arrive at Sounion.'

Ten minutes later they were on the road heading south towards sunset at the Sounion peninsular.

Chapter 24

October 27th 2010 – 13.00 – Vouliagmeni

Gregory sat under the sun awning of the Ithaki Restaurant Bar on Apollonos Drive, which was the only access by road to the Astir Palace Hotel in Vouliagmeni, where in a few hours the dignitaries attending the Bilderberg meeting were going to gather. It was the perfect spot to keep an eye on the cavalcade of cars that would soon be bringing some of the most powerful people in the world to the annual meeting. The speed limit was twenty kilometres an hour on this stretch of road up to the main entrance of the hotel, which was five hundred metres away to Gregory's right. There was no wind and as always in Greece the light was perfect. The sea, sparkling in the early afternoon sun, was like a mirror, only disturbed by the odd seagull touching down or one or two autumn swimmers braving the cool sea. Mostly though sunbathers stuck to the beach and soaked up the autumn sun.

Not for me, thought Gregory. Although he was a good swimmer he was bored by swimming. It wasn't the cold water that would put him off. His body was honed to not feel anything as mundane as hot and cold. No! Put him on a tennis court or a squash court where he could compete and he was a happy puppy.

Gregory took a sip of his Turkish coffee as his practiced eyes swept the scene in front of him. Nothing has changed, except that the two girls at a nearby table were eyeing him up and down more blatantly now. He smiled at them and they hurriedly turned away. He wasn't surprised at their interest because he knew he was handsome in a carefree sort of way. Blonde unruly hair, piercing blue eyes and a wide smile, coupled with a slim but athletic body and tall at six foot two inches, he was often chased by the opposite sex. He was tempted to go over to their table but thought better of it. He might miss something important if he became too distracted. Besides, he was after bigger game this evening. Yesterday's referendum result had been a small majority on the remain side which had shocked the whole of Europe at its closeness and he was waiting for a word from Sir Peter that the coup should not be hampered.

Ten kilometres north of central Athens in the suburb of Maroussi, Kostas Triandafilos sat together with Stavros and Christos his co-conspirators in the planned military coup. He had just announced the death of his friend Michalis, whose body had been found in the Milos bunkers.

'How did he die?' asked Stavros as he signalled a waiter for some beers. 'By the look on your face you suspect foul play.'

'It looks like a heart attack. After the incident on Daskelos island and the death of Ariadne, I have been very careful to make sure I have not been followed but on Milos a few days ago, I had a feeling that I was being watched.'

'Somebody was following you?' exclaimed Christos. 'Us as well?'

Costas could see that they were both getting jumpy at the news he had just given them. He didn't blame them. If they were caught they would all suffer an ignominious and lonely death by a firing squad. 'It was just a feeling, nothing concrete, however. Just in case I called in a favour of a friend of mine who is a forensic expert and she is doing an autopsy at this very moment. Hopefully, she will call me within the hour.'

'If Michalis's death is not by natural causes are we still going ahead with the coup tomorrow?' asked Stavros.

'It's too late to stop now. If his death is murder it won't jeopardise the operation because there would be no point in killing someone outside the armed forces. They would come after us,' finished Costas.

'Then why?' questioned Themis. 'Why kill Michalis?'

'A warning maybe,' ventured Christos.

'To whom?' questioned Costas. 'If it was a warning for us it's not been very successful, has it? No, I don't believe it was a warning, it's something else.'

They sat in silence for a while sipping their beers, deep in thought. Gradually, their thoughts turned to the next day and their roles in the coup. Kostas broke the silence.

'Stavros, is everything ready your end? No hitches I should know about?'

'I'll be one tank light. Engine trouble and it can't be repaired before we roll out tonight,' said Stavros.

'Twelve tanks should be adequate for your purposes, shouldn't it?' asked Kostas.

'Yes,' agreed Stavros. 'It's easier to conceal twelve tanks than thirteen of them...'

Stavros was interrupted by the sound of Kostas's cell phone ringing. 'Yes,' answered Kostas. For a couple of minutes, he said nothing, only occasionally nodding his head. Finally, he said 'ευχαριστω πολη φιλοι μου', thanking his friend. He turned to the others. 'It was indeed murder,' he announced.

'How was it done?' asked Christos.

'Well,' answered Kostas. 'My friend had a lot of trouble finding anything, but eventually she found a tiny hole on the side of Michalis's neck. Apparently, there are only a limited amount of chemical substances that can simulate a heart attack and she concentrated her search on finding traces in his body. She finally found a trace chemical which leads her to believe this was introduced into Michalis's body via a hypodermic.'

'So, he was killed,' stated Christos. 'But why? Who was he a danger to? It doesn't make sense.'

'I think we're looking at it the wrong way,' suggested Kostas. 'He wasn't working for any agency or Government, so in that sense he wasn't a danger to anyone. However, if someone thought that Michalis had overheard what we were planning, they might have been frightened that he would talk.'

'But no-one was there in the building with us so how would they know what we were talking about?' said Stavros.

'Exactly,' agreed Kostas. 'So, it was someone who not only knew we were in that building, but also knew what we were planning. That someone must have followed us.'

'We're blown then,' said Christos. 'Who could it have been? The Greek secret service, the CIA, who?'

'None of those otherwise we would have been arrested or terminated by now,' explained Kostas. 'What did Alex's mother and Michalis have in common?' asked Kostas.

'Nothing,' declared Christos.

'Yes, they did. Not directly, but Ariadne was in on the coup and someone mistakenly thought that Michalis also knew about the coup,' said Kostas. He leaned forward towards his two friends and co-conspirators and whispered 'Someone doesn't want any loose ends when this is all over. It can only be Lighthouse. They don't trust anyone to keep mum about their involvement.'

Christos and Stavros looked at each other then back at Kostas. 'That means that we're all in danger,' Stavros said.

'Agreed,' Kostas said. 'But I don't believe it's a Lighthouse sanctioned operation. It's one agent acting on his own.'

'You don't mean.....'

'Exactly, it's Gregory! He does their wet work and has gone rogue.'

'What does that mean for us Kostas. We must be in danger too!'

'Yes Christos, we are all in danger but don't worry we have an angel looking after us.'

'Who?' asked Christos.

'Do you remember when we had finished our meeting on Milos, Michalis and I had walked along the sea front where I expressed my sixth sense feeling that something was not quite right. I asked Michalis to come to Athens and watch our backs. He declined saying that he felt he was too old for that sort of job. He did however remind me of an alternative. A Mossad agent that had been part of my team in Afghanistan five years ago, and who is now attached to the Israeli Embassy in Athens.'

'How does Michalis know this agent and how does he know the agent is working in Athens?' questioned Stavros.

Kostas could see that Stavros was agitated because he didn't like someone else knowing more than he knew. He'd have to tell them the truth about Michalis. 'There is something I can tell you now that Michalis is dead. He was in the Greek secret service before he became caretaker of the museum on Milos. And he never lost touch with his contacts. That's how he knew Michelle Devereaux was working out of the Israeli embassy in Athens.'

'A woman,' breathed Stavros.

'Yes,' said Kostas. 'She's sitting behind us two tables back.'

Both Stavros and Christos turned and looked at the table which Kostas had indicated. They saw a woman who looked to be in her forties, wearing a pair of blue jeans, white trainers and a short sleeve jacket over a white tee shirt. She smiled at them, her white teeth seemingly brilliant against her dark skin. Her hair was jet black and hung effortlessly on her shoulders while dark eyes stared unflinchingly across at them. Michelle slung her bag over her shoulder and walked over to their table.

'Yasou,' she said as she slid into the seat next to Kostas.

'Hello Michelle,' acknowledged Kostas. 'Do you have any news for us?'

'Yes, one of my assets has located Gregory. He's in a coffee shop near to the entrance of the Astir Palace Hotel.'

'We have only just deduced that Gregory is probably responsible for a couple of murders, so how come you are tailing him?' said Stavros.

'My fault,' admitted Kostas. 'I called Gregory after our meeting on Milos and he told me that he was in Kolonaki in the centre of Athens.

135

While we were talking, I heard a ship's siren in the background so I knew he was lying. Of course, he could have been in any port around Greece but the fact that Michalis met his demise on Milos led me to the conclusion that Gregory was on Milos also. What other news do you have for us Michelle?'

'Two things which are causing concern in Europe and across the pond. Firstly, the American gas pipeline was destroyed early this morning near Soufli in western Thrace. No-one knows who the perpetrators are and no-one has owned up to it yet. However, there is a lot of unrest between the minority Turkish Muslims and the locals, with reports of clashes in several towns.'

'Don't the Russians have a pipeline running near Soufli too?' asked Kostas.

'Yes, that was unharmed. There are rumours they have another pipeline which will come on-line within a few days. If that is the case they will be doubling their capacity for transporting gas through Greece into Italy and on into central Europe.'

'Suspicious,' observed Kostas.

'Very, especially when it seems that the crashing of the Euro over the last two days seems to be driven by three institutions including a Russian bank. Still, we will know more later after your new finance minister does his press conference.'

'You said three banks, who are the other two?' interrupted Kostas.

'Oh, one is Greek and the other German.'

'Isn't that worrying?'

'Yes very,' replied Michelle. 'The wires have been buzzing. The CIA, MI6, and the French Secret Service have all contacted me asking if I knew anything. Of course, I don't, but the people who do have been conspicuously quiet.'

'The Russians, the Germans and the Greeks,' said Kostas.

Michelle's phone pinged. She looked at the screen. Then stood up saying. 'Have to go. I'll be in touch.' Kostas nodded and watched her glide between the tables before disappearing around a corner.

'Well lads everything that Michelle has said only emphasises that we are correct to act as we intend tomorrow. Themis Xenakis is knee deep in some shitty stuff and by all accounts he is dragging Greece into the mire with him. Alex's press conference will tell us more of course, but I doubt it will ease our fears. More likely it will make our actions tomorrow imperative. You know the plans so let's execute them with precision. Good luck! Tomorrow we say 'no'!'

With that they clinked their beer bottles, stood up and hugged each other, then left the café in three separate directions.

Chapter 25

October 27th, 2010 – 18.00 – Sounion Greece

Alex and Gitta stood hand in hand in the centre of the Temple of Poseidon gazing out across the azure blue Aegean Sea. They were waiting and hoping to see one of its famous sunsets to which thousands of tourists and Athenians flock to this sacred place every year. Cape Sounion was the most southerly outcrop of land on the Greek mainland, which was adorned by one of the most beautiful and hallowed temples of ancient Greece.

The temple itself was typical of many Greek temples, the building was rectangular, with a colonnade on all four sides. The total number of original Doric Order local marble columns was thirty-four with fifteen of those columns still standing. Poseidon was the God of the sea and the temple built in 450BC was a gift to Poseidon in the hope that he would allow the sea and winds be kind to Greek ships.

When the Greek hero Theseus sailed off on his famous adventure to kill the Minotaur in the palace of King Minos in Crete, his father King Aegeus reminded him that if he returned safely his ships should have white sails but if he had been killed his ships should have black sails. Although successful in defeating the Minotaur, Theseus forgot to change his sails to white. When King Aegeus saw this, he flung himself from the Temple of Poseidon onto the rocks below, killing himself. It is from this the name Aegean Sea is derived, named after the King.

'It's beautiful,' breathed Gitta looking out at the setting sun whose rays cast a mauve glow amongst the marble columns. 'I can see why tourists come to this temple. And the myth is so romantic. It is a myth, isn't it?'

'Greek myths are often entwined with reality to the point where it's difficult to tell between historic events and fiction.' Alex pulled Gitta gently and led her away from a crowd of tourists. 'Have you ever visited Crete?' Asked Alex.

'No, I've never had the opportunity. I've been to Rhodes and Andros but not Crete.'

'Then you must go and visit Knossos, the great palace of King Minos on Crete. It's an amazing place. The Minoan civilisation who built the palace around 1300BC were an advanced civilisation. They had flushing water closets, running hot and cold water and a form of air-conditioning using shades and blinds in a particular pattern around the palace.'

'I'll put it on my bucket list Alex, but for now we should call Langley and get an update.'

They moved back to their car which was parked in the small car park near the Temple of Poseidon. Inside the car Gitta retrieved her mobile and dialled the SCIPTS number for the Overlook section. After a few beeping noises and a few rings the phone was answered by Barry Lightfoot.

'Alex?' said Barry.

'No it's Gitta. I have Alex here with me. I'm putting you on speaker.'

'Are you clean?'

'Yes we have dry cleaned the area, no one can overhear. What's the latest?'

'We have put into place a plan with the help of Sean. The European Central Bank, The Bank of England and the Federal Reserve have coerced several major banks in helping them to pull up the Euro by its coat tails before Xenakis and company can react. The markets in Europe have already closed, London will close in an hour and a heavy hand has been laid on the biggest banks not to sell Euro before close of play here in the States.'

'Then what?' interrupted Alex.

'Well Alex, in all probability the announcement you'll be making this evening at the Bilderberg meeting will serve to push the Euro even further down overnight if we did nothing to stop it. And most likely the consortium of Greek, German and Russian banks will buy back the Euro some time tomorrow at an extremely cheap price and make billions in profit. However, we are orchestrating what is called a 'gap up' overnight by leaking news that the Federal Reserve will lower interest rates and the ECB will raise them. The differential in the two rates would cause a massive sell off of dollars against the Euro. The gap would regain twenty five percent of the Euro's value and the Greek, German and Russian banks involved in this scheme would take a hit of billions of Euro.'

Gitta and Alex looked at each other while Barry was explaining this, both with expressions of complete amazement tinged with bewilderment, as neither really had a clue what Barry was talking about. Alex had been trained as a lawyer with a degree in law and Gitta certainly wasn't an investment banker. As long as it worked they didn't need to understand. Barry sounded confident and seemed to have complete faith in Sean's advice and expertise.

'Sounds great,' ventured Alex. 'If it works the way you described it Xenakis and his co-conspirators will be wounded.'

'Yes but not mortally wounded. They might still be able to get away with whatever they are plotting. In all probability we will need the Government in Greece to fall, or Xenakis resign or……'

'Eliminated,' cut in Gitta. 'That is a possible option right?'

'We don't assassinate heads of Government. You know that – well not intentionally anyway. It's not US policy.'

No thought Gitta as she listened to Barry, but it has been done even if it was never an official sanction. She had done it herself in the past on her third assignment when she was ordered to compromise the second in command of the Stasi in Leipzig, Maria Gruber. She had spent days following her around in the hope of finding something to compromise her. She could not uncover anything that would get her sacked or demoted and in the meantime she was running a cell in West Germany that was embarrassing to the west. If she was out of the picture the cell would be headless and the authorities would be able to turn a couple of the cell members and imprison the rest of them. It would take years to train and form another cell.

So Gitta decided to sanction her. Maria was a lesbian and a stunning blonde, often spending evenings at one of the more up-market lesbian clubs in Leipzig. One evening Gitta started to go to the club and over several days flirted with Maria until eventually Maria agreed to go back to Gitta's apartment for a drink. Gitta had planned to spike Maria's drink early in the evening before Maria made any advances towards her. However, curiosity took over and she decided to wait until after Maria had made a move. That was a mistake! Maria made her move on Gitta quite unexpectantly and Gitta, who wasn't a lesbian, didn't have time to prepare herself from the sexual onslaught. Maria's tongue was in her mouth and one hand under her skirt before she realised what was happening. She involuntary pulled away not only out of surprise but also because she suddenly realised that she had forgotten to remove her thigh holster.

Maria pulled back with a triumphant look on her face, her right hand holding the Beretta and pointing it at Gitta's chest.

'I suspected it!' cried Maria. 'I thought you were not the real ticket when I saw you at the club. You did not attempt to pick anyone up and rebuffed anyone who tried to flirt with you which completely defeats the object of attending such clubs. I had my suspicions and wasn't surprised when you made your move on me.'

'Now what? What are you going to do?' said Gitta as she measured the distance between her foot and the gun in Maria's hand.

'Arrest you of course. I'm going to call it in and you will be taken to Stazi headquarters.'

As Maria reached for her bag, which was lying on the low coffee table in front of the sofa where she had made her move on Gitta, her gun hand wavered slightly. It was enough for Gitta, her foot shot up and the gun flew from Maria's grasp. Gitta was on her in a second, landing the edge of her hand at Maria's throat who went down like a sack of potatoes. Gitta followed up by sitting astride her chest, her hands around her throat squeezing the life out of her. Maria thrashed around for a minute but she was no match for Gitta and her thrashing slowed till eventually she stopped moving.

Gitta sat astride her for a moment or two gathering her thoughts. She had just completely disobeyed orders. Instead of compromising Maria she had killed her albeit unwillingly. There was no way she could hide this as there was a body to get rid of and the Stazi would probably start a city wide search when she didn't turn up for work. She had to get rid of the body and the only way was to call in the cleaners.

'Listen Gitta there are no circumstances which would warrant Xenakis being terminated,' insisted Barry interrupting her reverie. 'Do you understand!'

'I understand Barry. Don't worry,' replied Gitta making a face at Alex. Alex smiled shrugged his shoulders and squeezed her hand. 'Anything else we need to know Barry?'

'This might be nothing but Laura and Jim have been noticing higher than normal tank movements around Athens. Of course this might be in preparation for the 'Ochi Day' celebrations and military parade. Keep an ear out could you just in case it's more sinister than that.'

'Will do.'

'One more thing Gitta, we are deploying a drone over the Astir Palace for the next twenty-four hours as a precaution in case things go sour.'

'That's comforting to know, it used to be men on horses riding to the rescue but now it's an eye in the sky – wonderful,' she said with a hint of sarcasm which Barry completely ignored.

Alex caught Gitta's eye and looked pointedly at his watch while at the same time nodding his head in the direction they should be driving.

'I have to get Alex to the Astir Palace. He needs time to get ready for his announcement.'

'Okay, Chris Horsman our Athens Station Chief will be somewhere in the hotel at around twenty hundred hours and we will talk again after Alex has made his announcement.'

The line went dead before Gitta could give an answer or question why Chris was turning up. Another body she had to look out for. Alex put the car into drive and headed down the coast road towards the Astir Palace Hotel. The coastline between Sounion and Vouliagmeni was quite spectacular, with a new fast motorway which recently had replaced the original two lane road offering an excellent panorama of the myriad of small bays, beaches and marina's along the coast. They passed Lagonisi, one of the most popular resorts for rich Athenians, a two mile stretch of luxury hotels and night clubs which only came alive at night. As they passed there were still bodies taking in the autumn sun on the beach and a few of the braver ones enjoying the sea which although not cold it certainly wasn't as warm as it had been a few weeks earlier.

They passed the lesser known resorts of Agias Marina and Vari where the not so rich played during the summer months and winter weekends if the weather was unusually warm. They passed the organised nudist beaches which had sprung up in the last few years, then onwards towards Vouliagmeni the playground of the really wealthy, to the Astir Palace, their final destination.

They turned off the motorway onto Apollonos Avenue slowing down as the road narrowed and they also had to traverse the numerous sleeping policemen located every few metres. As they passed the Ithaki Restaurant Bar Gitta told Alex to stop the car one hundred yards further down the road.

'Why? Said Alex as he slowed the car down even further. 'Where are you going?'

'I've just recognised someone who shouldn't be here. You drive on to the Astir Palace and I'll catch you up when I've finished.'

'Right, but be careful, don't get into trouble.'

Gitta slipped out of the car carefully making sure the car was between her and the Ithaki. She then made her way towards the bar always keeping a palm tree or a group of people between her and her target. Unbeknown to her, far above, the drone that Langley had deployed was already doing its work. She was being tracked because the face recognition system had identified her on its database. Within seconds the drone had transmitted the capture to Langley and received a command from Jim Broadbent to track Gitta.

Gitta manoeuvred herself, without breaking cover, until she was directly behind Gregory. She was about to make her move when Gregory signalled to a waiter. She waited, not knowing whether Gregory was about to pay his bill and leave or was ordering another coffee. Gregory started giving instructions to the waiter at the same time pointing to the table where the two women who had been looking over at him were sitting. The waiter left and a few minutes later took two drinks over to the table where the women were. The drone meanwhile was transmitting it's face recognition signals to Langley. Gitta and Gregory were known to Jim. A third face, one of the women whom Gregory had bought a drink for, was not, but identified in the database as Michelle Deveraux of the Israeli Intelligence Service, a Mossad operative.

Gregory's attention was fully on the two women who were now holding up their glasses and saluting a thank you to him. Gitta saw her chance, broke cover and before Gregory could react had pulled a chair next to him, sat down and pressed her Derringer into his left side.

'Hello Gregory,' she said smiling at him with her mouth but not her eyes. 'What are you doing here? On vacation maybe!'

Gregory had not moved a muscle even when he felt the muzzle of Gitta's gun in his side. After a moment he turned his head and shrugged his shoulders.

'Vacation of course. What are you doing here? He answered.

Gitta had noticed the shrug and knew that Gregory had tested the firmness of her hold of the gun against his side. She was not worried as they were in a public place and doubted he would attempt to disarm her. Taking no chances she pressed the muzzle even harder against his side hoping he would at least wince. Not Gregory he was as hard as nails.

'Work, she replied. 'I'm part of the American Secretary of State's bodyguard team at the Astir Palace.'

'Oh what's going on at the Astir Palace I thought I saw more security than is normal for a hotel.'

Gitta chuckled and prodded him even more firmly. If you expect me to believe you don't know what's going on you've another think coming. Lighthouse operatives especially their top man are never on holiday and never in a place for no reason. I'd be careful if I were you.'

'I'm always careful and would you mind terribly taking your gun away from my ribs it's getting very irritating. You are spoiling my evening with those two attractive women,' Gregory nodded in the direction of the women.

Gitta glanced over to the table to which Gregory had nodded towards. I know one of those women she thought to herself. Her brain delved into her filing cabinet of Government agents and within seconds she had it. Michelle Devereaux one of the best Mossad agents Israel possessed. What on earth was she doing here? She glanced over again giving Gregory another prod to remind him her gun was still in his side. The woman called Michelle had left her seat and was heading towards their table. Gregory obviously had no idea who she was because he was smiling broadly at her as she approached.

'I'd put your gun away now. You don't want to upset this pretty lady do you. Perhaps we can finish this conversation another time,' suggested Gregory.

Gitta laid her Derringer along her thigh just as Michelle reached their table.

'Hello Gitta,' she said as she slid into the chair opposite Gregory, drawing her Glock 43 from her shoulder bag as she placed it on the ground beside her chair. 'And you must be the infamous Gregory,' said Michelle grinning at Gregory. 'Thank you for the drink, I don't normally drink on duty but as it's you I shall make an exception.'

Gregory almost let his calm demeanour drop. Who the hell is she? He said to himself. He like Gitta dredged into his memory banks searching for some clue to who she was. Nothing! He drew a complete blank. Now he was at a big disadvantage which he hated.

'I'm afraid you have me at a disadvantage, have we met before?'

'Once a long time ago in London but you won't remember the occasion because I was blonde then and a lot younger. It was at a boring embassy party,' Michelle smiled at Gregory showing him a set of perfect white teeth. 'I know you are working for Lighthouse. How is Sir Peter these days?'

Gregory managed not to show any sort of surprise on his face at the revelation that this woman not only knew him but also knew who he worked for and the name of his boss to boot. 'I'm afraid you have me there,' said Gregory. 'I really don't know what you are talking about.' He was thinking quickly now. If this woman knew Gitta then she must be working for some agency. But which one? he asked himself. Furthermore, if these two bitches knew each other then he couldn't keep up the pretence of being innocent for more than a few minutes before one of them decided to maim him or worse, to make him admit who he was working for and why he was in Greece.

'I think you have the wrong person,' he continued. 'I'm on vacation in this beautiful land.' While Gregory was talking he was thinking through his options. He could do nothing and continue to lie but he was pretty sure they were both armed. So to take both of them on would be foolhardy and he'd probably end up hurt. No-one would hear the sound of a muzzle silencer above the noise of the traffic and coffee conversations. The second option was to leave the table quickly before they reacted and make for the indoor area of the café, leave the café via the kitchen, and hopefully disappear over the small drop into the sea. Anticipating this option Gregory began flexing his leg muscles in readiness for flight, his eyes flicking between Michelle and Gitta waiting for the right moment to move.

Far above the drone was transmitting its pictures to Langley where Jim Broadbent had called Barry in from his lunch in the officers restaurant to look at the drones' pictures.

'What the hell is she up to,' exclaimed Barry. 'And who is that other woman and the man?'

'The man is Gregory Mitchell. He used to work for MI6 but then three years ago he dropped off our radar. The suspicions are that he works for a clandestine Government agency in the UK, probably the agency which is run by Sir Peter Bogart. However, no-one is certain and he covers his tracks very well. The woman is a Mossad agent who is attached to the Israeli embassy in Athens,' explained Jim.

'Something really stinks here Jim. What are three field agents doing having a friendly cup of coffee only a few hundred yards from the hotel where heads of state and captains of industry are about to meet?' said Barry.

'I don't think it's that friendly,' replied Jim. 'That drone is our latest surveillance one. It doesn't carry weapons but it does carry some very high tech instruments. It's a Lockheed Martin Stalker HALE (High Altitude Long Endurance) drone and it has amongst other things heat sensors which can identify materials according to their unique heat signatures,' explained Jim.

'What has it identified?' questioned Barry.

'Firearms.'

'Firearms!' exclaimed Barry. 'They are all field agents of course they have firearms Jim.'

'Yes,' said Jim. But these firearms are not in their holsters, they are drawn and pointing at Gregory.'

'Fuck!' shouted Barry. 'What now?'

Just at that moment there was a commotion at one of the tables on the other side of the café where an irate customer was remonstrating Greek style waving her arms at a bemused waiter.

Instinctively both Gitta and Michelle turned their eyes towards the shouting. Gregory saw his chance. He leapt up while at the same time tipping the table downwards so it blocked any shot either of the two female agents might fire.

He sprinted towards the entrance to the café not even bothering to weave to avoid any bullets that might be coming his way. Instinctively he knew that they would never cause an international incident by staging a shoot out in broad daylight in a popular tourist spot. Gregory slowed as he approached the open entranceway to the café, stopped and looked back. Both Gitta and Michelle were still seated at the table, which was now the right way up. He jauntily gave them a salute and slipped into the darkness of the café walked quickly through to the kitchen area, through the kitchen and out the back door.

Back in Langley Barry breathed a sigh of relief. 'Panic over Jim! Keep the drone on Gregory for a few more minutes I want to see where he goes, then send it back over the Astir Palace.'

'What about the two women?' asked Jim.

'They both have their specific assignments Gregory was just an unfortunate distraction for Gitta. She will join Alex at the Astir Palace while Michelle will continue to keep a distant eye on Gregory.'

They watched as Gregory made his way between the tree lined walkways surrounding Vouliagmeni Bay towards the chic Hotel Margi. The terrace at the front of the hotel offered an excellent view of the road which led to the Astir Palace Hotel and enabled Gregory to see all the comings and goings of importance. Meanwhile, Michelle who had seen where Gregory was heading had found herself a bench which gave a her a great view of the Margi's terrace but also, as she intended, gave Gregory a reminder that she was not far away.

Fuck! thought Gregory. How am I going to get rid of the bitch?

However, Michelle had no intention of staying long. She had other plans to keep Gregory honest. She dialled a number on her cell phone.

A white phone in the operations centre in the Israeli Embassy in Paleo Psychiko Athens rang once before it was picked up. Each operative attached to the embassy has their own colour coded phone to facilitate identification of the operative calling in.

'Yes,' grunted a deep voice. 'Your move.'

'White knight to bishop two,' said Michelle.

'Thank you. One moment please.'

The phone went quiet for a few seconds and then a voice said 'Bishop two here. What is it Michelle?'

Bishop two was the second in command in the operations centre in the embassy. Identification codes were all based on chess. The agents were the knight chess piece, colour coded according to their designated telephone colour. The designation bishop one was the head of the operations centre, the queen was the head of security and the king was the ambassador.

'I need a drone to keep tabs on a Lighthouse operative,' explained Michelle.

'What has Gregory been up to now,' asked Bishop two. 'Before you ask me how I know, we were tipped off by Chris Horsman that he might be acting on his own agenda.'

Michelle chuckled. 'He is very close to the Astir Palace where the Bilderberg meeting is taking place and I believe he is a security risk that needs watching.'

'Are you close to him?'

'Yes I am. Use my cell phone location for the coordinates.'

'ETA ten minutes,' said Bishop two. 'Launching in one minute.'

With that the line was closed. On the roof of the embassy an Israeli military drone pilot pulled out of a six inch tube a fully operational Prioria Robotic's Maveric unmanned aerial vehicle. He launched it by throwing it aloft and controlled it using a stick controller. The drone sped away from embassy towards Vouliagmeni where Michelle was waiting.

On the terrace at the Margi Hotel Gregory watch as Michelle moved towards him. What the hell is she up to now? Gregory asked himself. Michelle reached the terrace, climbed the steps and took a seat about ten feet from Gregory. Five minutes later she received a text message that the drone had locked on to her cell phone and was on station above the hotel. She got up, winked at Gregory and left the terrace.

Gregory stared after her for a few seconds and then he understood. He was now being watched by a drone. There was no way he could escape the prying eyes of that asset.

Chapter 26

October 27th, 2010 – 19.30 – Astir Palace Hotel

'Someone pulled a lot of strings to get you on this detail,' remarked Major George Spanos of the Greek Marine Corp, as he appraised Gitta who was standing in front of him on the other side of his desk.

A few minutes earlier Gitta had been shown into one of the more secluded family bungalows that were scattered through the expansive gardens of the Astir Palace Hotel. The bedroom furniture had been thrown out and replaced by several desks and work tops. Over twenty new secure telephone lines, and a super high speed satellite broadband connection had also been installed. The work tops were covered in monitors which displayed information from all the security feeds from the extensive cam network in and around the hotel as well as feeds from satellite surveillance cameras. Each monitor had two men assigned to them covering three hour shifts.

'I didn't request this sir,' said Gitta shrugging her shoulders as if she didn't care one way or another. 'I just do as I am told.'

'Glad to hear it. Just remember that here you report to me. You're assigned to the detail covering Alex Kalfas. Sergeant Trakas will escort you to your post immediately,' said Spanos as he beckoned over a young marine. 'Take Ms Lehrer to the Kalfas detail at once marine.'

'Thank you sir,' said Gitta as she turned and followed the young marine out of the communications bungalow.

As Gitta was led through the gardens of the hotel towards the main building she took the opportunity to look around. She noted that although it was exceptionally well landscaped with the marble pathways winding between the trees and small stone outcrops to each of the fifty bungalows dotted throughout the garden. The landscaping was a major security headache as a small army could literally hide in the grounds without being detected.

151

Once inside the hotel's main building she was led through the huge lavish reception hall that that was the hotel's trade mark. Marble columns rose sixty feet above the circular hall, framing a domed ceiling which like Michelangelo's Sistine Chapel was covered in frescos, not of the Revelations, but of Mount Olympus the home of the ancient Greek gods. The floor was covered in a marble mosaic and the reception desks dressed in white marble. Sargent Trakas ignored the lifts and headed for the wide stairway that led up to the mezzanine floor.

'Kalfas is on the mezzanine floor,' he ventured. 'It's the only floor with access to these stairs, lifts and a fire escape.'

The marine walked smartly up the stairs with Gitta in his wake. At the top he politely waited for her to catch up and then pointed to three suited men sitting at a small square table outside room number M10. 'Your detail,' he said before saluting and retracing his steps down to the reception area.

Gitta walked over to where the men were seated and introduced herself. 'Good evening apparently I have been seconded to the Kalfas detail. My name is Gitta.'

One of the men stood and shook her hand. 'We've been expecting you Gitta. I'm Jack and this is Stubbsie,' he said pointing to the man on his right. Then indicating to his left he said. 'And this is Foxy.' Gitta smiled as she extended her hand to each of the men in turn. After the formalities she sat down in the spare chair and addressed Jack.

'I take it Kalfas is inside, is there anyone with him?'

'Yes,' said Jack, quite a party by the look of it. The Greek PM is in there, also Elena Davilova, Dominik Vogel and Brigitte Neumann, all accompanied by a couple of their own security people.'

'I expect they are finalizing the speech that Kalfas will give later on at the Bilderberg meeting. I know Kalfas quite well having been part of his security detail after he was sworn in as finance minister.'

'Oh. That's why you were parachuted into a CIA detail at the last minute. We were wondering about that. You are the only non-CIA

152

operative except for the Greek major who is running the security in and around the hotel.'

Little do you know thought Gitta. She was relieved that her cover had not been blown and the CIA operatives on the ground at the hotel didn't know she was one of them. Alex was certainly being leaned on by all accounts she thought. Quite a party going on his suite.

'Do you mean that every security detail at the meeting is CIA manned?' said Gitta.

'Yes,' replied Jack. 'Seems that they heard some intelligence that one of the heads of Government attending the meeting was a target.'

'Do they know who?' asked Gitta.

'If they do they are not saying,' he replied.

Gitta wondered if that was true or in fact they did know. She needed to find an excuse to get away from the three men for a few minutes to find out if Michelle was still keeping tabs on Gregory and contact Langley for an update. I'll have to use the oldest excuse in the book. she thought.

'I'm busting,' she announced to no one in particular. 'Where's the nearest rest room?'

'Just off the reception area but don't be too long they could finish their meeting any minute now,' said Jack.

No worries I won't be long,' Gitta acknowledged as she rose from her seat and began walking towards the staircase leading down to the reception area.

Earlier she had noticed a couple of small reception rooms just off the guest services desk. She flashed her CIA badge at the receptionist and walked into the room furthest from the desk. Closing the door behind her she sat at the far end of the small table making sure she was out of sight of any casual passer-by and also facing the door.

Taking out her cell phone she text Michelle.

'Still have eyes on Gregory, Michelle?' she wrote.

'He is still holed up in the Margi,' replied Michelle

'Probably waiting till dark,' wrote Gitta.

'Yes, but I have a drone on him so he can't give us the slip,' wrote Michelle.

'Good thinking Michelle, that should keep him honest. Good luck' Gitta wrote.

Gitta closed her phone flipped open the back, took out the sim card and slotted it into a specially designed compartment next to the sim card holder. This compartment was standard in all CIA issue cell phones and used clever technology. It worked like the Microsoft Update system on Windows PC's. Whenever there was an update from Langley it was automatically downloaded de-encrypted and became available as a voice message to the user.

Gitta listened intently to the update on the latest developments from Overlook in Langley.

Chapter 27

October 27th, 2010 – 12:30pm – Langley

Barry Lightfoot welcomed the people sitting around the conference table in the Balkans section of Overlook. They were Sean Hughes head trader at Citicorp New York, Jacque DuPont head of the International Monetary Fund, Stephen Matthews head of the Federal Reserve Bank, Terence Palmer Governor of the Bank of England, Pierre Bernard head of the European Central Bank, Jim Broadbent and Laura Foot.

'I invited you all here because we think that what is happening in the currency markets is a part of a suspected conspiracy between three countries, Greece, Germany and Russia. We don't know for certain what the end game of this triumvirate is but we suspect that it has something to do with the oil and gas resources which are under the Aegean. There is a Bilderberg meeting starting in Athens in an hour or so and some sort of announcement will be made by the Greek finance minister during the meeting. Now Sean will recap what has happened to date in the currency markets and give us his thoughts on how we can stop the Greek, German and Russian Governments from profiting from their little game,' said Barry. 'The floor is yours Sean.'

'Thank you Barry,' said Sean. 'We know that Deutschland Bank, the Moscow Trade Bank and Alpha Bank are selling the euro at an alarming rate. It was three percent down when the European markets opened this morning and since then it has fallen another three percent. Strangely, not many other banks have jumped on the bandwagon. Most likely they don't understand why the euro is being sold as there are no technical or fundamental reasons why this should be so and they are afraid to commit to a selling strategy. We are now halfway through the USA markets session, European markets have closed and the euro has fallen by eight percent against the dollar since the Asian markets opened yesterday. Other market participants have jumped on the bandwagon in this morning's New York session.'

'Do we have an estimate of the total investment by the three banks,' asked Laura.

'We estimate between nine and eleven billion dollars,' Matthews replied. 'If they chose to buy back the euro at the current exchange rate level they would be making hundreds of millions in profit.'

'Sean has an idea on how to stop them and at the same time really hurt them,' said Barry. 'But it would be up to the rest of you to agree to it or not as it needs your directives to your respective regions. Go ahead Sean.'

'It's a simple idea really,' said Sean. 'But could be difficult to coordinate and implement. What I'm proposing is for the currency markets to be suspended just after they close tonight, and when Asia opens up gap up the euro against the dollar, pound sterling and yen.

The men around the table looked at each other. Each one trying to read the face of the others. Gapping up or down was not unknown to them. It often happened in the stock markets where a stock would open either higher than the previous days close or lower than the previous days close. This was usually due to either heavy buying or selling pressure, or earnings announcements, or a big change in an analysts outlook on that particular stock before the market opens.

Occasionally it also happens in the currency markets but only on weekends. The currency markets are closed from Friday evening to Monday morning and they open first in the far east. Sometimes, again due to some economic event occurring over the weekend a currency can open from a few pips to a couple of hundred pips change from its Friday close. However, what Sean was proposing was completely different. It was not a weekend. It was a Thursday morning. And the number of pips involved were nearer six hundred or more.

Terence Palmer was the first one to recover from Sean's little shock.

'I think Sean is right,' he said. 'There is no other way we can stop this. We will have to put pressure on the Australian Central Bank to suspend the market for a few minutes and gap up the euro to a higher level than it was this morning at the opening of the Asian session. I suggest an extra two hundred points'

'That would certainly hit the three banks hard but what about the other banks that have jumped on the bandwagon?' Asked Bernard.

'Good point,' said Matthews. 'Particularly if there are Australian banks who have been heavy sellers. The Australians won't be too happy with a gapping up strategy.'

'No they won't unless,' said DuPont.

'What!' said Bernard.

'Unless we compensated them for their losses,' finished DuPont.

'That would cost millions,' said Palmer.

'Think of it as a bailout. It might be the only way to persuade the Australian Central Bank to play ball,' explained DuPont. ' We could facilitate the purchase of call options from the three banks involved if we tempt them with a high premium and they write the call options. If we time it right and exercise the options at the Asian opening tomorrow, they will be hit with a double whammy. We talk to the other banks who have been heavy sellers of the euro and persuade them to buy into the strategy. By purchasing the call options they will recoup all their potential losses and probably more.

'I agree with you,' said Bernard. 'We have to offer the Australians and everyone else that cherry.'

'Are we all in agreement that gapping up is the way to go?' said DuPont.

All the bankers around the table nodded their heads in unison.

'Thank you,' said Dupont. 'I'll go back with Stephen to the IMF and set up a conference call with the Secretary of the Treasury, the Australian Finance minister and the Australian Central Bank. Terence and Pierre both of you go and talk to your respective finance ministers and advise them of what is going on. They probably already have an inkling from the markets that something is going on. Tell them that whatever the level of the euro before the Asian markets open we will gap up to the level, plus two percent, it was at Asian opening this morning. We have four hours to make this work gentlemen. Good luck'

After thanking Sean and Barry the bankers left to get on with their individual assignments. Palmer headed for the British Embassy in Washington where he would conduct his conference call while Bernard headed for the Belgium embassy. He would normally have used the German embassy but thought that doing that would certainly tip the German's hand. Barry thanked Sean and they agreed that he would call with the news once the dust had settled.

'Jim,' said Barry after Sean had left. 'Would you transmit a synopsis of the meeting to Gitta's cell so she is up to speed on what's going on.'

'I'll get on it right away.'

'Is the drone showing anything?' asked Barry.

'No,' replied Jim. 'Nothing out of the ordinary. There is another drone in the area though. A small surveillance Maveric which Michelle Devereaux called up it seems to be keeping an eye on Gregory.'

'Okay let me know if anything breaks. Laura didn't you want to get off for a while. Nothing much is happening in the next few hours. Off you go.'

'Thanks,' said Laura. Yes I do have something to do. I'll be back in a couple.'

Chapter 28

October 27th, 2010 – 13.45 – Hoover Field Virginia

Fifteen minutes later Laura was driving her 1979 red Pontiac Firebird south on the George Washington Memorial Parkway towards Hoover Field. She loved her classic car especially the long flat bonnet which made it look so streamlined. She was excited to be seeing Arcady. He was taking her flying again. One of her ambitions was to learn to fly a Cessna 152 the two seater single engine that many would-be pilots learn to fly in.

Arcady had already taken her flying in a Cessna 152 a couple of times and let her handle the controls. She loved the landing phase and one day when Arcady was heading back towards Hoover Field he said to her.

'You have control,'

'I have control,' answered Laura as she took the wheel and automatically scanned the instrument panel. The altimeter showed she was at fifteen hundred feet. She checked the horizon making sure she was flying level.

'Call Hoover Field,' said Arcady. 'You know the callsign.'

Laura gulped, cleared her throat and keyed her radio mike.

'Hoover Field this is three seven eight Charlie Papa requesting full stop landing.'

'Roger three seven eight. Where are you?'

'Eight miles south west. Field in sight Cessna three seven eight.'

'Report back on left downwind leg at five hundred feet. Traffic at twelve o'clock is number one, you are number two three seven eight.'

'Traffic in sight. Number two for left downwind leg at five hundred feet. Cessna three seven eight.'

Laura pushed in the throttle lever and let the nose of the aircraft drop until the craft was descending at two hundred feet a minute. Seven minutes later as Hoover field drifted by her right hand wing Laura had the Cessna at five hundred feet.

'Well done,' said Arcady. 'Now make a right turn where the traffic in front has done it then call the tower and report.'

Laura glowed with pride at Arcady's words. She carefully watched the traffic and gauged when to turn right to bring her about two miles behind it. When the moment came she began a right turn careful to make sure she pulled the nose of the Cessna up to keep it in level flight. Once she was satisfied that the manoeuvre had been done correctly she thumbed her microphone and called Hoover Field tower.

'Cessna three seven eight on downwind leg for full stop landing.'

'Cleared to land runway 27 one mile final three seven eight'

Laura continued on her course until she was one mile from Hoover Field. She then turned the plane to the right in a gradual one hundred and eighty degree turn until she was lined up with the runway. She eased up on the throttle and let the nose drop so it was pointing at the big number 27 which marked the beginning of the runway. She opened her flaps ten percent and checked her speed.

'Good girl keep it on the numbers,' said Arcady.

The traffic ahead had cleared the runway so she it was safe for her to land.

'Continue approach cleared to land three seven eight,' said the control tower.

As soon as the Cessna was over the runway threshold Laura pulled the nose up while easing up on the throttle and let the plane settle down onto the runway. 'Yes!' screamed Laura as she let the plane roll out towards the end of the runway.

'Perfect,' said Arcady grinning at her.

Today Arcady was taking her up in his Cessna 172 the four seater version of the 152. Hoover Field had been the original airfield that serviced Washington DC before Dulles or Ronald Reagan were constructed but now it serviced private plane owners and ran a training school for pilots.

As Laura approached the airfield she recalled that Arcady had told her to head for hanger number three. As she drew up to the gate she spotted the gatekeeper who was lounging in a chair dragging on a cigarette. She slowed and came to a halt opposite him and lowered her window.

'Could you direct me to hanger three please,' she asked.

The man eased himself off the chair, flicked his cigarette onto the tarmac and strolled over to the car. He stopped and nonchalantly leaned on the car door sill. He was young probably in his early thirties Laura guessed. Not bad looking but definitely not her type. The young man's eyes were glued to her cleavage which was bra-less just as Arcady preferred.

'Hanger three you say,' leered the young man as his eyes never left Laura's cleavage. 'Turn first right and then continue down past a bunch of planes and hanger three is a quarter of a mile further on. Mr Jones is already there.'

Laura hoped that this lecher had not figured out that Mr Jones was in fact a Russian. Arcady was a linguist though and very capable of speaking in an accent that would hide the fact that he was a Russian. Anyway this guy didn't look too bright she thought. She engaged her clutch and started to edge forward with the young man still attached to her window. 'Thank you,' she said as she fully engaged the clutch and the car leapt forward forcing the young man to push himself away from the car window before he was pulled to the floor.

'Bitch!' he shouted after her but his shout was lost in the roar of her three point eight litre engine.

A quarter of a mile away Arcady heard the sound of the Firebird's engine as he prepared his Cessna 172. There were thirty two pre-flight checks most of them outside the cockpit. They ranged from ensuring the correct documents such as airworthiness certificate, were visible in the cockpit, to checking fuel levels, checking that all control surfaces moved without hindrance and that the tyres had adequate air. Arcady was standing in front of his airplane just ticking off in his mind the thirty two points just in case he had missed one when the side door into the hanger opened and Laura stepped in.

She spotted Arcady standing in front of his ex-trainer Cessna 172 and ran towards him. He turned at the sound of her footsteps opened his arms welcoming her before kissing her passionately on the lips.

'Hello darling,' she gasped as she hugged him tightly. 'I've been so looking forward to this afternoon.'

'Hello baby,' said Arcady. 'Let's go. You're flying today I've done all the pre-flight checks.'

'Oh thank you darling,' gushed Laura. 'Can I take off?'

I tell you what,' said Arcady. 'You can have twenty minutes at the controls and also attempt a landing, Don't forget it will be your first flight at the wheel of a Cessna 172.'

Laura reluctantly agreed to Arcady's suggestion. He was right of course she had a couple of hours flying time on the Cessna 152 but the Cessna 172 was a different animal, maybe similar but different enough that she needed more time before she undertook the take off and ascent phase on the plane.

Arcady led her to the right hand door of the plane and invited her to climb in. As she did Laura noticed that Arcady's car was not in the hanger and she didn't recall having seen it outside when she drove up.

'Where's your car?' she asked.

'It wouldn't start this morning so I had to cab it.'

'Oh bad luck,' she said. 'Never mind I'll give you a lift when we get back.'

With that Laura got into her seat, strapped herself in and put on the pair of head phones which were draped over the steering column in front of her. Arcady walked round the back of the plane then climbed into the left hand door. He too strapped himself in, put on his headphones, flicked the 'on' switch on the radio and tuned into the airports Automatic

Terminal Information System for weather, wind and active runway information. He then tuned into the tower and said, 'Cessna nine seven two with Zulu ready to taxi.' By mentioning Zulu Arcady was acknowledging that he had listened to ATIS.

'Cessna nine seven two cleared to taxi to apron of runway 09 for pre-take-off checks.'

'Cleared to taxi to runway 09 nine seven two,' acknowledged Arcady.

Fifteen minutes later, having completed his pre-take-off checks and been given permission to take-off by the tower, Arcady gentle pulled back on the yoke causing the Cessna 172 to lift off the tarmac and begin to climb due east. As the plane passed 1000 feet Arcady turned south to avoid the no fly zone around the White House area.

'Where are we heading? Asked Laura.

'I thought we could fly down the coast today, said Arcady. 'What do you think darling.'

'Good idea it's a lovely day for flying.'

'You have control Laura. Take her up to two thousand five hundred feet. Trim her for level flight and then fly in a ten mile box with first leg heading ninety degrees.'

Laura repeated the instructions then confirmed she had control. Fifteen minutes later with Laura still in control they were heading out to sea on the first leg of the box. Arcady leaned towards Laura put his hand on her thigh then said in a low voice. 'Are they suspicious of anything or are they still in the dark about what's going down?'

'Well,' she said trying to concentrate on keeping the plane level as the ocean updrafts kept putting the plane out of trim. 'They know something is going to happen and they have reasoned that Greece, Germany and Russia are strange bed fellows but that's as much as they have at the moment.'

Arcady slid his hand towards the inside of her thigh feeling her smooth skin slid under his hand. He let his finger rest against the femoral pulse on her inner thigh, then asked her. 'What about the selling of the euro?' He felt her pulse slightly quicken. He watched her face intently.

'They certainly have not discussed while I have been in the room,' said Laura.

Arcady felt her pulse quicken a touch again. She was either very good he thought or she was telling the truth.

'Why would they discuss something so important without you in the room,' asked Arcady watching her face intently.

'They wouldn't debate anything without me being there unless I was sick or....something,' said Laura. She could feel the sweat gathering under her armpits from her efforts to keep her pulse on an even keel. She hoped he would not notice. His gaze was penetrating. It was if his eyes were boring into her thoughts. She was glad that flying the plane had given her a distraction.

Arcady noticed a slight increase in her pulse once again but not enough to make him think she was lying. He sighed. It was time he thought. What a shame. He almost felt sorry for Laura but he was a professional and from their first meeting he had known it was going to end this way. He took his hand away from her thigh and pulled out the Glock that was in the pocket of his flying jacket and pointed it at Laura.

She turned and looked at Arcady. Suppressing her fear and nerves she said. 'You wouldn't, how would you explain the blood in the cockpit, you'd never get rid of it all. Forensics would find a trace and you would be caught eventually.'

Arcady smiled. 'Nice try darling. Look down there.'

Laura looked down and saw a freighter steaming at a slow rate of knots moving out to sea. 'So,' she said. 'This has all been planned to end today.'

'Yes, said Arcady. 'That ship is my ticket back to Europe. I will land the plane on the water close to the ship and by the time they have gotten me aboard it will have already started to sink to the bottom taking you with it,' he finished smiling.

'You bastard!' shouted Laura. And before Arcady knew what was going on she had turned the plane sharply to the left which caused his gun hand to point up to the cockpit roof. He fired but the bullet passed harmlessly through the roof. Laura cut the throttle and pushed the nose down causing the plane to go into an almost vertical high speed dive. Again Arcady was caught off guard and he was thrown forward against his seat belt. The gun went off, the bullet nicking Laura's arm. She hardly felt it she was so intent on what she was doing. She slammed her foot hard on the left rudder pedal and the plane started to rotate as it dived towards the sea. Laura managed to catch a glimpse of the altimeter needle as it sped around the dial showing the plane passing through fifteen hundred feet. She passed out from the vortex and slumped against her seat belt.

Arcady was shaking his head trying to clear his dizziness. Too late he grabbed the controls and started to heave up on the control wheel but the spinning of the plane and its vertical attitude defeated his efforts. He gave up trying and just stared at the sea rushing up towards him. His last thought before being crushed by the engine cowling a fraction of a second after the plane had plunged into the sea at over one hundred miles an hour, was that it had been good.

Chapter 29

October 27th, 2010 – 20:30 Astir Palace

Alex left his suite in the Astir Palace with some trepidation. He glanced at the bodyguards who were outside his room and gave them a brief smile but even the sight of Gitta did not lighten his mood. The conference centre where the Bilderberg meeting was being held was located in a purpose-built building adjacent to the main hotel. It was accessible through a glass corridor leading from the lobby area which terminated at the reception lobby of the centre.

As Alex walked, the bodyguards took up their places around him, Jack leading, one guard bringing up the rear, Gitta on his right side and the fourth guard on his left side. Gitta allowed her hand to brush Alex's as they walked and give it a squeeze of what she hoped was assurance. It didn't help much as what he was about to announce on behalf of the Greek Government was going to send a shudder through Europe, the rest of the world and plunge the stock and currency markets into chaos. He prayed that Langley had managed to put strategies in place which would stop the potential chaos.

Five minutes later Alex entered the conference centre lobby to be greeted by an over-exuberant Xenakis who proceeded to shake his hand enthusiastically probably more for the portion of the seated audience who were able to see into the lobby, rather than his own emotional state.

'Are you ready Alex?' Xenakis enquired. 'Everyone in the hall is eagerly awaiting your announcement, a select few with excitement and the rest with perhaps some trepidation after hearing some of the whispers going around. Not least because they and the media have before them copies of your graphical slides.'

'I am ready,' said Alex rather stiffly. 'But not enthusiastic about what I am going to say. However, I shall do my very best as a patriot and true Greek,' he lied.

166

'Bravo,' said Xenakis as he turned on his heel and led Alex into the huge conference hall.

As Alex entered the conference area he looked around noting that the front row was populated by Dominik Vogel, Bridgette Neumann and Elena Davilova the representatives of the countries that would be the beneficiaries of Greece's substantial otherwise unused assets. They were joined by specially invited journalists from the worlds' media. The rest of the auditorium comprised captains of industry, a couple of CEOs from top investment banks, a few newly elected prime ministers, some foreign ministers and Bertrand Chevrolet the president of the European Union Commission.

On stepping up to the podium the delegates gave Alex a warm round of applause. Will they applaud me at the end of my speech thought Alex as he checked that the speech was on the autocue on the television camera in front of him.

'Good evening,' started Alex. 'My name is Alex Kalfas and I'm as you probably know the new Finance minister for Greece.' He glanced to his right as his peripheral vision caught a movement. It was Gitta stationing herself more comfortably just inside the exits double doors. She caught his eye and smiled. Alex smiled back then turning towards the front he continued his speech.

'Tomorrow is a national holiday in Greece as it celebrates 'Ochi' day. On the 28th October 1940 at 03:00am the then Greek prime minister Ioannis Metaxas was presented with an ultimatum from the Italian dictator Benito Mussolini to allow Italian troops to enter Greece and occupy strategic areas of the country. Metaxas uttered one word, No! At 05:30am the Italian army which was based in Albania crossed the Greek border and Greece entered the second world war.' Alex paused for effect.

'That act of defiance and national pride epitomises how Greeks respond to troubled times and adversity. The last two years have not been kind to Greece. The global economic crisis has plunged Greece into recession and further into debt. Yet underneath the Aegean Sea lie untold riches in the form of oil and gas assets which if exploited would elevate Greece's economy into the heights of the current G7 economies.'

Alex glanced around the room at the sea of faces. He had their attention now, especially Don Sharples the CEO of American Oil and Gas and Peter Amblin CEO of Amblin Hedge Fund. He could see the dollar signs spinning like a one armed bandit in their eyes.

'Right now schools, communities and the Greek army are preparing for tomorrows celebrations and parades,' continued Alex. 'Even though the austerity program that the IMF has imposed on us in return for lending us money last year has cut pensions by a third and civil servants salaries by the same ratio, Greeks everywhere are looking forward to tomorrows festivities. However, unbeknown to our people the latest round of discussions with the IMF has resulted in an offer of another tranche of funds in exchange for an increase in austerity measures. The Greek Government cannot and will not accept further hardship on its people, therefore it has sought to partner allies that will enable it to hold its head up high and rise like a phoenix from the country's current predicament. Who are these allies and how will this be done?'

Alex picked up the carafe of water to the side of the lectern and refreshed his glass. As he took a sip he debated with himself whether to ask if anyone wanted to ask any questions on what he'd said so far or continue with his speech and take questions at the end. No he thought, let me deliver the bombshell now and have questions later.

'So, ladies and gentleman let me introduce you to Greece's new friends and allies,' resumed Alex.

In Langley Jim Broadbent and Barry Lightfoot were glued to their television feed with bated breath. They were about to learn why a consortium of banks were driving the euro down and why an important pipeline in northern Greece had been destroyed. When the names of Greece's new partners were revealed by Alex but more particularly the obvious implication that Germany and Greece were about to leave the European Union and form an economic pact with Russia, Barry immediately called Stephen Matthews on his cell phone.

'Hi Stephen, where are you?' Asked Barry.

'Hello Barry, still at the IMF,' answered Stephen.

'Have you been watching Kalfas's press conference?'

'Yes and it gets worse. The revelation that Greece and Germany are planning to leave the European Union has accelerated the euros decline. We have managed to get Australia, Tokyo, Singapore and Hong Kong on board. London and Europe are closed now and the Bank of England and the European Central Bank have agreed to suspend trading until 11am Greenwich time tomorrow.'

'What euro exchange rate will they use when they do open?' asked Barry.

'The closing rate in Asia. They won't need to gap up as it will already have been done in the Asian markets.'

'And here in the States?'

'As it's still only 3pm here normally the foreign exchange markets would be open however, we could not allow any trading to continue after the press conference in Greece because that would have facilitated the strategy of the Greek, German and Russian banks to drive down the euro even further. So, we came up with a computer glitch which gave us the excuse to close the foreign exchange market. Unfortunately, we've also had to close the stock markets too as the glitch was caused by our own home made virus which we unfortunately could not control as well as we'd like and it crashed the stock market and the futures market IT systems too.'

'You mean the markets are now closed?' said Barry.

'Yes, at this moment in time there is no trading anywhere in the world and there won't be until the Australian markets open in five hours' time with the euro eighty hundred and sixty points higher, which is just over a eight percent rise in value.'

'Ouch!' exclaimed Barry.

'Exactly,' said Stephen. 'The troika will take a huge hit. But what about the other matter which Kalfas is announcing. Surely Turkey won't allow the Aegean to be raped of all its assets particularly as it is a self-imposed claimant on a good proportion of them.'

'No and that's the worry,' agreed Barry. 'Listen Stephen I need to go. Thanks for the update on the markets. Let me know if anything drastically changes with your plan although I doubt it as you seem to have got it well covered. No doubt the media will be full of this and the Aegean story before very long if not already.'

'Don't worry we'll be in touch,' assured Stephen putting the phone down.

Chapter 30

October 27th, 2010 – 19:00 London

Sir Peter Bogart was transfixed by what he was seeing on the television screen in front of him. He had supported the Greek army's determination to organise a coup against the Greek Government because he had thought that Greece was moving too far left. The rise of the extreme left Syriza party in Greek politics worried not only Britain but also several European Union countries too.

Since the Greek civil war which ravaged Greece between 1946 and 1949; a war between the communists the National Liberation Front/National Popular Liberation Army (EAM/ELAS) and the Greek Democratic National Army, Greek politics had continually been infiltrated by extreme left wing parties. This situation led in the late sixties to the colonels coup, a coup that led to Greece being ruled by a military junta from 1967 to 1974 and the King exiled to the United Kingdom.

After a failed attempt of a military coup on the island of Cyprus against Archbishop Makarios which led to the Turkish invasion of northern Cyprus and an internal coup in the junta itself. Shortly after, following the students uprising in the Athens University Technical School and with the Turkish army massing at the Greek border, the junta fell. The leaders of the junta fled knowing that the ill-equipped Greek army was in no position to win any war. In July 1974 senior Greek army officers called on ex-prime minister Karamalis to come out of exile in Paris and form a civilian Government. The seven years of the colonels' junta was at an end.

There followed a period of relative political calm with left centre and right centre Governments taking turns to govern Greece. However, the global financial crisis which hit the world in 2008 conspired to move Greek politics to the extremes seeing the rise of the extreme left wing Syriza party and the extreme right wing Golden Dawn Nazi-style party. But it was the rise of the extreme left wing party that Britain and the USA feared the most. However, mused Sir Peter, for a Greek centre left party to jump into Russia's lap completely and in doing so becoming partners in crime was definitely not a scenario that had been contemplated by London or indeed Washington.

Sir Peter picked up his phone and thumbed the button that called Janet.

'Yes Sir Peter,' answered Janet.

'Janet can you find Gregory and put him through on my satellite phone please.'

'Yes sir,'

'As quick as you can Janet.' Peter replaced his handset, opened his drawer, pulled out his own satellite phone, placed it on his desk then sat back waiting.

In the Hotel Margi Gregory was into his third Greek coffee in the last two hours. He was fidgety, angry and frustrated. He wanted to move, to continue on his mission but that damn drone was still hovering one hundred feet above the hotel. He had tried to escape earlier by moving into the hotel and then leaving by another exit under cover of darkness but when he emerged from the kitchen area where they deposit the trash, the damn drone was there not thirty feet in front of him. He understood then that the drone had his heat signature and he couldn't escape without it tracking him down. It had crossed his mind to shoot it but he had thought better of it. A drone was an expensive bit of kit and shooting one down would certainly fetch the wrath of the drone's owner.

A sudden ringing of his satellite phone startled him.

'Hello Janet,' said Gregory answering the phone. 'Is Sir Peter worried about me?' he continued with a sarcastic tone.

'Very funny, I'm sure Sir Peter knows that you can look after yourself but he does want to talk to you. I'm putting you through now.'

'Where are you Gregory?' questioned Sir Peter.

'I'm not doing well sir, thanks for asking,' answered Gregory trying to keep the peevishness out of his voice.

'Come now Gregory, believe it or not I was getting concerned as I haven't had an update from you all day. What's the matter are you hurt?'

'No sir but I'm trapped in a hotel close to the Bilderberg meeting's hotel complex. A Maverick type drone is tracking me, a type I don't know that well, so I have no idea if it is armed or not.'

'Was your cover blown?' asked Sir Peter.

Gregory paused to think. He dare not tell Sir Peter that his killing of Kostas' friend on the island of Milos had somehow been traced back to him and Kostas now suspected that Lighthouse were cleaning up. It was Michelle Devereaux who had called in the drone guard. But whose drone was it?

'Gregory?' said an impatient Sir Peter.

'Sorry sir. No my cover was not blown but I was recognised by a Mossad agent I knew from some years ago,' said Gregory. He then updated Sir Peter on the meeting and his subsequent escape to the hotel he was now in.

'She was probably part of the security operation around the Bilderberg meeting as was the other women and they suspected that you might be trying to infiltrate the security cordon around the place. You were lucky to get away. The Americans will know who that drone belongs to, but I'm betting it's Israeli. Stay where you are I'll be back in ten minutes at the most.'

Gregory went back to his table on the hotel terrace where a television had been wheeled out so that guests could watch the Kalfas speech. It was now over except for the mandatory questions which were being taken not by Alex alone but by Davilova, Xenakis and Vogel who all had joined Alex at the podium. The low babel of sound as the guests discussed what they had been hearing subsided as the first question was asked. Gregory turned towards the television, watched and listened.

'Prime Minister, John Brand Sky news. For years now the biggest hurdle for harvesting the oil and gas from under the Aegean has been Turkey. How are you proposing to appease them?

'Thank you John,' replied Xenakis. 'Our friends and partners have been negotiating with Turkey and I believe we are near a solution.'

Themis Xenakis looked out over the show of hands from the

journalists and Bilderberg members. He pointed to a dark haired woman in the second row. I'm not going to be accused of sexism by the media he thought to himself.

'Prime Minister, Judy Murray Reuters. Can you comment on the reason why the euro has been heavily sold over the past forty-eight hours?

'Thank you Judy. I'm afraid I cannot as the machinations of the currency markets are beyond me. However, I'm sure Dominik Vogel will be happy to answer your question as best he can. Dominik?'

'Thank you Themis,' said Dominik. I am as in the dark as you are. Both the technical indicators and fundamentals don't support the unexpected slide in the euro. There are no political or economic factors to warrant such a slide.

'Some people are worried though Mr Vogel because I have just heard that the American markets have been suspended for the day'

Vogel visibly blanched at the news. He looked over at Themis and Elena as if seeking help. Why would the Americans suspend the markets? Have they worked out who the main participants in this exercise are or have the markets been so volatile that the authorities decided to suspend them. It doesn't matter he thought, almost visibly sighing with relief, when the markets open in Asia in the morning we shall be free to buy back all the euro we have previously sold and make millions in profit.

'Sorry Mr Vogel,' apologised Judy Murray interrupting Vogel's thoughts. 'I gave you inaccurate information. In fact the markets were not suspended but instead forced to close by a computer glitch. My apologies again.'

'No need for apologies,' mumbled Vogel waving his hand as if shooing Judy Murray away. 'Any more questions?'

In the Hotel Margi, Gregory felt the vibration of his satellite phone.

'Sir,' he said.

'Gregory the Americans have identified the drone as belonging to the Israelian Embassy. They put pressure on the Israelis to pull it which they promised to do immediately. Has it gone yet?'

Gregory looked up into the night sky looking for the tale tell running lights on its underside. The running lights which the Israelis had switched on to let him know that he was being watched had been switched off. He spotted them moving in a slow circle around the hotel about one hundred feet above the hotel. Even as he looked he saw the drone move off in a northerly direction as it gained height.

'The drone has gone sir,' announced Gregory.

'Right now listen carefully Gregory. In the light of the press conference announcement the army coup must definitely take place tomorrow morning as planned. Your assignment is to make sure it does and eliminate anyone who attempts to stop it.'

'Understood sir,' said Gregory. 'Do you have intel on who, apart from Kostas Triandafilos, might know of our involvement in the coup?'

'We think that he has probably told his immediate lieutenants Blounas and Mavrides. It's probable that Michelle Devereaux also knows because of her past connection to Triandafilos and Michalis Louisos in Afghanistan.'

'Who is Michalis Louisos,' asked Gregory.

'He is ex-Greek secret service, now the curator of the Bunker Museum on the island of Milos.'

On hearing those words Gregory's mouth went dry. Learning that he had assassinated a comrade secret agent, an ally of Britain and someone who had worked closely with a Mossad agent, made him nervous. He was confident that Devereaux and Triandafilos had realized that he had killed the museum curator. That explained her behaviour towards him. She would have killed him given half a chance, he was sure of that now. Damn, he thought, now she had to go on his hit list, still he would enjoy killing the bitch when the time came.

Chapter 31

October 27th, 2010 – 16:00 Langley

'Jim any word from Laura yet?'

Jim looked up from the bank of monitors in front of him. 'No Barry nothing yet. Do you want me to run a search on her car plate and see if a cam has picked her up?'

'Good idea. See if that yields her whereabouts. Anything worth reporting in Greece?'

'Not a lot,' said Jim. I'm monitoring our drone over the Astir Palace and the Israeli drone which is keeping Gregory pinned down on the veranda of the Hotel Margi.'

'See if the western Mediterranean region will share information on anything unusual going on in Turkey will you. After Alex's announcement the Turks will be seething. There's bound to be something going down soon, they are a hot-headed lot.'

'Wait a minute,' interrupted Jim. 'The drone over the Hotel Margi has been pulled. It's moving away.'

'Looks like Sir Peter has friends in high places,' Barry said. 'Who do we have in the field in Greece?'

'Only Chris Horsman and his team,' replied Jim.

'Right get onto him and tell him to recruit a few friendly faces for a couple of days. Michelle Devereaux could be his first enlistee for a start.'

'On it,' said Jim.

'Good lad. I've got a budget appropriations committee meeting and then I'm going to see Geoffrey Stevens. He wants an update and I want resources on the ground.'

Ninety minutes later Barry was heading towards Geoffrey Stevens office. He had always maintained, half-jokingly, that walking the corridors of the Pentagon was an opportunity to think because associated departments never seemed to be close to each other. So as he walked towards Steven's office he turned over in his mind the options available to stop what was effectively a breakup of the European Union and an act of war against Turkey.

'Come in Barry,' beckoned Geoffrey Stevens as Barry approached his open door.

'Good afternoon sir,' said Barry. 'Looks a bit nippy out there what with the nights drawing in so early now.'

'In another month the nights will start to get shorter Barry,' replied Geoffrey. 'What have you got for me?'

Barry sat down on the two-seater sofa in front of Steven's desk and waited for Stevens to take up his customary position half sitting on the front edge of his desk facing his guests. On cue Stevens got out of his chair, moved round his desk and perched himself half standing half sitting on the edge of his desk. His long lean legs stretched out and crossed at the ankles, hands at his side seemingly supporting himself by gripping the desk edge. Barry thought that Stevens bore an amazing resemblance to Clint Eastwood. The same tall slim frame, long legs and arms, an angular elongated head covered in a mane of brushed back wavy hair with even a mole just above his top lip on the right hand side.

'I was watching the press conference in Athens just before you came in. Has that prompted your visit?'

Same physical frame but not the Clint Eastwood relaxed drawl thought Barry. Voice too high for that. 'Yes sir,' replied Barry. 'I'm afraid we have a mess on our hands in southern Europe.'

'When didn't we have a mess down there. Question is what can we do about it?'

'Well sir, we are already doing quite a bit. Things are beginning to move fast. The financial markets have closed early to stop anymore selling of the euro. The major central banks around the world have agreed that when the markets open tomorrow in Australia the euro exchange rate against all other currencies will be set at the rate it was at opening three days ago.'

'What will be the impact?' interrupted Stevens.

'We have calculated that the Greek, Russian and German banks who were leading this scheme will suffer billions in losses.'

'Will there be any collateral damage?' asked Stevens.

'Some sir. However, central banks will be compensating most of the heaviest losses. We were lucky that most major banks and corporations stood back and watched the carnage.'

'You were lucky that the central banks agreed to compensate. What is our next move? Is there any way we can stop them. Legally that is.'

'I don't think so, maybe overthrowing the Greek Government, ' said Barry sarcastically.

'A little late to organise that,' said Stevens. In 1967 it took us eight months.'

Before he could answer Barry felt the vibration of his cell phone. He took it out of his pocket and glanced at the screen.

'Excuse me sir but I should get this, said Barry.

'Go ahead.'

'It had better be good Jim, I'm in with Geoffrey,' said Barry as he put his phone to his ear.

'I'm afraid it's all bad news Barry. Laura has been found dead.'

'Wait,' said Barry. 'I'm putting you on speaker. Where was she found?'

'In the ocean trapped in the cockpit of a light aircraft.'

'I didn't know she was a pilot,' said Barry. 'Was she alone?'

'Well here's the kicker,' Barry responded. 'There was another person in the cockpit. A Russian from their embassy here in Washington.'

'Have they identified him yet?' interrupted Stevens.

'Apparently both bodies were pretty banged up from the impact but they found an overnight bag with a passport inside. The name of the Russian is Arcady Yershov.'

'Shit!' exclaimed Barry. 'That looks bad for Laura. Could she have been leaking information to the Russians I wonder.'

'Only one possible way to find out and that's to hoover both their homes,' said Stevens. 'But do it quietly. And do it before the Russians realise that their boy isn't coming back. Do we know what they were doing over the ocean?'

'The coastguard informed the Feds that they were tracking suspicious movements of a Liberian freighter in the crash site area which immediately after the crash left the area. The Feds and the coastguard chased and caught the vessel just before it entered international waters and boarded her. They found evidence that Yershov was expected as a passenger.'

'So he was scarpering,' said Stevens. 'Where to?'

'Marseilles was the freighter's first port of call.'

'Let me know as soon as you get more information on the Laura story please Jim,' said Barry.

'Of course,' replied Jim. 'One more thing. There are signs of a bullet injury on Laura's upper left arm. We'll have to wait for the post-mortem examination to be sure though.'

'Looks like there was some sort of struggle. Do you think Laura was trying stop him leaving the USA?' asked Stevens to no-one in particular. 'Okay let's wait for more information like we said and stop speculating. What else have you got for us Jim?'

Jim paused for a few seconds before he spoke again. 'There will be an army coup against the Greek Government tomorrow morning.'

Both Stevens and Barry looked at each other each one trying to grasp the purport of what Jim had just disclosed. Barry recovered first.

'Who is your source Jim?' asked Barry.

'The Israelis,' replied Jim. 'Apparently they have known about this for some time through Devereaux who is a close friend of the colonel who is leading the coup. Lighthouse is the sponsor and the Israelis were under the impression that we were in the loop also.'

'What made them realise that we weren't, asked Stevens.

'Do you remember the incident between Gitta, Michelle and Gregory,' said Jim. 'Well Gitta mentioned to Devereaux that she had no idea what Gregory was doing in Greece. She thought that he was there for the Bilderberg meeting.'

'But why tell us now,' said Stevens.

'Because of the revelations by Alex at the meeting. The Israelis figured that a coup was the best way to stop the Greek Government from forming a troika with the Germans and Russians. And it would be delivered on a plate.'

'Yes it would damn it,' enthused Stevens. 'Now we can just sit back and let it happen.'

'One other piece of news is that John Dexter has been spotted on the national highway between Salonika and Athens.'

'How was he picked up and where?' asked Barry.

'After you left for the budget meeting I spoke to Chris Horsman about resources in Greece. As luck would have it one of his operatives in northern Greece was at a filling station when six black SUV's drew up to the pumps. His man recognised Dexter.'

'Six SUV's,' queried Stephens. 'How many men? Any idea?'

'Thirty Six.'

'That's very precise,' said Barry

'Yes well, after Chris's man reported the sighting Chris contacted the Israelis. They had a Reaper, formerly Predator, drone on station on the Turkish coast near the island of Lesvos and agreed to divert it to Greece.

'What were they doing over Lesvos?' asked Barry.

'After the revelations at the Astir Palace the Israelis figured that if Turkey were going to cause any trouble they would initially send troops to invade the Greek islands off the Turkish coastline.' Said Jim.

'So how are they watching that area now that the drone has gone?' asked Stephens.

'Chris has a contact at Tanagra, the Greek air force base near Athens, and they told him that they were on a high state of alert already. They have a platoon of marines based on Lesvos, on Samothraki and also on Limnos.'

'That's close to one hundred and twenty marines on those islands,' Barry said giving out a sharp whistle between his teeth.

Yes, so anyway the drone is now tracking the SUV convoy. It has all the scanning instruments which detected thirty six warm bodies and the heat signatures of automatic firearms and smaller sidearms, in addition it also carries two hellfire missiles.'

'I don't like the sound of that,' said Barry. 'That's a well-armed small army unit. I wonder what they're up to.'

'Up to no good that's pretty obvious,' said Stephens. No-one said everything for a long minute as Stephens screwed his eyes shut tight in his customary thinking poise. After a minute his eyes snapped open again. 'There are only two targets which I can think of that warrant such firepower,' said Stephens. 'Either, word of the coup has somehow reached Dexter's ears and he has been told to stop it. Or, to bolster Xenakis's nasty plans Dexter's men will be used as some kind of leverage at the Astir Palace.'

'Both of those scenarios are tantamount to civil war,' exclaimed Barry.

'Quite so,' said Stephens. 'Look let's join Jim down in your area. We have the all the communications equipment down there including 'eyes' over Greece. Jim get hold of Chris and have him patched in to our audio and live streams will you. We are on our way.'

181

Chapter 32

October 27th, 2010 – 23:00 Astir Palace Greece

Gitta lay in Alex's arms her head buried in his chest hairs, her free hand caressing his stomach. She found his 'bump' as she liked to call it 'quite sexy'. Unlike many women she wasn't fond of six pack shaped stomachs but more preferred the rotund version. She had managed to climb up to the veranda outside Alex's first floor suite by standing on one of the many golf carts that were available for the guests of the hotel. She had parked it in the shrubbery and Alex who was waiting for her helped her up over the balustrade. She had been lucky enough to wangle her way onto the night detail watching the outside of the ground floor suites. The details were six hours long so she didn't have too much time to update Alex on everything that had happened in the last few hours.

After a long lingering kiss the moment Alex had helped her over the balustrade they sat on the edge of the bed listening to the latest podcast that Langley had sent her. At first Alex couldn't take his eyes off her very toned thighs. Gitta had debated with herself what to wear whether trousers, jeans or a blouse and skirt. In the end because it was a mild night even though it was the end of November, she plumped for comfort despite her reservations that Alex would be panting to get his and her pants off at the earliest opportunity.

'Listen darling,' she said playfully pushing Alex away from her. 'You have to concentrate on what Langley are saying, I promise that once we have discussed the next steps we can play as long as you like. Well at least until my detail has finished.'

'Can't we listen, then play and then discuss,' said Alex pouting in the childish way that Gitta adored.

Gitta burst out laughing at this. 'Seriously Alex,' she playfully rebuked him. 'Let's do this now and get it over with.'

Gitta switched on the podcast from her cell phone and they both listened intently to the information. When the section about the impending army coup started to play Alex glanced at Gitta with a look of disbelief on his face.

'Can things get any worse?' he said, more to himself than to anyone else.

'Surely that's good for us darling,' said Gitta as she took his hand. 'Think about it. There is no way legally Xenakis can be stopped can he?'

'No,' agreed Alex smiling ruefully. 'You are right. Most likely the only way to stop him is either for Turkey to declare war on Greece, which incidentally, they might still do, or the coup to succeed. I can think of no other way. Can you?'

'Well there is assassination but that is illegal too nowadays,' said Gitta coyly, knowing full well that if she had the chance she would kill Xenakis, as long as she could get away with it.

'In a couple of hours Xenakis, Vogel and Davilova will know that their foreign exchange project has completely failed. Surely that will stop their mad-brained alliance,' ventured Alex.

'It might,' agreed Gitta. 'In all probability though the raping of the gas and oil assets under the Aegean will compensate more than tenfold for their foreign exchange losses. Being a small country Greece would be the hardest hit of course and would need Germany and Russia to lend them funds until the revenues from the Aegean came in.'

Gitta and Alex sat quietly for a few minutes each deep in their own thoughts. Finally Alex broke the silence.

'What do you think Langley would want us to do,' asked Alex, taking Gitta's hand in his.

'Nothing, we stay as we are. You continue to be at Xenakis's side and feed me information whenever you can. I shall continue to be on your guard detail until the conference ends after the gala dinner tomorrow evening. I think we can leave Langley to pull the necessary strings at their end and Chris Horsman has enough assets on the ground here in Greece to help disrupt whatever ideas Dexter has.'

'Yes the Dexter news worries me,' admitted Alex. 'What on earth could he be planning that he needs so many men?'

'Darling we'll find out soon enough. Stop worrying,' said Gitta. 'Now I'm supposed to be meeting Michelle at the Moorings café bar just down the road, at four thirty tomorrow morning. Wait no its past midnight already, it's morning.'

'Let's have a drink,' suggested Alex. 'I have a bottle of bubbly in the drinks fridge.'

'Nice idea. By the way will your wife be coming to the gala dinner?'

'Unfortunately yes,' admitted Alex. 'I am a public figure I can't not take her it would look strange.'

'I understand darling but it will be interesting being on your detail and watching you and your wife. Don't worry I'm not the jealous type. Now you pour the drinks while I tidy myself up.'

Gitta disappeared into the bathroom as Alex turned his back, walked to the drinks fridge, took out a bottle of Moet Chandon Imperial, two champagne flutes. He opened the bottle and poured the drinks, then, with a glass in each hand he turned around. He hadn't heard Gitta come out of the bathroom. She stood facing him, smiling and naked except for her thigh holster. Alex looked at her letting his eyes feast on her flawless body.

'You scrub up well,' he said as Gitta stepped slowly towards him.

Chapter 33

Ochi Day - October 28th, 2010 – 01:00 National Highway E75 Greece

The black tarmac ribbon of the Salonika to Athens motorway stretched out ahead of the six SUVs as they passed the one hundred and ninety seven kilometres from Athens mark. They were driving well within the one hundred and sixty kilometres an hour speed limit in order to keep under the radar of any police patrols. John Dexter sitting in the passenger front seat of the lead vehicle was exchanging texts on his mobile phone.

'All arranged,' he said to the driver next to him. He switched on his radio-mic and spoke to his men. 'Operation Switchback is a go. Rendezvous in five minutes. Maintain radio silence.'

Five minutes later the SUVs entered the road tunnel which cut through the mountains above the spa town of Karmena Vourla. The lead SUV convoy slowed down and turned onto the emergency lane drawing to a halt behind a parked auto transport trailer which was empty of cars. In front of the parked trailer were six black SUVs - identical to the ones which Dexter and his men were using - with their engines running, one driver in each, except for the sixth vehicle which had an additional passenger in the back. He was attentively operating an Advanced Protection Anti-Drone system, a very high tech military-grade piece of equipment which detects and can destroy drones.

Dexter left his SUV and ran up to the sixth vehicle parked in front of the transporter; opening the rear door he said, 'Are you still locked onto the drone?'

'Yes,' said the operator. 'Do you want me to knock it out?'

'No not yet,' explained Dexter. 'I want them to think that we don't know a drone is watching us. I will let you know when you can interrupt and jam the signal between the drone and pilot.'

With that Dexter slammed the door shut and waved at the lead SUV signalling him to move. He watched as the six SUVs moved out in convoy picking up speed and moving across into the fast lane. Dexter looked at his watch. It had been less than a minute since he had alighted from his vehicle. He had calculated that as the tunnel was just over a kilometre in length, by the time the SUVs emerged from the end of the tunnel they would have made up the lost minute by moving at a faster speed than that of his convoy when it had entered the tunnel. He had estimated that the drone controllers would not notice anything unusual about the convoy when it exited the tunnel, such as a huge variation in speed. Dexter was also hoping that the drone would not need to use its scanners on the SUVs as the watchers would not see anything out of the ordinary to warrant another scan. If they did they would get a big surprise at seeing thirty odd bodies and an array of armaments missing from the vehicles.

The plan was to confuse the operators of the drone. At regular intervals one SUV would leave the National Highway and head west towards the mountainous spine of Greece. There was no way that one drone could follow all six SUVs and neither the British or the CIA had an abundance of drones to throw at him.

Dexter looked over his shoulder and saw that the trailer was being loaded up with his six SUVs. Already in were three on the top row and one on the lower row. He looked towards the entrance to the tunnel and saw headlights in the distance. He wasn't worried because by the time they had reached the trailer all SUVs would be loaded and all they would see was a parked transport trailer with its hazard lights on. If they were good Samaritans and stopped to help then Dexter would be prepared to kill them. Four minutes later the owner of the headlights, a Lexus RX Hybrid, sailed passed the parked trailer without so much as a glance.

Dexter watching from the drivers cab in the trailer let out a sigh of relief. So far so good he thought to himself.

'Right, let's go,' he said to the driver. 'Don't drive too fast or too slow. Keep to the nearside lane.'

With that the transport's gears screeched as the driver pulled away from the emergency lane into the slow lane heading south towards Athens.

Chapter 34

October 27th, 2010 – 18:00 Langley

Three men were glued to a bank of high definition screens covering one large wall in the operations room of the Balkans Station Section of the CIA in Langley. The screens were displaying vital information transmitted from various sources on the ground in Europe and hundreds of miles away in space.

One screen was relaying pictures from a US satellite flying over Greece. It was being used to relay audio from any assets on the ground. At the moment it was following the six SUVs on the National Highway. Jim Broadbent was coordinating the satellites and drones and was constantly in touch with the drone pilots. The satellite window of operation was about three hours but Jim had already rented time on a European Space Agency satellite which would be passing over Greece in two and a half hours from now.

Another screen was showing a relay from the drone following the SUVs on the National Highway to Athens. They watched intently as they waited for the vehicles to exit the tunnel above Karmena Vourla.

'Here they come right on time,' said Jim as the six SUVs sped out of the tunnel.

Another was relaying a picture from the drone which was above the Astir Palace Hotel. Nothing much was happening which was hardly surprising as it was one o'clock in the morning in Greece.

A third was relaying a picture from a dashcam in Chris Horsman's Lexus RX Hybrid, which was desperately trying to catch up to the six black SUV's. As they watched Chris entered the tunnel above Karmena Vourla.

'What's that to your right Chris,' asked Barry. 'The lights are a little glary. Some sort of large vehicle isn't it?'

'It's a transport trailer,' answered Chris. 'Looks like its broken down and waiting for assistance. Should I stop?'

'No, definitely not!' exclaimed Stephens. 'We are not good Samaritans. Dexter's SUVs are two kilometres ahead of you, try and get within five hundred metres and stay at that distance. Careful not to arouse their suspicions. If the drone loses them at least we have another pair of eyes on the ground.'

'Chris we've arranged for you to pick up some help when you pass through the rest area at Livanates,' explained Barry. 'Two fast cars, four armed men in each car. They have orders not to engage unless you get into trouble.'

'Understood,' said Chris. I'll keep far enough back so as to avoid being unduly noticed.'

'Good man,' said Barry. 'You're about twenty kilometres from Livanates so not long now.'

Chapter 35

Ochi Day - October 28th, 2010 – 01:00 Astir Palace

Although Themis Xenakis had not had any sleep he did not feel the least bit tired. Now showered and shaved – one of the banes of dark Greek men was that many had to shave twice daily - he was lounging bare-footed in white chinos and a pale blue polo shirt, watered down whisky in hand, in one of the luxurious armchairs in his hotel suite. Reflecting on yesterday's evening events at Bilderberg meeting he allowed a smile to play on his face. Alex's announcement certainly had the impact that his three partners Vogel, Davilova and Neumann had hoped for. When the currency markets opened in Hong Kong in an hours' time they would start buying back the euro they had sold over the last forty-eight hours and make millions. His partners would be here soon to share in his and their triumph.

He was looking forward to seeing Elena again, she had looked stunning at the meeting earlier. Xenakis had heard that she was bisexual but if she was he had no evidence to support the rumour. He hoped that he would get a chance to flirt with her and see where it led. The sound of the telephone ringing on the secure line his security services had rigged up, startled him. He picked up the receiver.

'Yes,' he said.

'Themis!' Xenakis immediately recognised the voice of his Minister for Defence, Panos Mavrides. 'Yes, Panos,' answered Xenakis. 'What's got you so excited?'

'Οι Τούρκοι,' said Mavrides.

'Ha ha,' laughed Xenakis. 'The Turks are forever getting you excited. What have they done now, taken one of our islands?

'Yes Themis, well almost. Two of their frigates are steaming towards Lesvos and I don't think they are planning to evacuate the refugees who are stuck on the island.'

189

'Sarcasm doesn't become you Panos,' chuckled Xenakis. 'What do you advise?'

'Firstly, a meeting of the security council to discuss our options. Secondly…..'

'Panos,' interrupted Xenakis. 'We don't have time for this fluffy stuff. They are obviously upset even angry about our plans for the Aegean that Alex so eloquently laid out yesterday evening. So we have to act fast. What are our options?'

'We have a platoon of forty three marines on Lesvos which have already been put on alert. They can be reinforced from Samothraki and Limnos by helicopter.'

'Navy?' asked Xenakis.

'Nothing in the immediate area,' replied Mavrides. 'Also we are going to lose our eyes over that area very soon. The French gave us some time on one of their satellites but that window closes in half-an-hour.'

'Wait a minute Panos. How did you find out about the frigates?'

'Old school,' answered Mavrides.

Xenakis burst out laughing. 'You don't mean smoke signals!'

This is serious thought Mavrides, why is the fool making jokes.

After all he is the one who made the Turks angry with his foolhardy agreements. 'A local out on his yacht spotted the frigates and radioed the harbour master in Mytilene, the harbour master contacted the marine base and they called headquarters in Tatoi,' replied Mavrides.

'Okay, leave it to me I'll talk to Vogel and Davilova and ask for time on one of their birds. In the meantime why don't you put the air force bases at Tatoi and Almiros on alert and get some planes over our islands.'

'I'll do that,' agreed Mavrides. 'I'll keep you updated.'

'Good,' said Xenakis as he put down the phone and reached for his whisky.

There was a knock on the door to the suite before one of the bodyguards stationed outside the suite opened the door and ushered in Elena Davilova. She smiled at Xenakis, walked over and kissed him once on each cheek making sure that each kiss also covered part of his lips too.

'You look beautiful as always Elena,' gushed Xenakis as he took her right hand and lifted to his lips and kissed the back of her hand.'

Putty in my hands thought Davilova. 'The others will be here soon,' she said stepping over to the chaise lounge and sat down.

'Drink?' asked Xenakis. 'Or do you want to wait for the others?'

Before Davilova could reply the door to the suite opened and one of the bodyguards shepherded in Vogel and Neumann.

Chapter 36

Ochi Day October 28th, 2010 – 02:00 National Highway E75 Greece

Chris Horseman had picked up the two black sedans as he sped past the rest area at Livanates half an hour earlier. They were following at a discreet distance behind him. They had discussed whether there might be less chance of being spotted as shadowing, if one of the sedans did a front tail. Langley didn't think there would be any advantage as these men were professionals. Chris had caught the convoy of six SUVs ten minutes earlier and was now keeping pace five hundred metres behind them.

They were now approaching the Kastro turnoff which led to Kastro and then onto Livadia to the west of the National Highway. Five hundred metres away the fifth and sixth SUVs peeled out of the convoy and shot down the exit road then turned right heading towards Kastro.

'What the fuck!' shouted Jim into Chris's ear. 'Did you see that?'

'Yes I did Jim. You almost broke my eardrum by the way.'

Barry said 'What the hell, we can't follow two convoys at the same time. Jim keep the drone following the four SUVs on the National Highway. Chris, where is Nikos Hathos your number two?'

'Driving point.'

'Okay Nikos, you can follow the two vehicles that left the convoy.'

'Roger that,' said Nikos.

'Good luck,' said Stephens. 'Now has anyone got any ideas where those two vehicles could be going?'

'I don't see anything out there that could possibly interest them,' ventured Barry. 'What do you think Chris?'

'I'm not sure. I think your right that there is nothing to the west that could possibly interest them. However, it could be a decoy move and once they get to Livadia they could take the Central Greece National Highway E3 and head for Athens. They have several options on how they get to

Athens but none of them are as fast as the road we are on. Perhaps they are trying to stretch our resources because somehow they know we are tracking them.'

'There is another reason,' suggested Barry. 'Wouldn't an army coup need to get the air force onside.'

'Stephens said, 'Most certainly, what are you thinking?'

'Does that other route into Athens go anywhere near any air force bases Chris?'

'Yes, Tatoi which is the headquarters of the Greek air force.'

'They might have got wind of the coup and are out to ruffle some feathers.'

Nikos Hathos broke into the conversation and announced 'They've stopped.'

'Where?' asked Chris.

'In the far corner of a municipal car park just the other side of Kastro.'

'Can you see what they're doing?' asked Barry.

'Tinted glass too dark to see inside.'

In the car park the driver of the SUV that had the Advanced Protection Anti-Drone system was speaking on his cell phone to Dexter.

'Not yet,' said Dexter. 'When we jam their drone they'll know that we know they are tracking us. You carry on and keep to the plan. I'll call you when I want the drone disabled. Pretty soon you'll be far enough away from the other four SUVs that if they tried to track both at the same time by going higher it wouldn't do them any good. So head on down to Delphi. We'll just confuse them for a while.'

'Yes sir, said the driver. 'Good luck.'

From a discreet distance away Nikos Hathos watched as the two SUVs exited the car park and headed west.

'They're off again.' reported Nikos as he followed after them.

Meanwhile Chris was sitting five hundred metres behind the remaining four SUVs. They were approaching the Schimatari rest area and he had to suddenly step on the brake as he realised the SUVs were slowing down.

They are human after all,' announced Chris. 'They're stopping for a pee break. I'm busting so I'm not surprised by that.'

The three men at Langley watched as the four SUVs took the exit lane from the motorway that led into the rest area. The SUV's parked very close to the lorry parking area and a man dressed in army fatigues got out of the lead SUV and disappeared into the main area where the restaurants, cafes and rest rooms were.

'Follow him in Chris,' said Barry. 'See what he is up to.'

'I was going in any way I'm busting. Anyone who needs to go to the restroom go now, I have a feeling it's going to be a long night. Keep a low profile and don't give them any inkling that they are being followed or watched. Best go one at a time, two minute intervals.'

With that Chris Horsman vacated his SUV and headed for the main building. Two minutes later one of the men in one of the black sedans got out and headed in the direction Chris had taken. Over the next twenty minutes each man in Chris's convey had visited the rest room and grabbed a bottle of water, a sandwich or a bag of crisps. They saw nothing suspicious happening from any of the four men that had vacated the four SUVs during that time frame. It had puzzled Chris however that not more men had vacated the SUVs.

'They must have bladders of iron,' voiced Chris to no one in particular. 'Slightly worrying.'

'Can you get a look inside any of those SUVs,' asked Stevens. 'Maybe the drones sensors were giving false readings.'

'It might be easier to get the drone to do another scan,' said Chris. 'We might tip our hand trying to see into their SUV's.'

' Good idea. Jim would you instruct the drone pilots to do another scan.'

Twenty kilometres from the Schimatari rest area, in the front cab of the transporter Dexter was talking to the driver of the SUV carrying the Advanced Protection Anti-Drone system.

'Disable the drone,' commanded Dexter. 'Then carry on as planned. We'll meet at the rendezvous point at zero six hundred.'

The driver signalled to the man manning the anti-drone system to start jamming the drone's signals. The man put his headphones on, fiddled with switches and sliders and then announced to the driver that the jamming had started. 'Drone disabled,' said the driver to Dexter.

In Langley the screens transmitting the pictures from the drone went dark.

'Oh shit,' muttered Jim. 'We've lost the drone signal.'

'Check with the drone controllers. Probably a malfunction,' said Barry.

There was an open satellite link between Jim and the controllers which was the usual system for communication between controllers and end users. The controllers are usually two pilots in a control centre in Nevada USA but recently controllers have been sited near the locale where the drone system is to be used. This one had been launched from the Harry S Truman American aircraft carrier based near Crete. Drones are launched locally to the area they are to be used. One pilot directs the drone at the request of the end user while the other makes sure that all satellite and radio uplinks and downlinks are functioning properly. If the drone is armed as this Reaper is with four Hellfire air to ground missiles, the second pilot also acts as a back-up to the main pilot in case he chickens out from firing the ordinance.

'No drone malfunction,' confirmed the controllers over the satellite link. 'We are being jammed. We can still steer the drone but we are blind until we move out of the range of whatever anti-drone system they are using.'

'Dexter!' exclaimed Stevens. 'He's one step ahead of us damn him. Well it's down to you Chris. You will have to be our eyes and ears until we have a fully functioning drone again. Stay with SUVs and keep your communications open. Nikos you continue shadowing the other two SUVs.'

Chris rolled his eyes at Stevens instructions. 'Right,' said Chris. 'I somehow knew it would be a long night.'

And he wasn't far wrong.

Chapter 37

Ochi Day October 28th, 2010 – 08:30 Deutschland Bank – Hong Kong

Forrest Collier, Treasury Head of the Deutschland Bank in Honk Kong, looked down from his raised up desk across the trading room floor below him. He was feeling very nervous because he did not know what was going on as the currency markets had not opened yet and they should have opened half an hour ago. His number two Head Trader Mike Mitchell was busy on the phones trying to find out why the delay. In the last half hour Collier had fielded two phone calls from an equally anxious Dominik Vogel inquiring if the markets had opened yet. Each time Collier had to tell him that nobody had a clue as to what was going on and each time Vogel had reiterated that they had to buy back all the euro that they had sold over the previous couple of days. They should make millions of dollars in Hong Kong and if everything went to plan the network of Deutschland Banks around the world would make millions too. Possibly the total profits from the whole Deutschland Bank network would be in the billions. Collier was unaware that two other banks, Moscow Trade Bank and Alpha Bank were involved in the same strategy.

Another thing that had him concerned was the activity in the currency options market the previous day in Europe and America. He hadn't voiced his fears to Vogel in case the news was too much for him. Vogel was anxious enough as it was. When he had come in this morning he was looking forward to the day's trading and making a lot of profit for the bank. During early morning 'prayers' Mitchell had informed the traders that the markets would be late opening due to some sort of computer glitch. Collier then asked, 'Anyone seen any unusual activity in the markets overnight?'

'There has been a lot of activity in the currency options market overnight,' one of the options traders announced.

'Are we involved?' asked Collier.

'Not this branch,' said the trader. 'But our branches in Europe and the USA have been writing calls on the euro.'

'Only that they haven't covered them yet. There's been no time. If they cover them this morning soon after the market opens I don't think the spot rate would have moved that much. The strange thing though is that the premiums are extremely attractive, a lot higher than they were yesterday morning.'

'We can't wait for them to cover the options when Europe and the USA opens; we'll have to do it when the market here opens.'

'What's the hurry?' asked the options trader.

'The hurry is that we are buying millions of dollars' worth of euro throughout our global network today so we don't want those call options to be exercised without being covered.'

The options trader blanched as he realised the enormous size of the hit the bank would take. 'I'll get right on it when the markets open,' he said sheepishly.

The meeting broke up after that and all the traders went back to their desks awaiting the market to open.

Now with the market opening delayed by half an hour Collier was staring at Mike Mitchell who was busy on the phone, almost willing him to bring him good news. Mitchell slammed the phone down.

'One minute boss,' he shouted over to Collier.

Collier let out a sigh of relief. 'Everyone listen up, we are in business in one minute. Get on those phones and start buying,' he barked.

He looked at his own monitors on his desk in front of him. One monitor showed him the final currency exchange rates traded at close of business by the major Hong Kong banks. This monitor was static as if frozen but once the market opened it would be flashing the latest buying and selling rates all over the screen. Another monitor was showing all the economic and fundamental data as it was announced around the world in real time. A third monitor had technical graphical tools and charts for the currency pairs he was interested in.

Collier held his breath staring at his rates monitor. Suddenly it came alive, currency exchange rates flashing all over the screen. Collier stared and the smile that was beginning to form on his face froze. His eyes widened, then he blinked and took a double take not believing what he was seeing. He turned to look at Mike Mitchell. His head trader had turned white and was staring wide eyed back at him. Collier looked across the trading floor and saw that all the traders seemed frozen, phones in hand staring at their own monitors. Collier could hear some of them uttering expletives. He turned again to look at Mitchell.

'What the hell is going on Mike. This can't be happening,' exclaimed Collier.

'The euro currency pairs have been gapped up to approximately two hundred points above the opening rate yesterday,' said Mitchell.

'What's the damage?

'Looking at the open positions reports from our branches worldwide I would say close to four hundred million dollars,' confirmed Mitchell.

'Are we able to cover the options that were written overnight?'

'It's too late. The options were programmed to be exercised on the opening of the market. They have all exercised.'

'Shit!,' exclaimed Collier. 'What's the damage on those?'

'Close to three hundred million I'm afraid.'

'So you should be. We should all be afraid. The bank has just lost seven hundred million dollars. We're bankrupt! I'm calling Vogel right away.

Ochi Day October 28th, 2010 – 02:00 Astir Palace – Greece

As soon as Vogel entered the room he could feel the sexual tension in the air. Elena is at it again he thought. Why does she always have to turn every project she works on into a sexual adventure. Mind you if he wasn't in this damn wheelchair he suspected that Elena would have flirted with him too. Would he have resisted, he thought to himself. Probably not.

'Here is fine,' said Vogel to Neumann who was wheeling him into the room. She parked him next to the desk where he had the whole room in front of him just as he liked. A legacy from his early days in the Stazi in East Germany where he always made sure that he had his back to the wall when he was in meetings or meeting someone he didn't know, in a public or private place. In East Germany before unification, trust was an unknown and dangerous commodity. Even now Vogel mistrusted most people he had dealings with. Even Bridgette Neumann wasn't on his trust list.

'Shouldn't Alex Kalfas be in this meeting,' asked Vogel. 'After all he did a reasonably good job last night during the press conference.'

'I don't think it's necessary for Alex to be in this meeting. He can't add anything to it as he was never a participant in the 'Sheepskin' project from the outset. He is just acting as our mouthpiece for now,' said Xenakis. 'What do you think Elena?'

Elena looked at the stern looks on the faces of Neumann and Vogel. Why can't they relax she thought. Elena actually felt that Alex should be in the room because for one thing she did not completely trust him, and two, earlier she had been walking in the grounds of the hotel when she'd spied Gitta being helped up to Alex's room balcony. But for all that she was feeling mischievous and decided to be contrary for a while.

'I agree with Themis,' she said giving Themis one of her best smiles whilst at the same time uncrossing her legs rather too slowly in making sure that Xenakis noticed that she wasn't wearing any underwear.

'I don't trust Kalfas,' said Vogel. 'And I would like to have him where I can see him.'

'You don't trust anyone Dominik,' said Neumann pointedly. 'Let's get down to the reason we are here. Shouldn't Collier have called us by now?'

'I called him a couple of times from my room,' revealed Vogel.

'Why?' asked Davilova.

'Because the Hong Kong markets should have opened twenty minutes ago. According to Collier there has been some kind of computer glitch and that needs to be resolved before the markets can open.'

'Should we be worried,' said Xenakis.

'I must admit I am slightly anxious,' admitted Vogel. 'There was a similar situation in the USA yesterday afternoon too and the markets had to close early.'

'What do have from Arcady,' asked Xenakis.

'Nothing,' said Davilova. 'I'm afraid he might have been compromised. Earlier my embassy confirmed his residence in Washington had been raided by Homeland Security. There is also a rumour going around in Washington circles that Laura Foot has been found dead.'

'And when were you going to tell us this information?' demanded Vogel angrily.

'Calm down Dominik. I was going to tell you when I had more information. I didn't want to worry you. We couldn't have done anything it's early evening in Washington. The Embassy called me just an hour ago.'

'Didn't Arcady and Laura Foot have a relationship?' asked Xenakis.

'Yes she was an informer for us. She was useful for a while. I quite liked her, in fact I couldn't resist having a fling with her when I visited Arcady in Washington. Arcady was supposed to kill her before he left the USA.'

'When was that?' asked Vogel.

'Yesterday,' said Davilova.

'How?' asked Neumann.

'He was supposed to give her a flying lesson, crash land into the sea near the ship that was his escape route, kill her, and then scuttle the plane.'

'For Homeland Security to raid his residence it's more likely the plan somehow failed, said Xenakis. 'Let's hope that 'Sheepskin' isn't compromised because of a mistake he's made.'

Their conversation was interrupted by a loud insistent vibration coming from Vogel's cell phone which he had earlier placed on the desk beside him. Vogel picked it up and checked the caller ID.

'Collier,' he said to the room.

He made the connection.

'About time too. I take it the market has opened. Hope your guys are working hard buying those euros back.

'I'm afraid not,' said Collier. 'Something has gone badly wrong.'

The others saw the blood drain from Vogel's normally ruddy face.

'How?' he just managed to whisper.

So Collier talked him through the whole thing from the gapping up of the euro currency pairs to the call options that were programmed to exercise on the Hong Kong opening and so not allowing enough time for the bank to cover them.

'They damn well knew didn't they? What's your estimation of the damage.'

'A best case scenario around half a billion dollars; worst case could be as much as seven hundred million dollars.'

'I see,' said Vogel. 'The bank is effectively bankrupt then. Thank you Collier we'll talk later. Shut down operations until you get further instructions from head office.'

'Yes sir,' replied Collier and cut the connection.

Vogel placed his phone carefully on the desk then turned to the others who were staring in his direction expectantly. 'The bastards!' he shouted burying his head in his hands.

'What the fuck.......'

'My god what's happened......'

'Talk to us...'

After a few seconds, as the colour started to come back to his features Vogel composed himself and began to tell them what Collier had related him. A heavy silence descended on the room after he had finished relating Collier's news to them. They were shell shocked deep in their own thoughts. Vogel decided to break that silence quickly and get them back on track. After all he reasoned compared to the billions they would make by raping the Aegean Sea, having three banks go bankrupt hardly put a dent in their combined profits. Anyway, a germ of a plan to save all three banks was beginning to form in his now keen brain.

'I suspect that Alpha Bank and the Moscow State Bank have had similar losses,' said Vogel to the group. 'Elena you had better get hold of Moscow State's headquarters and find out the damage. Themis you should talk to Alpha Bank and find out what the damage is on their side. Elena I suspect Igor will need to be appraised of the situation too.'

'Yes,' said Elena 'and he won't be pleased.'

'If you remind him that the profits from the rape of the Aegean's resources are in billions he will realise that the few hundred million lost from the euro currency project won't matter at all. Tomorrow Themis and the President of the Republic of Greece will take the salute at the Ochi Day parade in front of the parliament building. Themis will escort Madam President to the Presidential Place and attend the traditional Ochi Day luncheon. At two-thirty Elena, Bridgette and I will meet with Themis and Katerina Prokopoulou to sign the Sheepskin treaty which will bind our countries together as partners for the exploration and extraction of all the energy resources in the Aegean Sea. Once the treaty is signed we can then worry about the banks.'

'Agreed,' said Themis. 'I'm going to get some sleep now and would like you all to go back to your rooms. I'll talk to the CEO of Alpha Bank on Monday when the banks open again.'

Davilova nodded her head in silent agreement then announced she was going back to her room to call Igor Putilov. Xenakis reluctantly watched her go but she did give him a stunning over the shoulder smile as went through the door.

'Bridgette,' said Vogel.

'Yes, I concur with you,' she said as she wheeled him across the room towards the open door and the waiting security guards. As they exited the door Vogel asked Neumann to stop and turn him round so he was facing Xenakis.

'Happy Ochi Day Themis,' he said with a reassuring smile.

Little did they know that Ochi Day 2010 would be anything but happy and for some would be the last sunrise they'd enjoy.

Chapter 38

Ochi Day October 28th, 2010 – 02:00 Marathon Attika – Greece

The stillness of the night was ruptured by the sound of forty-six V12 twin-turbo diesel engines roaring into life. The engines belonged to Leopard 2A6 battle tanks, of which Greece had one hundred and seventy six and all were state of the art with digital fire control systems and laser targeting. Stavros Blounas led the first squadron of twenty three tanks out of the base onto highway eighty-three turning north towards historic Marathon Town. The town where in 493BC the heavily outnumbered Athenian army defeated the Persians and Pheidippides ran the twenty-six miles from Marathon to Athens to announce the victory.

Stavros's squadrons route would take them passed the huge man-made Marathon Lake, then west towards the highway eighty-three junction with the National Highway at Agios Stephanos some twelve kilometres away. At the same time Christos Mavrides was leading his squadron of tanks onto Highway eighty-three, but unlike Blounas, he turned his tanks south towards Athens Airport thirty kilometres away.

Just over an hour later Stavros Blounas was instructing three of his tanks to take up a position on the eastern perimeter road of Athens airport and make like they had broken down. Another three took up position on the south of the airport on the overpass which straddled highway sixty four, the only major highway into the airport. The rest of the squadron took up their positions on the western edge of the airport in some scrubland.

At the same time, Christos Mavrides's tank squadron entered the Tatoi Forest from the east and was making its way towards the Tatoi Military Base to take up position in a holding area four kilometres from the base.

Both squadrons went silent waiting quietly, no digital signatures until their designated times when they would implement the next phase of the planned coup.

Chapter 39

**Ochi Day October 28th, 2010 – 02:30 National Highway E75 –
Schimatari - Greece**

The transport trailer carrying Dexter's six SUVs pulled into the rest
area at Schimatari and parked up in the area designated for trucks. From
his SUV parked four hundred metres away Chris Horsman recognised the
trailer as the one which he had passed in the tunnel above Karmena
Vourla. He watched as the passenger door of the trailer opened and Dexter
still wearing army fatigues stepped to the ground and walked towards the
complex where the rest rooms and fast food restaurants were.

'Barry,' said Chris.

'Listening,' said Barry. 'What is it?'

'Do you remember that tractor trailer that had broken down in the
tunnel near Karmena Vourla? The one I asked if I should give them help.
Well they have just drawn into this rest area and the man in the passenger
seat is wearing army fatigues.'

'Is the trailer carrying army vehicles?' asked Barry.

'No, funnily enough it's carrying SUVs, six of them and in this light
they look black.'

'Bit of a coincidence,' mused Stevens. 'Can you follow that passenger
and see what he does?'

Right, I'd better go now or I'll lose him in the crowds. These rest
areas are overflowing with people even at this time of the morning.'

Chris alighted from his SUV and headed for the entrance to the eating
complex. While talking to Langley he had kept his eyes on the man in
fatigues and he could still see him hovering around the entrance as if
waiting for someone. Perhaps he is going to have a cigarette thought Chris
to himself. Most rest areas in Greece had smoking zones furnished with
wooden tables, sun umbrellas and chairs next to the entrance of the fast
food complex and this one was no exception. Chris slowed to a stroll as he

approached the area where the man was standing. There was fairly good light in the smoking zone and Chris was able to study the 'mark' as Chris liked to call people he was tracking. He was stocky, looked strong and was fairly tall, probably one metre ninety-five. But what Chris couldn't fail to notice was the mane of blonde swept back hair on his head.

'I've seen this man before,' whispered Chris into his mic. 'I can't place him though. He exudes leadership and toughness. He could be a marine.'

'Take a photograph with your cell phone and send it to us,' said Stevens. 'Jim will put it through his face recognition software. Whatever you do disable your flash and don't make him suspicious.'

'I've got a selfie stick. He'll just think I'm some sort of whacko taking pictures of the rest area.'

'Be careful,' reiterated Barry.

Chris took a couple of selfies at different angles whilst positioning himself in such a way that he could take a picture of Dexter without him being suspicious. He manged to take a profile and an almost full face picture which he thought should be enough for Jim's box of tricks in Langley. He transmitted the pictures then moved just inside the complex's doors so he could still continue to watch Dexter. As he watched, another man also dressed in army fatigues, who Chris recognised as one of the SUV drivers, walked up to Dexter and started talking to him.

'Interesting development,' said Chris. 'The driver of the lead SUV has just met with my 'mark' and they are chatting like friends.'

'It just got even more interesting,' said Stevens. 'The passenger in the car trailer is non other than Dexter himself,'

'I knew I had seen his face before but I couldn't put a name to it.'

'Listen Chris, while those two are chatting could you go over to that trailer and see if you can get a look into the drivers cab. Also, take a closer look at those SUVs it's carrying. See if you can spot anything unusual and take a few plate numbers. We'll trace who they belong to.'

Chris strolled towards the car trailer keeping vehicles between him and Dexter as much as he could. By the time he was within a few yards of the trailer there were enough vehicles between them to obscure Dexter's view. Chris seemingly studying his phone intently, strolled around the front of the trailer's cab to the driver's door. The driver wasn't in his cab. Probably off taking a piss somewhere thought Chris. He jumped up on the running board and peered in the window. It was dark and at first he saw nothing but as his eyes got used to the dark he spotted the outline of what looked like a machine gun lying flat between the passenger and driver's seat. He recognised it, from the unusual carrying handle which had the rifle sights built into it,

as a German made Heckler and Koch G36. Only the best for John Dexter, he said to himself.

'There is an automatic rifle in the cab of the trailer,' reported Chris. 'I'm going round to the back of the cab to get a couple of plate numbers now.'

Chris walked away from the trailer in a direct line from the bonnet. He had this uneasy feeling that he was being watched, consequently he made doubly sure that he couldn't be seen by anyone, if there was indeed anyone, on any of the SUVs sitting in the trailer. He thought it very irrational that there could be, but why was Dexter in the driver's cab? Did he stop to help the driver of the broken down trailer and allow his men to drive on in their SUVs? Would Dexter be that magnanimous with his time? Chris paused his thoughts, he was now amongst the parked trucks in front of the trailer and hidden from any potential prying eyes. He made his way around behind the trailer in a very wide circle, always keeping trucks and cars between himself and the trailer. After five minutes he was positioned beside a truck directly behind the trailer. He used the zoom on his mobile phone camera app to read the plates of the rear-most SUVs on the trailer.

'Barry, I've got two plate numbers for you,' said Chris.

'Fire away.'

'ΔΣ 5488 and ΔΣ 5487. I recognise the ΔΣ prefix as diplomatic plates.'

'Interesting,' said Barry. 'Jim is running them now. Get back to your vehicle and keep a watch on Dexter. You might have to move fast.'

'Well I'll be damned,' said Jim. 'The plates are registered to Black Hawke. John Dexter's company. I've got another four in the same sequence registered to the same company.'

'We have got to see inside those SUVs,' said Stevens.

'There is only one way. We have to knock out the SUV with the drone jamming equipment. Then we can scan the SUVs on the trailer,' said Barry.

'If we do that they will know we are on to them, won't they?' questioned Chris.

'Yes maybe but it won't matter. What they don't know is that we are interested in the SUVs on the trailer. It's too much of a coincidence that a trailer which seemingly broke down in a tunnel on the National Road has six SUVs registered to Black Hawke on it and gave Dexter a lift to the Schimatari truck stop. Where he met with one of the drivers of one of the other SUVs. My betting is they have done a switch and the SUVs we are interested in are on that trailer. But we have to be sure. We can't see into the SUVs from the ground so we have to scan them to get our proof,' said Stevens. 'Do you all agree?'

'Makes sense,' said Barry.

'Yes I agree,' said Chris

'Jim as soon as we obtain visuals get onto the pilots of that drone and instruct them to scan the SUVs on the trailer. Nikos are you still behind those two SUVs?'

'Five hundred yards back. How do you want me to do it?' asked Nikos.

'Rocket propelled grenade, terminate them quickly,' said Stevens. 'There shouldn't be anyone around where you are now. What have you got?'

'We have two Mk 153's shoulder launched assault weapons,' said Nikos. 'Do you want me to take out both of them?'

'Yes and once you have taken them out make your way to the National Road and liaise with Chris on a meeting point.'

'On it,' affirmed Nikos as he swung into the side of the road and screeched to a halt.

The two men riding in the back alighted from the car, opened the boot, removed the two American RPGs, then returned to their seats in the rear of the car. Nikos gunned the engine of his S-class Black Mercedes and chased after the two SUVs somewhere on the road in front of him.

Chapter 40

Ochi Day October 28th, 2010 – 02.30 Highway 962 – Greece

Three vehicles approached the outskirts of Erythres village lying on the eastern side of Highway 962, the road from Thiva to Oinoi. Ahead of them was a narrow mountain range three kilometres wide traversed by a switchback like road that wound its way across the range. The two leading vehicles were the black SUVs that had split off from the main group of which the trailing SUV housed the anti-drone equipment. Five hundred yards behind them was the Mercedes driven by Nikos Hathos.

'Right,' said Nikos. 'we have another five kilometres before the road starts climbing up through the mountains ahead. We haven't seen another car since we left Thiva so I doubt if there will be any traffic in the mountains. It will be very dark and as the road winds through a forest we won't be seen from below either.'

'Where do you think we should take them out. Firing from behind them makes it tricky to take out both SUVs at the same time,' said one of the men holding an RPG.

'About halfway down the other side of the mountain the road is like a switchback and in several places doubles back on itself like an inverted 'S'. Where the road doubles back we shall be above them and they will be sideways on, making it a far easier shot.'

'I like that,' said the other second man.

'I'll close up gradually until we are one hundred and fifty yards behind them. That should be far enough back for them not to see us when we stop at our firing position.'

The three vehicles raced on as the Mercedes gradually reeled in the SUVs. By the time the road started climbing Nikos had manoeuvred his Mercedes to within two hundred yards of the trailing SUV. Satisfied that the two SUVs did not suspect anything Nikos began to creep within one hundred and fifty yards of the two vehicles. Nikos figured that although the maximum range of an RPG was five hundred yards for a stationary target, they would need three hundred yards for a moving target to be effective and take them out in one shot. So he figured one hundred and fifty yards behind at the entrance to a bend that doubled back on itself would give them enough time to stop, alight from the Mercedes and get into firing position before the SUVs were out of range of a killing shot.

Thousands of miles away in Langley the Balkans team were watching the pictures relayed from Nikos Hathos's dash-cam with growing nervousness. What they had asked Nikos to do contravened international law and was tantamount to murder, even though there were mitigating circumstances that the two SUVs were a clear and present danger to US security and the security of NATO. A greater test of our resolve would come later reasoned Stevens, as he watched the action unfold, when we decide on how to deal with John Dexter.

'Two minutes,' said Nikos. 'Get ready you two.'

The men in the back of the Mercedes were loading their RPGs with some difficulty whilst trying to brace themselves against the movement of the car as it took the curves in the road. Nikos concentrated on the road ahead as it began to drop into the valley below. The headlights ahead would show him where the S-bend started. The SUVs ahead took the right curve at the beginning of the S-bend and then as they took the next left hand curve their headlights disappeared from view.

'Ten seconds!' shouted Nikos as he steered the Mercedes through the right hand curve and then swung the car into the left hand curve of the S-bend. He stamped on the brakes and swung the car out so it sat across both lanes, its headlights on full beam lighting up the road below. The two men jumped out and knelt down just as the two SUVs took the right hand bend at the top of the S and came into full view of the marksmen. The two whoomphs of the rocket grenades leaving the barrels were barely milliseconds apart as the rockets sped across the gap between the launchers and the SUVs at two hundred and ninety metres a second. Barely one second after the rocket grenades were launched they struck their targets, entering the SUVs just behind the central pillar separating the front door from the back door. The ensuing explosions blew the SUVs

212

apart throwing burning metal and charred flesh high in the air, spreading burning debris over the road and down the mountain.

'We're back,' shouted Jim as the monitors which were relaying the pictures from the drone burst into life. 'I'll get on to the pilots and instruct them to lock onto that trailer and scan the SUVs.'

'Good work Nikos,' praised Stevens. 'Get back to the National Road as quickly as you can and liaise with Chris for a meeting point.'

'On it,' replied Nikos. He was already weaving his way through the debris of the two stricken SUVs as he headed down the mountain towards the small town of Oinoi where he would take the road that led to the National Road.

'How long before the drone is above the truck stop Jim?' asked Barry.

'It's over the truck stop right now,' said Jim.

'That's quick.'

'When the drone goes off-line its onboard computer instructs it to go into a holding pattern similar to that of an airliner in a stack waiting for a slot to land. So the drone has been circling the truck stop since it went off-line,' explained Jim. 'Scans coming in now.'

The monitors showing the pictures from the drone now showed fuzzy infra-red type images overlaid by text confirming that the six SUVs each had a complement of six men and assorted firearms.

'Bingo!' exclaimed Stevens. 'We have them. So, they don't know that we have eyes on them yet and they won't until they try to communicate with the SUV that had the anti-drone equipment. The chances are that it probably wouldn't cross Dexter's mind that we would have the balls to take his two SUVs out, so he would simply think that communications were down for some reason. Chris your mission is to stay out of sight and when the trailer moves, follow it. Liaise with Nikos to decide on a meet point somewhere closer to Athens. We have you on the ground and the drone in the air so there is no way Dexter can slip through unseen as he did in Karmena Vourla tunnel. We are hoping to talk to Gitta and Alex in a few minutes to bring them up to speed. Good luck.'

213

Chapter 41

Ochi Day October 28th, 2010 – 02:30 Astir Palace Hotel - Greece

Gitta stopped right in front of Alex, her expressive green eyes boring deep into his. She had a look of shameless lust on her face as her tongue slowly traced a line along her upper lip. Alex felt a stirring in his loins as Gitta ran a finger from his lips down his chest to just above his groin, She inched forward until she felt his hardness against her pelvic bone. Alex placed a hand on each of her buttocks and pulled her hard against him. Gitta gently pulled his hands away and then knelt down in front of him.

'Loosen your trousers Alex,' she said gruffly.

Alex undid his belt and let his trousers fall to the floor showing her the pronounced bulge in his underpants. Gitta looked up at him locking onto his eyes as she deftly released his now rock hard penis from its prison. She gently cradled it in her hands before leaning forward, still looking directly into Alex's eyes, and tracked her tongue in a circle around the head of his penis. Alex gave out a small moan as he felt the exquisite sensation of her tongue on his manhood. Gitta slowly slid her mouth up and down his shaft while her tongue sent sensation after sensation coursing through his groin area until he could hold himself no longer and he exploded his semen down her throat.

As he stood there convulsing like a series of earthquake after-shocks Gitta released his member and stood up murmuring 'Oh darling…..oh baby.' Alex was speechless, with just a stupid grin on his face, so she gave him a long lingering kiss, then led him to the bed where she undressed him and lay together in each other's arms on the bed. Alex snuggled his head into Gitta's neck as she caressed his stomach which she loved.

Alex couldn't believe they had met only four days ago in Vogel's office. Since then they had made love just three times but each time had been more intense than the last. He was in a quandary for he was married to a beautiful woman, an Athenian socialite who was not very exciting in fact a little boring. He knew deep down that when this business was all over Gitta would have to return to her CIA duties. Even if she loved him, and indeed he did love her, she would forfeit her love for him for her duty to her country. Right there and then he vowed to enjoy the short time he would have with her and treasure the memories they had made together for the rest of his life. Gitta broke into his reverie and spoke.

'Darling, it's time. We must conference call Langley before my meeting with Michelle at the Mooring.

They both dressed hurriedly and Alex retrieved the drinks he had poured before Gitta had seduced him. Gitta closed the open sliding doors leading to the balcony and joined Alex at the desk. She completed the necessary protocols to link with Langley and waited for the connection to be answered.

'Hello Gitta,' said Barry. 'We have Geoffrey Stevens here and of course Jim. Good morning Alex quite a speech you gave earlier this evening. You certainly put the cat amongst the pigeons.'

'I felt bad for a while there but knowing that I had the support of Langley and Gitta got me through it. Certainly Xenakis and his gang have no idea that I am working for you guys.'

'Isn't Chris Horsman coming in on the call,' asked Gitta.

'He is rather busy, at the moment you have a lot to catch up on,' replied Barry. 'Shall I start Geoffrey and you jump in whenever you want.'

'Go ahead.'

'So, let me start with the currency project. In a co-ordinated effort between central banks and financial authorities in several major economies we managed to do some financial jiggery pokery and three banks who initiated euro sell-off were hit very hard. We estimate the damage to each bank was approximately half a billion dollars.'

'Wow!' exclaimed Alex. 'Some hit.'

'Yes, but we don't think it is enough to force them to dissolve their partnership or dampen their ambition but it lets them know we know we are not taking this lying down. Besides all they would do is nationalise the

215

banks and bail them out. On the Laura issue, unfortunately when homeland security searched both her and Arcady's homes they found evidence that they had been working together. As they are both dead we will never know exactly what information Laura gave Arcady but we feel it was low level stuff. Our theory is that he tried to get some high level information from her during the fateful plane flight, she resisted and paid the ultimate price, as did he. Michelle Devereaux has been giving us more information about the coup. We now know the timelines for its execution. It will be bloodless thank god. By the way Alex you will see it first hand I'm afraid because you will be on the saluting rostrum with Xenakis and other cabinet ministers.'

'I'll look forward to that,' said Alex sarcastically.

'The coup will put paid to their devilish triumvirate we think but we are uneasy about John Dexter and Gregory Mitchell,' said Barry. 'Sir, do you want to carry on?'

'Thanks Barry,' said Stevens.

'We have John Dexter and his men on surveillance from the ground and the air. By the way Chris did a marvellous job in taking out two of their decoy SUVs, one of which was carrying the drone jamming equipment. We don't know where Dexter fits in all this so we are keeping close to him. He is on his way towards Athens by now, but where in Athens is he going we can only guess. I suspect at some point he will have to be stopped somehow but we shall see. Gregory on the other hand must be stopped. We had a call from Sir Peter Bogart, the head of Lighthouse, the clandestine MI6 arm and he is afraid that Gregory is now a loose cannon and is likely to try and terminate Michelle and you Gitta.'

'I'm meeting with Michelle in a couple of hours,' said Gitta.

'Well be careful and watch your back. He is a dangerous man.'

'Thank you for the information. I'll stay vigilant.'

'That's about it for now,' said Stevens. 'We will let events run for now but the most important thing is that we must ringfence both Dexter and Gregory from any interference in them. 'Let's talk again at nine o'clock later this morning.'

With that Stevens broke the connection.

'I must go darling,' said Gitta. 'I need an hour before my meeting with Michelle. Don't forget I'll be riding with you to the Ochi Day Parade as part of your security escort.'

'Be careful,' said Alex kissing her on the lips. 'See you later.'

With that Gitta went out onto the balcony and climbed down to the flower beds below. Alex watched her until she had disappeared into the darkness. He couldn't help wondering what the next few hours would bring them.

Chapter 42

Ochi Day October 28th, 2010 – 04:00 - Moorings - Vouliagmeni

Gitta approached the outer door of The Mooring supper bar. It was a restaurant by day but a supper bar until the early hours, with a panoramic view over Vouliagmeni bay. It was a favourite place for the Athens elite who regularly adorned its modern glass and mirrors interior. It boasted the largest square bar in the Athens area which on its seaward side looked out onto a large patio where customers could enjoy a wonderful view over Vouliagmeni Marina and the bay beyond. The ceiling above the bar area was mostly covered in one huge mirror something which the patrons enjoyed using when checking out the talent. However, Gitta was not thinking about the interior of The Mooring at this moment because all her instincts were telling her that she was being followed. But by whom she thought. She glanced around but although she could see no sign of anyone, she was certain that during her walk of four hundred yards from the Astir Palace grounds entrance to this bar, somebody had been staring at her back. Gitta decided that if the person who was following her had wanted to do her harm they'd had a perfect opportunity during her walk to here. She shrugged her thoughts off just as the doorman opened the door and invited her in.

'Welcome madam,' said the doorman, resplendent in his green and braid uniform, as he smilingly extended his arm towards the interior of the supper bar. He was a black Greek American; a big man but fit. Gitta couldn't help but notice that he was six foot three of hard muscle. She didn't mind betting he was ex-army. She was right, he was an ex-marine from Philadelphia where his adopted Greek parents had lived until he had entered the marines. He had finished a couple of tours in Afghanistan and was just about to start a third when he heard that his mother had been stricken with cancer and had returned to Greece with his father. He was given indefinite compassionate leave and he travelled to Greece to be with his parents. Six months ago he realised that he needed a job to enable him to support his parents particularly as his mother was responding well to

218

her treatment. A friend of his father gave him the heads up about the doorman job so he applied and the same day was given the job.

'Thank you,' replied Gitta stepping passed the doorman and walking into the main bar area. She looked around eventually spying Michelle sitting in the far corner of the huge square mirrored bar which could seat fifteen people on each of its sides.

Outside The Mooring, Gregory stepped out from behind a huge rhododendron bush, followed by two men from the Golden Dawn extreme right wing Greek Nazi Party.

Earlier that evening Gregory had taken a taxi from Vouliagmeni to Saint Pantaleimon an area of Athens which was very rundown. The last two years of economic turmoil, had seen several inner-city neighbourhoods of Athens become visibly poorer; a decline that some people blamed on immigration. Saint Pantaleimon and the surrounding streets became notorious for racist attacks. So-called "assault squads" of men, who witnesses often said wore T-shirts bearing the name Golden Dawn together with their logo depicting a golden sun rising above some hills with a castle in the foreground. They would beat Afghan, Pakistani and west African residents with sticks and knuckledusters. Even local Greek people who spoke out against Golden Dawn, were threatened, too. The locals were told that after the immigrants, the targets would be leftists and Jews. In this atmosphere, Golden Dawn campaigned hard to position itself as the defender of the nation.

Its activists staged "Greeks-only" food banks and blood-donation drives, and forced their way into hospitals to check the residence permits of immigrant nurses. It staged glorious rallies, with hundreds of members marching with torches and Greek flags at night, in order to boost its prominence in the media. One talk show host told his viewers he believed a Golden Dawn MP's claim that what appeared to be a swastika tattoo was, in fact, a "Trojan symbol". The party's public statements frequently appealed to more mainstream Greek nationalism: incantations to ancient Greek history and Orthodox Christianity; resentment of Turkey and Germany, the former oppressors; and many conspiracy theories about who was responsible for Greece's economic woes. Golden Dawn's leadership came from the far-right environment that surrounded the junta. Michalakis, the party leader, once led the youth wing of a party founded by the former leader of the dictatorship. Now he led a fledgling, sometimes violent, extreme right wing party comprising of twelve MPs who were a constant thorn in the current government's side.

Gregory had managed to make contact with Michalakis fairly quickly once he had let word out that a female Mossad agent had been hired by the Xenakis government to assassinate Michalakis himself. He was soon escorted to Michalakis's office where he managed to convince them that he had once been a marine and security officer for the British diplomatic corps with a posting in Israel. There he had met this agent at an Embassy garden party. He told Michalakis that he now worked as a freelance agent with no particular loyalties to any organisation or country and the reason for this was the "Jewish bitch" had reported him to the ambassador after she had caught him shaking down a known drug dealer for his stash.

Michalakis had bought his story hook line and sinker and had assigned two of his best security people to accompany him to wherever the Mossad agent was hanging out. Of course Gregory didn't exactly know, but his instincts told him that if he followed Gitta she would lead them to Michelle Devereaux. So here he was outside The Mooring supper bar where he could see, through the huge plate glass window, Gitta and Michelle deep in conversation. Gregory pointed Michelle out to the men.

'Go inside and settle down at the bar opposite the women,' instructed Gregory. The "bitch" is sitting to the right of the blonde. Just act naturally as if you are two friends having a late night drink. I'll give you five minutes to settle down then I will come in and join you.'

The doorman held the door open for the two men and they stepped through into the foyer.

'May I take your jackets sirs,' asked the doorman.

'Όχι, ευχαριστω, ' said the taller of the men declining the invitation. 'We prefer to keep our jackets on thank you.'

'Of course sir,' replied the doorman. 'By the way if you need me at all sir, my name is Nate.'

The two men nodded and continued through to the bar area where they picked two seats directly opposite Michelle and Gitta. Nate watched them intently. He knew why they did not want to take their jackets off even though the temperature for the time of year was a balmy twenty degrees Celsius. He had noticed the bulges of their jackets: both under the left armpit. They were both right handed and carrying. In addition he had also noticed that the taller of the two, when putting his right arm out to help the door open, had a tattoo on his wrist which he recognised as that of the Golden Dawn. These two were not the usual clientele of The Mooring; he would keep a close eye on them. Nate did not carry a gun but out of habit he always kept his hunting knife in his locker. A knife that was so finely balanced that he could throw it with great accuracy and had often done so on duty in Afghanistan. He decided to retrieve it from his locker just as a precaution as he felt a little uneasy.

Gitta had brought Michelle up to date on all the news of the past few hours and then had a good chuckle when Michelle told her about the drone and Gregory.

'I think you have made him an enemy,' laughed Gitta.

'Yes, but I don't care. He killed my colleague and friend on Milos. I should be the one out to kill him.'

'Don't worry you'll get your chance one day I'm sure,' said Gitta as she beckoned the barman over. 'Two Expresso Martinis παρακαλουμε,' she ordered practising her minimal Greek. Please and thank you were the only Greek words she knew.

At that moment Gregory entered the supper bar; exchanged a few words with the doorman before sauntering over to the bar where he made a big display of suddenly seeing the two men at the bar and went over to them enthusiastically greeting them like long lost friends. However, it didn't fool Gitta or Michelle for one minute because they had earlier heard the two men ordering their drinks in perfect Greek, besides in Gregory's line of work one didn't make friends. So what was Gregory doing consorting with two Greeks in the same bar they were in. Too much of a coincidence.

'This is not a chance encounter,' ventured Michelle. 'He is up to something as usual.'

'I agree, however in that get-up; smart tight fitting jeans and a short sleeve shirt, he can't be carrying unless of course he is using an ankle holster.'

'I think we have to assume he is,' said Michelle. 'If you look at the mirror above their heads; where the shorter of the two men's jacket has caught on the bar, I fancy I'm seeing a flash of a shoulder holster strap.'

'Right,' said Gitta. We'd better stay vigilant. Should we try and leave the building?'

'No, too exposed in front of the door. If something does goes down we are better off with a bar between us.' 'Who do you think the two men are? They look as if they can look after themselves. Bodyguards perhaps?' said Gitta.

'Most likely,' confirmed Michelle. 'I don't think anything will happen while that couple on the veranda are still around.'

I wouldn't count on that,' said Gitta. 'Anyway they look as though they are oblivious to anything apart from themselves.'

Nate had been sitting by the front door trying to figure out what was going on. He had noticed that even though the guy in the jeans had greeted the two Golden Dawn guys with unbounded enthusiasm their subsequent interactions were practically non-existent. So, what were they here for? Both Golden Dawn guys were packing and although it wasn't obvious he was certain that the other guy was packing too. Probably an ankle holster. Why were they so interested in the two women one of which he was certain he had met before. He recognised the dark haired one but where from. He had been delving deep into his memory bank for ten minutes when abruptly he remembered. Of course he thought; Afghanistan! She had been a Mossad liaison officer on a CIA team attached to his base at Lashkar Gah. He remembered she had been very chummy with a Greek on the team. Then he remembered her name; Devereaux. So, now it was fitting together. The Golden Dawn being a neo Nazi party hated Jews and somehow, probably through mister smart jeans, they had found out she was here in this bar.

Nate decided he had to warn the dark haired woman so he wrote on a scrap of paper "two suits Golden Dawn – ex-marine Lashkar". He screwed the paper into a ball then started walking towards their side of the bar. He passed behind them and headed out onto the veranda towards the couple canoodling in the corner, but not before he had flicked the screwed up piece of paper onto Michelle's lap. She flattened out the paper ball and read the message. She understood at once.

'We have a problem,' said Michelle. 'The doorman has just given me the heads up on our two friends with Gregory. They're Golden Dawn.'

'Why would the doorman give you that information,' asked Gitta.

'We were posted to the same base in Afghanistan and he recognised me. He knows I'm Mossad.'

They watched, as Nate who had come in from the balcony with the young couple, escorted them out of the front door followed by the barman. Now except for the two of them, Gregory, the two members of Golden Dawn and Nate there was not any other customers.

'Time,' said Gitta. 'You take the two Golden Dawn guys and I'll take Gregory.'

Gitta and Michelle pulled their Deringers from their thigh holsters and were about to stand up when the shorter of the two Golden Dawn members let out a load grunt, stood up and then slumped forward onto the bar counter. A hunting knife was clearly visible protruding from his back. Behind him, about five metres back Nate was standing with his right arm extended towards his target. Instinctively, both Gregory and the taller Golden Dawn member stood up and half turned towards where Nate was standing. Too late they realised their mistake and before they could draw their weapons both Gitta and Michelle had made their shots. One shot each was all they needed, Michelle's shot caused the Golden Dawn member to fall backwards as her bullet struck him on the forehead, killing him instantly. Gitta's shot had struck Gregory in the heart area severing an artery. He slumped forward onto the bar bleeding profusely. He stared in disbelief at Michelle as she walked towards him.

'Too bad Gregory,' she smiled at him. 'And I was just beginning to get to know you better.'

'Jewish fucking bitch,' he mumbled through flecks of blood coming from his mouth. He shuddered once as his eyes became vacant and he expelled his last breath.

They both went over to Nate and thanked him for helping them.

'No worries,' said Nate. 'Best excitement I've had since I left the Marines.'

'We'll send a team of cleaners to clear up the mess and get rid of the bodies. No need for you to worry about anything,' said Michelle.

With that they left The Mooring and headed up towards the Astir Palace Hotel both looking forward to crashing out for a few hours.

Chapter 43

Ochi Day October 28th, 2010 – 05:00 - National Road E75 - Greece

The car trailer with its six SUVs with Dexter sitting in the passenger side of the cab was now forty kilometres from the truck stop at Schimatari nearing Agios Stephanos in the direction of Athens. Two kilometres behind Chris Horsman and his escort Mercedes driven by Triandafilos Mitsotakis were parked up in the small town of Kosmothea waiting for the imminent arrival of Nikos's Mercedes.

In Langley three very tired men were trying to orchestrate the appropriate responses to events on the ground in Greece. They had just received an update from Gitta on the happening that had taken place in The Mooring's supper bar. Stevens had not been happy. Not because Gregory had been killed; he had gone rogue anyway and Sir Peter had given them the heads up that he feared Gregory was not himself and might do something stupid. Which he of course did in miscalculating the skills of Gitta and Michelle. It was the two Golden Dawn members that concerned him. They were obviously lieutenants of Michalakis the leader of the party and if Gregory had told him who he was working for, then the repercussions could lead to very violent demonstrations indeed.

'We are about to lose the drone that's following the trailer,' announced Jim. 'Apparently it has almost completed forty hours flying time. The drone pilots have instructions to take it back to base for refueling.'

'Is there time for Chris to catch up with the trailer,' asked Barry.

'I don't know,' said Jim.

Ten seconds later the monitors displaying the pictures transmitted from the drone went dark.

'We're offline,' announced Jim. 'We should be back on line in two hours.'

'Can we get access to a satellite passing over the Athens area at all?,' asked Barry.

'I'll try and grab a feed from GEO32 it should give us a nice overhead view.'

'What's its ETA and how long will we have?' asked Stevens.

'Should be online in half an hour,' confirmed Jim. 'We'll have about twenty minutes use.'

'Probably too late but better than nothing. It's up to Chris now to catch up and get eyes on.' said Stevens.

On the National Road the car trailer with the six SUVs onboard was passing through Agios Stephanos the northernmost suburb of Athens. John Dexter sitting in the front cab had been attempting to communicate with the SUV with the anti-drone equipment. He had no idea of course that they had been destroyed and there wasn't any reason why he should be suspicious. He simply assumed that they were still in the mountains where communication was at best poor and at worse non-existent.

'There,' John Dexter pointed out to the driver. 'Take the Ikali turn-off and follow highway 83 north.'

The driver did as he was told and trailer headed north almost back the way it had come on the National Road. Now it was passing through another suburb of the Athens wealthy with tree-lined avenues, luxury villas each with a swimming pool and high walled security fences. Although many villa owners, in an attempt to avoid the swimming pool taxes, camouflage their pools from the prying eyes of the tax inspectors' drones which swarm over Ikali and other rich suburbs of northern Athens. The trailer continued north till it reached the outskirts of Ikali and entered the suburb of Drosia. Here it turned east and headed towards Dionysus in the foothills of Mount Penteli, the mountain which encircled Athens to the north. The trailer turned south into the lower reaches of the mountain and was soon hidden from view by the thick canopy of the overhead branches of the Penteli Forest. Where the road started to curve upwards towards the summit of the mountain, Dexter spotted a dirt road leading into an area where the forest had been cleared to accommodate an olive plantation. The

226

trailer turned off the main road and drove onto the dirt road stopping when it was out of sight of the main road.

The moment that the trailer stopped Dexter ordered the driver to release the clamps holding the SUVs and all six were driven off the ramps.

'Listen up soldiers,' shouted Dexter addressing the thirty six men who had vacated the SUVs. 'Sorry about the facilities but clean yourselves up the best you can. There's an electricity generating station for this plantation one kilometre up the track. It's got running water and a couple of portable toilets. No food I'm afraid but you can get some after you leave here. Now, here are your orders. The Greek prime minister is concerned that a rumour circulating of an imminent military coup might actually be true. So we have been authorised to guard the likely targets of a military takeover in this country. If the rumours are correct then the most likely day for it to happen is today; Ochi Day. Probably just before or during the military parade in Athens which commences this morning at ten hundred hours. Each one of you has been assigned a specific target which if a coup does take place you must protect at all costs. Now, Black One will be under my command and we will take up station in the vicinity of the Astir Palace Hotel. We will guard the prime minister's and other dignitaries cavalcade when it sets off for the Ochi Day parade in Athens. Black Two, you will take up station outside the government TV and radio station ERT. Black Three and Four, you will take up position at Athens airport and keep it open if the military tries to close it. Black Five, take up position at the residence of the President of the Republic and Black Six take up position outside the Maximos Mansion, the offices and residence of Xenakis. It'll be light soon so don't hang about. I want you all out of here in twenty minutes and don't travel in convoy, you'll attract attention.'

Eighteen minutes later Dexter swung his SUV south and headed for the summit of Mount Penteli. He was the last to leave the site. Once over the summit and down the other side into the suburb of Maroussi, he took Highway Six towards the airport and Vouliagmeni beyond.

As Dexter drove through Maroussi, Jim, Barry and Stevens were watching the monitors displaying what satellite GEO32's cameras could see, as it crossed over the northern suburbs of Athens from east to west.

They were looking for a vehicle trailer not six SUVs and the trailer was well hidden under the forest canopy of Mount Penteli.

'We've lost them,' said Jim.

'What are our options,' asked Stevens.

'Not a lot,' said Barry. 'But we could try something. We can't find the trailer so it's safe to assume Dexter has hidden it somewhere not far from the National Road otherwise Chris would have caught up with it. Why would he need to hide it? Because they have unloaded the SUVs. Even if we find the trailer it wouldn't do us any good.'

'I wager they are not in convoy now,' said Stevens.

'I agree,' replied Barry. 'Jim would it be possible to use GEO32 to find car plates?'

'If we had the drone it would be easier because we would have more time. The satellite window is closing as we speak. It's a NASA bird so theoretically we can use it but I need the techies to reprogram it to recognise the SUV plates.'

'Go ahead Jim,' said Barry. 'While Jim is sorting that, any ideas Geoffrey on what those SUVs are going to do? They have obviously split up for a good reason. Have they split because it's less risky to be detected or have they split because each of them has a separate assignment?'

'Suppose Xenakis is fearful of a military coup on Ochi Day and he is using Dexter and his mercenaries to thwart such an event. How would he use the SUVs? For a coup to succeed certain buildings and senior officials need to be nullified. So, which buildings would be prime targets?'

'Airports,' said Jim. 'Radio stations too, maybe railway stations.'

'Key military installations,' offered Barry. 'Key government buildings.'

'Right,' said Stevens. 'So if the satellite does not pick up a registration plate on this pass we should choose three locations we think might be targets for a coup and send Chris, Nikos and the other Mercedes to stake them out.'

228

'Triandafilos,' said Barry.

'What?' exclaimed Stevens.

'The name of the driver of the second Mercedes is Triandafilos,' repeated Barry.

'Oh yes I had forgotten his name, sorry,' apologised Stevens.

'The name Triandafilos means "friend of roses",' piped up Jim.

Chris Horsman smiled when he heard this. He had just turned into one of the main Athens thoroughfares heading south towards the centre of the city and the coast. During his time in Greece he prided himself that he had managed to learn both conversational Greek as well as colloquial nuances. One of the most enjoyable facets of the Greek language for him was understanding the meaning of names as in the case of Triandaphilos "friend of roses" or Parthena meaning "virgin". He had been so engrossed in thinking about his Greek language prowess that he hadn't noticed the black SUV that had been parked alongside a café which served hot breakfasts, suddenly move out into the road in front of him. He realised that he must have been behind it for a couple of kilometres and berated himself because it could have quite easily turned off onto another street and he would have missed it.

'I've struck lucky I think,' he announced to Langley. 'Can you verify this plate for me?' he said, then read out the plate number.

'It's a match,' confirmed Jim. 'But it's not Dexter's SUV.'

'Where are you Chris?' asked Barry.

'On Avenue Mesogeion approaching the General Hospital.'

'Their target must be the radio station. It's not far and it's on Mesogeion about a kilometre and a half farther south. Take care how you choose your stakeout position. Not too near for them to get suspicious and not too far that you are unable to intervene if necessary.'

'No worries,' said Chris. 'What about Nikos and Triandafilos?'

'What do you think Geoffrey?' asked Barry.

'If I was staging a military coup I'd hit the airport and the head of the civilian government.'

'Right, Nikos you take the airport and Triandafilos, you stakeout Mansion Maximo, the residence of the Prime Minister. Let us know when you are in position.'

'Jim, what time will our drones come back on-line and any luck with the satellite?' asked Barry.

'The drones will be back online at one hundred hours eastern standard and eight hundred hours central European time. That's in two hours' time.'

'Can you confirm we'll have a drone over the Ochi Day parade in Athens, one over the Astir Palace Hotel and one tracking Dexter's SUVs?' said Barry.

'Yes they are all booked. I've also booked time on GEO46, a European Space Agency satellite which will be passing over Athens at the time the Ochi Day parade commences. We should get a good hour of use with that particular bird.'

'Well done Jim! Right let's relax and get some caffeine inside us. It's going to be one hell of a night!'

In an adjoining room to the operations room were several comfortable armchairs and sofas, plus a couple of shower cubicles. Designed precisely for nights such as the one the Balkans region team were facing tonight. Barry and Geoffrey availed themselves of the facilities leaving Jim to man the shop. If they were hoping for a couple of hours rest and relaxation they were going to be very disappointed.

Chapter 44

Ochi Day October 28th, 2010 – 07:00 - Astir Palace Hotel - Greece

The mobile phone on Xenakis's bedside table buzzed angrily as it danced its way towards the edge and finally dropped with a load crash onto the marble floor and stopped vibrating. Xenakis stirred at the sound and groped for the clock which had once been a companion to his phone. The clock indicated seven hundred hours. He rolled onto his back looking towards the bathroom where he could hear the sound of the shower running. Who the hell he thought. Then it came to him, Elena Davilova. She had come back to his room after the very unsatisfactory discussion on the losses from the euro project had been terminated and Vogel, and Neumann had retired to their rooms. Xenakis was tempted to join Davilova in the shower but he knew that would lead to other things leaving him without time for breakfast before the cavalcade left for Athens.

The urgent buzzing started again from his cell phone which was moving across the marble floor. It was then he realised that what had woken him up was not as he had thought the sound of Elena Davilova in the bathroom but his phone hitting the floor. He picked it up, seeing it was his Defence Minister Panos Mavrides, he let out a sigh of exasperation. As Defence Minister Panos never made a decision of any importance.

'Yes Panos what is it?' he said.

'Themis haven't you been watching the news,' Panos asked.

'No Panos., tell me what's happened.

'Turkey has a squadron of fighter jets over Lesbos supporting their two frigates. I tell you they will invade the island,' said Mavrides.

'Have you managed to transfer the other two platoons of marines from Samothraki and Limnos?' asked Xenakis.

'Yes, they were helicoptered in a couple of hours ago. We have just over a hundred marines on the island.'

'Fighters?' questioned Xenakis.

'On alert,' said Mavrides.

'Why didn't you scramble them?' asked Xenakis angrily. 'Where are you?'

'In the command centre on Irodou Attikou where else would I be?' said Mavrides in exasperation. 'I called you over an hour ago and then again ten minutes ago. I even sent you a couple of text messages. You know I can't scramble the air force or any arm of the armed forces to go into combat without the authority of the President of the Republic, which I have, and the Prime Minister, which is you if I'm not mistaken!'

'You can't talk to me like that. I forbid it!' shouted Xenakis down the phone.

Just at that moment Elena Davilova walked out of the bathroom.

'Darling,' she said. 'You'll have a heart attack shouting like that.'

Xenakis turned and put his fingers to his lips signing her to be quiet, but it was too late Mavrides at the other end of the phone heard and recognised Davilova's voice.

'I see that you had more important matters of state to attend to than a mere attack on our territory by Turkey,' said Mavrides with as much sarcasm as he could muster in his voice.

'Scramble our fighters from the Almiros airbase at once,' said Xenakis ignoring the sarcastic remark made by Mavrides. 'I'll call the President and appraise him of the situation. Keep him and myself up to date on what is happening in that area of the Aegean. By the way do we have any friendly assets in the Aegean?'

'The only friendly we have is the frigate HMS Stallworth, the British floating listening platform,' said Mavrides.

'Does it have any offensive weapons in addition to its powerful passive electronics?' asked Xenakis.

'I believe it has a couple of drones, both Reapers I believe.'

232

'Can we get them to help?' asked Xenakis.

I've got some backdoor channels I could approach.'

'Do what you can,' said Xenakis. 'I'm going to call Konstantinos now, so get those planes off the ground.'

Xenakis didn't really relish the idea of calling Konstantinos Karras the President of the Republic, a man whom he didn't like and as far as he knew the feeling was mutual. The president did not have any real authority but it was customary to keep him informed of affairs of state on a daily basis and if he was a man of wisdom and was respected, prime ministers and members of the inner cabinet would go to the president for advice. Essentially the presidents had been afforded the role of pseudo royalty since democracy was restored to Greece after the fall of the junta in 1974 and a referendum was in favour of exiling the royal family in favour of a democratic republic. The president was elected by the members of parliament after one candidate had been nominated by each main party. This of course led at times to friction between a prime minister not of the same party as the president. Unfortunately, Karras was not respected by Xenakis for the reason that Xenakis considered his politics too liberal. Xenakis had kept Karras in the loop regarding the euro project and the Aegean project by informing him of the bare minimum knowing that if he went into detail he would have faced a lot of opposition and quite possible a censorship, which was the only legal avenue that the president was able to go down if he thought it was for the good of Greece.

Xenakis dialled the number for the president's mansion and asked to be put through.

'Good morning sir,' said Xenakis. 'Mavrides has appraised you of the problem we have on the island of Lesbos, I believe. As a consequence I am calling to ask that you sanction the scrambling of a fighter squadron with live ammunition instead of our usual dummy ammunition whenever the Turks enter our airspace.'

'Good morning Themis. I was wondering when you would call me. With the announcement of the arrangement between ourselves, Germany and Russia broadcast all over the news last night what did you expect?'

233

'I didn't expect a reaction so soon sir. However, we have enough men on the ground to repel any invasion of the island, but as they have scrambled their fighters we should do the same to at least give a show of strength.'

'It is with some misgivings that I am going to call Mavrides and give him the permission to scramble our fighters. But when the Ochi Day parade is over later this morning, you are to come to my office. Don't expect a warm welcome either. I want a full account of your actions and why you chose not to give me all the details.'

'Yes sir, thank you, I will,' said Xenakis and terminated the call. Stupid old man he thought to himself.

'Was that Karras,' asked Davilova who was now dressed after her shower.

'Yes, he might try to make trouble for me especially after I probably pissed off Mavrides earlier and he would have gone running to Karras.'

'Don't worry Themis, don't forget we have Dexter to do our dirty work for us. If needs must and Karras needs to be quietened I'm sure Dexter can come up with a plan to make it look like Karras had an accident.'

'Another death Elena. I've never met anyone particularly a woman that can be so passionate and loving yet hard as nails when it comes to removing unwanted people.'

'I'm Russian and a woman so you can't get to my position in life within Russia without being ruthless darling,' Elena smiled at Xenakis and for a brief instant Xenakis thought he'd glimpsed the devil in her eyes.

Chapter 45

Ochi Day October 28th, 2010 – 07:30 - Forces Command Centre - Greece

In the command centre Mavrides had just taken the authorisation from Karras to scramble fighters from the Almiros air force base near Volos in central Greece. It was obvious to him that Karras had been reticent to give the orders and was as angry with Xenakis just as much as he was right now. He had scrambled the fighters five minutes earlier and he could see from satellite feeds displayed on the huge wall-to-wall multiscreen array that the Turkish F16 were heading west to intercept the Greek Mirages. Would this turn out to be one of the many phantom dog fights that the two nations had fought in the last few years or would it be the real thing? The Turks were well into Greek air space now so the Greek Air Force had every right to be the aggressor. Not long now he thought.

Mavrides watched as twelve Mirage-2000 Greek fighters raced towards fifteen F16 Turkish fighters at a closing speed of just over two-thousand miles an hour. Suddenly a couple of flashes emanated from one of the Mirages and two fiery trails propelling air-to-air missiles sped towards the F16s. One F16 released chaff and began weaving through the sky. But the two Sidewinder missiles were closing on the single F16 at almost two thousand miles per hour . It was no contest; both missiles hit their targets and the F16 exploded into fiery fragments before tumbling towards the blue Aegean Sea.

The F16s which had started to break out of formation when the missiles were fired were all now diving towards the ocean below and wheeling back towards Turkey. The Mirages followed chasing them back towards the Turkish coast.

'Strike leader two-six, why are they running away?' said Mavrides to the squadron leader of the Greek fighters.

'I believe they don't have live ammunition sir. They were not expecting a real fight.'

'So, they thought it was to be another phantom dog fight. They'll be back though. They won't take this lying down,' said Mavrides. 'Are you carrying air-to-surface missiles?'

'Five of us carry sir, including myself,' replied strike leader. 'Each of us has an AGM Harpoon anti-ship missile.'

'Good, five should be enough. I want you to hit the two frigates' that are shelling Lesbos. We have a hundred of our boys defending the island against an invasion, but they are being bombarded by the frigates seventy-six millimetre guns. Don't sink them now, just chase them off. Can you do that strike leader?'

'I'll give it a good try sir,' said strike leader.

'Good hunting,' said Mavrides closing the communication.

Mavrides immediately called Konstantinos Karras and reported what had happened.

'What options have we got Panos?' asked Karras. 'Who's on your team there?'

'General Peponas, Admiral Lapantzi and Vice Marshall Reka, plus the rest of the defence committee except for Xenakis.' replied Mavrides.

'Have you come up with anything?' repeated Karras.

'We have one option sir because there is only one that will prevent a war,' began Mavrides. He was thinking on his feet now. He had been hearing for several days, through the grapevine, rumours that an army coup might be in the offing. As Defence Minister he had felt obliged to dig further. He was torn between duty to his government and his growing concern about the behaviour of Themis Xenakis. He had decided to call in some favours from old associates who had been with him in the marines. The marines were like a family, loyal to the end even if they were unhappy with some of their colleagues, so he was convinced he would learn more. He was right, although no-one said outright, not even his son Christos who was a colonel and a tank commander, that it would definitely happen; or when it would happen, plenty was said that made it clear that certain elements of the armed forces were unhappy with the political direction of Greece. He also learned that it appeared that Xenakis was using a mercenary group to carry out certain activities within Greece's borders.

He decided to sit on what he had learned and not let anyone in the government know, not even Karras. Last night's announcement by Alex Kalfas was the straw that broke the camel's back and he then realised that the only way to stop Xenakis was a coup by the armed forces. Then during his conversation with Xenakis earlier where he heard the voice of that Russian harlot who masqueraded as their Finance Minister, any reservations he might have had were completely dismissed from his mind.

Earlier, after he had spoken to Xenakis he called Alex Kalfas.

'Good morning Alex, sorry to interrupt you, no doubt you are getting prepared for the Ochi Day parade.'

'Who is it?' asked Alex.

'It's Panos Mavrides the Defence Minister.'

'Oh, hello Panos. What can I do for you?'

'I felt I had to call you after watching your press conference yesterday evening, especially as it seems it has precipitated an angry response from our noisy neighbours.'

'Really,' said Alex. 'I didn't think the response would be so soon.' He had told the truth, he really had not expected the Turks to move so quickly. What could he say to Panos? Somehow he had to convince him that in a few hours' time Turkey would not be interested in a war, without being explicit about what would happen at ten-thirty during the Ochi Day parade.

'No-one did, but the point is they have and the blame is firmly at Xenakis's and your door. We had to shoot down one of their F16s earlier. At this moment I'm looking at a satellite feed showing five of our fighter planes getting ready to hit two of their frigates.'

'Look Panos I know you knew my father very well. You even followed in his footsteps and attended the advanced officers academy at West Point in the States.'

'Yes,' said Panos. 'I also know that your father was working for the CIA at the time you were being educated in the States. So my thinking is that what you seem to have aligned with ideologically is completely out of character, and not something your father would have been proud of.'

'Panos you have to trust me on this please. There are greater forces in play than us two. It involves several governments and their secret services. All I can tell you is that an event this morning will negate the reasons that Turkey would want a war with us.'

'So it is a coup,' said Panos

'As I said Panos, trust me and this will all be over in the next few hours.'

'I am going to trust you for the sake of your father who was also a mentor and friend. Don't let me down Alex,' said Panos and disconnected the call.

Now, as Mavrides scrabbled for the words that would ease the anxiety for the President of the Republic, he saw from the satellite feed that the five Greek Mirage fighters had managed to turn both Turkish frigates around and they were heading west towards the Turkish coast.

'Panos!' shouted Karras. 'Are you still there?'

'Sorry sir, I was watching the action on the satellite feed. It seems our fighters have been successful in chasing the Turkish frigates back to Turkey.'

'Congratulations flight leader two-three, come on home now,' said Mavrides.

'Thank you sir,' replied flight leader two three.

'It looks like no casualties and no great damage to the frigates sir,' reported Mavrides to Karras. 'The Harpoon missiles were strategically placed to cause as little damage as possible, yet frighten them enough to disengage the battle.'

'What do we do now?' asked Karras.

' I suggest you call the Turkish Prime Minister and tell him that we have no ill intent towards Turkey and that the motives behind his country's attack on Lesbos this morning will have evaporated by lunchtime today. Please don't ask me why or how sir, just trust me on this. In fact not a word to anyone and I mean anyone about what we have discussed.'

'Not even Xenakis?' asked Karras.

'No sir especially not Xenakis.'

After the call was disconnected, Karras sat back in his chair for a moment before he called the Turkish Prime Minister. So, he thought, could it be that the plan that Xenakis has put into play is unravelling? With lighter heart he hit the intercom to his secretary.

'Maria, get me the Turkish Prime Minister will you?'

Chapter 46

Ochi Day October 28th, 2010 – 02:00 - Langley – Virginia

Both Geffrey Stevens and Barry Lightfoot managed one hour's relaxation before Jim called them back into the operations room of the Balkans Region. On their satellite feeds they had watched with ever growing concern the dogfight between the Greeks and the Turks and the ensuing attack on the two frigates using air-to-surface missiles. They relaxed a little once they realised that war had been averted for the moment but knowing how volatile the Turks were there was no telling when they would respond. They were considering calling Alex to ask his advice when Gitta rang.

'Hello Gitta,' said Barry. 'We were just going to call Alex to see if he had an idea to stop the Turks from retaliating before the coup takes place.'

' Already taken care of,' replied Gitta. 'Alex spoke with Mavrides the Defence Secretary and convinced him to encourage Karras to speak to the Turkish Prime Minister. Which he did and got the Prime Minister to delay any retaliatory attacks for eight hours. Are you ready for today?'

'Jim, tell Gitta about the technology we'll be using to cover today's events,' said Barry.

'We have eyes everywhere over Greece today. Live feeds from three satellites which will enable us to cover Athens from the Astir Palace hotel to the northern suburbs of the city. We also have smart phone GPS trackers on all individuals in play today and our heavy firepower if needed is three fully armed Reaper drones.'

'Impressive,' said Gitta. 'I'll be leaving the Astir Palace in the cavalcade of cars taking the dignitaries to the saluting rostrum that's set up opposite the parliament building in Syntagma Square. Of course I'll be in Alex's transport. What news of Dexter?'

'Long story,' said Barry. But we've tracked three of his SUVs, one is in the vicinity of the ERT national radio station two SUVs are in the locality of Athens airport. Also, we tracked one which is in the neighbourhood of the Mansion Maximo, but we've lost Dexter and the other SUV. We haven't picked them up yet. We are still unsure as to what Dexter and his mercenaries intentions are. However, one theory which is the most likely is that Xenakis is worried that a coup could scupper his plans for Greece and has hired Dexter and his mercenaries to try to stop it.' Anyway, we are ready. We have Chris staking out the radio station, Nikos is at the airport and Triandafilos is at Mansion Maximo.'

'Thanks for the update and good luck. Hopefully, the next time we talk the coup will be done; Xenakis will have resigned and an interim civilian government will be in place with Alex as Prime Minister,' said Gitta.

'Let's hope. By the way Jim has arranged that you and Alex will have comms which will allow you to be in the same audio loop as us here at Langley, as well as Chris and his team and Michelle in Athens,' said Barry. 'You will be fitted up by your transport driver when you enter the vehicle. Good luck!'

As Barry cut the connection to Gitta, Jim switched on the array of wall monitors. Three monitors displaying the satellite feeds and three monitors displaying the pictures from the three Reaper drones.

'Thanks Jim,' said Stevens. 'What fire power do the Reaper's have?'

'The drones we are using today have two Paveway II laser guided bombs, two AGM II Hellfire air to surface missiles and its camera can read a vehicle number plate from two miles away. Of course it also has the usual thermographic sensors. All three drones are being piloted out of Creech air force base in Nevada and have a maximum twenty three hours of flying time, sir.' Explained Jim.

'Do you know where their base is Jim?' asked Stevens.

'Akrotiri in Cyprus sir,' answered Jim. 'The USA has an arrangement with the British Air Force to base several drones there.'

'Okay let's see what we can see,' said Barry. 'Can we position the drones as cover for Chris and his team Jim? Particularly as they have the firepower which we will probably need if things go belly-up.'

241

'Anticipated that strategy,' said Jim smugly. 'They are already on their way. Look at the display on monitor five. That's the airport below.'

' Good man Jim. Now what we need to do is to decide what we want each monitor to display. I know it's a movable feast but we have to start somewhere. I'd much rather we are proactive than reactive. It's now nine thirty in Athens, the Ochi Day parade commences at ten hundred hours, so the cavalcade of dignitaries from the Astir Palace must be setting off. We should monitor their progress. What do you think Barry?'

'I agree sir. We must also monitor the saluting rostrum opposite the parliament building. The same feed can also show us what Kostas's platoon are doing at the back of the parliament building. A look at what's happening at the Tatoi Air Force base would be helpful too.'

'Right, get on that please Jim,' said Stevens.

Within twenty seconds the feeds from the three satellites showed the areas they were interested in and also that the drones were now on station with the monitors showing clearly the terrain below. Jim also switched on the comms feeds to those on the ground in Athens.

'The fun begins,' murmured Barry to no one in particular.

The teams on the ground however, will definitely not describe the next few hours in Athens as fun.

Chapter 47

The cavalcade of motor vehicles, mostly SUVs but a few Mercedes and Audi limousines; all with armoured bodies and bullet proof windows, trailed at a sedate pace around Vouliagmeni Bay before turning onto Vouliagmeni Avenue, a high speed dual carriageway, where it picked up speed. There were fifteen vehicles in total all carrying dignitaries except for two of them. The lead vehicle carried four Greek secret service agents all heavily armed, while the vehicle immediately behind them had invited members of the media riding in it. The Greek press joked that this vehicle carried the sacrificial lambs as any attack on a cavalcade would try to take out the secret service first and they would be caught in the crossfire.

The third, fourth, fifth and sixth vehicles were Xenakis, Bridgette Neumann, Elena Davilova, and Dominic Vogel with their bodyguards. Behind them were the dignitaries that had something to gain from the rape of the Aegean project. Two prime ministers, four CEOs of oil companies, the CEO of the biggest law firm in the USA and the CEO of one of the most popular social media company. The last vehicle in the cavalcade was the SUV in which Alex and Gitta were travelling and they of course unlike the rest of the cavalcade were keen on stopping the Aegean being plundered. Before they had boarded the vehicle Michelle had appeared with their comms equipment. She fitted them out with a tiny but powerful earpiece and on their wrist, under the watch band, a microphone.

The dignitaries who were in the cavalcade had all attended the Bilderberg meeting the previous evening. They had been specifically selected by Xenakis to join the consortium, together with Greece, Germany and Russia, of the Aegean project. It had been important to Xenakis not only that they were some of the best in class but that they had no allegiance to any particular political creed or to any religion or nation. The oil companies would be directly involved in surveying and extracting the gas and oil from not only the Aegean but also the Adriatic. The prime ministers of Cyprus and Albania needed to be on-side to allow the oil companies access to their extended coastal waters.

With such a large project the legal issues needed to be covered to ensure that contracts were watertight. Several lawyers from the law firm were present when Xenakis had met all the selected dignitaries, twenty minutes before he left for Athens, to have a pre-contract and non-disclosure agreements signing ceremony. So the occupants of vehicles three, four, five and six were feeling pretty confident about the future of the consortium and the riches that it would bestow on them, little knowing that a satellite far above them was transmitting to Langley high definition pictures of their journey towards Athens.

'Everything seems pretty quiet at the moment,' said Barry as he scanned the three monitors showing the feeds from the satellites.

'Seems like it but I don't trust quietness,' said Gitta chuckling.

'Perhaps we spoke too soon,' said Stevens. 'A black SUV has just caught up with the cavalcade, it is now sitting a hundred metres behind your vehicle Alex.'

'Do you know who they are?' asked Gitta as she tried to see into the SUV, but the windows were too tinted to see in. All she could make out were the reflections of the passing cars and scenery.

'Wait, just zooming in on the number plate,' Jim said as he manipulated the picture from the satellite. 'Well, well, well our old friend Dexter has just shown himself.'

'Dexter!' exclaimed Alex. 'You don't think he is going to attack the cavalcade do you? Immediately Alex realised what he had said. 'Σιγνωμη,' said Alex apologising in Greek for his idiotic remark. 'I panicked, of course Dexter wouldn't attack the cavalcade,' he finished ruefully.

Gitta smiling at him took his hand and said 'It does beg the question as why Dexter is tagging the cavalcade though. Anyone got any ideas?'

'No idea at all,' answered Barry. 'However, it just might be that he is protecting Xenakis.'

'Xenakis must be feeling very nervous if he is not relying on his secret service and using Dexter to augment his security,' reasoned Chris from his stakeout position at the ERT radio and TV station.

'Glad to see you're awake Chris. We have you on a drone feed,' said Barry looking over at one of the monitors. 'Not long to wait now.'

Ten minutes later the cavalcade of cars turned off Vouliagmeni Avenue onto Syngrou Avenue passing Hadrian's imposing arch which is the unofficial entrance to the centre of Athens. At that point Dexter's SUV left the back of the cavalcade and turned towards the Athens Zoo which is situated in the park at the back of the parliament building. The cavalcade then passed Zapion Gardens and the National Gardens before drawing up opposite the parliament building on their right and the saluting rostrum on their left. The dignitaries were ushered from their vehicles to the rostrum and invited to their assigned seats. Xenakis was at the front flanked on his left by Konstantinos Karras the President of the Republic and on his right by the Defence Minister, Panos Mavrides. The rest of the front row was made up of Vogel, Neumann and Davilova, the heads of the army, navy and air force. Alex was sitting in the second row together with other members of the Greek cabinet and the leaders of the opposition.

'Congratulations sir,' said Xenakis. 'I don't know what you said to the Turkish Prime Minister earlier but you certainly bought us some time and averted a war.'

'For the time being,' said Karras his eyes boring into Xenakis's making him feel uncomfortable. 'It wasn't that difficult in the end once Panos here had prepped me on what to say,' as he flapped his hand towards Mavrides.

'I would love to hear what you discussed. The Turkish Prime Minister is not one to step back without a large cherry being offered,' said Xenakis trying to read Mavrides eyes.

'Of course Prime Minister once the parade is over I would be happy to update you on what Mr President discussed,' said Mavrides trying not to show the contempt he felt for Xenakis, even managing a faint smile.

'Thank you, I shall look forward to that discussion.'

245

As Xenakis turned to the front, the crowds which were ten deep on either side of the rostrum and which had also filled Syntagma Square behind the rostrum as well as the opposite side of the broad avenue, began to wave their Greek flags and the words "Bravo" could be heard being shouted out towards the oncoming parade. Xenakis looked at his watch it showed ten hundred hours. The parade was starting dead on time. For Xenakis however, his tenure as prime minister of Greece had only half an hour left to run. He looked over the avenue and beyond the flag waving crowd; seeing the two Evzones, wearing their traditional skirt, who were guarding the tomb of the unknown warrior in front of the parliament building, he felt a sense of pride that he would be leading Greece through the next chapter in its glorious history just as the Evzones had during the Greek War of Independence in the early eighteen hundreds.

As Xenakis was puffing his chest out in pride, Konstantinos Karras stood up ready to take the salute. Already they could hear the sounds of a massed band playing the Greek National Anthem getting ever nearer. But what they couldn't hear was the sound of tanks starting up in the National Gardens to the side of the parliament building. Nor would they hear the roar of the tanks near Athens Airport as they rumbled out of the trees beside the airport. Or, the sound of the tanks in Tatoi Forrest crashing their way through the trees towards Tatoi Base, the headquarters of the Hellenic Airforce.

However, thousands of miles away in Langley they saw all of this on their monitors.

'It's game on,' announced Barry to those in the room and also to those on the ground in Athens.

Chapter 48

In the National Gardens under the canopy of trees and clear autumn skies, Colonel Kostas Triandafilos was positioned in front of his tank squadron, standing in the commander hatch of a Foxhound protected patrol vehicle. The vehicle, equipped with a 7.6 mm heavy machine gun turret, has a complement of commander, driver and four crew. It is capable of travelling at seventy miles an hour. He had just sent texts to Stavros Blounas commander of tank squadron two and Christos Mavrides commander of tank squadron three, giving them the go ahead to hit the Tatoi Airbase and Athens Airport respectively. Confident that both tank squadron's would be in position at about the same time as he was detaining Themis Xenakis he turned his attention to matters at hand. He would lead his squadron out of the gardens to take his place in the Ochi Day parade in the next few minutes. Three tanks from his squadron would not follow however, as they had been assigned to break through to the gardens at the rear of the parliament building where one would stand guard in front of the rear entrance and the other two would head for Mansion Maximo the Prime Minister's official home. At that moment a second Foxhound drew up beside his. When the time came this vehicle would be used to transfer key people from the saluting rostrum.

His thoughts turned to Michelle Devereaux who should have been here by now. She was due to bring him some key information about a small mercenary army operating in the Athens area. Sir Peter Bogart the head of Lighthouse had called him the previous night, not only to wish him luck; the United Kingdom supported and wanted the coup to be successful as well as bloodless. He had also told him about the mercenaries and his fear that they might try and prevent the coup happening. Now he was impatient for Michelle to arrive.

On cue, the front door of the vehicle opened and Michelle Devereaux stepped in.

When the people at Langley had spotted Dexter at the back of the cavalcade, they had contacted the Israeli Embassy security team and requested Devereaux to be temporarily assigned to the CIA. They readily agreed because not only did they support the coup but also regularly worked with Chris Horsman on security issues in the Balkan area. Devereaux was asked to follow Dexter. She picked him up as the cavalcade entered Athens and when he left the cavalcade she was right there behind him. For a moment she thought that Dexter was going to ground in the National Gardens where most of the participants of the Ochi Day parade were gathering. However, he took the road towards the Athens Zoo, which was closed, and as with most places on Ochi Day it would stay closed until lunch time. However, the car park was accessible and it was there that he parked the SUV. It was that news she was bringing to Triandafilos.

'I've done as you asked,' she said as Triandafilos came down from the hatch. 'Dexter has parked up at the Athens Zoo.'

'Good work Michelle,' said Barry.

'Who are you talking to?' asked Triandafilos.

'Langley, earlier they asked me to follow John Dexter.'

'Do you mean the John Dexter the CEO of Black Hawke?' asked Triandafilos thinking that Sir Peter had not mentioned that.

'The very same. He has been hired by Xenakis for some sort of protection. We are tracking six vehicles so far with six armed men in each. We think they may try to stop the coup because they have positioned themselves at key points in and around Athens. Nothing for you to worry about though, we have CIA operatives watching them plus drones. If they try anything they will be sorry. It's better than getting your tanks involved in a fight; then you can honestly say that it was a bloodless coup. We will let the blood if needs be,' Devereaux said. 'Would you mind if I rode with you?'

'I trust you Michelle, and yes I would like you to ride with me,'

Far away in Langley Jim, Barry and Stevens were glued to their monitors watching and waiting. One monitor feed showed John Dexter's SUV sitting in the car park of the Athens Zoo with six men lounging around the vehicle some smoking and some drinking from bottled water. No sign of any weapons not even a hand gun.

'What the devil are they waiting for?' commented Barry.

'The same thing we are waiting for,' said Stevens. 'Some sort of movement, something to happen.

At that moment Stevens phone rang.

'I'm putting this on speaker it's the CIA chief,' said Stevens as he hit the speaker button.

'Yes sir,' answered Stevens.

'I've spoken to the President and appraised him of the situation in Greece. He is concerned that the Baltic region could de-stabilise without any intervention from the USA or the UK. But he doesn't want any action to be seen as overt. Only if the Greek army is unable to neutralise Xenakis and his mercenary army, should the CIA take military action. If the action is needed it should be positioned as protecting the Greek citizens and keeping them safe. Is that understood Geoffrey?'

'Yes sir, completely. Thank you,' replied Stevens disconnecting the call. 'Did you hear that Michelle?'

'Yes sir I did,' replied Michelle.

'Please update Colonel Triandafilos and fix him up with a comms set,' said Stevens turning back to the monitors with a growing sense of anticipation.

After Michelle had fixed him up with comms, Triandafilos looked at his watch. Ten twenty five; time to go he thought. He climbed back up into the hatch, looked behind him at his squadron of fourteen tanks, then feeling like John Wayne leading a wagon train, he raised his right arm and signalled them forward. There was a jolt as his driver moved the

Foxhound forward as behind them a sudden crescendo of fourteen tank engines and metal tracks engulfed them.

The squadron trundled down the tree lined asphalt roadway that was just wide enough to take four tanks abreast. Ahead of them, marines in full combat gear were marching to the strains of a tune played proudly by their own band. A couple of minutes later the Foxhound turned right onto Vassilisis Amalias Avenue heading for Syntagma Square and the saluting rostrum opposite the parliament building. The crowds were more than ten deep, waving their flags and shouting their approval of the marines and the tank squadron. As they approached the rostrum, Triandafilos could see the President of the Republic resplendent in his Hellenic navy uniform, proudly displaying his service medals, taking the salute from the marines. Around Syntagma Square the balconies of the several large hotels were filled with flag waving watchers.

'When we reach the rostrum stop the vehicle,' Triandafilos shouted down to the driver.

'Yes sir,' shouted back the driver over the noise of the crowds and the clatter of the tanks.

As the Foxhound drew abreast of the rostrum the driver did as instructed and came to a halt. The second Foxhound halting directly behind it. The front row of the tank squadron did not stop but continued forward, two tanks moving in front of the Foxhounds and two staying immediately behind. All four turned their vehicles to face the rostrum, their turrets turned imposingly onto the dais.

Triandafilos alighted from the Foxhound as six marines exited one of the tanks and took up position directly in front of the dais their M27 automatic rifles pointing at the front row. Taking his Beretta M4 from its holster he walked to the rostrum and stood directly in front of Konstantinos Karras and Themis Xenakis.

'I'm sorry sir,' said Triandafilos addressing Karras. 'But I'm afraid for your safety I need you to come with me.'

'Am I under arrest?' asked Karras as he sat down pulled out a handkerchief and wiped his brow.

'No sir, you are not under arrest, however for your safety you must come with me. There are forces in Greece that pose a threat to you,' said Triandafilos beckoning Karras to join him as Michelle Devereaux exited the Foxhound and stood next to Triandafilos ready to escort Karras to the vehicle.

Reluctantly Karras stepped off the dais and stood next to Triandafilos, who noticed for the first time since the parade had come to a standstill that the crowd were now silent and many were beginning to drift away to their homes. Triandafilos thought that Xenakis looked decidedly sick, his eyes were staring, his face white as a sheet, his fingers playing nervously with each other as he constantly looked over to where Davilova was sitting as if asking her to save him. At one point he mouthed something to her but neither she nor Triandafilos understood what it was he was trying to say. Later Devereaux would tell Triandafilos that he had mouthed "Dexter". Most other guests on the rostrum were just sitting there, bemusedly watching what was going on, some though were having animated conversations and the Defence Minister looked decidedly confused probably trying to decide how he should react. Alex and Gitta looked the calmest of the lot of them. However, Vogel, Neumann and Davilova sitting on the front row as special guests of Xenakis were looking very uncomfortable at what they were witnessing. Well they will be even more uncomfortable in a few minutes, mused Triandafilos to himself. He turned to Karras and requested him to follow Michelle Devereaux to the Foxhound. At that moment his phone gave out two distinct pings.

'Excuse me,' said Triandafilos as he retrieved his phone from his pocket and read the texts he had just received. He allowed a faint smile to cross his face before turning to Xenakis he said.

'I have just been informed that the Tatoi Air Force base and Athens Airport have been successfully taken over by my forces without any bloodshed at all. Now Mr Xenakis I am arresting you in the name of the Hellenic nation for premeditated treacherous acts against the people of Greece and the murder of Christos Antonopoulos former Greek Finance Minister and Michalis Louisos former member of the Greek Secret Service. Please step down from the dais.'

In a daze Xenakis stepped from the dais where he was immediately taken by the arm by two marines and marched to the second Foxhound.

Alex and Gitta joined Triandafilos in front of the podium.

'Congratulations Kostas,' said Alex. 'This is Gitta, a CIA operative whose been helping us with this mission here as well as acting as my bodyguard.'

'Hello Gitta glad to have you onboard.' Then turning to the Defence Minister said.

'Sir, would you like to join Alex and Gitta in my Foxhound? You should be involved in discussions we have over the next few days.'

'I knew it! I told you I didn't trust him,' screamed Davilova pointing her finger at Alex. 'You fools he has been playing us all along. There will be repercussions for all of us.' She was shaking now. Her usual sophisticated ice cool demeanour had completely vanished.

'I'm afraid you and your companions are going to have to come with us,' said Triandafilos.

'You can't arrest us we have diplomatic immunity,' said Vogel.

'I'm afraid I can,' insisted Triandafilos. 'Greece is now under military rule and I have rescinded your right to immunity.'

'When did you do that?' screamed Davilova completely losing her cool.

'This minute,' said Triandafilos smiling. 'Now get in that Foxhound and join your friend Xenakis.'

Triandafilos signalled to the marines to escort them to the Foxhound in which Xenakis was sitting. Once they were in with three Marines guarding them Triandafilos went to his vehicle. As he boarded the Foxhound he was feeling buoyed at the thought that the taking of Tatoi and Athens Airport had been so straightforward. If the blowing up of the generator at Papagou and the transfer of power at Mansion Maximo go as smoothly he thought, today would be a major success for him as well as the country.

'Mansion Maximo please driver,' instructed Triandafilos as he settled himself into his seat for the short journey to the other side of the National Gardens.

A few thousand miles away in Langley they were just seeing the first signs that would not please Triandafilos. Things were about to become bloody.

Chapter 49

Ochi Day October 28th, 2010 – Athens

It was three-forty-five in the morning in Langley and even though they had plied themselves with coffee all night Jim, Barry and Stevens were feeling the strain. In Athens it was ten-forty-five in the morning. Langley watched as the two Foxhounds left the rostrum in Syntagma Square and Triandafilos' tank squadron encircled the square taking up position with their barrels facing the parliament building. Fifteen minutes earlier they had watched as Stavros Blounas had led his tank squadron into the Tatoi Air Base. No-one tried to stop him, not a shot was fired in anger and it looked as though they had been welcomed by many of the airmen on the base. However, at Athens airport, although at the outset it had looked as though the tank squadron had prevailed without a fire fight, that was not the case now.

Exactly on time four of Christos Mavrides's battle tanks burst through the western perimeter fence of Athens Airport taking the control tower staff completely by surprise. Luckily there was a skeleton staff because of the countrywide air controllers' strike and very few commercial aircraft landing at the airport or flying over Greece. Two of the tanks took up position in the centre of the nearest runway which is designated Zero-3-right, and 21-left, while the other two tanks threatened the control tower by positioning themselves one hundred yards from the tower, with both barrels facing it. At the same time two battle tanks breached the fence of the eastern perimeter and positioned themselves in the centre of the parallel runway to Zero-3-right designated Zero-3-left and 21-right. The remaining three tanks of the squadron had positioned themselves so as to block the only highway leading to the arrival and departure terminals.

Langley saw this through the feeds being transmitted by the Reaper drone circling the airport and a satellite. Then suddenly where the two tanks had breached the airport's eastern perimeter fence two black SUVs sped through the gap stopping two hundred metres from the runway.

254

'They know their stuff,' commented Barry. 'Kostas we've got two of Dexter's SUVs threatening the two tanks positioned on the runway on the eastern side of the airport. They are about two hundred metres away. How effecting are the tanks gun at that range?'

'Not very effective at all. The gun's range is approximately three thousand five hundred metres down to about five hundred metres. The shell will whistle over their heads. Mind you it might make them deaf.'

The mercenaries left their SUVs machine guns in hand. Two of them started loading their RPGs.

'Okay I've got a visual,' shouted Nikos as his Mercedes screamed up the perimeter road with dust billowing out behind it.

'Be careful they have RPGs,' warned Stevens. 'Can RPGs damage your battle tanks Kostas?'

'Hardly make a dent but if they hit the tracks they could disable them. I have told Christos to tell the tanks under his command to not fire in anger. Only warning shots.'

'Thank you,' said Stevens as he watched Nikos's Mercedes slide to a halt just inside the perimeter fence about five hundred metres from the SUVs. 'Time to call in the big guns. Jim we need to take out those two SUVs with the drone.'

'On it sir,' said Jim. He switched frequencies and instructed the drone pilots to hit the SUVs with the Reaper's AGM II Hellfire air to surface missiles. 'Thirty seconds to target sir.'

They watched as the drone's monitor feed displayed two cross-hairs in the centre of the picture at the same time magnifying the view.

'Nikos we're hitting the SUVs so stay in the car; you should be quite safe where you are,' instructed Steven.

'Ten seconds to target,' announced Jim.

They watched holding their breath as each cross-hair fixed onto an SUV. All of a sudden two large brilliant flashes, silent to the watchers, exploded over the SUVs and the men around them. 'Bingo!' shouted Jim.

As they continued to watch the debris raining down the smoke began to clear revealing two large craters intersecting each other, but of the SUVs and the mercenaries there was no sign that they had existed at all.

'What shall I do now there is nothing here to accomplish or even check, the SUVs and the mercenaries were obliterated. A pathologist is going to have an impossible job identifying anyone.'

'Go straight to the Mansion Maximo and join Triandafilos,' instructed Stevens.

'Good idea,' interrupted Michelle from the Foxhound that was heading slowly through crowds dispersing from the parade and traffic heading towards uptown Athens. 'We might need the support. Dexter is at the zoo, he might be intent on taking the building and rescuing Xenakis.'

'On my way,' confirmed Nikos.

'Chris any sign of the mercenaries moving into the radio station?'

'No, said Chris. And as you can probably see there are no tanks here either. The radio station's programme schedule has not been interrupted.'

'It will be shortly,' said Kostas Triandafilos from his Foxhound. 'Our plan is to sabotage a section of the electricity substation in Papagou. The radio station will not be able to transmit when that blows.

Jim punched in some coordinates and a picture feed from one of the satellites centred on the substation. The monitor also showed a solitary tank slowly making its way towards it from the north.

'A shot from the tank's gun could cause quite a lot of collateral damage,' said Barry. 'Is it really necessary Kostas? We are trying to prevent any civilians being injured during the coup, especially by the Greek army. The President specifically commanded it. That is why we are helping you and if needs be admitting to culpability if there are any casualties.'

The tank was now stopping by the substation.

'Don't worry,' reassured Kostas. 'We are not going to shoot the station. On board the tank are demolition experts who will only disable the part of the grid that feeds the radio station.'

'Thank you,' said Barry breathing a sigh of relief.

As they watched, three men in marine fatigues exited the tank and made their way to the metal double doors that was the only entrance to the substation. It didn't hold them up for long. One of the men moulded a small piece of C4 around the lock, then inserted a detonator and stood back. There was no big explosion, just a puff of smoke accompanying a small "whoof" like sound and the doors swung open. Quickly the three men made their way directly to one of the large boxes which looked more like a metal cupboard.

'They have obviously got the inside track on this. They went directly to that particular box,' said Barry.

The metal cupboard-like box was breached as quickly, and with the same method as the double doors earlier. One of the men reached into the box and pulled down a lever, then the box was shut and the men left the substation returning to their tank. The whole thing was accomplished in less than three minutes.

'Radio station has gone dead,' said Chris who had been monitoring one of the programmes. 'What do you want me to do now. Our friends are still parked up near the radio station. Oh! Wait a sec they're moving. They must have been listening to the radio too. Do you want me to keep on their tail?'

'Yes Chris. I just hope they are not heading for Mansion Maximo to reinforce their friends,' said Stevens. 'Jim can you reconfigure the monitors so that we can follow both Chris and Nikos; also I want a satellite view of the area around Mansion Maximo and all three drones policing that area too.'

As Jim reconfigured the feeds the three men in Langley saw that Nikos was approaching the Hilton Hotel which was a couple of kilometres from Mansion Maximo. On Irodou Attikou street where both Mansion Maximo and The Presidential Palace were situated, there was one tank positioned at the rear entrance of the Greek Parliament building and two tanks blocking the street either side of the entrance to Mansion Maximo. On Vasileos Georgos II street, which runs down the left hand side of Mansion Maximo and right hand side of The Presidential Palace, the two Foxhounds were parked side by side in the centre of the road two hundred metres from where the street met Irodou Attikou. At that junction, a black SUV was parked with its engine idling.

'Looks like a stand-off to me,' said Stevens. 'At the moment you have the advantage Kostas but there are two more SUV's heading your way plus Dexter's SUV parked for the moment in the Zoo.'

'The marines in the other Foxhound will transfer their prisoners into the side entrance of Mansion Maximo where for now they will be guarded and confined to their rooms. Alex, Gitta, Michelle, the defence minister will escort President Karras into his palace, again through the side door, and stay with him.'

'Is the President under house arrest?' asked Stevens.

'Of course not,' said Kostas. 'We are simply keeping him safe. In the meantime, with all the civilians secure, we can go about planning our response to Dexter and his men. We don't want a shooting match in the centre of Athens that's for sure and will try to avoid such a situation. We will make the necessary risk assessment and strategies accordingly on the least risky route. Don't forget the Foxhound is configured for a 7.62mm machine gun and standard equipment of two RPGs. Quite enough to knock out an SUV and also to act as a deterrent to anyone thinking of storming the palace.'

'We shall watch with interest from here and let you know if Dexter makes a move. If you need the drone's fire power at all let us know, although using its missiles in open spaces as we did to knock out the SUVs at the airport is a far cry from using them in the centre of Athens. If there is going to be a firefight, it should be the CIA team led by Chris who should get involved. Remember what the US President requested. We have Triandafilos on station in front of the Presidential Palace on Irodou Attikou street just out of your sight, and another two vehicles on their way,' said Stevens.

I'll wait for them don't worry,' confirmed Kostas. 'They'll be an important part of our risk assessment.'

Langley watched as the civilians in both Foxhounds were escorted to their temporary quarters split between the Mansion Maximo and The Presidential Palace. The tank which had been stationed opposite the rear door of the parliament building left its position and drove round the back of the Megaro Maximus stopping behind the two Foxhounds. Two marines carrying RPGs alighted from the tank and one each boarded a Foxhound while Kostas remained in his hatch on his phone no doubt talking to Christos Mavrides and Stavros Blounas his trusted lieutenants on strategy.

Unfortunately for the watchers in Langley, Kostas had turned his comms off.

Chapter 50

Ochi Day October 28th, 2010 – Presidential Palace – Athens – 11:30am

The President of the Republic sat behind his ornate desk in his equally opulent office staring out of the window into the immaculately landscaped gardens of the Palace. The building had originally served as the royal palace before the army coup in 1967. Built in 1897, it is a three-storey, neo-classical building with an austere and symmetrical facade. The central section of the building is flanked by two slightly protruding wings. On the second floor, there is a row of double windows. All sides of the building are clean and simple with the only embellishment that protrudes being the porch with the Ionic columns, located at the main entrance of the Mansion on Irodou Attikou Street. There were two Evzone guards at the main entrance and one Evzone guard at each of the other two side entrances.

'How long will I be confined to this building,' asked Konstantinos Karras to no-one in particular. With him was the Defence Minister, Panos Mavrides and Alex Kalfas, Minister of Finance. Both Gitta and Michelle had left them to go and freshen up and check security. Alex figured that being women they had really gone off to have a good look round.

'It's only for your safety, nothing else,' replied Alex. 'You are still in danger; we all are. We can't be certain if Dexter will try to take the building intent on taking you hostage to force Kostas to take his tanks back to barracks and reinstate Xenakis as prime minister.'

'From what you told me earlier about what he has been getting up to in Northern Greece to support Xenakis I fear you may be right. Although it would be a suicide mission against tanks and highly trained men,' said Karras.

'Sorry sir but they are amongst the most elite marines in the world; I wouldn't bet on them losing a fight,' interjected Mavrides.

'I agree,' said Alex. 'Sir, what you should do now is call the Turkish Prime Minister to inform him that Xenakis is not in power and he can lower his anxiety levels. The Xenakis project is now dead and buried.'

'What if he asks me who is in charge? I can't tell him the army, he won't like that one bit and it's sure to increase his blood pressure.'

'Tell him the truth sir. As soon as the Dexter threat is out of the way and Xenakis and his partners are in police custody, I will be sworn in as an interim Prime Minister of a civil government with the support of the army. The current cabinet will retain their positions including Panos here until such time as we have national elections. Kostas Triandafilos has agreed to this timetable; his only reason for organising the coup was that he saw the gradual ideological shift to the left, particularly the closer relationships Xenakis was forging with Russia. He had no idea of what Xenakis was planning and incidentally neither had the United Kingdom nor the USA.'

'How soon do you think it will be all over?'

'I think it's safe to say that I will be sworn in as prime minister by this evening. You can tell Turkey that. But it won't be all over sir. We have to deal with Vogel, Neumann and Davilova who have done immense damage to our country, both financially and criminally. We have to decide what we are going to do. Ah, here are the girls,' said Alex as Gitta and Michelle walked back in with Kostas.

'We should speak to Langley,' said Gitta. 'Our comms have been off for a while now. Chris and Nikos are back and parked up outside the main entrance to Mansion Maximo chatting to the two Evzones guarding the main gate.'

'And the other SUVs; have they joined the party yet?' asked Alex.

'One of the SUVs has arrived outside this building and parked up on the opposite side of the road about three hundred metres from the main gate of this building. His mate who was parked at the junction has now joined him. The other SUV has not arrived. Perhaps mechanical failure, who knows,' said Kostas

'That's worrying. If it's not mechanical failure then we could have an SUV with six armed men on board running loose around Athens,' said Gitta. 'That's another reason to talk to Langley because they must have tracked it.'

Okay,' said Alex. 'I think one of us should go over to the Mansion and check on our prisoners. Are they being closely guarded in separate rooms, or altogether in one room?'

'Neither,' said Kostas. 'Xenakis is in a separate room from the other three; he is confined to his bedroom suite. Phones disconnected and mobile phone and laptop confiscated. He can't communicate with the outside world but he is not restrained in any way. The other three are confined to the main reception room where the investitures take place. Again, no phones or computers and not restrained. One marine outside each room. I'll go over if you like.'

'No it should be me,' said Kostas. 'After all they're my marines guarding them.'

'No not you Kostas. You should be out there in the street with your men. Don't you think it strange that nothing is happening? What are they waiting for and why is Dexter hanging around in a Zoo car park? I'll go, you don't need me here at the moment,' insisted Gitta.

'At least let Michelle go with you,' said Alex.

'No, there is no need; I'm perfectly able to look after myself,' protested Gitta.

Alex was slightly startled by her outburst. He thought that Gitta would have jumped at the chance of having Michelle as company. Perhaps she is tired. After all it had been a long five days. My god he thought has it only been five days since this all started? Reluctantly he said 'Fine Gitta, go on your own but switch your comms back on.'

Gitta left them with a brief wave of her hand and made her way out of the Palace and out of the building's side entrance. Outside on the street she took some deep breaths sucking in clean Autumn air in an attempt to steady her nerves. She was angry with herself for losing her cool back there. It wasn't professional. Her excuse was that the next few hours would be fraught with difficulty and she had to tread very carefully. She looked down the street towards the junction with Irodou Attikou Street. The two Foxhounds had moved further down towards the junction and were now only five metres from it. Beyond the junction was the wall topped with railings that separated Irodou Attikou from the grounds of the zoo, where, somewhere in there, Dexter was waiting. Well, he would have to be patient a little while longer, just until the optics were right. Gitta crossed the street, showed her ID card to the guard, gave him a smile and entered the side entrance to the Mansion Maximo.

Back in the President's office in the Presidential Palace Alex had taken Michelle to one side.

' I don't know what got into Gitta just now but even though she insisted she be alone I think you should wait ten minutes and then go across and join her. You have comms so you can join in the Langley conference when we convene it.'

'Okay Alex, I'll take a walk in the street to get some fresh air and then slowly wonder over to the Mansion. I'll see you later,' agreed Michelle tapping him on his arm.

As Alex watched her go he had a bizarre sensation that scared him a little. He went to call her back but stopped; thinking himself too sensitive he turned back into the office of the President little knowing that his fear was prophetic.

Chapter 51

Ochi Day October 28th, 2010 – Mansion Maximo – Athens – 12:15

Gitta made her way up to the main hallway. It was her first time in the neoclassical building which had been built between 1912 and 1921, on land which had been part of the royal gardens belonging to the current presidential palace. She vaguely recalled that over the years it had served many uses and it was not until fairly recently used as the residence of the prime minister. Initially it was a private house owned by Dimitrios Maximos, who had completed building the mansion in 1921, and lived there up to the second world war. After the war it served as the residence for the American Ambassador for a while; a guest house for foreign dignitaries, such as Margarete Thatcher; but not till 1982 did it become the residence of the Greek Prime Minister.

Gitta found herself in an rectangular hallway with several doors leading off. At the far end of the hallway to her right, was the main reception room which now served as a prison for Xenakis's three partners. To her left at the far end was the main entrance to the mansion. The side entrance where she was standing, opened out to the centre of the hallway, opposite a marble staircase winding its way up to the right. Another staircase also of marble, descended down under the main staircase to the basement area. Here the Greek States art collection was stored, as well as many vintage wines, ports and liquor. Gitta knew that upstairs were the residence rooms and it was there that Xenakis was confined. To the left of the main staircase was a door which clearly was a kitchen as Gitta could hear crockery and cutlery noises coming from within. To Gitta's right was the prime minister's office. Gitta headed for it; opened the door and stepped inside.

Nice office she thought, the whole office being furnished in dark oak and brilliant white material covering the chairs and one sofa. Behind the desk a huge set of French doors led out onto a marble veranda which offered a view of the immaculately landscaped gardens. Gitta moved over to the desk and sat down. Taking out her mobile phone she punched in a number.

'It's me,' she said.

Is everything going as planned?' the voice asked.

'More or less, I shall talk to Alex tonight.'

'What if he doesn't go along with it?

'We'll have to use heavier hitters.'

'You mean London.'

'Yes, and if that doesn't work we still have Protos,' said Gitta.

'I hope it doesn't come to that; Protos won't like getting directly involved.'

'Isn't he calling the President of the Republic?'

'No, the State Department is.'

Well let's see,' said Gitta. 'I have to go.'

'Bye,' said the voice and cut the connection.

Gitta got up from the desk and went to the door. For a few minutes she stood listening. Satisfied there was no-one in the hallway she went back to the desk and punched in a different number.

'Have you received the package?' she asked when the phone was answered.

'Yes,' said the voice at the other end.

'Is it what they agreed?' asked Gitta.

'Everything is good.'

'Is what I asked for here?' Gitta asked.

'It arrived with the morning delivery of bread and flour. It's in the flour drum. You'll have to dig deep.'

'No problem, see you in the morning,' said Gitta and broke the connection.

She smiled to herself as she left the office that Xenakis once had but would now be Alex's office. Walking over to the marine guarding the reception room she asked him if everything was alright. He told her that it had been quiet most of the time except when Davilova had started demanding a phone. She had been refused of course and eventually quietened down. They all had eaten lunch shortly after her outburst. Gitta thanked him, returned to the staircase and made her way up to the first floor to Xenakis's suite of rooms.

'Take five,' she said to the guard who was on the door. 'I'll only be a few minutes.'

The guard nodded and headed for the stairs leaving her alone outside the door to the residency.

'What are you going to do with me,' slurred Xenakis the moment she stepped in the room. He looked dishevelled, distraught and scared sprawled as he was in a large armchair. She noticed he had not touched his lunch and apart from his speech an opened half bottle of whisky betrayed the fact that he had been drinking heavily.

'You will be put on trial I expect,' said Gitta. 'But it's not up to me. Alex will be sworn in as Prime Minister later today. Technically you have been sacked as you are under arrest. I expect at some time tomorrow you will be handed over to the authorities.'

'Why not today?' asked Xenakis.

'I don't know whether you have noticed but your friend Dexter is still outside waiting for something. Probably for you to be transported out of here to the authorities and no doubt ready to try a rescue attempt. Would that be close to the truth?'

'Maybe,' said Xenakis trying to sound nonchalant but failing miserably. 'I can't believe that Kalfas would betray the cause like that. I thought he was loyal to his country,' he whined.

Gitta laughed and said. 'You must be joking, he is the one being faithful to his country not you. He has effectively stopped you and your friends from one, breaking up the European Union; two, allowing Russia unfettered access to the Aegean Sea; three, going to war with Turkey and four, bankrupting Greece. Add to that lot, being complicit in two murders. It doesn't bode well for your future does it?. If you are not sentenced to death, it will be life at the very least for you I'm afraid. Unfortunately for you and what you didn't know, Alex is working with the CIA, his father was a high ranking CIA official in Washington and his mother was CIA liaison with MI6 in London.'

At that revelation Xenakis buried his head in his hands. 'And you,' asked Xenakis. I suppose you belong to some agency too.'

'Yes!

'Am I allowed to speak to my lawyer?' asked Xenakis.

'You are not under arrest yet, so why do you need a lawyer?'

'But you are keeping me here against my will,' said Xenakis whining through slurred words.

'We invited you to stay here. No-one is forcing you to stay. Anyway it's your home.'

Xenakis took another mouthful of whisky. 'So I could walk out of here?'

'Of course you are free to walk out of here. However, you should be aware that the marines have orders to shoot you if you step outside this room.'

Xenakis's face turned white on hearing this; he took another gulp of whisky and stood staring at Gitta before saying. 'You can't do that, I'm an unarmed civilian,' said Xenakis raising his voice a little.

'Technically until Alex is sworn in as Prime Minister of Greece you are commander of the Greek armed forces, so not a civilian. However, this is all semantics; the bottom line is that you have a choice; stay in this suite of rooms and stay alive or leave and be shot. It's up to you,' finished Gitta.

Gitta's phone started vibrating. 'Excuse me,' she said to Xenakis. 'Hello Alex.'

'Hello Gitta, we are starting the conference call with Langley over here in the palace.

'Right, I'll join you there immediately,' confirmed Gitta as she closed the connection. She gave Xenakis a big sarcastic smile; turned, left the room and made her way down the marble staircase to the side entrance.

Chapter 52

Ochi Day October 28th, 2010 – Presidential Palace – Athens

It was one o'clock midday in Athens and six o'clock in the morning in Langley, as Alex, Gitta, Defence Minister Mavrides and the President of the Republic Karras, were gathered around a circular table in the conference room of the palace.

'Are Michelle and Kostas joining us?' asked Gitta.

'I have ordered Kostas to remain with his men while Dexter is still a threat,' said Mavrides.

'Michelle is puzzling,' said Alex. 'I had asked her to go over and keep you company because your outburst had got us worried that you were not yourself. Before she could go, she received a text instructing her to urgently return to the Israeli Embassy. We have not heard from her since and have no idea what is going on.'

'Don't worry about me, I was just a little tired and irritable. I'm perfectly fine now.'

Just at that moment the red light on the conferencing telephone in the centre of the table started to flash.

'We're on,' said Alex as he reached forward and depressed a button that opened the connection to Langley.

'Everyone present?' asked Stevens. There was a chorus of yeses.

'I have Barry and Jim with me. Alex can you just cover the state of play as you see it please.'

'Sure, we have Gitta, Panos Mavrides the Defence Minister and Konstantinos Karras in on the call. Xenakis has been under house arrest in his residency in the Mansion Maximo since this morning. Tomorrow we hope to hand him over to the police authorities who will be charging him with various criminal offences. We also have Vogel, Neumann and

Davilova in the same building. They are being kept together in one room and we are waiting to see what we should do with them. The most worrying issue is the standoff which we currently have outside. We are unable to work out why Dexter is sitting over in the zoo on his own and not joining the rest of his men on Irodou Attikou Street. Knowing that the drones are overhead is most reassuring though,' finished Alex.

'Dexter has one other SUV keeping him company and the other two as you know are sitting on the opposite side of the street some two hundred yards from you. At least that was the case half an hour ago before we lost the drones,' said Stevens.

'What do you mean, lost the drones?' interrupted Alex.

'They were pulled,' said Jim. 'They went off-line without warning. When I tried to find out why, I came up against a brick wall. I was told that orders came from someone way above their pay grade.'

'So we are fucked,' said Alex in exasperation.

'No,' replied Stevens.

'What do you mean no? What is happening?'

'I can't tell you yet.'

'Why not?'

'Because at the moment it is way above your pay grade as Jim has said,' reiterated Stevens. 'We have some good news for you though. Dexter has now withdrawn his men. They are not a threat to you anymore.'

'And Dexter himself,' asked Alex.

'He has gone too.'

'What made him go? He must have had some incentive,' asked Alex.

'You will learn the whys and the wherefores in due course Alex.

'I am about to become the next Prime Minister of Greece shouldn't I be the first to know or at least consulted on happenings that effect my country?'

' Of course Alex. After you have been sworn in you will learn everything,' explained Karras.

Alex turned to Karras in surprise. He had wondered why both Karras and Mavrides had been keeping quiet. Now he understood, this was not new news to them, they had prior knowledge of this. Alex had an idea. He walked over to a window that looked out onto Irodou Attikou Street. Stevens was telling the truth, Dexter's men weren't there. He looked towards the main entrance to Mansion Maximo. No tanks! They had gone too. So too had the two Foxhounds. It's as if they had all quietly slunk away in the night. Except that is, it was in broad daylight. What the hell was going on he thought. Had some deals been struck. If so what deals? He turned to Mavrides and addressed him. 'How the hell did you get Kostas to pull his men out?'

'He received a phone call,' said Mavrides.

'Do you know who from?' asked Alex.

'No,' replied Mavrides. 'But it was obviously from someone high up because he didn't argue.'

'Yet you are his boss aren't you?' said Alex with a puzzled look on his face.

'Technically I'm not. Once Xenakis was arrested all members of his cabinet had no authority. Besides Kostas was the leader of a coup which actually took place so for that period of time the coup was in force Kostas was the highest authority in Greece. But now the coup is over the President of the Republic is the highest authority.'

'Spot on,' said Stevens. 'Now, Mr President sir, have you decided when Alex will be sworn in?'

'It will be at four o'clock this afternoon in this building,' confirmed Karras.

'In that case please all of you gather again for a conference call at five o'clock your time.'

'Who will be participating your end?' asked Karras.

271

'It will be myself and someone from the United States government,' replied Stevens. 'Bye for now have a good afternoon.'

After the connection was broken President Karras said that he needed to work on his speech in preparation for facing the nation at three o'clock. The people must be completely confused about what happened at the Ochi Day Parade. Was it a coup or wasn't it a coup? Has Xenakis been arrested? Who will be the next Prime Minister?

'Not an easy speech,' agreed Alex. 'Why don't you have Panos here by your side to reassure them that he is still in charge of the armed forces. I will want him to stay on as the Defence Minister anyway when I'm Prime Minister.'

'Excellent idea,' beamed Karras for the first time since he was escorted off the dais at the parade. 'Are you up for that Panos?'

'Of course sir, and thank you Alex for believing in me,' said Panos.

'Right that's settled, let's go and prepare Panos. Alex and Gitta make yourselves at home you have enough time before the Archbishop gets here for the swearing in ceremony. There's a heated swimming pool in the garden if you fancy some exercise,' said the President as he swept his arm towards the large bay window which overlooked the garden.

Once the president and Panos Mavrides had left the room, Gitta went over to Alex and gave him a lingering kiss on his lips. She sat astride him on his lap, while giving him more passionate kisses. Alex began to squirm as he felt himself get harder.

'Let's go to a bedroom,' he gasped barely getting out the words.

'Tonight the bedroom but now let's go to the pool. The temperature is quite warm now, besides a cool dip will do us both good.'

'I haven't got any swim wear with me though,' said Alex.

Gitta let out a saucy chuckle. 'Neither have I Alex, not even underwear under this trouser suit. Come on; race you.'

She swung off his lap and headed for the door with Alex in hot pursuit. After several attempts at finding the exit out onto the gardens they eventually found the right one and stepped out onto a long wide marble veranda. Steps, which were also the same white marble led down onto a pebbled area which had an intricately chiselled fountain in its centre. Beyond was a huge lawn, the size of half a football pitch, bordered all around by the most beautifully coloured Azalea bushes, except for two treelined pathways leading off in opposite directions, both signposted. One said "tennis courts" and the other "pool area". They took the one to the pool, Gitta leading Alex who was beginning to tire.

'Please Gitta slow down I can't run anymore. I'm not as fit as you,' shouted Alex between panting breaths.

'Perhaps you need an incentive,' Gitta shouted back as she peeled off her jacket; stepped out of her trousers; picked up her shoes and ran, revealing her completely naked body to Alex, towards the swimming pool. Alex somehow finding extra energy ran after her. When Gitta reached the pool, without any hesitation, she dived straight in. Alex arrived at the pool in time to see Gitta, demonstrating a very good crawl stroke, disappearing towards the other end of the pool, her white behind moving from side to side seemingly beckoning Alex to join her. Quite remarkably the pool was full size, fifty metres in length, not the usual social pool usually found in private residences; pools with nice friendly curves, shallow with nice potted plants all the way around. This one had loungers spread around its edges each with a small table and an umbrella. There was also three Jacuzzies, outdoor showers and what looked like changing rooms. The pool area itself was perfectly secluded from prying eyes from the street and the palace windows. Something Alex was glad of as he proceeded to remove his clothes.

Alex dived into the pool and came up gasping for breath as the cold water took him by surprise. He started to swim leisurely towards Gitta who was now speeding back towards him. Alex stopped and trod water waiting for Gitta to swim into his arms, but she had other ideas and as she reached him, she dived under him and was gone. She reached the edge of the pool; pulled herself up and out onto the surrounding stone, then went to the nearest sun bed, lay down on her back, legs akimbo, offering her body up to the sun.

Alex swam to the steps as he was sure he didn't have the strength to pull himself up. He walked over to where Gitta lay and stood looking at her for a few moments. Her eyes were shut and he couldn't be sure she was asleep or not. He knelt at the foot of the bed between her legs and bent forward towards her inner thighs still glistening with water droplets.

'No, darling,' said Gitta without opening her eyes. I want to feel you inside me. I want you to make slow sensuous love to me. Come here, let me make you hard while you use your tongue to make me wet. When Alex entered her a few minutes later Gitta gave out a low throaty moan as she grabbed his buttocks and pulled him in as far as he could go.

'Don't move,' she whispered. 'Stay still and let yourself relax darling.' She kissed him tenderly as he felt the muscles inside her vagina contract onto his penis giving him amazing electric sensations. After a while she planted her feet flat on the sunbed and started to use her strong thigh muscles to slowly thrust and gyrate her lower body. 'Stay where you are love, I'm going to try and twist us round so I'm on top.' She threw one leg over his buttocks and using her other leg as a lever slowly twisted them round till she was astride him sitting on his penis. She started to ride him. 'Caress my nipples darling,' she panted as she rode him harder and harder. It was then that they both went to heaven as they came together, Alex exploding inside her like he had never done before, and Gitta screaming through her ecstatic orgasm, till finally she collapsed on top of him exhausted. They lay there catching their breath in the now weak sunlight sweat droplets covering their skin. Alex looked into Gitta's emerald green eyes and saw love there, but he knew from the way they had made love that this was the last time.

'Darling, you're leaving aren't you?' he said.

'Yes my sweet. It has to be this way. I love you but you are about to become the Prime Minister of Greece. You have a wife waiting for you and I have a career with the CIA. You don't need a scandal in the first months of your premiership do you? I will come back I promise, perhaps in a few years. If you are divorced by then we could continue our love affair where we left off here in this garden. Just remember me as you see me know completely exposed to you and loving you with everything I have lover. Now go and get sworn in. Fulfil your destiny. Goodbye my sweet.'

Gitta kissed Alex on the lips, then sprung up, slipped on her trouser suit and walked out of his life.

Chapter 53

Ochi Day October 28th, 2010 – Presidential Palace – Athens

At precisely four o'clock Alex in his best bib and tucker was with Konstantinos Karras and Panos Mavrides, in the palace ceremonial room, waiting for the Archbishop of Athens to arrive. While waiting Alex pondered the role of the church in Greece, it being one of those countries where the church and the state were still not separated, and where no important civil ceremony ever takes place without the blessing of the Archbishop of Athens. Alex believed, that as Prime Minister, he would have to up the narrative about separating the Orthodox Church from the Greek State. If nothing else, the economics of such a move would relieve the state's budget of the huge payroll for the ten thousand priests which it currently pays, and also allow the state to reclaim, for development, the huge tracks of land which the church had allowed to go uncultivated.

His revere was interrupted by the sweeping entrance of the Archbishop in his black clothes accompanied by his entourage of three priests. Alex was asked to step to an ornate table where a large black book similar to an old fashioned accounting ledger, was laid open. He laid his right hand on the book while the Archbishop offered up some short prayers to God asking him to give Alex wisdom and strength to carry out his duties as Premier. He then blessed Alex who then signed his name at the appropriate place on the page duly witnessed by the signatures of the Archbishop, the President and finally the Defence Minister. Once the formalities were over there were congratulations all round as the President's butler entered the room with a tray of the traditional tsipouro for such occasions. Alex kept to himself that the un-aged brandy tasted like petrol and it wasn't a drink of choice for him.

By the time all the niceties were over it was almost time for the five o'clock conference call. As they moved to the conference room Alex took the opportunity to ask Karras how his press conference had gone. A press conference that Alex had missed because he was otherwise engaged in the gardens of the palace.

'It was difficult Prime Minister,' said Karras. 'There are so many unanswered questions that I could not give a satisfying answer to. They pressed me on Xenakis and what would happen to him. They pressed me on the three people we have under house arrest in Mansion Maximo. Neither of these questions could I answer. However, the good news is that Turkey is happy that Xenakis is out of the way and the people are happy that the very short lived army coup was bloodless and the civilians were back in charge. Hopefully this conference call will make things clearer. By the way, I was expecting you to be at the press conference somewhere in the background but I didn't notice you.'

I'm sorry sir, but I was showing Gitta around. She wanted to swim as you had suggested to us earlier.'

'Ah, yes I remember now,' acknowledged the President as they entered the conference room.

Alex noticed the camera and the large monitor at one end of the room facing the round table and at each seat there was a microphone and camera. Now he thought, I will see the people in Langley who up 'till now have only been at the end of a telephone. A technician, probably some IT geek thought Alex, was fiddling around with wires and cameras. The technician turned to Karras and said. 'It's all ready sir. As soon as they connect the monitor here will display a picture. If more than one location joins the meeting the monitor screen will automatically split into smaller screens so everyone can see everyone in the meeting. Your microphones and cameras are already on. If you need anything or something stops working I shall be in the next room.'

'Thank you,' said Karras.

A minute later the monitor turned blue and then cleared showing the head and shoulders of Geoffrey Stevens.

'Good afternoon gentlemen,' he greeted. 'Is this everyone Mr President?'

'Yes,' confirmed Karras.

'Good, firstly let me congratulate you Alex on your appointment to Prime Minister. I and indeed my President is confident you will do a good job.'

'Thank you Geoffrey,' said Alex.

'Right, let's get on. I'm going to bring in Dominic Ferrari the Secretary of State and Sir Peter Bogart the Head of Lighthouse in the UK. If you could just bear with me a second or two.'

Why the heavy hitters? Alex questioned to himself. Neither Mavrides nor Karras turned a hair at hearing the names. So they obviously knew this was coming. Alex was wondering if some sort of deal had been broached already to Karras and Mavrides and because he was not the Prime Minister till an hour ago, whatever they spoke about was above his pay grade. Alex's thoughts were interrupted by the monitor splitting into three windows, one showing Stevens, another Ferrari and the third Sir Peter. Ferrari spoke first.

'Good afternoon,' said Ferrari. ' I would like to also congratulate you Alex on your promotion to Prime Minister of the Hellenes. Now down to business. We, that is the President and I are very grateful to all those involved in stopping the former Prime Minister of Greece from completing his scheme. If he had succeeded we would have seen the Aegean region and Europe destabilize very quickly, and it would have provided the catalyst for Russia to hold sway in the Mediterranean. The European Union with the exit of Germany would very likely have collapsed, causing untold economic hardship in that arena and would have greatly weakened NATO. Oil and gas prices would have become very volatile due to Russia trying to manipulate the market. A war in Europe, Turkey and the Middle East would not have been just a fear but a stark reality. We have to thank Geoffrey's Balkans Overlook team, Sir Peter's insight in supporting a military coup, which as it turned out, did a lot more than just stopping Greece drifting too far left. And you Alex, following in your father and mother's footsteps as you have, starting to work in the CIA under extreme duress, have our special thanks for your fantastic efforts.'

278

'Yes,' interjected Sir Peter. ' I fully agree with what Dominic has just said, and also want to congratulate you Alex, on your appointment to Prime Minister.'

Alex murmured his thanks as he looked at Karras to see if he knew beforehand what he had just heard about Alex's alternative career. He saw that Karras had not changed his expression nor had Mavrides for that matter. With an unheard sigh of relief he realised that they both had been briefed some time before.

'We understand that you have Xenakis under house arrest in Mansion Maximo and will be handing him over to the authorities tomorrow. The United States government agrees that is the best way to deal with him. Transparency throughout the charging and trial process is very important. As for the other three whom you also have under house arrest, we have arranged a military plane, which is now at Tatoi Air Base, to take them back to Germany later on this evening. Chris Horsman has been assigned to take them to the base and escort them onto the plane,' said Ferrari. 'He will pick them up after dark at eight o'clock. Someone has already been to the Astir palace and picked up their belongings. They are on the way to Tatoi as we speak.

'Shouldn't Chris have an escort?' asked Mavrides.

'I don't think that will be necessary,' said Ferrari. 'They don't pose a threat to anyone anymore.'

'I agree but what about Dexter,' asked Alex. 'He might try to rescue them or intervene in some way.'

'Dexter is not a threat either. He is working for us now.'

'What!' exclaimed Alex. 'What happened there? With respect sir he is a very dangerous man to be friends with.'

'Dexter is more dangerous when he is working for your enemy,' continued Ferrari. 'We can use him on your eastern flank, protecting Greece from any possibility of an invasion which after we are about to discuss with you now, might be a substantial risk.'

Now what thought Alex. Here comes the fly in the ointment. 'I'm all ears,' said Alex, pretty sure that whatever it was, it had already been broached with Karras and Mavrides.

'Earlier President Karras had a telephone conversation with our President in which the subject I am now going to talk to you about, was briefly discussed.'

Ah, so Mavrides wasn't in on that conversation thought Alex.

'Strategically, Greece has always been important to the west because of its proximity to Turkey, the Middle East and North Africa. Historically, America has had a big presence in the area but as you know after the coup of 1967, over the years our bases have been closed down. With the Middle East continuing to be a flashpoint and Turkey flexing its muscles every once in a while, we need more permanence in the area. We and the British should never have left Gladio to just Greece and Germany. A fresh Gladio Protocol must be created. One way we can achieve that while helping your country grow, is to become strategic partners in the exploration of the natural resources in the Aegean. We are asking for the exploration rights and a share in the income from the resources extracted. We would also like to have the only pipeline access into northern Greece and on into Europe.'

Alex looked at Karras and Mavrides. Nothing on their faces suggested whether they agreed or disagreed. So Alex said. 'You mentioned that you had lost all your bases, is having a base here going to be part of the agreement?'

'Yes,' said Ferrari. 'We would like to reactivate Souda Bay on Crete and share your air force base at Almiros in central Greece.'

'And in return what would we get,' asked Alex.

'Security foremost because we would guarantee your protection as a nation both physically and financially. The first thing we would do is to bail-out the bank that Xenakis bankrupted and indemnify any issuance of perpetual bonds by the Bank of Greece to ease your debt mountain; so as a nation you will only have to pay the interest but not the capital. We would also re-arm your armed forces with the latest equipment.'

'And our share of the income from the resources extracted from the Aegean and Ionian?' questioned Alex.

'Sir Peter, perhaps you could come in on this as Britain has done major research in this area.'

'Thank you Dominic. We estimate that twenty two billion barrels of oil are under the Ionian Sea and forty nine billion barrels under the Aegean Sea. Gas reserves under the Aegean are approximately in the region of thirty three trillion cubic metres. We estimate that all the resources are worth eight hundred billion dollars in total. We, that is Great Britain and the United States would want forty percent of the income. Your share of sixty percent is certainly much more than enough to wipe away Greece's current debts.'

'It sounds very generous, in fact the whole package sounds generous and very importantly it does not harm the integrity of our membership of the European Union or NATO. But do we have to give you an answer during this call,' asked Alex.

'I'm afraid so,' said Ferrari. 'This is not a business negotiation. There will be no negotiation on this very generous offer.'

'If we decline the offer?'

'We would have to look for another partner in the region. There are options available to us such as Cyprus, Israel and possibly Turkey. You understand it would make it much more difficult for you to extract the resources from the Aegean and Ionian Sea if that were the case,' said Ferrari with a forced smile on his face.

Alex looked at President Karras and Mavrides in turn. Both of them gave a small nod of assent.

'We agree to your generous offer,' said Alex, feeling a nasty taste in his mouth.

'Fantastic,' said Ferrari. 'We shall transmit a general agreement document to you immediately for your signature. I look forward to visiting your lovely country very soon. I'm sure that I am speaking for Sir Peter too.'

With that two of the three windows on the monitor faded out and left Geoffrey Stevens on his own.

'Mr President sir and Alex, I'm happy you accepted the offer and in the next few days I will ask Chris Horsman to contact you to discuss how you can use them as this project unfolds. I'm signing off now. Enjoy the remaining hours of Ochi Day,' said Steven with a wave of his hand.

How ironic thought Alex saying No to the Italians entering Greece at the beginning of the second world war was heroic and quite rightly celebrated all these years. Today the Americans and British asked to enter Greece and this time Greece said yes. Should we have said no? Only time and history will tell thought Alex shrugging his shoulders. He turned to Karras and said. 'Sir I'm going over to Mansion Maximo to tell our three unwelcome guests that they will be taken to Tatoi air base and flown to Germany tonight.'

'Very well Alex. You can stay here tonight obviously. After Xenakis is taken to the authorities you will be able to move into your apartment in the Mansion Maximo. Dinner at eight o'clock? You too Panos.'

'Thank you sir, said Alex as he turned and left the conference room. Leaving the President and Mavrides discussing the menu.

As Alex walked towards the side exit of the palace his thoughts went back to Gitta. He wondered where she was and what she was doing. Little did he know how close she was.

Chapter 54

Ochi Day October 28th, 2010 – Athens Vicinity – 21:00

The black Mercedes, driven by Chris Horsman, majestically wound its way up the mountain road towards the Tatoi Air Base. His three passengers had been picked up from Mansion Maximo after being escorted to the car by two marines at precisely eight o'clock. Dominic Vogel was sitting in the front passenger seat while Elena Davilova and Bridgette Neumann sat in the back. All of them had morose looks on their faces as they tried to figure out when, where and why it had all gone wrong and what they were going to tell their respective governments when they reached home.

'How far are we from the base,' asked Davilova trying to break the miserable atmosphere in the car.

'About half an hour,' said Chris.

'I have landed at the base on previous visits to Greece and do not recall these mountains,' said Davilova. 'Unless the darkness has disorientated me of course. However, previous trips have lasted around the hour mark, not an hour and a half.'

Shit! Thought Chris, why didn't anybody think to mention this.

'Don't worry the most direct route has been blocked by a traffic accident, so we have to take a more roundabout route. Would you like me to switch on the GPS?'

The mention of GPS reminded Davilova that she hadn't got her phone and she was very late in reporting in to Igor Putilov.

'No, it doesn't matter. I hope our phones were picked up and are with our luggage,' said Davilova. 'I need to make arrangements for my journey onwards from Germany.'

'Your phones are with your luggage,' Chris assured her.

That seemed to allay her fears as she didn't say anymore. Chris peered ahead up the road looking for the small layby he knew was coming up. The road was a two lane black top, so passing was very difficult and as the Mercedes climbed the mountain road it came, on several occasions, perilously close to the offside barrier which was, as is typical on many mountain roads in Greece, mostly a two metre high metal netting fence. Only on dangerous bends did the road have proper crash barriers. Suddenly, Chris spied the layby and he drew to a smooth stop.

'Why are we stopping,' asked Vogel alarm on his face.

I need a toilet break,' smiled Chris. 'Too much wine at lunch time. I'll just be over there in the trees,' he said pointing to the forest which hugged the other side of the road. 'Look you can stretch your legs too if you like. How about you Dominik?' asked Chris. 'Do you need a toilet break?'

'I do but I think I'll stay this side. The women can close their eyes.'

'Fine, I'll be two minutes at most,' said Chris getting out of the car. He crossed the road and headed into the trees. Twenty yards in, Chris found the laser tag instrument which had been hidden there a few hours earlier. He pointed it at the Mercedes and set the timer for a two minute countdown. Leaving it there, he hurried a further two hundred metres into the trees; found a thick trunk and hunkered down behind it.

Far above the Mercedes unseen and unheard in the still night air a Predator drone was circling like a bird of prey. Back in Tatoi, Dexter was sitting in one of the Greek Air Forces remote piloting rooms watching the monitor showing the feed from the Predator drone Black Hawke had in operation in Thrace. He was no stranger to the skills of piloting a drone; to him it was like driving a car. Part of the bargain he had struck with the Americans and British was to personally compensate for his lost payments for Black Hawke's services rendered to Greece, Germany and Russia in the last year. Financial payment was out of the question now that Gladio had been shut down and a new protocol was in place. Still he mused, now that the Americans and British have a substantial stake in Black Hawke, I am a very rich man.

He saw that the drone's sensors were picking up the heat from the Mercedes engine and the heat signatures of its passengers, who were standing next to the car stretching their legs, except for Vogel who was a few yards away having a pee. Amazingly, the drones sensors picked up his stream as well. The heat signature of Chris could be seen some three hundred metres inside the forest.

Dexter instructed the drone to display a wider angle. The new angle revealed what looked like a petrol truck struggling up the road five hundred yards behind the layby where the Mercedes was parked. The truck was driverless, the latest technology innovation developed in the Black Hawke laboratories. The truck, carrying gasoline and the belongings of the Mercedes passengers, was using GPS for most of its journey but for more intricate manoeuvres, a pilot needs to guide it.

Dexter guided the petrol truck into the layby and pulled it in behind the Mercedes it's headlights lighting up the car and the three passengers like malevolent eyes. Davilova, Vogel and Neumann stared at the truck. 'No driver,' exclaimed Davilova. Just as she said it, a laser beam emanated from the trees; stuck the boot of the Mercedes; bounced off and shot up into the night sky. Davilova immediately realized the import of the beam. 'Run!' she screamed.

Dexter commanded the drone to release its laser guided bomb at precisely the same time that Davilova screamed. A millisecond later the laser guided munition dropped from the drone, it's surface controls already responding to the signals received by it's photodiodes on its outer surface, aligning itself to the laser beam. Within another half second, the bomb was hurtling down the centre of the laser beam towards the Mercedes.

Davilova, Vogel and Neumann had only taken a couple of strides before they realized that they could never get far enough away in time. They looked up towards the night sky, perhaps foolishly hoping to see the bomb hurtling towards them. Then, oblivion; no pain, no feeling, simply blackness, as the bomb struck the Mercedes and exploded with such force that everything in a fifty yard circle around the explosion vaporised, including the truck and with it their belongings.

Dexter watched Chris leave the forest safely before he instructed the drone to go to its home and shut his control over it down.

Chris had stepped out of the trees onto the road fifty metres from the explosion. No-one can get passed this piece of road now he thought. Two minutes later Nikos Hathos drew up beside him and a grim faced Chris got in the passenger side. Nikos expedited a U-turn and headed back the way he had come. Neither man spoke during the whole journey back to Tatoi.

Mansion Maximo – Athens 23:00

The shadow suddenly moved; taking the form of a human dressed all in black, a balaclava covering face and head. The intruder had gained access to the grounds of Mansion Maximo, by climbing the wall at the back of the property, where the garden's trees grew tall and obscured the brick wall which surrounded the Mansion. The intruder knew that the gates were guarded day and night by marines and an hourly patrol of two marines around the grounds ensured the security integrity of the property. The intruder wasn't worried about alarms as the Mansion wasn't alarmed before midnight. Reaching the kitchen storage entrance the intruder was relieved to find the lock was not as strong as it should have been and had it unlocked in two minutes. There were no lights switched on in the short corridor leading to the main kitchens so the intruder was able to slip inside without being observed.

Inside the kitchen the barrel containing flour was easy to spot in the torchlight and the intruder pushed their hand deep down into the flour and the fingers found the package. With a sigh of relief the intruder retrieved the package and opened it. Inside was a small vial of liquid and a cutthroat razor. The intruder made their way out of the kitchen onto the hallway, then up the marble staircase. The door to Xenakis's residential apartment was un-guarded. The intruder listened at the door for a few seconds, then satisfied Xenakis was not in the immediate vicinity of the door, drew a Glock from an armpit holster, quietly opened the door and slipped into the room.

The small hallway was empty but beyond that the intruder could see that Xenakis was not in bed. He was sitting reading a book in front of the huge lounge picture windows that opened out onto the veranda. The intruder removed their balaclava and stepped into Xenakis's eyeline.

'Gitta,' exclaimed Xenakis. 'What are you doing here this time of night?' Then his eyes widened when he noticed the gun. 'Are you going to shoot me?'

'Don't worry,' replied Gitta. I won't shoot you, although you deserve it. I came to talk.'

'What about?'

'Sheepskin.'

'What about Sheepskin? It's shut down isn't it.

'Is it?'

'Why don't you ask the others?'

'They're gone.'

'What do you mean gone? Dead?' Xenakis had gone ashen.

Gitta laughed. 'No, they have gone back to Germany, so I can't ask them.'

'Let's have a drink,' offered Gitta. 'What would you like? I'll be mummy.'

'Whisky straight. Thank you.'

Gitta went over to the drinks cabinet and started to prepare the drinks. 'You know that the police authorities will grill you don't you, and they might even torture you. There is no way you can hold back any information. There has to be others in Greece who were involved. What about your cabinet ministers?' said Gitta as she handed Xenakis his drink.

'Tell me and maybe we can do a deal.'

'What sort of deal?'

'Well, your charge sheet includes the murder of the former Greek Finance Minister and accessory to murder of the family in Thrace.'

'Not me, that was Dexter,' interjected Xenakis.

'Prove it,' challenged Gitta. 'Anyway the American's have bought him. He is working for them now so he won't help you. I could get the accessories to murder dropped and lessen the murder charge to accessory to murder. You will probably get life but you will escape execution.'

'I can't move my arms,' groaned Xenakis.

I know,' affirmed Gitta taking out of her pocket a vial of clear liquid. 'I put this in your drink. It's a poison which stiffens all the muscles in your body. Your legs will go next then your speech will suffer, then your internal organs will start to fail. Tell me and I'll give you the antidote,' said Gitta holding up a syringe which she had retrieved from her pocket.

Xenakis looked at her with obvious fearful apprehension in his eyes. Gitta could see he was wrestling with himself as to whether she was telling the truth and would let him die. He tried to move his legs and failed.

'Okay, I'll tell you. Give me the anecdote I beg you,' beseeched Xenakis, his voice reducing to a whisper as the poison began working on his speech muscles. Gitta went over to Xenakis, bent down and put her ear to his mouth. She could just about hear what Xenakis said but she understood. So a cabinet minister of little consequence and.....well the other name stunned her.

'Thank you,' said Gitta looking into Xenakis eyes. He was now looking horrified, his eyes pleading for the antidote. Gitta took the glass that was in his disabled hand and commenced to roll up Xenakis's left arm shirt sleeve.

'Sorry Themis, I lied,' admitted Gitta taking a cutthroat razor from of her pocket. She opened it and then proceeded to run the razor down the centre of the inside of Xenakis's arm from just below the elbow to the wrist. Xenakis stared mesmerized at the blood streaming from his lower arm and pooling on the floor. Gitta sat down again and watched as his life ebbed away. When she was sure he was dead she went over to him and making sure she didn't tread in his blood she placed the razor in his right hand. She then wiped her prints off everything she had touched, donned

288

her balaclava and slipped out from his apartment. She made her way out using the same route she had employed to get inside the mansion, then crossed the gardens, scaled the wall and vanished into the night.

Later a post mortem on Xenakis found no trace of the poison and a verdict of suicide was announced.

Chapter 55

October 29th, 2010 – Athens

SKAI News - Announcement

Three prominent dignitaries who were attending the Bilderberg Meeting at the Astir Palace Hotel were involved in a tragic accident with a petrol truck on their way to Tatoi military base. There were no survivors. A spokesperson from the Greek government announced that the dignitaries were Bridgett Neumann the German Chancellor, Dominik Vogel the German Finance Minister and Elena Davilova the Russian Deputy Minister of Economics. The driver of their car has not been identified as yet. Greece's thoughts and condolences go out to the victims loved ones.

An office in the Greek Parliament Building – 11:00

'Xenakis was found dead this morning. Apparently suicide,' said the minister. 'And the car carrying Vogel, Neumann and Davilova met with a tragic accident last night. All fatalities.'

'So they take our secret to the grave?' said the other party. 'My sources tell me that it wasn't an accident.'

'But we have not been compromised,' said the minister. 'Otherwise they would have been knocking at my door.'

'Agree, keep a low profile until I get back to you. Sheepskin is still very much alive. Just needs a change of players.'

'Don't worry,' said the minister closing the connection.

21st December 2010 – Berlin -10:00

'I'm pleased to confirm that you are definitely pregnant,' announced the doctor. 'You must be pleased.'

'I am,' smiled the young woman. 'Although, it is too soon. The father does not live in Germany he lives abroad, and I am unable to join him for at least a year.'

'That's a shame but please let me know if you can't cope on your own. I'm sure the practice can help in some way.'

'Thank you. I'll book an appointment for a month's time.'

A few minutes later as the young woman was walking out of the practice a voice hailed her from behind.

'Where have you been? I haven't seen you around for a long time Gitta.'

About the Author:

Philip was born and educated in the United Kingdom. He joined Citibank in London before moving to Athens where he worked as a foreign exchange trader for both Citibank and Chase Manhattan Bank. Philip was then posted to Citibank's Middle East North African Training Centre in Athens/Beirut as the operations manager and a foreign exchange trader.

After returning to the United Kingdom Philip joined Union Bank of Switzerland as the Head of Learning and Development. He was later appointed Head of Learning and Education for UBS in North America. He subsequently left the bank and went into partnership with two colleagues and set up a successful financial training company (New Learning Developments) in New York City.

Returning to London he worked as a training consultant to financial services institutions and the Ministry of Defence. After which he moved to Greece where he wrote books teaching English as a second language as well as developing knowledge databases for on-line brokerage houses.

He returned to London in 2012 where he began his writing career. To date he has written a children's book, two fictional erotic short stories, available on www.smashwords.com, and a poetry book available on www.amazon.com. He recently had two financial books, Competing in the Financial Markets and Mastering Options, published by Business Expert Press in New York www.businessexpertpress.com. also available on www.amazon.com The Gladio Protocol is his first novel.

Printed in Great Britain
by Amazon

72914168R00175